The Domesday Book
(No, Not That One)

ALSO BY HOWARD OF WARWICK

The Chronicles of Brother Hermitage:
The Heretics of De'Ath
The Garderobe of Death

The Domesday Book

(No, Not That One)

Howard of Warwick

First published in 2014 by
The Funny Book Company
Dalton House
60 Windsor Ave
London SW19 2RR
United Kingdom
www.funnybookcompany.com

A catalogue card for this book
is available from the British Library.

ISBN 978-0-9929393-2-8

Cover design by Double Dagger
Typeset by Lodestar Editorial
Printed in the UK by Albury Books

Contents

Chapter		Page
1	A Field North of Hastings	9
2	A Treasure Hunt	21
3	Hic Irritatus Ranulf Est	34
4	A Spare Saxon	44
5	Northern Lights	55
6	Hillhill Woodwood	66
7	Salehurst by Night	80
8	Vikings to the North of Us	92
9	Normans to the South	101
10	To the Rescue	111
11	De Sauveloy *vs* Toll-man	123
12	The Vikings are Coming!	136
13	More's the Pity	145
14	Freya's Tale	155
15	Through Rain and More Rain	165
16	Ferry Risky	178
17	Roman Down the Road	188

Chapter		Page
18	Fourpence Again	198
19	Old Zeb	207
20	The Night Legion	220
21	Aefred the Absent	232
22	Avoiding the Slice	245
23	Saxons in the House	253
24	The Advantages of Being a Filth-man	263
25	To Horse … and Cart	274
26	The Very Short Battle of Spalding	282
27	Collision Course	291
28	North or South?	303
29	Heels, Hard on the	313
30	Epilogue 1	324
31	Epilogue 2	328
32	Epilogue 3	339

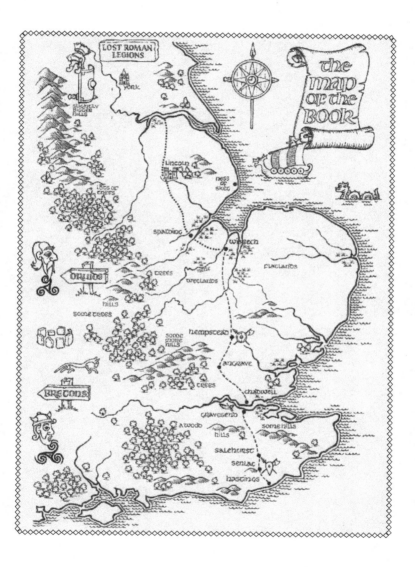

Chapter 1
A Field North of Hastings

14 October 1066, about 4 o'clock

THE SLOPES OF SENLAC HILL were green and sparkling in the cold of an autumn afternoon. Or at least the bits that could be seen between the bodies looked a bit green and sparkling. A lot of the place looked red, and most of it was mud, but a discerning observer could still pick out some speckles of green and sparkle if he looked hard.

True, most of the discerning observer's attention would be focused on trying to discern a way out of this awful place. If you didn't care for the bodies of dead Saxons, this was not the spot for you. And if you cared for neither the bodies of dead Saxons nor dead Normans, you really needed to be somewhere else.

The battle had been long and it had swung back and forth, or rather it had run up and down modest hills until eventually the Normans killed the Saxons. They didn't kill all of them, but there seemed to be a point in the afternoon when those Saxons still capable of fighting realised they weren't capable of fighting the much larger number of Normans who were still capable of fighting.

And when King Harold took an arrow, they decided they had better things to do with their day. The Saxons who were still capable of fighting ran away.

No one was really sure where the arrow that took the King came from. The archery phase had appeared pretty much over when one lone shaft seemed to come out of nowhere and make straight for Harold.

The King dropped, and his men dropped with him.

Thus the Battle of a Field a Few Miles Outside Hastings was won.

Yet after such a great victory, the tent of Duke William of Normandy did not feel very victorious. It certainly didn't sound very victorious; the air was full of the groans and grumbles of men who had suffered. Men who had suffered cuts, bruises, breaks and amputations. Amputations at the hands of wickedly blunt instruments.

The suffering would fade as the hours went by. Some would get over the shock, and start the natural healing process – the first stage being to boast how utterly blood curdling their injuries had been. Others would stop suffering as the shock of their injuries reached their brains, which promptly told them to get on and die.

Of course, this tent was only for the well-connected injured. The common soldiery would still be out on the field, tending their common wounds among the blood and the mud. Meanwhile, in the hastily-assembled veterinary yard, injured horses were either being tended or put out of their misery. Misery out of the way, they were passed to the camp butcher to make ready for that night's celebratory meal. There were plenty of them, which was fortunate. The Normans had worked up quite an appetite.

The groaning and moaning of field and tent were pretty much all in Norman French. Saxons capable of running away had done so, while those not capable of running away weren't capable of anything at all any more.

One or two of the better-dressed Saxon wounded had been brought to the tent as prisoners, there being a good chance their families were wealthy and would pay ransom. This had been before William realised he had actually conquered the country, and so everything belonged to him anyway. The better dressed Saxon wounded swiftly became the better dressed Saxon dead.

❖   ❖   ❖

The Duke himself had left his tent to examine the battle's out-come in closer detail. He was striding up and down Senlac Hill again, taking in the moment and glorying in his power and majesty. He roared now and again, clapped Norman soldiers on the shoulders in congratulation, if they still had shoulders, and generally gloated all over the place. Whenever he came upon a groaning Saxon he despatched him with his mighty, magisterial sword, just to make the day absolutely perfect.

William was not the sort of leader to stand at the back and direct his forces. He *was* one of his forces and wanted to be in there, forcing things. Mainly metal things and mainly into other people.

He was not a large man, not for the time anyway, but there was a certain something about him – the sort of something that made other people look away. Even those of a naturally aggres-sive disposition found themselves unable to hold the Duke's eye. It wasn't that he could out-stare you: it was that he looked at you as if you were already dead.

Not that trying to out-stare William was advisable. It helped to know that he would leap into the most pointless and hideous violence at the drop of a ... well, he didn't really need anything to drop at all. He just did pointless and hideous violence when he felt like it. Which was most days.

And of course he was a duke. His title gave him natural auth-ority while his behaviour rammed it home, often literally.

He had a cadre of confidants; no leader could operate alone, but William's group was small and select. There was strategy in it, too. The men around him, particularly the ancient warmonger Le Pedvin, survived close to William because they were just like him. When he screamed that he would cut their heads off for some perceived insult, they would reply that he was welcome to try as they'd spread his guts on the floor before he'd taken a step.

And if he did take a step he'd slip in his own guts, which, by the way, were putrid.

William would roar his delight at such insults, and there would be much slapping and punching, and the occasional light stabbing.

If anyone else tried this approach they'd be dead. Others had, and they were.

If the man had simply been an average mad duke, he could have been avoided. It was his intelligence, ambition and single-mindedness that made him really scary. Years of rankling hatred between William and Harold had led to this day on Senlac Hill. If you had a really major grudge you needed bearing, William was your man. That a generous scattering of Norman and Saxon manhood now lay leaking into the soil of England was a sign that William's grudge had been a good one.

Into the Duke's tent, one particular leaking Saxon was being dragged on a bier. He was very well dressed indeed, and was leaking from a very specific wound. The leaking was no longer copious, though, as the Saxon heart had stopped beating some time ago.

'Fetch the Duke,' the ambitious young Norman in charge of one half of the bier called to some guards standing nearby.

The guards appraised the man and weighed him up: ambitious, rich, but not well connected. They ignored him and carried on talking about one another's injuries, particularly whose had been the most blood curdling.

'All right,' the ambitious Norman snapped, 'I'll go and tell the Duke that I have the body of King Harold, shall I? And that you couldn't be bothered to take him the news?'

The two guards left.

◆　　◆　　◆

When he received the news, William's striding came to a halt. With some scowls at undespatched Saxons, he redirected it towards his tent. It was an entirely equitable stride; live, dead, Saxon, Norman … William trod on them all in his haste to get to the body of his vanquished foe.

On his way across the field of ruin he spied his old companion Le Pedvin, busy robbing the dead.

'Ho, Le Pedvin, you rat's arse. Come and see Harold's body.'

'Ha ha!' Le Pedvin roared his own roar and joined his Duke. Patting his purse to make sure the newly severed fingers with rings on them were safe, he clapped the Duke on the shoulder. 'Dead, then?' the older man asked.

'Seems so,' said William, with some disappointment.

If our discerning observer had loitered until this moment, he would wonder why the victorious Duke was talking to one of the corpses, and why the corpse was talking back. It was also walking pretty well for corpse.

Duke William certainly looked like a duke. His small pieces of armour shone, the sword at his side gleamed, his helmet was close fitting and looked comfortable, and his chest bore his sigil for all to see. This was a dangerous foible for a duke in a battle, one might imagine, but then William was largely mad.

Le Pedvin looked like the corpse. He always had. For as long as anyone could remember the man had been pale, pock-marked and as dour as the dead. As the years went by, more and more lines creased his face as if they were trying to fold him to death, and in some old battle he had lost his right eye. Where another grizzled soldier might have worn his patch with pride, Le Pedvin just used his to keep the wind out.

Both men were built of fighting muscle, though. This was clear from the way they quickly trampled over the dead to get to the tent.

At the entrance, where two poles topped with wooden bosses held up a sheet of canvas, the ambitious Norman stood. The look on the man's face was one of grim seriousness as he bowed before his Duke.

'You've got him, then?' William asked.

'Yes, sire.' Giles Martel, ambitious young Norman, nodded his head sharply, in that respectful but sycophantic manner William was used to. The manner that said the man wanted something in return for his service, probably a small county. There would be plenty to go round, after all.

William raised an arm indicating that Martel should lead the way. He and Le Pedvin ducked their heads through the entrance of the tent and followed.

◆   ◆   ◆

'Tent' is a bit of an understatement for William's canvas construction – it was more like small village. Various tents had been joined together to create an accommodation befitting a duke. There were separate spaces for cooking, for storing clothes, for dressing and for receiving audiences. William's sleeping space was grand, his resting space was comfortable and the space for his weapons was just plain large.

Most of this space was occupied by Norman nobles, groaning mightily over one injury or another. The tent was well run: as soon as anyone became a dead Norman noble, he was neatly escorted from the place. Space for the accommodation of corpses was not part of the design. In any case, the smell would soon become unpleasant.

An exception had been made for the body of Harold. His bier had been placed on the banqueting table, a twenty-foot long monolith of oak which had come across the channel in its own boat. The cook had protested at this location for a corpse, but Martel had promised the decoration would be moved before the dinner began. Unless William wanted it there as a trophy.

A confidently smiling Martel led the Duke and Le Pedvin through the winding ways of the tent. They paused, momentously, on the threshold of the new mausoleum.

The body had been covered with a sheet, as befitted the remains of a king. Granted he was not a real King in William's view, but the Duke had made it clear that the remains of Harold were to be treated with due respect. His living body, people could do whatever they wanted with. Once he was dead, though, decency and decorum was the order of the day.

William knew that after winning the battle he would have to negotiate with the wretched English assembly, the Witan, if he wanted the throne. Hacking the old king's body about and using it for some healthy sport would be just the sort of thing to get some snotty English backs up. And they'd go bleating to the Pope, who'd have one of his quiet conversations with William. All agreement and nodding, but full of hatred and threat. This was where William's intelligence came in handy: he knew that stabbing a pope in the head would get him nowhere.

Once he was crowned King though, he could do what the hell he liked. Until then, he'd play it straight.

◆　　◆　　◆

The anomaly of the sheet covering the body on the table was that it stuck a good two feet up in the air where the head was.

'Did no one think to take the arrow out?' William demanded of no one in particular.

'Er,' Martel muttered.

'For God's sake, give the man some dignity in death.' William was clearly pained.

The look on Martel's face was that of a man whose county was getting smaller by the minute.

'Did we find who shot him?' William asked this of Le Pedvin.

'Nope,' the old soldier answered, 'not one of ours. At least not one who's owned up,' he shrugged.

William had made it perfectly clear that if anyone got the chance to finish Harold, they should pass that chance to their Duke. Anyone killing Harold themselves, either in the heat of battle, or just because they fancied a go, would find themselves joining him almost immediately. Hardly surprising that no one had owned up.

The three men stood in silent contemplation for a moment. William even bowed his head toward the body on the table. Martel followed suit, but Le Pedvin just looked through his single eye. 'Right,' said William, his moment of respectful reverie despatched, 'let's have a look at the bastard.'

Martel skipped forward, took hold of the sheet and swept it away in a flurry. Unfortunately the edge of it caught on the flight of the arrow lodged in Harold's head and Martel had to give a good tug to get the thing free.

The sheet fluttered to the floor. William and Le Pedvin stepped up to survey the symbol of their victory.

The body was well dressed, there was no doubt about it. Le Pedvin eyed some of the accoutrements with interest and a single raised eyebrow. Solid fighting boots clad the feet. They were covered in a lot of the blood and mud at the moment, but they'd clean up nicely.

The legs were tightly clad in brown material, overlaid with patches of leather. This might have been helpful in giving Harold the freedom to manoeuvre about the battle, but wouldn't stop an arrow or a sword. Even a well placed kick could do some damage.

Above the legs his jerkin was similarly solid and workmanlike, just of very high quality. No blazon like William's chest, but many hours of tailors' effort had gone into this thing.

Le Pedvin reached out to feel the quality of the weave.

'Get out of it,' William snapped and brushed Le Pedvin's hand away.

There was a bit of mutual snarling and staring, as if two dogs were about to start fighting over the body of a cat.

Le Pedvin drew his hand back, but not without a contemptuous snort towards his Duke, who appeared to have gone soft.

'Where's his armour?' William asked. Harold would hardly fight the whole battle in so unprotected a manner.

'We left some padding and his helmet behind. It was a bit heavy,' Martel explained.

'Oh dear,' said William, in a very specific tone.

'But we'll go and get it,' he added quickly.

William simply grunted. Which was a good sign.

Martel's sheet tugging had pulled on Harold's head so he was turned away from them. Like some shy maiden caught in bed, the ex-King looked to the wall.

Le Pedvin reached out, this time with a half-hearted check to his Duke. William nodded and the older man leaned over and gently took the flight of the arrow between his finger and thumb. He used this lever to pull the head over so the reluctant corpse would have to face its visitors. Over it rolled.

'Ah,' said Le Pedvin.

William said nothing.

Martel looked at them both and then at the corpse. Yes, the face was a mess, but then that's what happened when an arrow went into the soft bits at some speed.

William turned to Martel, his hands on his hips. This looked bad for some reason.

'Who the hell is this?' Duke William demanded. He brandished his arm to show which corpse he was talking about.

Martel's mouth flapped a bit. The connections from mouth to muscle had all run off to avoid the Duke's question.

'Er, King Harold?' Martel suggested, without actually moving his lips.

'No. It isn't,' William said, in a very matter of fact manner.

'But ...' Martel began, then tailed off. He knew better than to contradict the Duke. 'The arrow?' he asked. 'We saw it. Everyone saw it. Harold was shot in the eye.'

'So was this bloke.' William was contemptuous. 'In fact, a lot of people have probably been shot in the eye. They simply pull the arrow out, sometimes with the eye still attached, eh, Le Pedvin?' William nudged the older man, who laughed. Clearly his experience of having his own eye shot out was a happy reminiscence.

'And then they get on with life,' William continued his contempt, this time directing it at people who got shot in the eye and then made a lot of fuss about it. 'I shouldn't think you could take a short walk out there,' he gestured towards the battlefield, 'without bumping into several people with eye problems they didn't have when the day started. With arrows falling out of the sky, it'd be quite common. Take this man, for example.' William gestured to the corpse on the table. 'Undoubtedly he has been shot in the eye.' The Duke leaned forward for a closer examination. He pulled the head back and forward and examined the wound at an unnecessarily close distance.

'Good penetration,' William commented approvingly, 'low angle of entry so it went straight into the brain. When they come down from high up there's always a chance the arrow will take the eye and then hit bone.' This was clearly a subject on which the Duke was most knowledgeable. 'Unless you're looking up, of course,' he nodded.

Martel nodded, much more cautiously now. He seemed not to know where this was going, but was anticipating its arrival would be uncomfortable.

'But then if you're on a battlefield during an archers' attack and you look up, you must be some sort of idiot.'

Martel shifted on his feet as he felt his Duke was now talking about him. Even though it wasn't fair as he had both eyes. For the moment.

'What we have here is a man who has most definitely been shot in the eye, eh, Le Pedvin?'

'Very little doubt, sire.' Le Pedvin checked the arrow to confirm the diagnosis.

'What we do not have,' William said calmly, 'is KING HAROLD.'

He did not say the name calmly. He did not reach out and grab Martel by the throat calmly, and he did not shake the man calmly until his eyeballs bounced either.

William carried on raging in a voice that could loosen the bowels of a constipated cow. 'What we have here is some well dressed Saxon stiff, and you have dragged me from the field to examine a total stranger. I want Harold.'

Martel did his best to nod agreeably – not easy as his feet had been lifted from the floor by William's throttling grip.

'Is this really the best you could manage?' William's voice was ferocious. It contained the clear suggestion that if this was the best Martel could do, Martel could be dead very soon.

The grip softened just enough to let some words out of the man's throat.

'We searched the field, sire,' he rasped, 'all the men with arrow wounds to the eye. This one was at the top of the hill. He was the best dressed. The rest were all common soldiers. I swear.'

'Had you ever seen Harold before today?' William growled.

'No, sire.'

'Then go out and search again. And take someone with you who knows what he actually looks like.' William released his crushing hold on Martel's windpipe.

'Er, yes sire,' Martel replied, trying not to rub his throat.

'Le Pedvin here will do,' William added.

'Excellent.' Martel tried to sound enthusiastic instead of terrified.

'Come,' Le Pedvin instructed, striding towards the entrance with natural assumption that Martel would follow in his wake.

William kicked Martel heartily from behind as he left. 'And if you can't find him, I'll take your eye out with an arrow. An extra long one so I can do it through your arse.'

Martel swallowed.

'Or perhaps I'll use this.' William extracted the arrow from the corpse with a soft plop. 'Oh look, the eyeball's come out on this one as well,' he said as he brandished the thing towards the departing figures. Le Pedvin laughed heartily. Martel fought to keep the contents of his stomach inside his bulging cheeks.

'Come, boy,' Le Pedvin strode off, 'let's find Harold or we'll never hear the end of it. Well, you'll never hear the end of it because you'll be dead. I'll hear the end of it, but I'll have to put up with it for months first.' He grimaced.

Martel managed to swallow his day's meal again.

Chapter 2
A Treasure Hunt

T HE SEARCH OF THE FIELD of Senlac Hill for Saxons with arrows in their eyes proved to be time consuming. Not all the defenders had been so stupid as to look up when the arrows were coming down, but a lot had. They pretty soon discovered this would be the last thing they ever saw.

The Norman tactic towards the end of the day, of deliberately firing the things up in the air to take out Saxon eyes, had met with alarming success. Arrows were sticking up all over the place, plenty of them still attached to eye sockets, but so far none belonged to the King. Corpses had to be turned and heads examined for signs of arrow damage. And there were lots and lots of corpses.

It soon became apparent that the two men would not be able to examine every body on the field, not unless they wanted to die of old age before the job was finished. So Le Pedvin and Martel narrowed their focus to the better dressed deceased, on the assumption that Harold would not have been mucking in with the common man.

At least the better dressed had kept together on one part of the slope – probably hoping to remain better dressed by keeping far enough away from the fighting. The Saxon tactic towards the end of the day, of running down the hill to chase the Normans, had proved their undoing. It helped Martel and Le Pedvin's search, however, as this meant they had all been undone in pretty much the same spot.

'Why don't we get some others to help?' Martel suggested as the magnitude of their task became clear. The magnitude of it plus the fundamentally depressing nature of a task requiring careful examination of dead people's faces. 'I mean most of our men are available, we could get the place covered in no time. And it'll be dark before long.'

Le Pedvin dropped the head of the latest corpse, which had come off in his hands, and stared at Martel with his disappointed eye.

'What?' the younger man asked.

'We'll go and round up a few men and get them to help us with the search for Harold?'

'Yes.'

'Get them to join in looking for the enemy King who everyone assumes is dead?'

'That's him.' Martel was bright with enthusiasm.

'The King whose apparent death brought the battle to an end and led to the surrender of the Saxons.'

'Of course.'

'The King whose body we seem to have mislaid? The one whose death we cannot actually display?'

'Ah.' Martel clearly wasn't that stupid, and he saw the problem. Eventually.

'Several witnesses saw Harold fall, the story is he was shot in the eye, but, as the Duke said,' Le Pedvin went on relentlessly, 'a lot of people were. There's no guarantee the wound was fatal anyway. If William is going to have trouble persuading the Witan to make him King when he produces Harold's pristine body, imagine the debate if he can't produce the body at all. Let alone if it turns up to dispute the claim in person.'

'And the fewer people who know we're having a bit of trouble finding him, the better,' Martel concluded. There was a depressing logic to this. 'So we keep looking.' Le Pedvin kicked another well presented but dead Saxon until he rolled over and showed his undamaged eyes. They were blank and staring, but didn't contain any arrows.

'What if he really isn't dead?' Martel thought it through. 'Suppose he left the battle and is even now gathering his men?'

'I may not know much about Saxons,' Le Pedvin speculated, 'but I do know about being shot in the eye. If Harold has survived, he will be in a fever somewhere, throwing up and howling. If he's conscious at all. Gathering his wits will be as much as he can manage, never mind his men. Chances are he didn't survive and you just got the wrong man.' He spat. The man he spat on was lying on the ground covered in blood and didn't seem to mind. (The body didn't mind rather than Le Pedvin.)

'What were you doing dragging bodies around anyway?' Le Pedvin asked, as he rolled another corpse over without success. 'I was on the left flank with my men and one them said he saw Harold fall. It was pretty quiet on the left flank and so I said we should go and get him. Present him to the Duke.'

'The left flank?' Le Pedvin frowned. 'Old Gerard Martel's men?'

'My father,' Martel confirmed. 'He sent me with our contingent to support the Duke.'

'I bet he did,' said Le Pedvin with another spit, 'and I bet he said "hang around on the left flank until you see who's winning and then come in on their side"?'

'Not at all.' Martel was outraged.

'Don't see why the Martel family tactics would change in 30 years.' Le Pedvin didn't seem particularly put out by this analysis. 'At least you're somewhere your father and grandfather never got.'

'Where's that?'

'In it up to your neck.' Le Pedvin wandered off to the next contender for the post of dead but missing King.

Martel looked worried now, with a hint of reminiscence at the advice his father had given him about the best place to be during a battle. 'Not too close' summed it up pretty neatly.

'Where was it your man saw Harold hit exactly?' Le Pedvin asked. 'And don't say "in the eye"', he warned.

'Definitely round here.' Martel scanned the field and the slope up to the hill. 'The royal banner was up there and the men were coming down the hill while the arrows were going up.'

Le Pedvin stood with hands on hips as he surveyed the site. The last well-dressed dead Saxon had proved another disappointment. 'Well, he's not here.' He sucked the dwindling afternoon air through his teeth, which sounded like it was going into the Norman against its better judgment. ''Course he could still be dead, and someone just took him away.'

'Took him away?'

'Make a shrine, to rally the Saxons to the sacred body of their dead King – that sort of thing.'

'Ah,' Martel nodded sagely.

'Or he could be mashed up in the mud somewhere. If any of our lads came across him they might have got a bit carried away.'

Martel had seen some of the Norman troops get a bit carried away during a skirmish. The human body was made of many parts, all of which came off, given the right encouragement.

'Whatever's happened, there's a difficult task to be done,' Le Pedvin said, his eye now beady as it drilled into Martel. He twitched uneasily.

'What's that?'

'We have to tell the Duke.'

Martel grimaced.

'Well, you do,' Le Pedvin concluded, his eye rolling nastily. Martel's spirits sank.

◆   ◆   ◆

In his tent, William was enjoying a quick bite to eat before dinner. A slab of horsemeat, thrown on the fire for a couple of moments to seal in the blood, lay on a wooden plate in front of him. Or rather the remains of it lay on the plate. A large piece was clearly still in his mouth and a lot of the blood seemed to have dribbled down his front.

At least the Duke had the grace to put the sheet back over the corpse before he sat at the table to eat. He had shoved the body of not-Harold to the edge of the table though, to make room for his meal. He looked up as Le Pedvin and Martel entered his presence.

'Don't tell me you can't find him,' William said, without waiting to swallow his mouthful.

'All right,' Le Pedvin replied amicably, 'we won't.'

William simply stared. Although it covered both men, the stare seemed to have most of its attention on Martel.

'You do recall what I said would happen if you couldn't find him?' William stood up, leaving the dead horse on the table with the dead Saxon.

'Of course, sire, of course.' Martel was gabbling rather.

'This is Martel's boy.' Le Pedvin spoke up. It wasn't clear whether this was in support of the man or as an encouragement to some hideous punishment.

William paused and his eyes widened rather. 'Gerard Martel?'

'Yep.'

'Old "left flank" Martel?'

'The same.'

'Ye gods,' William snorted a laugh, 'a man never troubled by the thick of battle because he always stayed near the thin bits.'

Martel said nothing.

'Well you're in it now, eh, boy?' William snorted again.

Martel nodded a reluctant acknowledgement.

'Or rather you got in it after the fighting was over. Came in at the last minute to harvest your glory from the work of others.'

'No, no, sire, I assure you,' Martel began

'Your father would be proud.' William actually clapped his hands to his knees and laughed out loud.

This news seemed to have distracted William from the plans

he had made for Martel. He stepped from the table and took a couple of paces away from the men, turning his back. 'What's to do then?' he asked the air.

'He could be dead,' Le Pedvin speculated. 'Probably is.'

William turned and looked Le Pedvin in the eye. He spoke slowly and deliberately. 'That's no good. He can't be probably dead, he must be actually dead. The wretched Witan will know what he looked like. I can't turn up with one of Martel's random bodies and say "Look, I killed the King."'

'No, sire,' Le Pedvin accepted the fact. William could not.

Martel kept his head down. Some of his father's advice had covered situations like this. The main piece being, don't get in situations like this. But if you were, keep quiet.

'We could take one of the damaged bodies and say it's him?' Le Pedvin offered.

'Of course we could,' William snapped back, as if he'd already thought of this, 'but I need people to *see* it's Harold. The country has to believe he's dead, and you know what people are like. If they don't see it, they don't believe it. Before we knew it we'd have rumours that it wasn't him, that he wasn't dead, that he's going to rise again and drive the Norman invader from the lands. Like that other one, what's his name? Half a?'

'Arthur?'

'That's him. Not that we are invaders,' William went on. 'We all know perfectly well that I'm the rightful King.'

Martel and Le Pedvin added hasty agreement to this.

'Problem is the common folk have all sorts of strange ideas in their heads. It doesn't seem to matter how many of them you cut off, they go on believing.'

Neither man had anything to contribute to the Duke's contemplations.

'And of course there is the possibility that he really isn't dead.'

'Unlikely, sire.' Le Pedvin did his best to sound encouraging, but his eye was not full of conviction.

'I wouldn't be so sure,' William was doubtful too. He took to pacing up and down the space of his tent. This did nothing for Martel's condition as every time the Duke approached, he feared for his life. 'All the years he lived in Normandy, all the times that killing him was so attractive for so many reasons, somehow he survived. I'd even have my sword drawn ready and he'd come up with some weasely reason why I shouldn't do it. How loyal he was, how much help he could be. Without really knowing how it happened I'd find my sword put away and Harold dining at my table again. The man has the most appalling habit of staying alive when you least want him to.' This recollection clearly annoyed William, who thumped the table with his fist.

Le Pedvin had no reaction to this, but it made Martel jump backwards slightly. It also made the arm of the corpse, which was already close to the edge of table, drop down and hang, like a pheasant waiting for the kitchen. William looked at the arm with disappointment.

'But the battle was pretty intense,' Le Pedvin ignored the arm. 'Remember the arrow flights, and the stupid Saxons running down the hill to get slaughtered?'

'The Harold I know could walk through the middle of it all without a scratch. He'd persuade the arrows not to hit him, he'd argue the swordsmen out of stabbing him and he'd bore the horses to death so they wouldn't trample him. No,' William had come to some sort of conclusion, 'until I see the body I won't believe it.' He paced up and down in front of the corpse on the table. 'In fact the more I think about it, and about him, the more convinced I get. If there's a battlefield without his body on it, the likelihood is he walked away.'

'That'd be trouble.' Le Pedvin was thoughtful as well.

'Trouble?' William's temper was pushing at its gates. 'Trouble? Of course it will be trouble,' he roared. 'If he's alive it makes replacing him just a bit more complicated, wouldn't you say?' William had moved his pacing to the front of the two men, waving his arms about and shouting. Crumbs of horse splattered from his lips and decorated the men before him. He turned now and kicked the table. Martel was grateful that the furniture was taking the punishment instead of him.

The dead Saxon appeared to object to this behaviour and shifted further, as if preparing to get up and leave in a huff. The left leg now slid from the table and joined the arm in its dangling.

'And if he is alive, he'll soon be out there telling people. Bit hard to conquer the country if the country believes their old King is going strong, isn't it? Even if they don't see him, even if no one sees him, he's trouble. Just the word that he's alive will be enough. He has to be dead.' William was barking an instruction to the two men now. 'Really, demonstrably, dead.'

Le Pedvin looked at his Duke, his eye thoughtful as he considered options. 'Martel's men saw him take one in the eye. He's not going anywhere quickly.'

If Martel's head had been down before, it was positively subterranean now. Why had he ever started this?

'How do you know it was him?' William barked the question at Martel. 'You'd never seen him and you couldn't get it right with a corpse close up.' He gestured at the body on the dining table and gave it another kick to emphasise the point. The Saxon's head bounced in annoyance at this treatment.

Martel decided to stand firm. 'It was him,' he nodded. 'Under the banner, giving orders, directing people here and there. One of my men had seen him before, and when he took the shot to the eye everyone gathered round. Must have been him.'

'Hmm.' William reluctantly accepted this description of events. 'He has got to be found.' The instruction was clear and serious.

'How long ago was it you saw him shot?' Le Pedvin directed the question at Martel.

'About three, I suppose,' the younger man replied.

'Won't have got far then,' Le Pedvin concluded. 'If we get the men out looking they'll find him quick enough.'

'Oh no,' William quickly bit the head off Le Pedvin's suggestion. 'So far only we three know the body here,' he gestured to
the sheet on his dining table, 'is not Harold. As far as the rest
of the world is concerned it *is* Harold. Am I clear?' Each word
of 'Am I clear' was accompanied by a thump of the ducal fist on
the table.

The poor Saxon was getting positively agitated and danced
about, as if trying to get away.

'But what if he's out there telling everyone he's Harold?' Le
Pedvin was worried by this plan.

'We won the battle,' William retorted, 'so we decide what's
true and what isn't. At least for now.'

Both men nodded acquiescence. This made sense.

'Martel's men clearly believe it's Harold,' Le Pedvin added.

Martel nodded vigorously. He was delighted the conversation had moved on from unwelcome plans for arrows and eyes.
Not to mention bottoms.

'So they're probably spreading word to all and sundry that
they took the body of Harold to the Duke,' William went on.

'Certainly will be, sire,' Martel confirmed. 'They were very
enthusiastic about the task.'

"Course they were,' William sneered slightly. 'The most activity they've had all day.'

Martel's head went quickly down again.

'So,' said William, 'I won't be telling anyone. Le Pedvin won't
be telling anyone. And if I kill Martel he won't be able to tell
anyone.'

The head came up even more quickly. 'Wouldn't tell anyone anyway, sire. Wouldn't dream of it. Not under any circumstances.'

William frowned.

'I mean,' Martel went pleadingly on, 'I'm the one who
brought the body of Harold to you. I told my men that's what

we were doing. I'd look pretty stupid if I told them I'd got it wrong and it wasn't the King at all.'

'You'd look better dead,' William observed.

'But that would leave only two people to find him, sire.' Martel was gabbling again now. If in doubt, gabble, his father had told him. Takes the anger out of a situation. Martel's gabbling wasn't calculated, though, it was the genuine article.

He looked around the tent and thought that this was not the place he wanted to die. He hadn't planned on dying at all, and his father had given him numerous tips on making sure it didn't happen. Dying in the service of the Duke was always a guarantee of good standing for your family, but Martel would rather stay standing himself. Anyway, dying for the Duke in battle was one thing. Being killed by the Duke in his tent while Le Pedvin and a dead Saxon looked on wouldn't do his family any good at all. Never mind what it would do for him.

'Go on.' William's hand was stayed. For the moment.

'You can't go looking, sire, you're the victor, got to be seen around the place, glorying in your triumph. That would only leave Le Pedvin. Bit of a task to do on your own I'd have thought, find a missing King?'

'Hmm.' William appraised Martel through narrowed eyes. Martel couldn't tell if the eyes were narrowed so that the order for execution would be more effective, or if the Duke was actually thinking.

'All right, you live.'

Martel sighed and shook slightly.

'Until we find Harold,' William qualified the reprieve.

'Of course, sire,' Martel bowed in gratitude. This was no time for quibbling.

William returned to his seat, put his feet on the table, which annoyed the Saxon further, and moved quickly on to the practicalities. 'The problem is going to be looking for him, when no one must know he's gone missing, and doing it quickly. We've got about a week, I reckon. The Witan will want to know he's gone, and his family will probably start bleating about wanting the body. I can hold them off by saying it's in a pretty horrible condition, but if we can't produce him in a week, word will start spreading.'

Le Pedvin rubbed his hands. 'No problem, sire. I'll simply round up a few locals and ask them if they've seen a well dressed man with a wounded eye, walking away from the battle.'

'But then they'll know we're looking,' Martel objected.

'If you'll let me finish?' Le Pedvin sighed with impatience. 'I'll ask them under threat of death, and then when they've answered I'll kill them anyway.'

'No good,' William concluded after a moment's thought. 'Word will soon spread that you're going round killing people.'

'It's what I was going to do anyway,' Le Pedvin shrugged.

'Word will still get out. Harold'll go into hiding and we'll never find him then. What we need is a good reason to be going round the country asking a lot of questions and looking at things. That way we can find out where he is and kill him before anyone else finds out we've lost him.'

Martel and Le Pedvin exchanged glances. They were sharing some confusion over this convoluted plan. It didn't sound like the Norman way. Straightforward and brutal, that was a proper plan,

'We won the battle, sire,' Le Pedvin protested. 'We can ask anyone anything we want, and we can kill anyone we like. What's the point of winning a battle if you can't do simple things like that afterwards?'

'Things are different for kings.' William sounded rather resigned. 'You have to behave yourself a bit. The Pope may be right behind us now, but he's a devious bastard. For all I know the next conqueror's right behind *me*. And getting Harald Hardrada to invade the north just as we came south? That took some organising, I can tell you. The Norsemen might be relatives, but they're still a difficult bunch. I can't risk them turning round in the middle of the northern sea and coming back for a go themselves. Bloody Vikings!' William mused for a moment on some personal recollection, a rather disturbing one by the look on his face. He shook the memory away. 'Which they will do if they get a sniff that I haven't had a total victory.'

'Pah.' Le Pedvin clearly thought being a king wasn't worth the effort. Better to be a duke who can kill who he wants than a king who has to talk and listen.

'We need to let the world know that I'm completely in charge. I won the battle decisively, and Harold is not wandering around looking for a physick who removes arrows from eyes. That's a thought.' William rubbed his hands. 'Isn't there a place round here full of nuns who make tapestry?'

Le Pedvin frowned for a moment. His eye looked confused.

'You know – big woolly things with pictures in.'

'I know what a tapestry is, sire. I'm just not sure I see the point?'

'The point is that we could get them to make a great big one showing me winning the battle and Harold getting killed. You know, *Hic Rex Anglorum Harold Est*, that sort of thing, only there's a man with an arrow in his eye. Fatal wound for all to see. We could show it round the country and everyone would believe it. I mean nuns don't lie, do they?' He didn't look too sure about this, not being familiar with the ways of nuns.

'I'm sure they would if you prodded them.' Le Pedvin nodded, thinking hard. 'It's somewhere round here – in Kent, I think.'

'That's the place. Send word to get a bit done with a dead Harold in it, something that'll be convincing, showing Harold's dead and I own everything. Simple stuff. Won't hold them for long, but every little helps. Then we can put it on show back home, at Bayeux or somewhere.'

Le Pedvin nodded acknowledgement of the order.

William pondered on. 'Next question is, what excuse do we have for wandering about asking a load of questions – some of which will help us find Harold?'

The Duke had a devious look in his eye, the one which usually shone when he'd worked out the most profitable order in which to murder his neighbours. 'I believe I have a marvellous idea,' he said slowly. 'Not only that, but I know just the man to carry it out.'

'Who?' Le Pedvin scoffed.

'Ranulf,' William replied.

Le Pedvin blanched. Le Pedvin, the great man of war and of violence in general. The man who knew no fear and bowed to no one, the ragged, one-eyed face which brought terror to the houses of his enemies and to the dreams of children; this face was itself a picture of anxiety.

'Oh no, sire, no,' he pleaded, 'you promised. Not again. Not Ranulf.'

William grinned at his idea and Le Pedvin's discomfort. He stood again and gave the table another hearty thump.

The Saxon took this as the final insult and the weight of the body made it roll completely off the table and on to the floor, leaving the sheet behind.

Martel could not contain a small squeal as all three men looked to the corpse to see if it was going to start crawling towards the door.

After a few moments of quiet, William snorted. 'At least this one's got the good sense to be really dead.'

Chapter 3
Hic Irritatus Ranulf Est

ANULF DE SAUVELOY HAD HIS OWN TENT at the battle site, but he wasn't in it. This was normal.

He had expressed great reluctance to join William on this venture at all. He knew where England was, of course, between Alderney and Iceland, but he had no desire to visit the place.

William had persuaded him, though. Not in the way William usually persuaded people to do what he wanted. He had actually asked, and asked nicely. In fact he'd positively pleaded. The Duke said the invasion would be a complete failure if Ranulf wasn't there, and of course he was right.

Ranulf's very particular skills and talents were essential to the success of the venture. From beginning to end, the conquest of England depended on Ranulf de Sauveloy. There was no one in William's force with a better head for planning and organisation, for attention to detail and coordination. No one else who could put an invasion force together in the right place and at the right time, and make sure they all turned up at the right battle. No one was more meticulous, thoughtful, careful and rigorous.

Nor was anyone more pedantic, officious, critical or difficult, irritating, infuriating, exasperating and just plain reviled.

Only Ranulf could look upon the work of others and pull it to pieces without ever offering anything approaching help or encouragement to get things right. He was the sort of man who would offer you a goblet of wine and you'd feel insulted. He'd say you had a nice house and it sounded like he hated your revolting hovel. He'd compliment your horse and you'd be convinced he thought the thing was only good for a stew. Basically whenever Ranulf opened his mouth, someone would want to hit him in it.

Many of William's nobles had mental lists of those they were going to despatch at the battle. For an awful lot of them Ranulf was further up the list than Harold.

The man was not actually impossible: it just felt like that. The impression was not helped by the overwhelming aura of self-importance which floated round him like a sycophantic fog.

Everyone knew William was a better fighter than most. They accepted the fact and William did likewise. He didn't spend his time going round reminding people how awful their fighting was, how they weren't really trying and how, if they put in a bit more effort, they could improve their standards. Yet that was how Ranulf lived his life. Yes, he was better organised and more thoughtful than everyone else. Yes, he knew where things should be, what they should do and when they should do it. He was better than everyone else at this. He also spent more of his time reminding people of this fact rather than actually organising things.

And he didn't do this by telling everyone he was better. He did it by telling them they were worse.

Ranulf knew that the battle master had disposed the forces wrong and was using wholly inappropriate tactics. He knew the quartermaster had designed most of the equipment wrong, built it poorly and wasn't maintaining it properly. He knew the cooks weren't preparing the victuals correctly, were distributing them inefficiently and hadn't cleaned up right. He knew the battle drills hadn't been thought through, weren't very good anyway and the men simply didn't do them. And he said so.

This approach alone was enough to make the man the most hated thing in the Norman army – but the most infuriating thing of all, the most appalling aspect of a thoughtless and appalling man was that he was usually right.

The ordinary men, the nobles, high and low, and even the Duke himself could have put up with Ranulf if he had been wrong now and again. Had there been some chink in his armour of perfection, his pomposity and pedantry would be bearable. As it was, all anyone could do once he started was sigh and say, 'Yes, Ranulf'.

Even when the man appeared to criticise you for doing something he had told you to do in the first place, there would appear to be some perfectly reasonable explanation. It was just that you weren't quite bright enough to follow him.

William recognised Ranulf's talents and used them to great advantage. The price was worth paying, particularly as he was the Duke and could delegate dealing with Ranulf to people he didn't like very much.

◆   ◆   ◆

Ranulf was not in his tent at this moment because he was in that of Robert de Beaumont, one of William's senior nobles. He was half way through a withering deconstruction of the failures of Robert's forces during the battle: how their shape and discipline had failed and how, frankly, Robert's leadership was not all it could be. He even had his toolkit with him, the small folder of bound sheets of parchment he always carried, and he was reading from what was clearly a comprehensive list. As he went through the catalogue of shortcomings he ticked them off with a quill pen, dipped now and again into his portable inkwell. People had to admit that even Ranulf's criticism was very well organised.

De Beaumont had tried to protest that they'd actually won the battle if Ranulf cared to look. He tried to explain how, if Ranulf had been anywhere near the actual fighting, he would have been able to see how complex the situation was, but Ranulf wasn't listening. As usual.

If Ranulf had any empathy, if he was in the least way capa-

ble of appreciating and recognising the reactions and feelings
of others, he would have noticed that Robert de Beaumont was
gripping the hilt of his sword very tightly indeed. Ranulf's value
to William was very high, and the Duke's instructions about the
man's wellbeing were very clear. Still, this was a battlefield, and
accidents did happen.

Of course, the one thing Ranulf didn't have a clue about
was other people. He just assumed they were like him and wel-
comed his comments. He assumed they were all ashamed of
their failures, which were so obvious they couldn't fail to notice
them, and were eager to improve their performance on the back
of his welcome observations. He assumed everyone respected
him and his opinions. He did not assume he was dicing with
death every time he said, 'Can I have a word?'

What he never realised was that his destructive criticism
actually prompted people to do exactly the opposite of what he
suggested. Which explained why things often got worse after
one of his visits. For everyone.

The tension of the moment was shattered by the entrance of
William's messenger. The look on Ranulf's face quite clearly said
that the messenger couldn't even walk into a tent properly.

'Duke William commands your presence,' the messenger
announced to Ranulf. Those weren't the actual words of his
instruction, but people took every opportunity to put Ranulf in
his place, even messengers.

Ranulf raised his eyebrows at the messenger and cast one
of his haughty looks at de Beaumont. 'We shall continue this
review later,' he said as he swept importantly from the room,
leaving the messenger to follow in his wake.

'Not if I cut your bloody head off we won't,' Robert de Beaumont hissed in a fit of wishful thinking.

◆　　◆　　◆

It was hard for the men of the Norman camp to avoid Ranulf

as he corrected his way across the ground. They never saw him coming.

He was not a prepossessing man in any way whatsoever. He was of no distinguishing appearance, being neither noticeably short nor tall. Neither fat nor overly thin, he had no squint, scar or disfigurement of birth. He didn't limp and even his clothes were plain and unremarkable. No one could even put an accurate age to the man. Some thought he was about twenty-five, others were sure he'd been around forever. The more imaginative even argued he had been in a certain garden, persuading Eve of the benefits of an apple-based diet. Others retorted that he'd have been hiding behind the tree, waiting to criticise the snake for its slithering and the woman for her choice of fruit.

This awful averageness was Ranulf's most awesome weapon. Those who didn't know would engage him in conversation as he looked pretty harmless. They would welcome him into their homes or introduce him to their families before they realised what they'd done.

After enduring comprehensive criticism of every aspect of their lives, possessions, pastimes, ideals, eating habits and decorative taste, even the mildest would be ready to commit murder. Then somehow the appalling memory of the man would fade when he wasn't there. It would be back within ten seconds of meeting him again.

The journey from de Beaumont's tent to William's was not a long one, but it was a fine opportunity to put a lot of things right. Soldiers were told to straighten their armour and their tents. Victuallers were told they'd put too much blood in the stew, or too little. Stable lads were given instruction on the care of horses and one minor noble was told that the griffon on his coat of arms was facing the wrong way. It was.

As the messenger followed behind the rampaging Ranulf, many in the camp made encouraging faces and gestures towards him. These all indicated pretty plainly that he should take out his sword and stick it through Ranulf's head. The messenger ignored them, knowing his approbation would be short-lived. Duke William would doubtless waste no time in sticking his sword through the messenger's head. And William knew how to make things like that last a long time.

◆ ◆ ◆

Le Pedvin had steeled himself for the moment, but he still twitched as he heard Ranulf's entirely normal and inoffensive tones drift through William's tent. As the noise drew closer it became apparent Ranulf was berating the camp master for not putting William's tent up in quite the right direction, without quite the right tension in the guy ropes, and without repairing some noticeable holes. 'Sire,' Ranulf announced himself to the room with a perfectly correct bow.

'Master Ranulf.' William held out his arms, with no invitation for Ranulf to come into them. 'The day went well.'

Ranulf released the most subtle, the most perfectly pitched sigh. 'Well, I suppose we won,' he said, making it perfectly clear that this was in no way sufficient to justify the conclusion that the day should be described as going *well*.

'We did,' said William, quite happy that this was perfectly sufficient.

'I have just been going over some of the major errors made by de Beaumont's men,' Ranulf sighed again, 'and as for the group who stood loitering on the left flank, I have some lengthy observations for their leader.'

Martel tried to vanish even further into the background. Even Le Pedvin kept his mouth shut.

'Is that the defeated King?' Ranulf said, looking at the sheet on the table, under which the Saxon had been replaced. He looked at it with an eye that wanted to go and straighten it.

'It is,' William announced, 'and we shall present the treacherous Harold to the Witan to prove our right to the throne.'

'Excellent, sire,' Ranulf nodded. Then there was that sigh again. 'Except, of course, the process is actually …'

'I have a job for you, Ranulf.' William interrupted before the plans for his coronation were torn apart.

'Indeed, sire?' Ranulf seemed puzzled, as if there was clearly enough to do here without being given another task.

William took himself back to his seat and pushed his plate away. It caught in part of the sheet, which he hurriedly grabbed to stop it falling off the corpse.

'Now Harold is gone, I have it mind to discover what this country is actually made of,' he said.

Ranulf said nothing. Martel and le Pedvin exchanged glances that said the country was made of the stuff all countries are made of.

'I've heard all about it, of course. We all think we know what's here, but do we really? Harold could have been pulling the wool over our eyes all this time. Telling us there was a shire here and a town there; could have been a pack of lies. Plus, of course, we want the conquered people to know they've been conquered.'

'Sire?' Ranulf still didn't get it.

'So I want the place counted.'

'Counted?'

'Yes, counted. And who better to count things than you? Who better to count them and make sure they stay counted?'

'Count the country?' Ranulf was lost. He was clearly resisting the almost overwhelming urge to tell his Duke he was babbling.

'Not count the country obviously: count the things in it. Write down how many there are and where they all are.'

'What sort of things?'

'People, castles, towns, farms, animals, everything.'

'Everything?' Ranulf was a bit daunted by this task. 'You want everything counted?'

'I do.'

Le Pedvin and Martel were clearly relishing Ranulf's discomfort. Even Le Pedvin's eye had a gleam.

'And Martel and Le Pedvin will help.' William soon put a stop to that.

Ranulf looked at them. He looked at them as if they weren't good enough to be standing in the same room as him, let alone be capable of assisting him in anything as complicated as counting. He had a point.

'It is a commendable aim, sire,' Ranulf began.

'I know,' William finished. 'Off you go then.' He flipped a hand to indicate they could leave.

'Sire.' Ranulf was all seriousness. Seriousness and instruction, instruction of his betters, which was his usual approach. 'While counting the contents of the country is a laudable and entirely sensible aim, it needs planning.'

William's lips were tight.

'We need to clarify the remit of the count. Agree some terms of reference and any exclusions, set boundaries and expectations. Where do we start? In what order should we proceed? What resources will we require? What is our timescale and how many men will it take? These are all matters which need to be resolved before we can start. I hardly think three men can count a whole country.' His look to Le Pedvin and Martel said he doubted they could count above one.

'I'm sure that's all very reasonable,' William managed to get out through his clenched teeth as he dragged himself back to his feet. 'Unfortunately it's not what I *want*.'

Le Pedvin took a cautious step backwards. Martel observed and did likewise.

'What I want,' William went on, stepping up to Ranulf and looking him in the eye to make sure the man understood the debate was coming to an end, 'what I want is for you, Martel and Le Pedvin to get out there and start counting. I want it done quickly so the wretched English know they're Norman now. I want them to know that this has been their Doomsday. Take your little book with you and write it down to show the buggers who's in charge. If we don't get to know what they've got pretty damn quick, they'll hide it all. How can we tax their arses off if we don't know how big their arses are in the first place? You don't need to count every blade of grass. Just head north and start with the big stuff.'

'Wouldn't it be better to send a force?' Ranulf asked. 'To let the English see your power?'

'No,' William replied simply.

'Oh.' Ranulf tried to make it sound like a question.

'Better to send you lot. Let the English see I'm so totally in control and confident I can send just three men into their heart.'

'Into the heart of the English.' Ranulf allowed himself a small complaint.

'Martel will stop them cutting your head off,' William promised, 'and Le Pedvin will stop them cutting his head off.'

Ranulf allowed his hand to creep up in question.

'One question, Ranulf,' William said deliberately. 'One final question.'

'How will we know the best places to look?' Ranulf asked. Anyone else in this situation would have asked timidly. Ranulf still made it sound like one of William's personal failures was not having a map of England in his head. 'I assume neither Martel nor Le Pedvin are familiar with the country.'

Martel and Le Pedvin shrugged to indicate this was indeed the case.

'Do I have to think of everything?' William growled. 'Find a tame Saxon to take with you. Find a map. Pull one of your eyes out and tie it to a crow. In fact let *me* pull it out and tie it to a crow.'

Ranulf bowed rapidly and retreated.

'We will leave first thing in the morning, sire,' he said, recognising when debate was to no avail.

'Now would be better,' William said simply.

'We will leave immediately, sire.'

'Excellent. Take a week and come back after that. Then I might let you plan how to do the full job properly.'

Ranulf shivered, probably at the thought of being asked to do anything which wasn't going to be done properly. He gestured imperiously that Le Pedvin and Martel should follow.

The men did so, but Le Pedvin gave William a deeply unpleasant look with his baleful eye as he passed. He even pointed a finger at William, making it perfectly clear that the finger was going to remember this. William now owed a great debt to Le Pedvin's finger.

'And make sure you find *everything*,' William snarled pointedly as his one-eyed companion passed.

With his King-finders dispatched, Duke William returned to his seat. He now had a dead Saxon he didn't want, cluttering up his dining table. Everyone thought it was Harold so he couldn't just get rid of it, but he didn't fancy the thought of it sitting there for a week while the search went on. It wasn't the idea of a week-old corpse which bothered him, it was the damage the thing might do to such a nice piece of oak.

He would have to get the thing moved. He could probably say that dead kings had to have their faces covered or something. Then he smiled that he would be King soon, so he could say whatever he wanted.

Chapter 4

A Spare Saxon

NUD MABBUT WAS IN AS SORRY a state as he had ever been. It was bad enough that his life was spent as a Saxon hostage in the Norman court. Now he had been dragged along to this field to witness the slaughter of his own kith and kin.

He had spent as much of his captivity as possible remonstrating with the Normans and speaking up for the Saxon people: their way of life, their culture, their music, their art, their clothing, their dance, their jewellery, their mountains and streams and fields and villages and, well, pretty much everything. He was usually listened to for about the first five seconds. If that.

And now what? The marvel that was the Saxon race, cut down by these ... these *Normans*. Mabbut couldn't think of a more denigrating title.

He had been optimistic at the start of the day as the Saxon line held firm. William had been unable to break the shield wall, and Mabbut was quite looking forward to going back to the boats at Hastings, and across the water. He was planning to say 'I told you so' at regular intervals.

Then some idiot had decided to break the Saxon line and chase the Normans down the hill. And that was that. The Normans turned and attacked, and the Saxons were lost. And what could he do? Nothing. He had to stand there while the hated enemy swept his people away.

Yes, someone had offered him a sword to go and defend his land, but it was too late by then. The day was lost. His duty now was clear. He would protect the Saxon ways and make sure his people were not forgotten. At a practical level he wandered round the battlefield seeing who was dead, He'd already found several cousins on his mother's side.

◆　　　◆　　　◆

'Is he mad?' Ranulf demanded when the three of them had gathered outside the tent.

'Yes,' Le Pedvin replied simply, 'you know he is. That's why we do what he says.'

Ranulf stared into the encroaching darkness, ready to pick it apart for not encroaching properly.

The moans and groans of the battle had died down as more and more of the people who had been doing the moaning and groaning expired. Torches flared here and there as William's men made their camps, illuminating a scene that should really be the property of the dark.

The colour had been stripped from the place by the departing sun. Night was falling, and those who had survived their wounds for a day knew that darkness was never so kind. Their silence hung over the place like the sheet which still covered not-Harold's body.

It looked as if the men lolling about had simply lain down at the end of the day in the closest convenient spot. It was a tricky place to lie down as there were arrows sticking up from every spare spot of land, but many had been assisted in lying down by an arrow or two that pinned them to the ground.

Crows and magpies hopped joyfully from place to place, trying to decide where to start their feast amongst such largesse. Despite the fact there was more than enough to go round, they still cackled and fought one another. After them the night creatures would emerge and make a much better job of dismantling the remains.

The more important Normans were being taken away for burial by their fellows, the sights and sounds of great mourning accompanying their passage. The less important were being dragged out of the way, the sights and sounds of men moaning at a job they didn't want to do accompanying their passage.

Saxons, high and low, were left where they were. Their people could come and get them in the morning and make whatever noises they liked.

It seemed unjust to many that their companions should be dead and buried in this strange land. However, the alternative of taking the bodies back with them to Normandy was even less attractive.

The whole country seemed bizarre and everyone assumed it would only get even more strange the further they went. The hills were the wrong shape, the trees and grass the wrong colour and the smells didn't bear talking about. No one had tried the food yet, but that was going to be a real shock.

Even the birds seemed to be singing in English, and the ones that dared a speculative peck at the odd corpse squawked in a most disturbing manner. A small group of men had liberated a cow from a nearby farmer, just after they liberated him of everything else of value. They had been on the verge of slaughtering the beast for a magnificent meal when the thing said 'moo' instead of '*meau*' and they all ran like hell.

The sooner they got back to Normandy the better.

◆　　◆　　◆

'Do either of you know anything about this country?' Ranulf asked the question with a hint of criticism. The same as the sea they had just crossed had a hint of wet.

Martel shook his head, 'Never been here before. Nor has Father. He just sent me to accompany William. I was surprised how far it was.'

Ranulf tutted at the completely useless man.

'And you, Le Pedvin? You must have known something? You came to invade the place, for goodness sake.'

Le Pedvin, the man who could slice the head off an enemy with a backhand, shivered in the face of Ranulf's withering question.

'Some,' he shrugged. 'We know our landing place at Hastings and the lay of the land round here. Apart from that, I only know what everyone knows.'

'Which is?' Even a simple question from Ranulf came across as a personal insult.

'The west is called Corny and it's full of Bretons. Weird lot.' He scowled at Martel who was himself of Breton stock, clearly thinking he fitted the description admirably. 'They're odd enough on our side of the water and I've heard horrible tales of what they get up to over here. The east is under water. The north is full of savages and lost Roman legions. Then there's Wales. No one knows what's there. People who go tend not to come back. Druids,' he explained with a shudder.

Ranulf frowned.

'Anyway,' Le Pedvin went on the offensive, 'you're the one who was planning the attack. How come you don't know what's here?'

'Of course I know what's *here*.' Ranulf spread his arms to take in the battlefield. 'I don't need to know what's everywhere. In fact, I don't want to know. Once this was sorted out I was heading home.'

'Bad luck.'

Ranulf snorted. 'I certainly don't intend to set off tonight. Ridiculous. We wouldn't even be able to see where we were going, let alone count anything of significance. First light will be quite adequate.'

A sound broke the silence. The sound of Le Pedvin's sword being drawn. 'Our Duke commanded us to leave immediately,' he said simply, his simple sword pointing simply at Ranulf, 'and so that is what we do.'

Ranulf observed Le Pedvin's blade and tutted at the state of the thing.

'As I see it,' Le Pedvin went on, 'I've been given a specific task. I have to keep you alive, while you carry out the Duke's orders. If you aren't carrying out the Duke's orders, I assume I no longer have to keep you alive. In my little book, not keeping someone alive is the same as making them dead.'

Martel stood to one side with eyes wide. Death was everywhere. Anyone's life could be like that of William's favourite jester who had led the Normans into battle: cut off very, very quickly. Time for a babble, clearly. 'Well, that's good, then,' he smiled, placating the opposing parties and rubbing his hands. 'Off we go. Didn't the Duke say something about getting a guide?'

Le Pedvin's sword lowered slightly and Ranulf gazed into the darkness, which was now gathering quite nicely.

'He did,' de Sauveloy scoffed, 'as if we can find a co-operative Saxon amongst this lot.' He gestured once more to the remains of the battle. This time he seemed to be having a go at Le Pedvin for allowing so many useful people to be killed.

The warrior cast his lonesome eye across the scene of devastation. Some idea came into his head and he lifted himself to scan the place with more purpose. 'There,' he pointed.

Martel and Ranulf followed his arm and saw a figure wandering among the dead. Every now and then the figure bent to examine one of the corpses before moving on. The shrouding evening made it impossible to identify the shape from this distance. Only the flickering torches revealed the movement.

'Is it a Saxon?' Martel asked, a hint of worry in his voice.

'It is,' Le Pedvin said with confidence. 'Mabbut. Cnud Mabbut.'

'Oh, not him,' Ranulf groaned. 'He's an awful man, constantly complaining about everything.'

Le Pedvin raised his eyebrows at this coming from Ranulf, the master complainer. Well, he raised one eyebrow and one brow.

'Who's Mabbut?' Martel asked.

'You'll soon find out.' Le Pedvin did not sound enthusiastic.

He stepped into the field and waved an arm to indicate the others should follow.

Martel and Ranulf swapped looks. Martel's was all puzzle, Ranulf's all annoyance. No change there then.

Stepping over and in between the bodies in the darkness, not through respect but from an earnest desire not to trip and land on anything unpleasant, the party made its way towards the shape which still dipped and wove among the bodies.

'Oy, Mabbut,' Le Pedvin called when they were in range.

The figure looked in their direction briefly, before turning back to whatever grizzly task it was carrying out.

'I'm talking to you,' Le Pedvin growled when they came up to the man.

Mabbut stood and tried to look like a haughty Saxon. Well, as haughty as was possible in a field of dead Saxons; but at least he had dressed the part. It was as if he'd gone to one of William's raucous parties dressed as a Saxon. His legs had crossed binding on them, his leather jerkin was cut Saxon style and he even wore a Saxon helmet.

He maintained his haughtiness as the figures of Le Pedvin and Ranulf drew close, together with another man. Le Pedvin he knew by face and reputation. It was a very bad reputation, or a very good reputation for doing very bad things, depending on your point of view.

Ranulf he knew as well. He had encountered that ghastly man on several occasions, and on every one he had been complaining and criticising. The only saving grace was that he did not discriminate between Norman or Saxon. All were potential targets for his withering tongue. The man had even been overheard suggesting that Mabbut should be sent back to England, as he appeared to be completely useless. Overheard because he was saying it very loudly to Duke William during a banquet.

Apparently he then followed it up with a letter and an itinerary for the journey.

Mabbut would have taken offence, but the planned expedition included a wide selection of Norman nobles, also deemed by Ranulf to be below standard.

Who the other one was, Mabbut had not a clue. He had never seen him before, in court or battle. Perhaps he was foreign. Mabbut couldn't immediately decide whether that was better or worse than being Norman. In this place at this time, anyone who wasn't Saxon was the devil's playmate.

'This is my uncle.' Mabbut gestured to the body he now stood over. He was pretty sure it was an uncle. Someone he'd called uncle anyway. He'd once asked his mother how many brothers she really had, but she'd been rather vague. He acknowledged numbers had never been her strong point.

'Really?' Le Pedvin either didn't believe it or didn't care. Or both.

'Yes, really, and you killed him.'

Le Pedvin studied the particular corpse carefully. He shook his head slowly. 'No,' he said, 'don't think so.' He looked around a bit and pointed to another body. 'I did that one.'

Mabbut let out a groan of pain and despair. He was still young and full of energy, but it all counted for nothing. He rubbed his beardless chin and then drew hands over his eyes, as shining blue as a Viking's. His face was even, and would have been handsome had his nose not been broken some time ago and put back together sideways, from the look of it. He had chosen the wrong Norman to lecture on the superior qualities of the Saxon. He rubbed his angular extremity and glowered at Le Pedvin.

'You could always have fought for them,' Le Pedvin goaded.

'You know perfectly well I couldn't,' Mabbut snapped back. 'William would have killed my parents.'

'How many times do I have to tell you, boy?' Le Pedvin threw his arms in the air. 'Your parents are not hostages. They live quite happily and comfortably in William's court. Your father is the Duke's agricultural adviser.' He looked to Ranulf for help.

'It's perfectly true,' de Sauveloy confirmed. He confirmed it grudgingly, making it perfectly clear that any agricultural advice given must have been wrong.

'Then why do I never see them?' Mabbut demanded. He heard this argument trotted out all the time. As if he would fall for something so transparent.

'I'm not going to get into this with you again. You don't see them because they don't want to see you. You are an annoying little turd, prancing around like a jester's version of a Saxon, going on and on about Saxon this and Saxon that. You're an embarrassment. You know your father disowned you – you got the letter.'

'A forgery!' Mabbut exclaimed.

'Ye gods above,' Le Pedvin shook his head, 'there really is no point arguing with you. Believe what you want about who you want. I really couldn't care less. The point is we've got a job for you.' He glared his most ferocious glare.

'I won't do it,' Mabbut said simply. 'I won't do anything to help the Norman invader.'

'You will or I'll chop your bloody head off,' Le Pedvin replied, equally simply. He drew his sword once more to emphasise the point. He felt the blade and frowned at the condition of the edge. 'Might take a few hacks, but it'll come off eventually,' he concluded.

Mabbut surveyed the weapon in Le Pedvin's hand. He surveyed his people scattered on the floor. He considered his options: side with the murderers of his people, or make one last glorious, defiant but ultimately hopeless gesture. 'What's the job?' he asked grumpily.

'You're going to show me, Ranulf and Martel here round this awful country of yours.'

'I'm what?' Mabbut was outraged. 'You've just slaughtered the best men in England and I'm supposed to give you a tour?'

'Well done.'

'And you're going to show us all the points of interest,' Ranulf added.

'Such as?' Mabbut was still having trouble believing what he'd been asked.

'Farms, manors, castles, anything of value really.'

'And you can point out any nobles or freemen,' Le Pedvin added, with a sideways glance at Martel.

'You've got all of *them* here.' Mabbut nodded his head towards his countrymen, his dead countrymen.

'Make that bit easy then,' Le Pedvin offered.

'So let me get this straight.' Mabbut had assumed the tone people use when they want to make it quite clear that what they are explaining is insane. 'You've just invaded the country and killed most of the army. I'm now supposed to show you where all the good stuff is so you can steal it, or tax it or just plain move in. Is that right? You're asking a Saxon to turn his country over to the enemy?'

Le Pedvin dug his sword into the ground. Or at least he thought it was the ground until Mabbut asked him to remove the sword from his uncle.

'Let *me* get this straight.' Le Pedvin said when he'd extricated his weapon from one of Mabbut's mother's many brothers. 'This is no longer your country. We have just invaded it. We have killed its army, so everything is now ours. That's how it works, invasion. All the good stuff as you call it, although from a first glance I haven't seen anything I'd actually want, belongs to us. That pretty much means we can do what we like with it.'

'But you can't seriously ask me to co-operate. I'd be betraying my people.'

'I think you'll be the least of their problems,' Le Pedvin shrugged. 'If you change out of those stupid clothes they'll probably think you're just another Norman.'

'You could be a sort of go-between,' Martel offered.

Mabbut looked at him with disdain. It was bad enough having to deal with Le Pedvin, never mind his lackey.

'If you don't accompany us we'll go anyway,' Martel continued, 'and if we do that, there's a good chance Le Pedvin here will do some more damage. With you to deal with the natives, there'll be a lot less trouble.'

'But what will they think of me?' Mabbut wailed a bit.

'I'm sure they'll be grateful,' Martel got in quickly before Le Pedvin could offer a response, which would doubtless include phrases like 'don't care' or 'no worse than they do already, you time-serving little toad'.

'I mean to say,' Martel went on, 'who'd want a great Norman like Le Pedvin here knocking on your door in the middle of the night? Or de Sauveloy turning up to count your chickens? Much better to have one of their own to deal with. I expect you'll save lots of lives. And of course this is Duke William's bidding. Who knows how grateful he'll be when it's complete?'

This did give Mabbut some pause. If Duke William actually owed him something, his situation might improve. Maybe he could use his service as a lever to get his parents' conditions improved. After all it was plain they were hostages, despite what Le Pedvin said. Which good Saxon folk would voluntarily leave the green pastures of England to go and live in Normandy, for goodness sake? The place was warm in the summer and mild in the winter, not a proper climate at all. As for the food ...

'What about the nobles and freemen though?' Mabbut objected. 'If I point them out to you, you'll kill them.'

'I thought you said they were all here?' Le Pedvin asked pointedly.

'Well,' Mabbut was evasive, 'there might have been a few who couldn't make it.'

'If they didn't come to the battle they're all right with me. As long as they spent the time practicing swearing loyalty to William.'

Mabbut paused as he weighed all this information up. 'This is ridiculous,' he concluded.

'Good, that's settled,' Le Pedvin sheathed his sword. 'Four horses!' he yelled into the darkness – the yell of a man who is used to getting exactly that he wants, immediately.

'Now?' Mabbut was alarmed again. 'It's the middle of the night.'

'That's what *I* said,' Ranulf put in. Then the shock of actually agreeing with someone made him choke.

'It's the Duke's will,' Martel said cheerfully as he strode off across the field of silent Saxons, following Le Pedvin.

'But what about my pack, my things?' Mabbut called after the departing Normans.

'Don't worry,' Le Pedvin called back, 'remember who won the battle. Anything we want, we just take it.'

Chapter 5
Northern Lights

FAR TO THE NORTH, BUT STILL SOUTH of the land of savages and lost legions, a night mist floated from sea to shore. It deadened sound and movement, and lent a haunted atmosphere to the strand. The fact that many men had died here, a lot of them drowned in the racing tides, added to the aura of dread.

It was easy to imagine bodies still drifting off shore, just out of sight in the enveloping mist, moaning gently as their watery graves denied them entry to their afterlife. The drowned man was a figure of terror to all, and a nightmare fear.

Through the muffling of the dank fog, noises emerged. They were quieter than they should be, the sort of noises made by people trying not to make any noise, and doing it quite well.

One patch of the fog suddenly lightened with a lonely glow, as if the bodies of the dead reared up as one to throw themselves in supplication on the shore.

The shape resolved itself quickly into a dim lamp, hanging like drool from a hideous gaping maw. The maw of an animal of power and hatred, looking for souls to devour as it scoured the fog. Probably for eternity, and doubtless under some curse or other.

If anyone had the fortitude not to run from this ghastly sight, they would soon see the maw was made of wood. Behind it a great boat forced itself through the mist and turned its unwelcome attentions on the coast. It slowed not one jot as it drew closer, until the stones of the beach cried out when the prow of the craft drove into them. Eventually they mustered their strength to resist the onslaught, and the mighty boat ground to a halt.

From the high prow, from one side of the dominating figurehead, great feet flew down and crunched the shore. The figurehead itself, a great roaring dragon, looked on as two more pairs of feet left its shadow and pummelled the ground of England. This was not the first time they'd done that.

'Meet at the agreed place in a week,' the voice belonging to the first pair of feet called back to the boat. 'If we're not there, if we haven't made it for some reason, don't you hesitate; You stay where you are until we arrive. I don't want you bloody clearing off and leaving us. Not after last time.' The voice was deep enough to pierce the fog and spoke in the guttural language of a people who didn't like to open their mouths very much. They didn't want the cold getting in.

'Pah,' a female voice from the boat called with some contempt. 'Don't worry about us, just you worry about yourselves. I thought you were going in disguise anyway?' An arm appeared with the hand on it gesturing impatiently, apparently waiting for something.

The three figures on the beach shrugged. One by one they reached up, grabbed their helmets by the massive horns which adorned them and took them from their heads. They handed them back to the boat.

'I still don't know what you're doing this for,' the woman said as she took the headwear. 'Let him rot, I say.'

'Honour,' the owner of the first feet replied.

'Honour!' The woman spat most effectively on to the beach. 'It would have been honourable to drown him when you had the chance; we could have been home by now.'

'Someone has to be honourable in this sorry business. We'll none of us be sitting in the halls of Asgard if this isn't put right.'

'Don't know why,' the female voice grumbled.

'His own brother.' The man on the beach spoke as if this were ample explanation. 'I knew Harald was in the wrong, but the Englishman's own brother? It's not right.'

'You didn't say that when you killed all them monks,' the woman pointed out.

'Ah well, they was heathens. Fair game, your heathen. Specially your heathen monks. But this is different.'

The woman had clearly given up an old argument. 'Well, just sort yourself out quickly. Sail east you said, no sail west you said, turning backwards and forwards, never knowing whether we're coming or going. Call yourself a sailor.'

'Be quiet, woman,' the voice retorted, with the air of one accepting defeat. 'You could nag the blubber off a seal,' it muttered.

'I could if you caught one once in a while you lazy, stinking, pile of herring crap.'

'Ha ha!' Male and female laughed raucously.

'If you come back dead, Erik,' the woman called through the mist, 'I shall be bloody furious.'

The two fellows with him dug Erik in the ribs and made a wide variety of suggestive noises.

He brushed them aside and indicated they should get their backs behind the boat. They did so, and heaved the craft off into the silent sea.

'And don't you cause any trouble,' Erik called after the departing boat.

'It's all right,' the woman's voice floated back through the mist, 'we'll just go and get a spot of plunder.'

Erik raised his eyes to the sky and tutted at his fellows. 'Well, don't come back with a load of rubbish you're never going to use. I know you and plunder,' he called into the shrouded air.

There was a reply, but it was pretty indistinct. Very rude, but pretty indistinct.

'Right.' Erik clapped his hands together. 'Let's go.'

They tramped away from the beach and headed inland.

Each had a short sword at their belt and a single round shield hung at the left shoulder. Knives were hidden away in various discreet and not so discreet places, and across each back a massive, double-sided axe was strapped. On top of this, simple packs bulged with supplies.

Huge arms, built into ramparts from the constant rowing, hung bare at their sides, even in this autumn cold. Legs were clad in tight animal skin and strong boots wrapped the feet.

The men's heads were now bare. Great blond beards bristled from their faces, themselves framed by long fair-haired locks, bound into tails that ran down their backs. From the middle of this confluence of blond, shining blue eyes pierced the darkness.

They revealed the combined intelligence of a group that thought simply taking their hats off would disguise the fact they were Vikings. They strode confidently away from the sea and towards the unsuspecting land.

◆　　◆　　◆

Reaching the top of the dunes that ran down to the beach they stopped. From here they surveyed the land as best they could. Surveying in the dark and the fog was not a sign of great military thinking – or of any great thinking at all.

'Which way?' Sigmund asked hopefully. He was the youngest of the group, the most enthusiastic and impetuous. He would have run off into the darkness at a moment's notice and kept going until he came to the western shore. He had been brought on the mission for his strength, his fearlessness and his ability to follow orders without question. His only problem was that if he had no orders he tended to make his own decisions, and these weren't usually very good. At all.

'We don't know, do we?' This was said with some feeling by Fregurd. This man was of slighter build than the massive Erik; slighter, but somehow carrying more intent. Fregurd's talent was a welcome addition to any expedition. If ever there was a battle, or a dispute of any sort, and you needed someone stabbing in the back, Fregurd was your man. He had a collection of knives for different occasions and different soft bits of the body. They all had names, and he spent many a happy evening in conversation with them. Everyone knew you should keep Fregurd in front of you in a fight. If you couldn't see him, you were probably his next victim.

'Look,' Erik said, 'I don't want to argue about this any more. He shouldn't have wagered if he wasn't going to pay up.'

'I know you have to pay up,' Fregurd said sarcastically, 'and I know that if you refuse to pay up, you deserve to die. Quite straightforward. What was not such a good idea was to throw the only man with a map overboard.'

'I beat him fair.' Erik was sulking rather.

'I know you did,' Fregurd agreed again. 'You also needed him to show us where to go.'

There was an awkward silence.

'We could ask someone,' Sigmund suggested.

The other two looked at him. The young man had his sword out and was swinging it around stabbing at pretend enemies.

'Ask someone?' Erik asked in some disbelief.

Sigmund looked puzzled.

'We're bloody Vikings,' Erik insisted. 'We don't ask people things. What sort of saga would that make? Great Erik, Fregurd and Sigmund did travel across the sea to the ravaged land of England, where they stopped to ask directions?'

'I'm only saying,' Sigmund grumbled.

'Well, don't.'

The group lapsed into thoughtful silence.

❖　　❖　　❖

'We could torture,' Fregurd suggested happily after a pause. 'That would sound much better. We find someone and stab them until they tell us.'

Erik nodded carefully. 'That could be told well.' He followed his thought through. 'In fact we could find a village, burn it to the ground and torture the last surviving person until they tell us what we want to know.'

Sigmund looked thoughtful now – not a look that visited him often. 'I thought we were supposed to be in disguise?'

Erik's shoulders fell. 'Bugger,' he said.

Fregurd voiced the problem. 'If we burn down a village and do a bit of torture, they'll guess we're Vikings.'

'And we're not supposed to be here,' Erik said with disappointment. 'If we're found out there'll be hell to pay.'

'Still don't know why we worry about that,' Fregurd mumbled into his beard.

'We are in the land of Danelaw,' Erik said simply. 'If we go round plundering and killing the King's own subjects, he's not going to be too happy is he?'

'Happy!' Fregurd was dismissive. 'Whoever heard of Vikings being happy when there's no killing? Ridiculous.'

'Modern times,' Erik shrugged. 'The world is moving on and we have to go with it.'

'More like "I've made a deal with William and if you cock it up I'll kill you".'

'Same thing.' Erik was resigned. 'Good King Magnus wants to keep William happy, so we'd better not upset him.'

Fregurd snorted. 'As if we should worry about upsetting the Danish King.'

'Upset him so much he has us all killed?' Erik asked.

Fregurd snorted again.

'In that special way he has?' Erik raised eyebrows.

'Ah,' said Fregurd, apparently registering the force of this argument. 'So we really have to go and ask someone?'

'I suppose so,' said Erik glumly. 'Still,' he added, brightening, 'we don't have to ask nicely.'

They strode off down the hill and away from the beach

without any direction in mind. Nor could they get any sense of where they were heading. No moon or stars could be seen; all they knew was they were heading away from the beach. The beach faced home which was east, therefore they were going west.

The Viking people had an unerring sense of direction, which served them well in their travels over the oceans of the world. They found new lands, explored uncharted waters and discovered new peoples. They then killed a lot of them. Still, they knew where bits of the world were that others didn't even know existed.

Put a bunch of Vikings in a boat and they could find their way to a named fish.

Put this lot on dry land, however, and they would struggle to find their horns on their heads.

In fact their boat had swung round on the tidal flow of the Humber, depositing them on the riverbank. They had then set off over land, heading due south.

Viking luck was with them, however. If they had headed west they'd have ended up in the swamps of the river. Due south was a safe track, and one which led directly to the nearest village.

✦   ✦   ✦

The nearest village knew the Vikings well. Even though this part of the country was still under Danelaw, marauding Vikings seemed to treat the place as some sort of entertainment, raiding and pillaging just to keep their hands in.

As is the Saxon way with things that are feared, the people here made many jokes about the Vikings. These were mainly centred around their apparent willingness to keep invading the same village time after time, despite having taken everything on any value with them on the first visit. The jokes were all about Viking stupidity and the same tales were repeated endlessly – unless there was a Viking to hand.

In the spring, when Viking blood was up, the jokes turned to the connection between their headgear and their loins. The subject of horny Vikings was an endless source of amusement.

This village, in fact, had got so used to incursions by the hairy men of the sea that it had built a special defensive system. It comprised a very well made and maintained track that headed off into the countryside. At the first hint of a Viking, the first blast of a horn, the first roar of Viking lungs, the entire village would drop whatever they were doing and run like hell.

When the season came for the tales of horny Vikings, the womenfolk of the village were usually first on the track and fastest down it.

This tactic only worked because everyone knew Vikings couldn't do sneaking up.

◆　　◆　　◆

On this particular evening the villager on guard duty was having an easy time of it. Since good King Harold had defeated the Danes at Stamford Bridge, word must have spread as the Norsemen's incursions had diminished. Only the occasional band of rogues still landed in England, and they probably only did so by mistake.

The weather was helping as well. Vikings had been known to come in the fog, but it was rare. This night was a still as a cockerel's corpse, and as quiet. A Viking battle cry would be heard from miles away. Guard duty should be peaceful this evening.

And so the village guard was taken completely by surprise as a large Viking hand clamped over his mouth. He could tell it was Viking from the smell of fish. Looking up from the ground where he now lay, he saw some large Viking faces staring down at him. They had no helmets on, which was a bit odd, but apart from that they fitted the description admirably.

Another thing which was odd was why he wasn't already dead.

'What do you want?' he asked in a shaking voice, shaking only as anyone who was lying at the feet of three Vikings can shake. He'd only been put on guard duty because things were safe now. If there had been any real threat of Viking invasion, no one would have put Siward Longstone in charge of anything as valuable as a small pile of half-burned sticks, let alone the whole village.

'Where's Lincoln?' The biggest and nastiest of the Vikings demanded in a deep and thick Norse accent – the type that most of the villagers could impersonate for their 'how many Vikings does it take to fell a tree' joke.

For a moment Siward thought this was some sort of riddle. 'Er,' he said, as he prepared to guess.

'Come on, man,' another Viking demanded. This one sounded more scheming and devious. And much more scary. 'You must know the way. Or do we have to dig it out of you?' The fellow produced a vicious-looking knife from somewhere and waved it threateningly.

'Oh, the way,' said Siward with relief. These were just three massive Vikings on a foggy night out who wanted to know the way to Lincoln. Fair enough.

'It's, erm, south.' Siward raised a slightly shaking arm, which shook in the general direction of Lincoln. 'It's a big place, though,' he added as an afterthought, remembering why Vikings generally turned up, 'and there's only three of you,' he pointed out.

'We don't want to conquer it, we're just going ...'

'To meet someone.' The largest Viking interrupted the youngest.

'Oh, right,' Siward acknowledged. That was all right then.

'Is it far?' The one with the knife asked, looking disappointed that he hadn't had a chance to use his weapon.

'Oh, erm, a day or two's walk, I suppose,' Siward guessed. He was only a filth-man, the lowest of the low in the village. He did all the jobs no one else would do; gutted the animals that had already gone off, cleared out the muck no one else would touch and dealt with anyone who'd died of something pretty revolting – usually quite a number. The full extent of his life's travel was to go as far away from the village as a stench could carry, and bury things. He had no idea about Lincoln, but it didn't seem sensible to let these gentlemen know that. He really didn't want to give them any bad news. They didn't look like they would respond well.

'Right,' the big Viking said, turning to face the road.

'Can I kill him now?' the one with the knife asked politely.

The big one stroked his beard. At least he was pausing to think about it.

'Be a bit obvious, dead guard,' he said.

'I could throw him in a ditch?' knife-man offered.

'They'd still find him in the morning.'

'We could take him with us?' the young one suggested.

Siward sat on the floor, watching his life debated backwards and forwards.

'Lot of trouble lugging a body along with us.' The man was polishing his knife now.

'Not dead,' young Viking explained.

'Not dead?' The Viking with the knife fixation couldn't understand that.

'No, he could show us the way.'

'I could, I could,' Siward offered, pretty sure he could work out the way to Lincoln from some of the talk he'd heard. Or at least lead a bunch of Vikings who didn't know the way round and round in circles until he could get away.

'And he might stop the locals bothering us,' the large Viking added.

'I would, I would,' Siward nodded enthusiastically.

'They'd still miss him in the morning.'

'This is my last turn of guard duty,' Siward said, seized with enthusiasm for the role of Viking guide, as opposed to the role of Viking victim. 'Come the morning I'm done for the week. I could be off and no one would miss me. I do all the horrible jobs, so no one wants to know what I'm up to most of the time anyway.'

'Horrible jobs?' The knifely Viking said this as if the activity was akin to interfering with fish.

'Dead things and muck mostly,' Siward shrugged.

The large Viking beckoned his fellows to join him in a huddle. There was guttural discussion in their strange language with much gesticulation, a lot of it with a knife. Several times they looked at Siward and then at the road stretching off into the dark fog. Eventually their minds were made up.

'All right,' the large Viking announced. 'You show us the way to Lincoln.'

The three blond, beweaponed men looked expectantly at Siward, clearly wanting him to get on with this straightaway.

'Excellent,' said Siward, thinking it was at least excellent that he was still alive, and might still be tomorrow with any luck.

Young and large Viking pulled some supplies from their packs and started gnawing on chunks of dried fish.

Knife Viking stood slightly apart, digging his knife into the palm of his hand and muttering about how Vikings weren't Vikings anymore, how in his father's day things weren't dealt with like this and how the whole race had gone soft. He muttered in English, so it was clear he wanted Siward to hear. He also seemed to be muttering to the knife rather than Siward. The knife he appeared to have named Ssaxon-Ssnuffer, which wasn't very comforting.

Siward made a note to spend the journey to Lincoln as far away from this fellow as possible.

Curiosity crept into a quiet corner of his mind. It asked what three Vikings, helmetless and in the dark, could possibly be doing asking the way to Lincoln, instead of demanding it and then leaving a trail of blood behind them.

Siward tried to tell curiosity to mind its own business, but it stayed in the corner of his mind, grumbling at him.

Chapter 6
Hillhill Woodwood

ITH HORSES SUPPLIED by nameless Norman grooms, it was only a few moments from the battlefield, over the ridge of Senlac Hill, before the woods thickened properly. England was really one big forest, with clear places where the people lived – or not, if they lived in the forest. Even when places were cleared, the trees quickly covered the effrontery, so there had to be regular weeding of saplings to stop the forest simply healing the space over.

Wearing only their single cloaks to keep out the cold, the band entered the edge of the wood in darkness. Here they found complete and utter darkness waiting for them.

'Can you find your way?' Le Pedvin asked Mabbut as they gathered just inside the first trees.

'You are joking.' Mabbut wasn't asking a question. He couldn't see the wood or the trees. 'I said it was mad to go at night.'

'So did I,' Ranulf reminded them.

'I thought you knew your own land?' Le Pedvin was scornful. 'You keep bleating on about it all the time. In fact I'm surprised to see the sun setting on it at all, given your descriptions.'

'Of course I know it. I know it like the back of my hand.'

'Perhaps we could cut your arm off and take that with us then; it would save having to put up with the rest of you.' Le Pedvin sounded like this was more realistic proposal than sarcastic remark

'When the sun is up in the sky and we can see some bits of it, we can find our way.' Mabbut felt bad enough that he was doing this at all; he wasn't going to put up with Le Pedvin's ridiculous demands as well. 'Put you in a pitch black Norman forest and you'd be lost as well.'

'What is it we're actually looking for?' Martel asked, riding into the middle of the group.

Mabbut grumbled, but at least this fellow behaved in a reasonably civilised manner. For a Norman, of course. 'There should be a track through the wood. We follow that until we find the old Roman road.'

Le Pedvin stood in his stirrups, as if he'd be able to see over the top of the darkness. His eyes went left and right, but nothing immediately came into sight.

His head suddenly stopped its questing and tipped to one side to allow some small sound into his ear. 'What was that?' he hissed.

'What was what?' Mabbut asked loudly, only to get a glare from Le Pedvin.

'In the wood, to the left.' Martel was much more quiet and more serious. He and Le Pedvin dismounted very slowly and very carefully, trying not to make a noise as they did so.

Ranulf raised his eyebrows and sighed.

Mabbut folded his arms at the inconvenience of soldiers who wandered off into the woods at the drop of a hat, or the snuffle of a hedgehog.

'Probably a hedgehog,' he said to Ranulf, as the two soldiers crept towards the undergrowth. 'Noisy so and so's in the mating season.'

'It's October,' Ranulf pointed out scornfully.

'Very fertile, hedgehogs,' Mabbut defended himself.

If this was a hedgehog, it was a very big one and had a good pair of lungs on it. It also spoke English.

Le Pedvin and Martel emerged from the woods, dragging a struggling Saxon between them. Though the man wasn't struggling very effectively as one of his arms wasn't working any more.

He was clearly a fighting man, although most of his accoutrements had been discarded. Mabbut imagined they'd been discarded pretty quickly, somewhere between the battlefield and here. He looked like he was getting on a bit for fighting age, must have been at least forty, and he also looked more like a man of the soil than a soldier. The fellow had probably been dragged from his land, pointed in the general direction of Hastings and had a sword thrust into his hand, with helpful instruction on which was the dangerous end.

The wound on his arm was clear as he was brought up to the horses. His sleeve had been torn away and used as a bandage across a nasty gash on the shoulder.

'Do you know him?' Le Pedvin demanded of Mabbut, holding the captive by the scruff of the neck.

'Do I know him?' Mabbut couldn't understand the question.

'Yes, he's one of your precious Saxons. Must be a relative of some sort.'

Mabbut was aghast, even Ranulf tutted.

'England is a big place. I can't possibly know who everyone is. Just because I'm a Saxon you assume I must know all the others? The country has, oh,' he thought about what massive number he could use, 'hundreds of people scattered about. It wouldn't be possible.'

Le Pedvin huffed at Mabbut's uselessness.

'You know every Norman by name, do you?' Mabbut muttered mostly to himself.

'Who are you?' Le Pedvin demanded of his captive with a vigorous shake.

'No one,' the captive responded, as if he was just passing Le Pedvin in the street.

'Well mister no one, what are you doing hiding in the woods after a battle, with a wound in your arm?'

'Has there been a battle?' the man asked, sounding very interested at this news.

'You know there has, and you were in it. On the losing side.

As for me, I was on the winning side, so I want to know what you're doing here and who else is hiding in the woods.'

'I was just out hunting rabbits and then you come and grabbed me,' the man protested.

'Big rabbit with a sword, was it?' Le Pedvin indicated the man's wound, which he slapped heartily.

'Ow, bloody hell, mind that,' the man protested, clutching his arm.

'Look,' Le Pedvin grabbed the scruff of the neck again and shook it about some more, 'as far as I'm concerned you're a fugitive from the battle, and an enemy, so I should just give you another wound, right where your head joins your body. I will then leave your body in this wood and your head in a different one. With me so far?'

The man nodded, hunching his shoulders as if this might keep his head joined on.

'I want to know if anyone has passed through here or if anyone else is hiding in the wood after they ran away from the battle.'

'Oh, the *battle*,' the man said, his memory returning, 'yes, I do recall something about a battle now. I was, erm, hunting rabbits down Senlac way and there did seem to be a bit of a commotion. 'Course I was going to leave them to it, but some big bloke accidentally cut me in the shoulder, so I made off for the woods.'

'I'm glad it's coming back to you,' Le Pedvin encouraged. 'Now, what about other people who might have wandered into the battle by mistake?'

'There's only me here,' the man said, 'some of the other, erm, rabbit hunters headed north. I thought if I stayed close, no one would notice.' He shrugged and winced at his wound.

'Martel.' Le Pedvin nodded to the woods and Martel vanished back into the undergrowth.

'And who exactly went north?' Le Pedvin demanded.

'It's like your friend says, I don't know everyone in the country.'

'I imagine quite a lot of them had been accidentally hit by something during the battle?'

'Could be.' The man was noncommittal.

Le Pedvin leaned in close so that only the wounded Saxon could hear.

'Anyone … special?'

The man looked worried, as if something far worse than a fight with a well-armed rabbit was about to happen. 'Special?'

'The well-to-do? Nobles? Anyone important, perhaps being helped along by a bunch of men? Might have had a wound to the eye?'

The man had looked increasingly concerned, but his face did light up slightly at this.

'Bloody nobles,' the man grumbled, 'horses when the rest of us have to walk.' He clamped his mouth shut quickly. 'Erm, there were quite a lot with head and eye wounds,' he went on quickly, nodding helpfully. 'Probably bumped into trees,' he explained.

Martel emerged from the woods now and shook his head at Le Pedvin. 'No sign of anyone else.'

'And these Nobles who'd bumped into trees went north?'

'I suppose so,' the man admitted.

'What's your name?' Le Pedvin snapped loudly. 'Quickly.'

'Oh, er, Aethur, Aethur Stockman.'

Le Pedvin looked to Mabbut for confirmation. Mabbut just shrugged. 'How the hell should I know?' he thought, but he kept it to himself.

'Well, Aethur Stockman,' Le Pedvin growled out, 'this is your lucky day. If, later on, I find that any little bit of your story is not quite right I shall come back and look for you. I shall ask around and find people who know your whereabouts. And your head and your body will cease to be acquainted. At all. Clear?'

Aethur Stockman nodded his head gratefully.

'We go north,' Le Pedvin announced to the company as he and Martel remounted.

Aethur Stockman looked at the four men on horses for a moment, before scurrying back into the woods as fast as he could go. Three rabbits emerged from their holes and scratched themselves derisively.

♦   ♦   ♦

'Who said we want to go north?' Ranulf questioned. 'This really is ridiculous. We can't just go wandering off into the woods to survey a whole country. Something like this should be properly planned, thought through, laid out in a number of options for appraisal and consideration.'

'Even determining the options needs time,' he went on. 'We need to sit down for a week or so with local scholars and maps, identify required outcomes, lay down measures for success, agree the record-keeping approach and allocate duties. We haven't even established a small group to consider the most advantageous route, let alone made appointments to organise supplies and equipment. No, we've been told to go and count the country and do it now, in the dark. The whole thing is headed for failure before it's even begun.' Ranulf was getting quite wound up at the inefficiency of it all.

'And now we go north for an equally good reason, namely none at all! Perhaps we should go east or west? Tell you what, we'll split up. I've give you each a quill and we can cover the country in a quarter of the time.'

Le Pedvin sighed. 'We go north.'

'Why?' Ranulf wanted to know.

The old soldier rested his hand on his sword and looked at Ranulf with disdain. 'Because we know the east – it's only Kent and then the coast. South we've just come from, so no point in going back and counting ourselves. West is wild and we don't want to bite off more than we can chew. North is towards London and that's where ...' He stumbled as he caught himself going too far. But Ranulf was on to him.

'Where what?'

'Where the capital is and where the richest pickings will be.'

'We're surely not going all the way to London?' Mabbut was aghast. 'It'll take days. And there's only four of us.'

'Oh, I get it.' Ranulf was all gloating criticism now. This was when he was at his worst. It was bad enough the man could examine the best efforts of a life, the proudest achievements of a man's brief passage through the world, and dismiss them as chaff with the arch of an eyebrow. When he was proved right it was appalling, but when he uncovered some aspect of your abject failure you had tried to hide, he was truly unbearable. These were the moments that brought him closest to a rapid death. Not that he noticed, of course.

'What do you *get*?' Le Pedvin was weary. And wary. Not a good combination.

'You want to find anyone who ran from the battle.'

'Do I?'

'Of course. William wouldn't want any Saxons getting away. As you said he *is* mad, he'd want them all dead. London's the capital, that's where they'd go. So you've been sent to make sure they don't make it. Your whispers to the funny little Saxon probably confirmed it. I wondered why you didn't kill him. That's not like you at all.'

'Ridiculous.'

'No it isn't.' Ranulf knew he was getting somewhere now. He usually knew he was right, but there were events which added an extra smugness. This was one of them.

Le Pedvin shook his head at the idea. 'How could four people, only two of whom are capable of fighting, no, I take that back, only *one* of whom is capable of fighting ...'

Martel looked offended. No one noticed or cared.

'... How could these people, one fighter, one loiterer, one Saxon whinger and a pedantic horse's arse, chase down fleeing Saxons? If that was what William wanted to do, he'd have sent a force. We're to do exactly as he said and we do it north.'

Ranulf scoffed. 'Off you go, then.' He gestured into the wood – the pitch black, impenetrable wood.

'Is this the track?' Martel called. He had wandered away from the group slightly and come across the clear signs of a track emerging from the forest. Or going into the forest.

The others joined him.

'That's it,' Mabbut announced.

'Right.' Le Pedvin urged his strong white stallion along, gesturing that the others should do likewise.

Ranulf shook his head in the way people do when they're criticising the riding of others, and followed on to the track. The steps of his mount were purposeful and solid, but the animal looked to left and right, with its head down, as if trying to find something suitable to eat. It clopped along, disappointed. The man had even been given a picky horse.

Mabbut came next, reluctant and cautious, his steed being the one that came supplied without anything at all. Not even a saddle. The giggling stable lads had not been disciplined by Le Pedvin.

Martel brought up the rear on his own horse. It was light and careful, as if trying to avoid being spotted.

'So what's this place then?' Le Pedvin called back.

'Eh?' Mabbut didn't understand the question.

'What's the name of this wood?'

'Oh right. Erm …' Mabbut looked about in the dark. 'This is Senlac Wood, I think.'

'You don't say.' Ranulf was his helpful self.

'Better write that down then,' Le Pedvin instructed.

'You want me to write down that at the top of Senlac Hill there is a wood called Senlac Wood?' Ranulf was dismissive. 'I think we can remember that.'

'That's not the point, though, is it? There's going to be lots of things we find, and even you won't be able to remember them all.'

'I think Senlac Wood will stick in the mind.' The shaking of Ranulf's contemptuous head could be felt, even in the darkness.

'We're not in Senlac Wood any more,' Mabbut announced.

'Eh?' Le Pedvin was confused.

'Oh yes,' Mabbut was confident. 'This is Drewhurst Wood now.'

'I thought it was so dark you couldn't find your way?'

'Once I'm on the path I'm fine.'

'And the wood we were in has now changed to a new wood?'

'That's it.'

'I didn't notice.'

'Oh well, you wouldn't. You have to be a local.'

'When exactly did the huge number of trees stop being Senlac Wood and become Drewhurst Wood?'

'It's very subtle.'

Le Pedvin's dismissive snort had a touch of Ranulf about it. Perhaps he was infectious.

♦   ♦   ♦

They rode on for several minutes in silence. The path was a clear one, and the darkness began to lift a little as a bright moon tried to push its way through the enveloping English cloud. The enveloping cloud was having none of it, but did allow a shrouded glimmer to reach the ground. It prepared to put a stop to that pretty soon, with a good heavy shower or two.

The trees of the woods bordered the path closely just here. Even in the dark, it would be hard to wander off without bumping into one of them.

'How long before we find this road?' Le Pedvin asked. 'Is Drewhurst Wood large?'

'Oh we're not in Drewhurst Wood any more. Haven't been for ages,' Mabbut explained.

'What?'

'Oh yes. We left Drewhurst Wood sometime ago. This is Hillhurst Wood now.'

'How many trees does it take before you people call it a wood?' Le Pedvin asked. 'I mean, the trees are all together anyway, what's the point?'

'Oh well, in ancient times …' Mabbut began. He enjoyed a bit of local history. Local Saxon history.

'Oh no,' Le Pedvin stopped him. 'It's bad enough you go on and on about Saxons. I'm not letting you go off on your ancient times again.'

'They are significant.'

'They are to you,' Le Pedvin agreed.

'The Saxons aren't the ancient people, anyway,' Ranulf explained, destroying Mabbut's heritage in a moment.

'I beg your pardon.' Mabbut's offence was clear.

'Oh no, the Britons were here first. Still are, of course, in the west. Saxons only arrived recently, just a long line of invaders. You should be in Saxony, with the other Germanics, if you want your people.'

Mabbut's spluttering offence could not find an adequate outlet.

'And why do you call all your woods "hurst" anyway? Drewhurst, Hillhurst. What is a hurst?'

Mabbut managed to put the offence to his people to one side, with difficulty. 'It means hill, or hillock,' he explained.

'Hillhurst wood?' Le Pedvin enquired. 'Hillhill wood. My God.'

'Or it can mean stream. Or clearing.'

'Stupid people, stupid language.' The Norman dismissed the whole country with a shrug and turned to happier matters. 'Is this the road?'

◆　　◆　　◆

It was certainly *a* road. They had moved from a trodden path, with rutted tracks where carts had rumbled and rolled their way over the grass. They stood now upon a smooth surface, paved with uncountable stones, each laid carefully in its place. In the struggling moonlight they could see that the way stretched ahead in a line as straight as an arrow on its way to the nearest Saxon eye socket.

The road curved gently over its surface, ensuring that rain would run off into the surrounding land. A white marker stone could be seen with Roman numerals on it, marking the distance, probably from London. The whole thing was wide enough for half a dozen men to walk side by side, or for a good-sized cart to travel with ease. Not far away a passing place could be seen – an addition to the road enabling carts to pass without having to leave the paving.

The thing was a marvel, and it was already a thousand years old.

The problem was that the marvel only lasted about fifty yards. After that it decayed into rubbled rubbish.

When someone wanted to build a house, they generally used wood. If it was for someone important, or for the church, they would use stone. There were two options for getting enough stone for a decent-sized construction: dig it from a quarry at great effort and expense, or pick it up off the floor of the nearest Roman road.

Many of the buildings hereabouts were constructed from the finest Roman cobbles. After all, you had to live in a house. You only walked on a road now and again.

'Not much of a road now,' Martel observed.

'The track is still there.' Mabbut gestured off into the distance.

'Write this down as well then,' Le Pedvin prompted Ranulf. 'One road, Roman, broken.'

Ranulf made no move to do anything.

'Where does this lead then, before London?' Le Pedvin asked.

'Are we likely to reach any sort of civilisation before dawn?'

'We might make it to Salehurst,' Mabbut offered.

'Another hill,' Martel laughed lightly.

'Ah.' Le Pedvin seemed to have a problem. 'Salehurst might not be so good,' he said seriously.

The others turned to face him.

'Well,' he looked rather sheepish, still corpse-like but corpse-like with a touch of sheep, 'we've been in the country a couple of weeks now. Some of the men went off to do a bit of a reconnoitre.'

'And they reconnoitred Salehurst?' Ranulf asked. 'To no good effect, I imagine.'

'Apparently one of the locals looked at them a bit funny.'

'So they burned the place to the ground, killed everyone, and left it a smouldering ruin.'

Le Pedvin shrugged. It was all history now. 'Pretty much.'

'So perhaps not Salehurst then,' Martel offered brightly. 'Where's next?'

'It'll have to be Salehurst.' Mabbut exerted what little authority he had. 'Even if you don't want to stop there, we'll have to pass through. There are a few peasant hovels about the place, but nothing substantial. Or rather there were a few peasant hovels last time I looked.' He snorted, contemptuous of this company's mission and its attitude to his people, his country and himself.

'And, of course, fleeing Saxons probably made straight for the place.' Ranulf was contemptuous as well.

Le Pedvin turned to him. 'Look, I have told you we are not chasing fleeing Saxons. There are not enough of us to chase fleeing Saxons. There will be plenty of time for that later. You may not agree with what the Duke has told us to do, but he has told us to do it and he is the Duke. I am the Duke's man and I make sure he gets what he wants. So …'

'So?'

'So shut up about fleeing Saxons.'

'Of course, if we came across any?' Martel offered.

'Obviously we deal with them,' Le Pedvin put hand to sword, 'but if we come across a whole army of Saxons we let them go their way.'

'Very wise,' said Mabbut.

'Unless they're in a very poor state,' Le Pedvin added, 'in which case we might have a go.'

'We could always make camp here and go to Salehurst in the morning. When it's light,' Martel suggested. 'That way we could see anyone approaching.'

'Camp on a Roman road?' Mabbut was aghast.

'What now?' Le Pedvin dropped his shoulders.

'No one camps on a Roman road.'

'Part of your precious history? Definitively not Saxon, though, are they? Roman roads. If they were, they'd be called Saxon roads and they aren't. Saxon track, Saxon bog, Saxon dung heap, yes. Road? No.'

Mabbut shook his head, expressing the unfathomable depths of his contempt for Le Pedvin.

'Spirits,' he said.

'Spirits?'

'Everyone knows the spirits of the Romans still travel the roads. They're looking for souls to carry off to the Night Legion, and if they find you sleeping on their road, let alone camped on it ...'

'Well, you really are an idiot,' Le Pedvin concluded with a laugh. It sounded more like the retching of a terminally sick stoat, but it counted as a laugh. 'The Night Legion. Ha.'

'It's true. The Night Legion still patrols the old roads. People have seen them. Cursed to walk the roads for eternity, they take anyone they find. Old men, women, children: no one's safe from the night legion.'

'You won't be safe from my boot in a minute. Anyway, we are not camping here. It's only about eight o'clock. We've got hours to go before we camp.'

'I'm not sure we should even be on the road after dark.' Mabbut looked about as if a ghostly centurion was going to come and conscript him at any moment.

'Mabbut, the whole world is covered in Roman roads. And it looks like your marvellous Saxons have stolen most of this one, like we all do. I don't think the night legion will be very happy if they turn up for a good night's walk and find bits of their path holding up your privy. Beside, in Normandy there are whole towns built on the roads, and the inhabitants haven't been carried off.'

'Ah, but Saxon roads …' Mabbut began.

'Right,' Le Pedvin said loudly. They all paid him attention.

'Ranulf has shut up about fleeing Saxons. Mabbut, you are going to shut up completely. I've never travelled so little distance with so much wittering and pointless gabble. You will know me as a man of very little patience. In fact I have a bit of reputation for cutting conversation short. The next thing I want to hear from anyone is "Look, there's Salehurst". Am I clear?'

They nodded.

'We go in perfect silence.' Le Pedvin rode away muttering to himself. It was mostly indistinct, but the words that did drift into the air were not complimentary.

Then silence reigned, apart from the clopping of tired and resentful hoofs. Soon rain began to fall. It was dark and cold on the road, and they were alone.

Chapter 7
Salehurst by Night

 ook, there's Salehurst,' Mabbut announced. He had not kept totally silent during the journey, but his voice had been quiet and out of Le Pedvin's earshot.

There had been much conversation with Ranulf about the nature of their mission, and what might really be going on. The two of them walked their horses together between Le Pedvin in the vanguard and Martel at the rear.

Mabbut supported the theory that this really was William stamping his authority on the country. The Normans had rampaged a bit since they'd landed, but this would be an opportunity to spread word of the outcome of the battle and show that the Duke was now really in charge. Of course, he went on at length about how appalling this was, but he seemed resigned to the fact there was very little he could do about it. Apart from moan regularly.

Ranulf doubted that four men could make much of a stamp. They both admitted that if anyone was going to stamp authority on anything, Le Pedvin was the man – but he was only one. Even Martel recognised that his own stamping capability was extremely limited.

He maintained his theory that they were after renegade Saxons who had run from the battle. William would want them dragged back and executed. That would be a far more effective stamp of authority than Le Pedvin going round shouting at the locals.

Neither of them could resolve the question of why only four, or why the four of them. Le Pedvin was a key man to William, so why send him away now? Why Martel, who seemed to add nothing to any group he was in? And why Ranulf and Mabbut? All right, Mabbut knew the country and yes, Ranulf was the most organised thing in the modern world. Even so, the whole exercise was bizarre.

They came to the reluctant view that carrying out a cursory check of the land, recording what was here and letting William know, did actually fit quite well. It could even be of military advantage as William pressed home the invasion. They still didn't believe it though.

♦   ♦   ♦

'That?' Le Pedvin gestured off into the darkness, where a slightly darker dark splattered the night. Slow lights flickered here and there, showing little strength or enthusiasm.

'Well,' Mabbut acknowledged with a dig at Norman reconnoitring, 'what's left of it, I suppose.'

'Come on then.'

'It would be more sensible to camp here and enter the town at dawn,' said Ranulf. 'I can't make anything out. If I really am to make a note of the place, I would be best seeing it from a distance first.'

'And entering a recently ravaged town in the dark might not be the safest option?' Mabbut offered.

'Safe? Pah.' Le Pedvin dismissed the suggestion. 'Martel, you're with me.'

Martel urged his beast forward to join Le Pedvin at the front. Tired and tense, the unhappy party walked on over the short distance to the edge of the town.

♦   ♦   ♦

It was hard to tell the edge of the town from the edge of the forest that surrounded it. There had clearly been an entrance at some time. The remains of some buildings squatted in the darkness, testament to the fact they used to be a lot taller. Light wasn't necessary to tell that these places had been burned to the ground. The thick smell of charred timber, soaked in English rain, swam through the air.

The main street, or what had once been the main street, stretched in front of them and it held what looked like a charcoal auction. Even in the dark, the jumbled shapes showed that bits of buildings had been dragged and deposited in the road.

'Norman conquest, eh?' Mabbut offered. The sincerity was clear in his voice. Le Pedvin kept silent but a rather alarming movement slid across his lips. Something akin to a smile but the sort of kin you hope don't turn up at a wedding.

The lights they had seen from a distance had all vanished. The place was silent and apparently deserted.

'We camp here,' Le Pedvin commanded.

'With what?' Ranulf was direct and accusing. 'You dragged us away from Senlac without so much as a backward glance. We've brought no supplies, no equipment, no food. The Duke's orders had to be followed immediately, it seemed, which gave us no time to prepare.'

Le Pedvin instructed Ranulf in the ways of Norman manhood. 'You find a spot where the wind is slightly less cold, and the rain doesn't come quite straight down. You cover yourself in your clothes and sleep. Hungry.'

'This is exactly why things go wrong.' Ranulf was off. 'There's been no planning and no forethought. If you'd put just a morsel of time aside to prepare, we wouldn't be in this situation. We'll be cold, hungry and unready for either the tasks of tomorrow or to deal with any attack in the night. If you'd just put a bit more effort in, you would have had a pack ready to go at any moment, just as I have. But of course that's in my tent, which I'm not allowed to return to. Ridiculous.'

Le Pedvin walked his horse over to Ranulf, leaned out of his saddle and grasped the man by the throat. 'Remember, we are out here on our own. If we came back without you, no one would be any the wiser. Martel has his own reasons for wanting to keep William happy and Mabbut wouldn't say a word. A lot of people would be grateful if you had some accident as we searched the new land. No one would ever find out I'd stuck my sword in your mouth to stop you talking.' He released Ranulf, but held him with his eye – an eye accustomed to issuing threats.

Ranulf tutted, giving the clear impression that Le Pedvin couldn't even do threatening right. He didn't say any more though.

'Martel, find a spot,' Le Pedvin barked, keeping his eye on Ranulf and his hand on his sword.

'Aye.' Martel dismounted, handed his reins to Le Pedvin and went off into the darkness.

The remaining three sat in awkward silence while Martel searched for their accommodations. Mabbut looked around in an accusatory manner while Ranulf took his notebook and quill from the small, purpose-made pack at his waist and started scribbling some notes. He only glanced at the place they were in, but looked half into the sky, as if thinking up the exact words for a withering report for William. Le Pedvin just sat.

'Here.' Martel's voice came from the darkness.

Le Pedvin dismounted and the others followed suit as he led the animals off toward one of the fallen buildings. Stepping over beams and piles of burned something or other, they came to a simple dwelling – so crude and simple the passing Normans had clearly not bothered to rampage through it. It was a single room, which might once have been a store of some sort. Its main attraction was that it still had half a roof and three walls.

'Mabbut, attend to the animals,' Le Pedvin ordered.

'Why me?' Mabbut demanded in a rather squeaky voice. 'Can't Martel do it?'

'God spare me.' Le Pedvin looked to the sky, apparently hoping that the Creator would lean down and spare him right now.

83

'Martel is a Norman gentleman,' the last word was squeezed out between reluctant lips. 'De Sauveloy is the adviser to Duke, now King William, and I am the King's liegeman.' Le Pedvin paused to make sure Mabbut had got all that. 'You, on the other hand, are an annoying Saxon turd. That's why you're doing it. And that's why you'll be doing anything else I tell you. And doing it without opening your annoying Saxon mouth.' Le Pedvin flung the reins at Mabbut, who grabbed them quickly.

'I'll take first watch,' said Le Pedvin, as he walked into the building. 'Martel, I'll wake you in three hours. You sleep.' He nodded towards the cover of the remains of the roof. 'I don't want either of you keeping watch. Mabbut'll probably engage any attack in a charming conversation about how much better things were when the Saxons were in charge, and Ranulf will get himself killed when he has a go at the attackers for not doing it properly.'

Amid grumbles and gripes, Mabbut attended to the horses while Ranulf cleared the ground to find some comfort. After several minutes of distant muttering about Saxons, Normans and injustice, Mabbut returned and sat near Ranulf. The two wrapped their cloaks about them and prepared for the night.

Martel had simply laid himself flat and fallen promptly asleep.

◆   ◆   ◆

Through a gap in the wall, or rather a gap where the wall used to be, the shape of Le Pedvin could be seen against the night sky. He must have been standing on a pile of rubble as he did look rather magnificent, no mean feat for a man whose shadow disappeared if he turned sideways. After a few moments he stepped down from his pile and moved off into the darkness.

'Gone to patrol, I imagine,' Mabbut speculated.

'I should certainly hope so,' Ranulf snorted. 'Small band in hostile territory? As the senior man it's his responsibility.

Frankly I have my doubts about his commitment to our protection, but I suppose he's the best we have.'

The two men lapsed into silence, hoping that sleep would join them.

Both heads dropped as their minds made the strange connections that are precursors to sleep. The hoot of an owl became a distant horn, blown by a Norman guard, who was himself being whisked away on the wind which carried its own wailing. The guard suddenly dropped from the sky with a loud crack.

Two heads shot up. They had definitely been asleep for some time, as it took several moments for their senses to make it back into their brains. Martel still slept on the floor and Le Pedvin was nowhere to be seen. The darkness was still dark.

But the crack had come from the land of the living. No doubt. They looked out to find no silhouette of Le Pedvin cut from the sky.

'What was that?' Mabbut whispered.

'Well, I don't know, do I?' Ranulf retorted.

A second crack.

'It was a crack,' Mabbut observed.

'Well done.' Ranulf was contemptuous. He reached out his right leg and kicked Martel on the shoulder. Hard. No response.

He then kicked Martel again on the shoulder. Really hard.

The Norman stirred. 'What?' he demanded, groggily awake.

'There's someone out there,' Ranulf hissed.

'A crack,' Mabbut confirmed.

All three listened in the best silence they could manage. Breath was held and movement halted.

The effort was rewarded by a further noise. This time a scuffle of sorts, like feet scrambling over the burnt out wreckage of a village.

'Could be Le Pedvin,' Mabbut guessed.

'I think he'd just come round the wall,' Martel replied as he got quietly to his feet. He drew a short knife from his belt and stood ready. What he was ready for was a mystery.

'They could be hostile,' Mabbut said helpfully.

'If I lived in a village burnt down by Norman soldiers, I think I'd be pretty hostile,' Ranulf scoffed.

Martel looked at the man who would probably criticise the knife work of the assailant who stabbed him to death. 'Quiet,' he snapped.

He looked around, moving his head this way and that, trying to pick something up by ear if not by sight. He took half a step back as the wall in front of him seemed to swim.

It carried on. Yes, the wall in front of him was definitely swimming. Not very well, but it was moving. Just a little bit, but certainly more than walls generally moved. This subtle motion, not being compatible with being a wall, came to an end as the whole thing lurched forward and collapsed on Mabbut and Ranulf.

Martel leaped backwards to avoid the collapsing wattle and daub. Groans of complaint could be heard from beneath the wreckage. At least the thing hadn't been made of stone. He couldn't see Ranulf, but guessed he would be complaining about the quality of wattle and daub used, and how it had never been maintained properly.

Martel flipped his dagger to his left hand and drew his sword with his right. He took another step back and came to the ready. From the darkness, two ragged and stick-thin shapes jumped on to the fallen wall.

'Get off,' the voice of Mabbut called plaintively from under the wreckage.

'Ha, ha,' one or other of the shapes cackled.

Martel stood upright, confident he could swat these two away with little effort. The sticks they brandished would be no match for his blade.

Unfortunately they both jumped him at once. No warning scream, no 'en garde,' nothing. Although they weighed only slightly more than the wind, they took Martel down by weight of surprise. He crashed to the ground and did not move again.

✦ ✦ ✦

From under the bulk of a pretty shoddy and lightweight wall, Ranulf and Mabbut struggled and fought against the tangled twigs and mud. Heaving the mess away, they dragged themselves into the clear.

'Le Pedvin!' Ranulf barked, clear that the man's failure to protect them would be going in his book.

'Where's Martel?' Mabbut asked, clearing the dust from his eyes.

'I don't know,' Ranulf snapped. His clothing was covered in dust and he was brimming with irritation at Mabbut, and Martel, and Le Pedvin. 'If you recall I was under the wall with you.'

'All right,' Mabbut snapped back, emboldened by his experience. 'What I meant was, look, Martel has gone.'

'I can see that. Useless man.'

'I am not …'

'Not you, Martel. Well, you and Martel. Le Pedvin!' Ranulf bellowed into the night.

'If I might suggest,' Mabbut offered quietly, 'shouting out Norman names in a ravaged Saxon village in the middle of the Saxon night isn't the brightest thing?'

Ranulf did pause at this.

'Particularly when the locals seem inclined to drag people off into the night? Even people who have swords?'

'This is intolerable,' Ranulf hissed into the darkness. He moved away from the collapsed wall to look up and down the street. 'Where is the wretched man?'

Mabbut joined him, but it was really too dark to be able to make anything out clearly.

Their straining ears eventually picked up some noises from

out there somewhere. The noises resolved themselves into steps. They became running steps, the running steps of someone large and with a clear intent.

They backed into what was left of the building and Ranulf drew a short dagger from somewhere. Mabbut took his apple knife from his belt; it was the only thing he was allowed to carry, and perhaps he would be able to peel their assailants to death. He looked around for another weapon and found a charred piece of roof timber the size of a decent club, which he picked up. It crumbled into charred pieces of timber about the size of poor toothpicks. He moved to stand behind Ranulf.

'Get in front,' Ranulf ordered. He stepped swiftly backwards and pushed Mabbut into the line of fire.

'Why me?'

'You're a local. They're likely to think twice before doing anything to you. That might give me time to get away.'

'Oh, thanks very much.'

Both men stood their ground and waited as the steps got closer and louder.

Ranulf gripped his dagger. Mabbut held his fruit knife between thumb and finger. He clenched his muscles and half-closed his eyes.

'Right,' a voice boomed in the dark.

'Le Pedvin,' Ranulf demanded, 'where the hell have you been?'

Le Pedvin strode into the space and cast a weary and disappointed look at the cowering Mabbut and the poorly armed Ranulf. 'I've been finding something very interesting. We have to go. Now.'

The man was all urgency and beckoned the others to follow him as he turned away.

'They took Martel,' Mabbut announced dramatically.

'Really,' said Le Pedvin with very little interest. 'I'm sure he'll catch up. Come.'

'Some people burst in and buried us in the wall. When we

got out, Martel was gone,' Mabbut protested insistently.

'These things happen.' Le Pedvin dismissed the problem with a shrug. 'Let's go.'

'We have to find Martel.'

'Why?' Le Pedvin stopped and turned now. He did not look happy.

His response threw Mabbut rather. 'Because he is a Norman gentleman and I am an annoying Saxon turd?'

'Yes, he is a Norman gentleman, and they can look after themselves. We, on the other hand, need to go.'

'Why?' It was Ranulf who asked the plain question.

'Oh, let me think,' Le Pedvin rubbed his chin. 'I said so,' he announced. 'There we are. That's why.'

'So there is something more interesting out there than the rescuing of a missing Norman gentleman,' Ranulf concluded. 'Something so important it will drag me away from following Duke William's express instruction to make a list of all the useful bits of the country?'

Le Pedvin glared at him.

'So this isn't a mission to make notes at all. You're looking for something else. What could William possibly have sent you to find that is so important?'

'All right,' Le Pedvin gave up, seemingly anxious to end the conversation. 'Just stop talking. We look for Martel. I just found a local cowering in the rubbish heap and heard about a group of fleeing Saxons, but you're right, of course. We should stay here and look for one rather ineffectual Norman. Much better that than defeat the King's enemies.' His voice almost collapsed under the weight of its own sarcasm.

'I rather think the battle achieved that,' Ranulf replied. 'The four of us wandering around in the dark is hardly the stuff to defeat enemies.'

'No, it isn't, is it?' Le Pedvin sounded very disappointed. 'Come on then, where is he?'

'I think "when we got out, Martel was gone" answers that?' Ranulf suggested.

'Ye gods,' Le Pedvin ground out through his teeth. 'Martel!' he yelled into the night. Mabbut looked very nervous.

'Martel, where are you, you godforsaken horse's arse?' Le Pedvin strode out into the street with Mabbut and Ranulf hard on his heels.

'If any of you poxy Saxon dung gatherers have got him, I'll slice you open like a pig in a slaughterhouse,' Le Pedvin yelled up and down the street.

Ranulf turned to Mabbut and held an arm out, clearly indicating Le Pedvin. 'This is why our battles are usually so costly. Not a thought about the nature of the problem and the best approach to solving it. Oh no. Spot the problem and go and hit it.'

'I'll hit you in a minute,' Le Pedvin responded, without looking round. 'We'll go and see my man on the rubbish heap. He seems to know where most things are around here.'

'You mean the ones that are still standing, or still alive,' Mabbut put in.

'No. He knows about the dead ones as well. And I'm sorely tempted to let you join them.'

'See what I mean?' Ranulf asked as they followed Le Pedvin. 'He'd kill you, and me, and only then would he realise he had no one to complete his mission. No brain at all.'

As they stepped off along the street, they passed over and around discarded bits of building, no longer needed because the people who used to live in them now occupied holes in the ground. Off to the east the sky was just showing the first signs of another troublesome day.

Le Pedvin led them round the back of some ruins to where the village's rubbish was piled. Old bones, picked dry first by men and then by animals, then by men again, were joined by scraps of cloth too small to be even a patch and broken shards of pots, all scattered over a rough area of ground. As the Norman strode towards the middle of it, the sound of hooves could be heard far off. It was vague and indistinct, and growing more so.

'Now we've missed them,' Le Pedvin barked. He kicked one particular heap of bones and pots.

'Missed who?' Ranulf asked deliberately.

Le Pedvin looked at him with a hearty glare. 'Probably just some Saxons.' He shrugged and kicked the bones again

Mabbut was torn between gratitude that some Saxons were escaping the Norman onslaught, and fear that they might turn round for a bit of onslaught of their own. If there was a chance of lopping the head of an invader, a group of Saxons on horseback might not pause to check exactly who each head belonged to. It might be a cunning ruse to gallop away and then come up behind them. He suddenly felt very alone in his own country. Alone and vulnerable and it was all the fault of the Normans. Like everything else. He had a horrible feeling that just surviving the next few hours could be a bit of a challenge.

Chapter 8
Vikings to the North of Us

AWN WAS ANNOUNCING ITS ARRIVAL in the north as well, caring not which invaders it illuminated, nor in what order. The whole country would receive its attentions, welcome or unwelcome as they may be, depending on your preoccupations in the dark.

Siward Longstone had at least performed his designated function. He had guarded the village through the night. Well, most of it. He had neither slept, nor wandered off home, nor to the tavern. Granted, there were now three more Vikings in the vicinity than there had been when his duty started. Yes, his prime function was to guard against the arrival of Vikings, and to raise the alarm if any turned up, but no one really expected any Vikings any more.

And these three weren't like Vikings at all. They looked the part certainly, but their behaviour was very odd. No one could expect him to raise the village alarm for three polite and inquisitive Norwegians who turned up asking the way. Well, two polite Norwegians and a worrying one with a family of knives, each of which had a very unpleasant name. They had walked for a few hours in the direction of Lincoln until at one point the Vikings had announced it was time to sleep. This point in time seemed the same as all the other points to Siward, but they were the ones with the weapons.

They had slept soundly under his guard. They hadn't killed him nor had they gone back to ravage the village or set fire to anything. They'd even offered him some bits of old leather to eat, which they assured him was fish. They seemed harmless – a bit of an odd concept when considering Vikings, but there you were. Siward never bothered with harmless things. If the magpies were rooting through the occasional corpse they weren't doing any harm, so why chase them off? Same with harmless Vikings. His was a simple world.

Naturally, in the circumstances, he had not stolen a weapon from the sleeping Norsemen and used it to stab them as they slept. Nor had he sneaked off when they started snoring, to get help. In fact he had lived up to the village's expectations of him and dozed off too. It was a fitful sleep, though, as it should be when tucked up in the company of Vikings, and he woke before they did.

He could see that Granar, the village headsman, might have some comments to make about this situation. The man had comments for all the situations Siward found himself in, mostly nasty. This time Siward wouldn't be there to listen, though: he'd be heading south with the Vikings.

Wandering about with strange Vikings didn't seem quite right now he thought about it in the cold light of approaching day. He often thought of what he should have done several hours after he should have done it, if not days.

He sighed as the large Viking stirred himself. He leapt instantly to standing wakefulness, as if he was used to things happening to him in the night.

'What?' he demanded of Siward.

'I don't know,' Siward replied. 'You just woke up.'

'Ah.' The Viking looked around cautiously and tugged on his beard, as if this was the bell-pull to his consciousness.

'Sigmund, Fregurd, up.' He kicked the sleeping figures in order.

The two men leapt up as swiftly as their leader. The one called Fregurd had a knife in each hand. He had probably slept like that.

'To Lincoln,' the large one commanded.

'Oh, er, right.' Siward hadn't really expected to start again quite so quickly.

Siward appraised Erik. Massive Erik with his axe. It was time to leave. 'Right oh,' he said, 'this way then.' He gestured them down the only track that he knew went south, and wandered off.

The three Vikings followed immediately, as if they'd been stamping to get away.

'Come on, man,' Erik gave Siward an encouraging kick. 'It'll be spring before we get there at this rate.'

Siward stepped quickly, trying to keep his pace ahead of the long strides of the Vikings. It was going to be a long day.

◆　　◆　　◆

The track was easy enough at this point, and the area Siward knew was soon left far behind. He amused himself by wondering what the reaction would be when the village woke and discovered he was gone. There would be no blood, no sign of a brave struggle as Siward fought off invaders.

They'd probably think the usual, that Siward had gone to do some horrible job for someone, and they really didn't want to hear anything about it. They'd expect him back in a day or two, probably covered in something unspeakable. Really unspeakable.

As he half-ran along the track to keep ahead, he thought that when he came back and told people he'd been off with the Vikings, they'd have to sit up and listen. They'd invite him to their hearths to tell his tales, not ask him to shut up about his day. The future looked brighter. If there was a future, that is.

'What's your name, man?' Erik asked. He paced along quickly and Siward, who had given up the struggle, scuttled up behind.

'Siward, Siward Longstone.'

'And your trade, Siward Longstone, what did you say it was?'

This seemed to be a very sociable Viking. They didn't usually ask questions.

'Village idiot,' Siward replied mockingly.

'Ah.' Erik nodded understanding.

'No, not really,' Siward hastily explained. 'I just do all the jobs that no one else will do. Clear the muck, dig privies, get rid of rotten dead animals, and people if they've had the pox – and you'd be surprised who has. That sort of thing.'

'Very important work.' The Viking nodded.

Siward looked at him. The man appeared to be genuine, and Vikings were not renowned for their sense of humour. They seemed to laugh a lot when they were killing people, but what they got up to afterwards was anyone's guess. There weren't usually any non-Vikings left to find out.

All Siward could do was give a shrug and make a face that said his was not a respected trade.

'Where we come from, this is important work,' said the chatty Viking. 'We live in a harsh world: cold, death and danger lurk at every turn. If villages aren't kept clean, well. You can imagine.'

No, Siward couldn't imagine. He frowned.

'What happens if you leave scraps of food around, or a dead body in its home for a day or two?'

'Gets a bit smelly,' Siward replied knowledgeably. 'Carrion birds, maybe foxes, they come and make a mess of the place.'

'Ha!' Erik roared in contempt. 'Foxes?'

'Maybe two.' Siward tried to make it sound a serious issue.

'Where we come from? Wolves.' Erik glared. 'Leave your village in a mess, with bodies unburied – before you know it the place is calling the wolves from the forest. And they don't come in ones and twos.'

'I'd heard.'

'Even Vikings have trouble with a pack of hungry wolves, you know.'

'I can imagine.' Siward *could* imagine this time.

'So the man who keeps the village clean and gets rid of the dead keeps us all alive.'

Siward rather liked the sound of that. He'd tell his village when he got back.

"Course they're usually old men or women.'

Maybe he wouldn't mention that bit.

'But they take the job after a life of battle. Highly respected people.'

For a moment Siward wondered if they had any vacancies.

'Your village does not respect such a job?' Erik asked.

'No,' Siward replied simply, 'not at all. Not a bit. Never.'

Erik was thoughtful. 'Sigmund could run back and burn them to the ground if you like?' he offered.

'That's very kind of you, but they'd only make a fuss.' Siward smiled at the power he held in his hands. He had prevented the village from being burned to the ground. One word from him and Granar would be running down the track, looking over his shoulder at his smouldering house. That would be another tale to tell when he went back.

If he went back. He was on the road to Lincoln, the furthest he'd ever travelled, and he was with a band of Vikings. As his situation sank into his head, he realised this must be an adventure. He'd heard all about them of course, tales around the fire, but he'd never thought he'd have one of his own. Always assuming his adventure didn't end with him on the wrong end of a Viking.

'So, erm, Lincoln?' he asked as lightly as he could, 'Got relations there?'

'Probably,' Erik grunted a laugh, which was taken up by Fregurd and Sigmund. 'We've got relatives in a lot of places.'

'Really?' Siward was interested.

'We try to leave several children behind whenever we pay somewhere a visit.'

The Vikings joined in a bout of raucous grunting. It was enthusiastic, if unconvincing.

'Ah ha.' Siward tried to sound light again. He'd never known who his own father was. Perhaps? No. At the age of twenty-three, or thereabouts, he was already balding slightly. What hair he had was jet black and he was about two-thirds the size of Sigmund, who was the smallest of the Vikings. No Norse blood troubled his veins.

'Anywhere particular in Lincoln we're going?' he asked. 'It's quite a big place, and I wouldn't want to take you to the wrong bit.'

Erik stopped walking, and it took Siward two or three paces to realise. He halted and looked at the Viking, who was appraising him carefully.

After a few moments, Erik gestured the other two to join him. They put their heads together in whispered conversation, accompanied by some nodding from Sigmund and low growls from Fregurd. Erik's head lifted briefly to look at Siward again, then it went back to the huddle. Eventually they broke up and Erik approached Siward.

'Do you know the bishop's house?'

'The bishop's house, the bishop's house,' Siward repeated thoughtfully. He tried to make it sound like he had been there once, but couldn't quite bring it to mind.

Of course he didn't know it. He didn't even know Lincoln had a bishop, although it was fair to assume that the man would have a house of his own if it did. That was bishops for you. Never mind its ecclesiastical population, though: Siward didn't actually have the faintest idea where Lincoln was at all. A fact that he wasn't about to share with his new companions. South he knew, but then there were a lot of places south. Probably.

'I think I know where it is roughly,' he said, through a very thoughtful face.

'Well, you can take us to the right area, point it out and then clear off,' said Erik.

Fregurd huffed a bit at this, as if he had a very different idea of how the relationship should end.

'Fine by me,' Siward nodded agreeably. He hoped to God

that he could find someone to ask, before they ended up back at the village by mistake.

◆　　◆　　◆

The day wore on. A pale autumn sun was climbing its tired way into an ominous sky as the group tramped along the path. The weather was cold and overcast, of course, with a strong hint of rain in the air, but the dull cloud was brighter to the left and so Siward was still pretty confident they were going south. He wasn't feeling quite so confident now that this was the road to Lincoln. For all he knew they could end up in Spain.

They moved into a more densely wooded area, the bare trees pointing fingers skywards, and Siward examined his surroundings carefully. None of the trees had 'Lincoln this way' carved on their bark. Although thick, the trees were reasonably well spaced, the leaves of a thousand autumns having most effectively killed anything that tried to grow which wasn't another tree. A bit like Vikings really.

As they moved along, Siward noticed a less well-trodden path weaving off to their right. Just in the woods at the junction of this and the main track, a cross was planted. It was a simple affair, wooden and crude, and not very well looked after at all.

Could this be …? Siward had heard of the place naturally, who hadn't? But did he dare go there to check the way to Lincoln? Surely that was insanity. Out of the frying pan and into the fire was a well used expression, but Siward had never considered its practical application before. With three Vikings behind him and this place in front, the only question was which was the pan and which the burning fiery furnace? He dithered.

'Problem?' Erik asked, in a tone of voice that said it really did not want to hear about any problems.

'Oh no, not at all,' Siward said, thinking as quickly as he could. 'It's just that this is a sort of holy spot.' He pointed to the cross in the wood.

'Pah,' Erik snorted. 'Heathens.'

'And it's traditional to seek a blessing for a journey. Won't take a moment.' He hopped off down the path before Erik could grab him. He could hear the Vikings following, though, and hoped they didn't think he was trying to run away. 'It's quite all right,' he called over his shoulder, 'there's a famous monastery just down here.' He prayed in his heart of hearts that he'd meet someone before he came to the famous monastery. He certainly had no intention of going anywhere near *that* place.

Just as he felt Erik closing on his back, probably with a weapon in his hand, Siward caught a glimpse of a black habit on the path.

'Father!' Siward called. 'A blessing for our journey?'

The habit stopped in some alarm and looked at the approaching band. The hood was thrown back and a young face showed a good portion of trepidation, as if people who rushed up to it in woods were generally up to no good. It had a point.

'A blessing on our journey, Father,' Siward repeated more quietly as he knelt at the feet of the monk.

The Vikings, apparently content that this seemed genuine, kept their distance.

'I am no Father, my son, just a humble monk.' The monk leaned forward and lifted Siward gently by his elbow.

'Oh, right,' Siward said, and tried to put a pleading look in his eye. 'Perhaps you could bless our journey then, Brother, erm?'

'Hermitage.'

'Where?'

'No, that's my name: Brother Hermitage.'

'Odd name for a monk,' Siward observed.

'A lot of people say that,' Brother Hermitage replied with a sigh.

'Is this …?' Siward hesitated to say the name aloud. 'Is this … De'Ath's Dingle?' He swallowed hard.

'It is.' Brother Hermitage confirmed.

Siward crossed himself vigorously.

'There's no need to come in,' Hermitage assured him. 'You need a blessing for your journey though?'

'Well, sort of,' Siward whispered. 'I don't suppose you know the way to Lincoln, do you? Especially the bishop's house? These gentlemen have an appointment there and I've promised to take them. To tell the truth, I've never actually been there.'

Hermitage smiled. 'As it happens I do know the way. I am only recently returned from a journey there myself and can let you have the most specific directions.' The monk almost seemed enthusiastic about this task.

Siward beamed.

He wasn't beaming quite so much when he had received the instructions. They included an awful lot of extraneous material – a lot of it about the Bible, which wasn't helpful and which Siward didn't really want to know.

With the route now clear in his head, along with a lot of other information which he sincerely hoped would fade as soon as possible, and a great weight off his mind, not to say his head still on his shoulders, Siward left the monk to do whatever it was monks did in the woods. He rejoined Erik, Sigmund and Fregurd and waved a hand in grateful farewell to Brother Hermitage.

The monk turned his rather reluctant way back to his monastery. He thought it odd that locals wouldn't know the way to Lincoln. He thought it even more odd that the three who held back looked a bit like Vikings.

They couldn't be, though, he reasoned. They weren't wearing helmets with horns sticking out. They had also held back, which he knew was not a Viking habit. Perhaps they were learning to behave at last? The influence of a good Christian country like England was having its effect. Always keen to believe the best, Hermitage hummed thoughtfully as he went on his way.

Chapter 9

Normans to the South

HERE ARE YOU?' Le Pedvin called towards the pile of rubbish, which seemed to be unoccupied.

'Are you sure Saxons in the dark who live on rubbish are a reliable source of information?' Ranulf asked as he appraised the empty space.

'He told me there were Saxons here, and then we heard them.' Le Pedvin continued to cast his eyes about for his contact.

'Yes,' Ranulf mused. 'He told you there were Saxons here and then we heard them galloping off in the other direction. Bit of a coincidence?'

'Pah.' Le Pedvin strode off across the space, scowling to left and right.

Mabbut watched him go. Neither he nor Ranulf made any attempt to help Le Pedvin as he scoured through the rubbish.

'You'd think he could leave the Saxons alone. The Normans won the battle after all. Why keep going on about it?'

'Oh, I think they'll keep going on about it for a long time to come. It's the sort of thing he and William do.'

'So you think we're really after Saxons?' Mabbut asked. Le Pedvin's behaviour was making it even more doubtful that this was all about counting sheep.

'I'm mulling it over,' Ranulf replied. 'It's true that four of us really aren't enough to chase down Saxons.' 'A Saxon treasure trove,' Mabbut breathed the words.

'What?' Ranulf seemed contemptuous of the concept. But then contemptuous came naturally.

'They could be after a Saxon treasure trove.'

'I rather think William owns the whole country now, he's hardly likely to send us off after some box of treasure.' The contempt was really in charge now.

'Could be very particular,' Mabbut went on, 'Harold had to come down from the north, probably had most of his court with him. There'd be a fair bit of royal treasure, I expect. Someone probably made off with it after the battle. That could be what we've been sent for. Any Saxons he happens to come across will be a bonus.'

'Hm,' Ranulf was actually giving this some thought. 'I suppose it might be worth chasing the crown of England if that was missing.' It was a shame he had no idea how close to the truth he was.

'He's going to steal our treasure,' Mabbut wailed. Every action the Normans took drove him deeper into despair.

'Well, of course.' Ranulf looked at him as if he was stupid. Well, even more stupid than most people. 'We've just won a major battle, defeated the King, taken over the country, of course we get the treasure. What's the point otherwise?'

'Our magnificent Saxon land.'

'Doesn't look very magnificent to me.' Ranulf gestured at the rubbish heap.

Mabbut lapsed into a sulking silence.

◆   ◆   ◆

In the middle of this pause, there was a noise. It was low and muffled, but definitely human. Both men looked around to locate the source.

'Over there,' Mabbut called as he noticed a movement among the shards.

Le Pedvin was on the other side of the space, so Mabbut and Ranulf picked their way over to an indentation in the ground. In the bottom of this lay a bound and gagged Martel, kicking his feet to attract attention.

'Le Pedvin!' Ranulf called and beckoned.

Mabbut knelt and drew his tiny knife. Cutting a rather poor piece of string was the sort of thing it was made for, and it made short work of the scraps that tied Martel's wrists and ankles. Once free, Martel ripped a disgusting piece of material from his face and spat several times to clear his mouth.

'What the hell happened to you?' Le Pedvin demanded when he joined them. It was clear that whatever it was that had happened to Martel was entirely his own fault and could all be put down to incompetence. It had also caused great inconvenience to Le Pedvin, and would be held against the young man for some time to come.

'They jumped me,' Martel defended himself, shaking his hands back into life.

'Some thin, raggedy Saxons in a burnt out village, jumped an armed Norman and tied him up?' Le Pedvin clearly thought this was unbelievable.

'How do you know they were raggedy?' Martel demanded.

'They're all raggedy, especially round here. And we've taken all their food, so they're bound to be thin.'

'More to the point, why didn't they kill you?' Ranulf asked, not unreasonably.

'Decent people,' Mabbut started to explain.

'Ridiculous,' Ranulf stopped him. 'Saxons capture a Norman, we never saw them, they carry him off in the night and leave him tied up? It's mad. As soon as they had him down they should have stuck a knife in his vitals.'

'Oy,' Martel objected.

'Well, wouldn't you? Why on earth leave your enemy where he can be found, let alone in a condition that he can become your enemy again? At least cut something off that he needs. Honestly, it's just very poor practice.'

'As I was saying,' Mabbut started, 'the Saxon people have a great respect for …'

'The Saxon people have a great nothing.' Le Pedvin was fuming. 'They left him here to delay us and give them time to get away.'

'The ones with the treasure,' Mabbut exclaimed before he could stop himself.

'What treasure?' Le Pedvin was confused.

Mabbut looked at the ground and mumbled a bit.

'Oh come on, Le Pedvin,' Ranulf was dismissive, 'we're clearly not here to take stock of the country. If that were the case we'd have waited till dawn when I could carry out a survey of this place. Instead, you want to go chasing after Saxons in the dark.'

'You heard the Duke's instructions,' Le Pedvin gave Ranulf half his attention, 'but if I hear of Saxons running away after the battle what am I supposed to do? You know me – it's not in my nature to let people live unnecessarily.'

'Hmm.' Ranulf was not convinced.

'There's nothing to stop us doing both. You can survey and write down, while I kill people. Seeing how Martel here has delayed us by getting himself knocked over by a couple of children, you'd better do a survey now while I get the horses.'

'They may have been raggedy, but they weren't children,' Martel protested, rubbing his wrists where they'd been bound. No one showed any interest, so he stopped again.

◆　　◆　　◆

The band trooped back into the remains of the village and took in its glory in the growing daylight. It didn't take long. There were a few piles of things here and there, and the odd wall was still standing, but that was about it.'

'There you are,' Le Pedvin held his arms out, 'won't take you long to count everything.' He stomped off to get the horses.

'Thank you,' Ranulf replied to his back. He took his book from his pack, his quill and portable ink well, sat cross-legged on the floor and settled down to note his findings.

Martel considered their surroundings, wary in case more small Saxons might be waiting to jump on him.

Mabbut drew up behind Ranulf to observe what was being written. As a minor landowner, his father had insisted on his education, wanting his son to take over his responsibilities when the time came. Doing his numbers and his letters had been an early ritual.

Even more unlikely, then, that his father would disown him. Granted they had not seen eye to eye on many things, or any things really. The father often criticised young Cnud for his lack of interest in farming, livestock management and this new-fangled crop rotation.

Cnud's response was to say that he found lambing and animal husbandry disgusting. Who wouldn't? The fields were boring and the life of the farmyard was dirty and smelly and laborious. It was not for him.

The father would then repeat his position, only louder, and the whole conversation would descend into chaos. Unless it was brought short by mother Mabbut screaming at both of them and throwing them out of the house.

Yet the young man had to admit that his father ran the most productive land for miles around. Even in times of famine, while there might not exactly be plenty, there was enough. His reputation spread, and soon visitors came to learn what they could of Mabbut's agricultural wisdom.

Sometimes young Mabbut even tried to listen, but as soon as talk moved on to strains of wheat his head would nod. As strains of wheat was usually the opening topic, he got very little from these events.

When his father was invited to Normandy, Cnud had been horrified. Farming was bad enough, but doing it for the Normans? His father pointed out that the nobles had agreed it, and that if he didn't go he would be taken anyway. That seemed to be some trigger to young not-farmer Mabbut. The Normans became the hated enemy and all things good were Saxon. Even his uncles.

Farmer Mabbut had agreed that his son could stay behind, as long as his cousin Bran made all the farming decisions, but no. Cnud saw it as his duty to accompany his parents into captivity, and use the time to berate the wretched Normans. It also made a change from rain and mud.

Mabbut's time at the Norman court had been well spent. He had berated repeatedly, and felt he had established the Saxon as a race to be respected and valued. He even had the honour to catch a glimpse of Harold Godwinson after the poor man had been ship wrecked and taken to the Norman court. It was only a glimpse as Mabbut had been quickly escorted from the chamber before he started annoying Normans and Saxons alike. He had also learned how to read and write Norman, and so could see what Ranulf was putting down.

'Salehurst. Gone,' he read. 'Is that it?'

'It's enough.' Ranulf gathered his book and writing materials together.

'It's outrageous,' Mabbut squealed. 'A whole Saxon village, gone.'

'I know it's gone,' Ranulf observed, 'and I've just written it down. Where next?'

'Are you going to say nothing else?' Mabbut couldn't believe this. 'Nothing about the wanton destruction wreaked by the Norman horde? Nothing about the death brought upon a peaceful people by a rampaging evil?'

'Seriously?' Ranulf asked. 'You seriously expect a Norman to write anything like that down? In a book that Duke William has commissioned? Are you out of your mind? Oh, I forgot, yes, you probably are. Tell you what, you write down what you want in your book and I'll write in mine.'

'I haven't got a book,' Mabbut grumbled.

'There you are then. I'm the one with the book, so I decide

what goes in it. Now, for the second time, where next?'

Mabbut gaped at this injustice. Until Le Pedvin came up behind him and pushed his mouth shut with the flat of his sword.

'Where next?' the soldier growled. 'It sounded like those horses were going north. Where would Saxons go north from here?' There was real menace in his voice, the sort of menace that told those who knew the man to avoid him, quickly.

'Wherever they liked, before their country was despoiled. Ow!' Mabbut recoiled as Le Pedvin slapped his face with the flat of the sword.

'Where are they going on *our* horses?' Le Pedvin added, slowly and deliberately. 'In Normandy you're just a nuisance and an idiot. Here you are a potential traitor, and we know what happens to them. I'm becoming less convinced we need you to show us around at all. The roads are pretty clear; if those horses went north, we'll go north. It's good enough. We can just write down what we find and I'm sure we could manage if you were, oh, what? Dead in a ditch? Or on a rubbish heap?'

'Could be anywhere,' Mabbut mumbled as he rubbed his cheek, now stinging like hell. 'London? Due north is the river.'

'River?' Le Pedvin prompted.

'The river Thames.' Honestly, the major river of the country and these Normans didn't even know that. They weren't worthy of the place.

'Is there a bridge?' Le Pedvin seemed very interested in the river.

'Not here.' Mabbut sort of indicated the general direction. 'London's the nearest. Closest this way would be the ferry at Gravesend.'

'Graves End? What sort of a name is Graves End for heaven's sake?'

Mabbut just shrugged. Sounded reasonable to him. He couldn't see anything wrong with it.

'Not London then.' Le Pedvin seemed to have reached a

conclusion about something.

'Why not?' Mabbut asked, wishing this man would make his mind up. 'London's our capital, surely that's where you'll want to go to find out what the country's got.'

Le Pedvin looked northwards. 'I may be a leader of the great Norman army, and Duke William's right hand man with all of his power and authority vested in me, but I'm not stupid. I'll take the whole army to London; I'm not wandering in there on my own. Anyway, I think if there were some Saxons running away from the battle they'd want to get across the river as quick as they could. They'll be to this ferry and gone before we've got halfway.' He glared at Martel.

Martel rubbed his wrists and ankles some more, adding a few groaning noises as he did so.

'Right,' said Le Pedvin. 'Martel, back to the camp for fresh horses. We'll start walking north and you catch us up.'

'But ...' Martel started to protest.

'And run,' Le Pedvin insisted, 'all the way.'

'Fresh horses?' Martel seemed to be having some trouble understanding the concept.

'We're hardly likely to find any here, are we?' He gestured at the bleak expanse of not-very-much.

'Why can't Mabbut go?' Martel asked. 'He's the Saxon.'

'Send a Saxon into the Norman camp asking to borrow some horses? They'd kill him.'

'Everyone knows who he is.'

'Like I say, they'd kill him.' Le Pedvin glowered at the man. He raised his sword and pointed at them all one by one, grinding words out between his teeth. 'I am getting fed up with people not doing what I say immediately. You all know what happens to those around me when I get fed up. There's no telling who will be first, but let me tell you,' he paused for breath before shouting in his best battle voice, 'I am going to chop the bloody head off the next person who answers me back.'

Martel left for the horses.

◆　　◆　　◆

'Right, north,' Le Pedvin ordered.

Ranulf packed his writing implements in the small, purpose-made pouch and Mabbut said nothing. He had an overwhelming urge to mumble 'bloody Normans', but thought better of it.

He followed Le Pedvin's beckoned instructions and set off up the road. He was assisted by the flat of the Norman's sword again, this time on his backside.

'Oy.'

'I can see what you're thinking.' Le Pedvin's face was a picture, a very nasty picture of something quite dangerous.

'Move!' He shouted at them both and they picked up their pace. 'God above, I'd rather deal with the whole Saxon army than you lot of bleating sheep,' he muttered, half to himself, as they walked off out of the village. 'And if you have one word to say, Mabbut, choose it carefully because it will be your last.'

Mabbut did have his mouth open and a very choice phrase on the superiority of the Saxon people was on his lips. He decided to save it for another time.

'You can tell me how far it is to this ferry,' Le Pedvin instructed.

'About forty miles,' Mabbut replied, hoping that this answer would be bad news. There had to be some way he could get at Le Pedvin without personal risk. He succeeded.

'Ahrgh.' Le Pedvin directed his guttural fury at England, at Mabbut and at every individual mile between here and Gravesend.

'Let them go,' Ranulf spoke up. 'The idea of chasing men on horseback across the country is ridiculous. We can do the job William gave us without rushing off after a bunch of Saxons.'

'Let them go?' Le Pedvin replied, as if he'd just been asked to release some Saxon prisoners. 'On Norman horses?'

Ranulf shrugged.

'I wanted to go off and just kill some more Saxons, but no, William wants the country checked out so that's what we're doing. But I'll bite my own ears off if I'm going to let a bunch of Saxons steal my horses and get away with it. We go after them. You'd better learn how to write things down pretty bloody quickly because we're not stopping.'

He strode off down the road. It was beginning to rain again, and a chilly wind blew. The autumn of England was going to join Mabbut in showing these invaders exactly what the country could do to you …

Chapter 10

To the Rescue

WITH EXCELLENT DIRECTIONS from the strangely named monk, Siward and his band of Vikings, as he now thought of them, headed down the road to Lincoln. He had no idea what he was going to do when he got there, though, not with a bunch of Vikings at his side. He didn't relish the prospect of taking them into a town that had had notoriously poor experiences of Viking visitors.

It was clear these men were powerful and Siward was sure they could take care of themselves in normal circumstances. Three up against a whole town, however, might be a different bucket of herring. Getting to the bishop's house, which unfortunately appeared to be in the middle of the old town, was going to be a challenge. What they did when they got there, heaven only knew. He assumed the Vikings had a plan; they would hardly have come this far just to pay a social call. He had no recollection of Vikings ever paying social calls. But maybe they were getting softer. He glanced at Fregurd and quickly put that idea from his head.

He speculated for a moment whether, when a Viking went to visit another Viking, his mother, or a relative perhaps, he burned the house down, slaughtered their livestock and ravaged their women. It seemed unlikely: if that was the case, the Vikings would have wiped themselves out years ago.

Whatever the circumstances, this was a very strange group of Vikings, on a very strange mission. Perhaps the bishop was a Viking? No, he was getting ridiculous now.

Of course, he might have another problem leaving Lincoln.

Erik had made it clear that Siward's work would be done once they had reached the town, but he wasn't sure the locals would be very supportive of a man who brought fresh Vikings to their midst. Once he was out of their protective aura, he might not fare very well. He could only keep plodding on, and hope.

◆   ◆   ◆

The sun was high in the sky now, although still buried in cloud, and Siward's normal state of continuous hunger was beginning to play games. His mind started to swim about inside his head, and his legs felt like they were flopping backwards and forwards, instead of having bones in the middle. He'd had a small bite last night, but it had been small. Granar had said that it would be best to spend the night hungry: it would keep Siward on his guard. Granar said a lot of things Siward didn't agree with.

'So …' Siward murmured, looking at the sun and hoping the Vikings would take the hint that lunchtime was upon them.

'So what?' Erik asked, without slowing his pace.

'I'd, erm, normally have something to eat about now.' Siward nodded, he hoped agreeably.

'Did you not feast last night?' Erik seemed contemptuous of something as feeble as eating.

'No, actually, I was on guard, you see? You remember? And coming with you I haven't got anything with me. Normally, of course, I'd go home and feast handsomely after the night on watch.'

Siward had never feasted handsomely in his life, but he hoped this approach might persuade the Vikings to give him something – ideally not another bit of fish that had the consistency of a shoe.

"Pah,' Erik snorted. 'Sigmund.' He nodded towards the young man who plodded at his side.

Sigmund nodded back and stopped. He drew a short-handled axe from his belt and adopted a pose of intense listening. At

112

some signal Siward couldn't detect, the man hurled his axe into the undergrowth of the all-encompassing forest. He smiled his satisfaction as the flight of the weapon terminated in a satisfying thud, followed by the terminal squeak of the animal that had caught the axe.

The Viking hopped off into the woods, scrabbled about a bit, and returned with axe in one hand and dead roe deer fawn in the other. The small deer was the size of a decent guard dog and had a very clear axe wound. The wound was so effective that it had wounded most of the top of the head off.

'There you go,' Sigmund said, as he threw the thing at Siward's feet.

'Erm, thanks,' Siward said, looking at it and wondering what the hell he was supposed to do now.

With a pained *tut* at Siward's failure to carry a full set of gutting knives with him at all times, Fregurd set to work with glee. Within moments the ex-deer was a neatly butchered series of joints. 'That's my Tendon Tickler,' the Viking whispered to his knife as he polished it and put it away

Fregurd stood and looked at Siward. He then looked at the deer expectantly.

'Oh, right, thanks,' Siward said as he knelt and gathered up all the edible bits of the beast.

'Are you going to leave that?' Fregurd gestured at a pile of very inedible bits.

'I was,' Siward offered.

Fregurd tutted again. He gathered up a steaming handful of soft, yet vital organs and passed them amongst his band. Each Viking tucked in with relish, the blond beards soon turning a very different colour all together.

'Aren't you going to eat?' Erik asked, gesturing at Siward's armful of deer as he chewed on the stringy bits which did something or other inside a deer. 'I thought you were hungry.'

'I'd normally cook it,' Siward explained apologetically. In

truth, the sight of the Vikings tucking into a deer's precious bits had put him right off his lunch.

'Ye Gods of Asgard,' Erik snorted, 'we're not stopping for a fire. You can keep going till dark.'

There was much muttering and laughter amongst the Norsemen at the weak and pathetic ways of anyone who wasn't a Viking.

Siward did manage to get some energy from his load, as the smell of fresh meat wandered around his nose. The thought that he appeared to have a whole deer to himself was positively cheering.

As the afternoon wore on, and the group continued its journey uninterrupted, Siward's hunger did get the better of him and he found himself first licking, and then nibbling on some of the raw venison. Eventually he even tore a small strip off with his teeth and found the chewing helped quell the pangs of starvation. This was handy, as there was a lot of chewing to be done.

◆　　◆　　◆

While it was true to say the journey was uninterrupted, as no one actually came to stop them, there was a good deal of scurrying out of the way by a number of locals.

People bent double under massive loads of firewood would look up as they came along the road. Seeing that there were three massive Vikings approaching, one and all decided to rush into the forest to put the firewood back on the trees.

Men pulling carts would suddenly conclude that the rough ground was a better route than the smooth path.

Even a group of three prosperous-looking merchants, with a band of least seven servants carrying their goods, apparently realised they were heading in completely the wrong direction. They turned round and headed back the way they'd come, at quite a lick.

'I think we've been noticed,' Siward commented when one youth, carrying a brace of rabbit, actually screamed, dropped his catch and ran off into the woods.

'Pah,' said Erik. It seemed to be a comment suitable for all occasions.

'Aren't you worried?' Siward asked. He felt some companionship with these men now, and had relaxed a little. He wouldn't go anywhere near them, of course, and took care not to look Fregurd in the eye, but he felt he could at least speak They didn't actually seem interested in him at all: they must realise he was as much of a threat to them as the fawn – after it had tried to headbutt the axe.

'There could be militia about. Some freeman's guard, and you just three Vikings?'

'There are no militia,' Erik grunted as they walked along.

Siward now had a leg of venison tucked in each trouser leg, one in each side of his jerkin and the rest of the corpse in his arms. It was even more difficult to keep up.

'Oh, for the gods' sake,' Fregurd snorted at the hobbling man. He took a length of twine from his pack and neatly bound the butchered corpse together so that it could hang comfortably across Siward's shoulders.

'Thanks,' Siward acknowledged, only to receive another snort of derision in reply.

'How do you know there aren't any militia?' he asked Erik as he now walked along comfortably.

'They all went south, didn't they?' Erik stated, as if Siward should know this.

'Oh, right,' Siward nodded. He had heard something about Harold heading south after defeating Harald Hardrada and the rest of the Danes at Stamford Bridge.

'Is that why you've come? No defenders left?'

Erik appraised the Saxon, as if weighing him up for some task, probably a dangerous one.

Anyone appraising Siward would not leap to their list of dangerous tasks. Any Viking appraising Siward would probably wonder which task they could take off one of their children and get the Saxon to do instead.

Of course the Vikings were larger than Siward, they were larger than everyone, but the poor filth-man had all the strength and vitality of a Norse thigh bone. He was still young, but really needed a good meal or two – if he had the strength to eat a good meal or two.

It looked like he had lain too long on his own filth heap, as the foxes had clearly had a go at his hair. This had no shape at all that could be discerned, but rather rambled over his head like some dark thicket looking for a place to settle and raise little bushes.

The eyes were lively, though. Dark brown and alert, they told of energy and potential which only needed the right outlet. He would have to make sure these Vikings didn't create a few new outlets which would do him no good at all.

As Siward looked expectantly at Eric he saw the exact opposite. The body was massive and purposeful. Smelly and dirty, but massive and purposeful. Rather like holding a shell to the ear to hear the sea, Siward found himself thinking that if he held this Viking close he could smell the sea. In fact close wasn't really essential. He was sure he had seen some flies buzzing around which were usually only associated with rotten seaweed.

The eyes, though, while clear and blue as water, were as vacant as fishes trousers – the water was the sort drawn in pictures, not the brown stuff that sloshed up and down the Humber. There was purpose in the eyes, but just the one. When that was completed there would be a pause while another one was brought up from the depths.

They were clearly very capable and practical men: dedicated, implacable and decisive. Rather like a falling tree which is going to hit the ground whether you are in the way or not. After it has landed you can do what you like.

◆ ◆ ◆

'Should I tell him?' Eric asked the other two.

Viking looks were exchanged, accompanied by a couple of shrugs.

'We can always kill him,' Fregurd offered helpfully, 'if need be.'

Siward's jaw dropped at this comment. If there was some piece of information that was so important that it meant death, the Vikings could keep it. He opened his mouth to say he really didn't want to know.

'He's bound to find out sometime, anyway,' Sigmund said darkly. 'What about when William's men come north?'

Erik grunted what seemed to be Viking assent.

'You've been conquered,' he said simply as their pace slowed not a jot.

Siward frowned, he didn't remember that happening. He knew he didn't get around much, but he didn't think being conquered was the sort of thing you'd miss. Of course, it could have been a big day with the filth. Anyway, even if they had been conquered, why was it such a secret? 'By you?' he asked.

'No, not by us, you fool,' Erik snorted. The other two joined in. A murder of crows, alarmed by so much snorting leaped from their tree top into the air

'By William.'

'Who?'

'William. William of Normandy.'

This didn't help much. 'Never heard of him.' Siward was sure if he had been invaded he'd recall the man's name.

'You will.' Sigmund gave a grim laugh.

Siward didn't understand. 'I don't understand,' he said.

'Your King Harold fought the Danish King Harald at Stam-ford Bridge, yes?'

'Oh yes, I heard about that.' He vaguely remembered something.

'Good.' Erik didn't seem impressed by Siward's lack of interest in events.

'After he'd defeated Harald,..'

'By guile and deceit,' Fregurd spat.

'After he'd defeated Harald by guile and deceit,' Erik confirmed, 'news comes that Duke William of Normandy has landed in the south. So your Harold packs up and heads off to deal with him.'

'How do you know all this?' Siward asked.

'We were with Harald, weren't we?'

'With Harold?'

'No, Harald.'

Siward frowned. This was getting complicated.

'Hardrada,' Erik said with some impatience. 'We're hardly likely to be fighting against the Danes, are we?' He held his arms out to indicate their allegiance was as plain as the axe on their backs.

'I don't understand,' Siward repeated.

'That's because I haven't finished,' Erik snapped.

Siward shut up.

'So,' Erik went on, 'Harold heads off south to defeat the Normans, except unfortunately he doesn't. William wins the battle and the Normans hold the south of the country.'

'What, Lincoln? Is that why we're heading there?'

'No, not Lincoln. Lincoln's not in the south, you weevil brain. It's just south of here.'

Siward worried that Erik's frustration was about to get physical. But he couldn't stop. Surely they didn't mean ...

'Not Sleaford?' He gaped at such a mythical place.

'You really know nothing about your own country, do you? Have you heard of a place called London?'

Siward nodded. Of course he'd heard of it. He'd no idea

where it was, but it seemed best not to say. He'd always thought it was near Africa, or just outside Jerusalem. Wherever they were.

'Well, even further south than London is your coast. Across the sea from there is Normandy, and that's where William came from.'

Siward nodded, very impressed. These Vikings really did get around.

'And William is a bastard,' Erik continued.

'Ah,' Siward nodded knowledgeably. He knew a few of them. 'Nasty piece of work, eh?'

'Very. And his father wasn't married to his mother either. He'll come rampaging north, mark my words, and you won't know what hit you. You think Vikings are bad?'

Siward thought it best not to answer that.

'William is worse. Vikings do what Vikings do, but we have some honour.'

Siward couldn't recall this being one of their defining qualities, but he didn't like to say.

'And when we've done what we do, we clear off. Until the next time. But William's a freak. He wants everyone under his thumb, all the time. If someone puts up a decent fight against a Viking, we respect them, we congratulate them on their courage and sing sagas about their brave deeds. After we've killed them and chopped them up, of course. That's only right.

But if William comes across anyone who puts up a fight he makes an example of them, usually by killing them slowly. Then he kills all their relatives, their friends, their livestock and anyone who knew them. Then he kills a few random people just to drive the message home. No honour, see?'

Siward nodded that this seemed very dishonourable. Though it didn't appear to matter very much whether you died on the end of an honourable Viking axe or a dishonourable Norman sword, or whatever it was Normans used to kill people. You'd still be dead. Very.

'But …' Siward had been thinking. There were big gaps in his understanding. Such things never usually bothered him, but this was a story, and he needed his stories to make sense. 'If you were with Harald, the Danish one, and he was defeated,' Siward quickly picked up the scowl on Erik's face, 'if he was, erm, the slightly less successful Harald at Stamford Bridge, what with all the guile and deceit going on,' the scowl faded, 'how do you know all about William? When did he win this battle of …?'

'Battle of?' Now Erik was lost.

'Yes, Battle of … It's got to be a battle of somewhere. All battles are of somewhere. You can't just have a battle, you can't say King So-and-so lost the battle. It has to be the battle of. Battle of Stamford Bridge, for example.'

'I don't know.' Erik clearly didn't give the name of the battle the same significance. It had just happened, that's all.

'Well, where was it? Where did this William land?'

'Place called Hastings apparently.'

'There you are.' Siward was happy now. Names were solid. Reassuring. 'Battle of Hastings, then.'

'If you say so.' Erik shrugged at this piece of nonsense.

'You never know,' Siward said enthusiastically, 'the name might catch on. So when was this battle?'

'Yesterday.'

'Yesterday! How could you possibly know what happened in this Hastings place yesterday?'

'Birds,' said Erik, as if this was obvious.

'What?' Siward looked to the sky.

Erik shook his head in some despair. 'I'm not surprised you people have been conquered. It's a miracle you manage to live from one day to the next without help. Messenger birds.'

Siward's mind was boggling. What was this Viking land like

– a place where birds could pass on messages?

'You carry a bird with you all the time and feed it and so forth, and it always comes home,' Erik explained wearily. 'Then you lend it to someone else, and when they want to send you a message they write it down, tie it to the bird and let it go. The bird flies home and you read the message.'

'Wow!' Siward was amazed at this sophistication. What was the world coming to?

'So you gave a bird to Harold?'

'One of his people.'

'Why?' Siward couldn't see why the defeated side would do that. He didn't like to raise the topic of the Vikings losing the battle again.

'Honour.' Erik looked to the sky in a rather grand manner. 'We were defeated by a great foe. Like I said, Vikings respect that sort of thing, and your Harold's own brother was on our side, which wasn't honourable at all.'

Siward was about to say he didn't know Harold had a brother. He knew he had a wife, a woman called Edith who had the neck of a swan apparently. Royals always were a bit odd.

'So when we heard Harold had been called south we gave him a bird, in case he needed to call upon us. Once he'd defeated us, we were his to command. Well, the honourable ones among us were.' He nodded at the other two.

Sigmund nodded acknowledgment and held his honourable head high. Fregurd looked a lot less impressed.

'Only three?' Siward said, before he could stop himself.

Erik mumbled a bit. 'Turns out our Harald had made a separate pact with William, and the others are sticking to that. We'd have the north, William the south. Except with us defeated, William will get the lot.'

'So you got the bird that said William had won. It still doesn't explain why you're going to Lincoln. Surely you'd want to keep away.'

'Ah, but that wasn't the whole message.' Erik nodded knowingly.

Siward nodded, a lot less knowingly. He was feeling alarmed, but not sure why.

'Yes. William won the battle, but not everyone was killed. Some people escaped and we're on a rescue mission.'

'A rescue.' Siward perked up again. This sounded quite exciting. 'Who are we rescuing?'

'Your King Harold, of course,' Erik said simply. 'We wouldn't come all this way for some peasant.'

Siward was amazed and gawped to show it. From his life of filth to the rescuing of a king. *The* King. This was fantastic.

'And if we have to go into the very teeth of the Norman horde and die in the doing of it, so much the better.' Erik roared and beat his chest.

Ah, thought Siward glumly, there was always a downside. Perhaps an adventure with a rescue at the end of it wasn't so good after all. Perhaps being a filth-man had its attractions. Like being alive.

Chapter 11
De Sauveloy *vs* Toll-man

ABBUT HAD BEEN WISHING Martel would turn up with the horses for *ever*. Well, at least for a couple of hours. The pace Le Pedvin insisted they keep up towards Gravesend was harsh, and whenever Mabbut made the slightest sound of complaint he got the flat of the sword again.

Ranulf said nothing, but did appear to be taking note of his surroundings. As these consisted entirely of trees, Mabbut couldn't imagine it wouldn't take a feat of memory to write them down when the time came – even for a Norman, who everyone knew the Lord had not troubled with brains.

Mabbut was about to let out another moan, despite himself, when behind them the sound of horses could suddenly be heard. He stopped and turned to see how far away they were.

'Keep going,' Le Pedvin grumbled out his order.

'The horses will be here in a minute.'

'And in a minute we'll be a minute further up the road and closer to a bunch of thieving Saxons.'

Mabbut shook his head. It must be really awful being a Norman. Horses, weapons and shouting: that was their world. Nice.

A few moments later Martel came clattering up behind. He sat on one large grey mare, while he held the reins of three others. It seemed the whole journey had been a bit of a mare itself. The reins were all tangled up and the horses looked like they'd spent the last hour bumping into one another.

'What's this?' Le Pedvin demanded.

'Horses,' Martel replied curtly.

'Mares,' Le Pedvin snapped back. 'I do not ride a mare. I ride a stallion.'

Martel frowned at him. 'Well, you should have said. You should have said fetch fresh horses and make one of them a stallion.' He had a point.

'You should,' Ranulf confirmed with a knowing nod. Knowing nods were the only ones he could do.

'I really, really need to kill something soon,' Le Pedvin said as he swung himself on to the horse with the sort of grimace he probably saved for a warm garderobe seat.

Ranulf and Mabbut mounted their steeds and the whole party set off once more. Mabbut started at a gentle walking pace, before an explosive 'yargh' from Le Pedvin had all four animals up to the full gallop and headed north.

It was starting to rain again, and the clouds were lowering. They were still quite alone on the road. It may have been well trodden a thousand years ago, but now it was like the road from nowhere to nowhere, stopping by in the middle of nowhere on its way. Four men and horses could disappear in these parts and not be missed for another century or two.

The world stretched away from them as they hurtled on through the misery which passed for weather.

◆   ◆   ◆

Mabbut shivered. He disliked the road being so empty, assuming it was because rampaging Normans had burnt down the nearest town. Word had spread that the battle had been lost and everyone had, not unnaturally, vanished. Any locals still alive were not going to concern themselves with the passage of an invader with a sword and his friends. There had been ample time for those fleeing the battlefield to make good their escape, if they were capable of walking at all, and for anyone else simply to hide.

'We're not going to be able to observe much at this pace,' Ranulf shouted over the buffeting wind and the clattering horses.

'You observe, we ride,' Le Pedvin instructed.

Their journey continued uninterrupted, although Mabbut couldn't imagine who was likely to try and interrupt them in any case. Armed men on foot were to be avoided, but armed men on horses, even on mares, were to be positively run away from. It wasn't even any good throwing yourself on the ground in supplication, as the really dedicated mounted warrior would get his horse to trample you to death. The horses of mounted warriors seemed to enjoy that sort of thing. They were as mean as their riders.

Horses were in any case relatively unusual beasts in these parts, so would scare most of the locals half to death before any trampling could get started.

The road became more established the further north they travelled. More village tracks fed into it and they reached a point where the nearest large town was Meopham to the north, rather than Hastings to the south. The road became a positive highway, broad, with several parallel ruts where the carts had bounced their way to market, or to the port itself. It was still not a patch on the original Roman road, but then the locals didn't have a detachment of Roman soldiers threatening them with death if they didn't maintain the carriageway. Little things like that made all the difference, so Mabbut's uncles had always said. He was sure they were right. Dead, probably now, but right.

✦   ✦   ✦

Le Pedvin had allowed the horses to slow from their head-long gallop, and take the chance to recover themselves before he drove them on again. He muttered a lot about mares and stallions and general incompetence, while casting dagger-filled looks at Martel. The young man ducked them with the ease of long practice.

They emerged from one densely forested area, where in summer the trees would create a charming tunnel of dappled green, shading the traveller and dropping a measure of sheltered peace upon a troubled world. Now, though, harsh autumn winds were ripping the remaining leaves from skeletal branches. They hurled them into the travellers' faces as if to say the departing summer was all their fault.

To their left the land now dropped away into a small but deep dingle, the sound of water drifting up from its depths. To the right the woods remained thick and impenetrable. The track narrowed until it was only wide enough for them to pass one at a time and they ordered themselves into single file. Le Pedvin barged to the front, of course. He said there would probably be a rude bridge of some sort ahead to get them across the stream. No one contradicted him.

Suddenly, squeezed into the space ahead, they came upon a wooden hut. Hut was a bit of a generous description. It rather looked like the autumn wind had blown the limbs of some trees together and a man had decided to live in them.

Outside of the hut, a large tree trunk blocked the path completely. Mabbut looked left and right. There was no way round into the valley of the stream, and behind the hut the wood blocked any hope of passage. He assessed the tree trunk and thought it was probably jumpable by an experienced horseman on an experienced horse. He knew that he was not the former and suspected his mount was not the latter. It was busy radiating lack of enthusiasm. So was he, to be fair. He also thought Ranulf probably didn't do horse jumping at all. Le Pedvin would do, of course.

He turned his attention back to the log and noticed something rather odd about it. Nowhere along its length did it seem to touch the ground. This was remarkable: a floating tree? He had never heard of such things, except in myths and fairy tales.

126

He noticed Le Pedvin was inspecting the thing as well. The Norman, more practical in approach, had promptly found a sturdy rope, which ran from the middle of the log up into the trees above. Letting his eyes follow the rope over a wooden pulley, he spotted another tree trunk of similar size, hanging in midair behind the hut.

Mabbut, considering this remarkably sophisticated system, now that Le Pedvin had pointed it out, reasoned that if the trunk in the trees was allowed to drop, the one blocking the path would rise, like some huge, crude gate.

A man emerged from the hut-conglomeration, stepped into the middle of the path and held up his arm.

'Toll,' he intoned in a very matter of fact manner, without bothering to look at those who were approaching.

'Four horses, four men, fourpence,' he droned, ignoring them altogether and instead examining the trees around him, as if suspicious that some of them had moved since he last emerged.

'Toll?' Le Pedvin asked. His tone clearly said he was not going to pay any toll. It also said, to those with some experience of the tones of the Norman fighting man, that anyone who asked him for a toll was also asking for a hideous fate.

This man was little better ordered than his tollhouse, being drab from head to foot. He had clearly spent so long in the company of rotting wood that the fungus was in the process of infesting him. There was no telling if this creature had a home to go to at the end of a day's toll gathering, or if he simply lived, ate and slept in the horrible hovel. He was probably required to collect tolls day and night, so it was very likely this *was* his home.

It was hard to imagine there would be a Mrs Toll-man and a collection of junior Toll-men inhabiting the tiny and unsanitary left-overs of a tree. Still, one could never tell; it was probably one of the steadiest paid jobs for miles around. Being a toll-man's wife might be better than being left to the vagaries of the seasons to put food in the stomach. Or it might not.

The toll-man sniffed at Le Pedvin. 'Yup,' he said, with very little interest. He held out his hand. This time he did look at the group, but only at their horses. He didn't have the slightest interest in who they were or why they were there. He just wanted, no, *expected*, his toll.

'Do you know who we are?' Le Pedvin asked.

The man raised his weary gaze to the faces of those mounted on their horses. Perhaps he was worried that this might be the lord who actually owned the road, or one of his men.

Mabbut observed him and concluded no, he wasn't, he wasn't worried at all. Mabbut had met his sort before. This man had a job to do and would do it, and that would be all he would do. He wasn't going to step out of his way to grant boon, or favour, or aid. Or engage in any discussion, consider explanations or take anything in lieu of the toll. Nor would he give any consideration to the rank of those who wanted to use his road. If the fearful night legion itself turned up, this man would stop them for the toll.

'Nope.' The man confirmed that he didn't know them. He also said, in that one word, that he didn't care who they were and really didn't want to be told.

'Fourpence.' He held out his hand again. 'For the upkeep of the road.'

'Upkeep?' Ranulf spluttered, appalled. 'Upkeep of the road? You call this upkeep?' He gestured at the rutted, muddy tracks that wound through the forest. 'Do you seriously expect me to believe that any toll has been spent on the upkeep of this road in the last hundred years?'

'Eh?' This did seem to throw the man. It was highly improbable that anyone had actually challenged the philosophy of the toll before.

'I don't mind paying a toll if I'm getting something for it, if I see any sign of improvement in travel conditions – but do I?' Ranulf went on. 'No, I do not. I have no idea what is being done with this toll, but it is most certainly not being spent on upkeep. Where's your bark for absorbing the mud, your stonework for filling in the holes and the top dressing?'

'Um.' Toll-man looked at Ranulf as if he was speaking Norman French. His English did have a terrible accent, but it was comprehensible. At least it was to Mabbut, but then he'd been listening to these ghastly people for years.

'All I see is a toll-man taking money I see no workmen, no supplies,' Ranulf scanned the surrounding woodland, 'no sign that anything is going to be done with my fourpence, and I therefore refuse to pay.'

The man looked very nonplussed at such a well-reasoned withholding of the toll.

'You can't,' was the best argument he could come up with.

'Oh, can't I?' Ranulf sat back on his horse and folded his arms.

Le Pedvin looked to the sky. 'Oh God, here we go,' he sighed. He clearly had some experience of people telling Ranulf what he couldn't do, and the memory was not a happy one.

'Where's your charter?' Ranulf asked.

Again the toll-man's face said an answer was not readily available.

'You have got a charter?' Anyone hearing Ranulf's tone would know that the response to this should be 'yes'. It should be prompt and clear, even if it was a lie. Anything other than 'yes' was going to mean trouble.

'Erm,' the toll-man said.

Ranulf sighed. When Ranulf sighed the world sighed with him. Even the wind seemed to howl in sympathy and the rain veered away to avoid what was going to be a very embarrassing situation. 'Are you seriously telling me that you have no charter to gather a toll at all?'

The man looked at Ranulf, and for a moment questioned what was going on. He seemed to recall his place and his role in life, which was to be as difficult as possible to anyone who passed by. He felt back on sure ground. 'No, I don't have no charter, and I don't know anything about charters. That's my lord's business and he tells me to come here and take his toll. I don't go questioning my lord, wouldn't be right.'

'Very well,' said Ranulf, who seemed half-satisfied with this. Only half-satisfied because he was never completely satisfied about anything. 'Where are your books, then?'

'Books?' Toll-man replied. His tone of voice said there was no question of him having any books, nor of him having a very clear idea of what a book was.

'Yes, man, your books. How do you keep count of the toll?'

From the look on the man's face, counting was another challenging concept.

'How many tolls do you collect each day? You must know that.'

Toll-man didn't.

'It's the most basic piece of information,' Ranulf ranted. 'How can you call yourself a toll-man and not know how many tolls you collect? You *are* a toll-man, I assume, and not some impostor who's just loitering here with not a clue what you're doing?'

Poor Toll-man didn't know whether to shake his head cautiously or nod vigorously.

'Can we get a move on?' Le Pedvin asked.

Ranulf turned his doleful stare on the Norman warrior, who found something of interest in his horse's mane.

Ranulf turned back to the toll-man. 'As far as I can tell, whatever your excuse for being here, you really do have not a clue what you are doing.'

Ranulf's withering look of disappointment, the one he used to great effect on nobles of the Norman court, let alone grubby toll-men in the middle of woods, caused the fellow to drop his eyes and study some of the leaf litter on the floor.

'I shall need full details of the toll,' Ranulf went on, getting out his parchment and quill. He waited. The toll-man looked, not understanding what was happening any more. Ranulf waited.

'How much is the toll?' He eventually broke the silence with a despairing question, aimed at an idiot and hitting its mark.

The toll-man continued to study the floor. 'Fourpence,' he mumbled.

'Pardon?' Ranulf spoke loudly. 'I didn't hear that.'

'Fourpence,' the man answered with a touch of irritation and impudence.

'Fourpence?' Ranulf repeated with a cartload of patronising contempt. 'The toll is fourpence.'

Toll-man nodded.

'That's it, is it?' Ranulf asked, and if there had been a class-room full of toll-men, this one would now be brought to the front as an example. He'd probably then be sent to stand outside the master's office. If he didn't shoot himself with an arrow first, that is.

✦   ✦   ✦

On their horses, the others were starting to look away, or study the leaf litter themselves. Mabbut knew what Ranulf in full flight could be like, he had been on the receiving end and understood what the toll-man was going through. The embarrassment, the inability to do anything about the situation or to wrest control of it from the ghastly Norman, who was denigrating you in front of an audience.

And there was no such glorious relief as the experience of watching it happen to someone else.

'So this fourpence,' Ranulf went on, pronouncing 'fourpence' as if it was a made-up word for something revolting, 'is charged for what?' He waited again, but there was no answer. 'Horses? Men? Carts? Nobles? Everyone pays fourpence?'

The toll-man mumbled something.

'What?' Ranulf snapped. 'We didn't hear that, speak up.'

'It's a penny,' Toll-man almost shouted.

'Oh, so it's a penny now?' Ranulf's sarcasm joined his other infuriating traits and laid waste to the toll-man, who clearly wanted to go back to his hut and leave these people to go wherever the hell they wanted.

'So four of us, fourpence.' Ranulf nodded, a smile playing on his face.

Those who knew him shivered at this development.

'Yessire,' the toll-man said, with some confidence.

Playtime over, the smile vanished like a child called in by an angry parent.

'A penny for a horse, a penny for a man, a penny for a cart?' Ranulf nodded slowly.

The toll-man picked up the nod and dared a smile back.

'Oh dear, oh dear,' Le Pedvin muttered.

'Wrong!' Ranulf exclaimed to the toll-man, his companions and the creatures of the wild wood. 'That is not how a toll works at all. You are quite simply the most incompetent toll gatherer I have ever come across. I don't know who your master is, but he is clearly as useless as you for letting you carry on. You do not seem to have even the most basic understanding of your task, other than to stand in the middle of the road saying "fourpence".'

The toll-man looked to the others for some support against this unjustifiable attack. He clearly thought standing in the road and saying 'fourpence' was most of the toll-man's art.

'Who is the beneficiary of the toll? How much is gathered in a year and what proportion is paid in taxes?' Ranulf looked at the toll-man expectantly, quill in hand.

'Er.' Toll-man had clearly never had such a troublesome customer. 'I shall report you to the lord.' He found some courage and resorted to what sounded like a standard response, as if this was usually enough to put the fear of God into the recalcitrant traveller.

'No, I think *I* shall report *you* to the lord,' Ranulf responded, not put out one bit. 'I am clear that you have absolutely no idea how much toll you have collected, and have therefore not passed the correct amount over to your lord. For that I imagine he will hang you.'

Toll-man's hand involuntarily went to his throat.

'Perhaps you have not heard the news from Hastings?' Martel stepped in. The humiliation of this very humble man was becoming unbearable.

'Nope,' the man responded, clearly very happy to have a change of subject.

'There has been a great battle,' Martel said dramatically.

'Oh, right.'

'And the battle was won by Duke William of Normandy.'

'Oh, really?' Toll-man said, sounding desperately interested in this news, offering, as it did, a topic of conversation which did not touch on his personal failures.

'And so there's a good chance that the lord who owns this land is now dead.'

'The lord who owned this land,' Ranulf corrected Martel to the past tense.

'Yes, owned this land. So really it all sort of belongs to, erm …'

'It all belongs to Duke William,' Ranulf finished off, 'so the toll belongs to him as well, and as you know so very little about your own business, I have a strong suspicion I'm going to have to report you to Duke William instead of the useless local lord who has done so little to manage the tolls hereabouts.'

The man looked at Ranulf, unsure whether this would be better or worse.

'Being hung by your own lord will be a positive pleasure compared to the sorts of things Duke William does to people.' Ranulf put that idea to bed.

Toll-man had run out of comments and expressions. He simply looked pale and worried.

Ranulf peered at the man in his very critical manner. 'Fortunately,' he went on, and the toll-man's face showed some spark
of distant hope at this word, 'I've been given a mission by the
Duke to assess the land for him and so we can spend a few useful hours getting this place in order.'

The spark died.

'We'll do no such thing,' Le Pedvin growled, finding his voice
in the face of one of Ranulf's onslaughts, 'we're wasting time. Put
this idiot on one of your lists and we'll get him on the way back.'

The Norman had started fiddling with his eye-patch and
those who knew him knew this as a very bad sign. A very bad
sign amongst very bad signs. The man was appallingly aggressive
and dangerous at the best of times, and they were few and far
between, but when he started fiddling with his eye-patch? Men
of courage, daring, and great size found something else to do
when Le Pedvin started fiddling with his eye-patch.

There was rumour that when the grim reaper was at a loose
end, there being no reaping to do, he loitered behind Le Pedvin's
eye-patch, knowing there would always be good business in the
vicinity. He had had enough.

Ranulf looked to Le Pedvin in some surprise at having his
plans questioned. He then took note of the eye-patch fiddling
and looked at the toll-man and the hut, and perhaps concluded
that a few hours spent in the man's company, and in his hovel,
was not so attractive after all. Even if there was the prospect of
getting a toll system properly organised.

Toll-man nodded some enthusiasm for this plan, it being
pretty clear he would be miles away when they came back.

'You may pass,' he announced in a grand tone and skipped
forward to lift the trunk out of the way, the counterweight dragging it upwards.

'Of course we may,' Ranulf scoffed as the horses stepped forward.

'Ranulf here is a very thorough man,' Le Pedvin observed as

he passed the toll-man. 'If he says he will report you to Duke William, you can rest assured that he will. I, on the other hand, am a man of action and I think that if I lower the gate, wrap the rope around your neck and then cut it, the counterweight will rip your head off before your feet leave the ground.'

Toll-man mumbled rather incoherently, but it sounded a bit like gratitude.

'I think your toll gathering days are over?' Le Pedvin suggested.

Toll-man nodded enthusiastically.

'And the log here will be long gone before we return.'

'Certain of it,' Toll-man said with confidence.

'Come on,' Le Pedvin called to the others, 'we've wasted enough time. Gravesend.' He spurred his horse forward. 'Although I'll be damned, with all this pointless chatter we've probably missed them.' He glared at Ranulf and galloped away.

Chapter 12

The Vikings are Coming!

ORD OF THREE VIKINGS walking down the road to Lincoln must have spread. As they approached the outskirts of the town, looking down from the Lincoln edge on to the river valley spread for miles below them, a deputation appeared.

It wasn't much of a deputation and Siward could understand why. When word that Vikings were approaching was received, sane people went in the opposite direction as quickly as they could. The suggestion that just three Vikings were approaching must have been a very odd message to deal with.

Doubtless Harold had taken the best body of fighting men south, so there wouldn't be much of a contingent left. Whoever they were, they were probably holed up behind the walls of the town, ready to defend should the need arise.

This deputation would be the expendable ones, old men mainly, who could try and find out what was going on and report back, or die in the attempt.

The first would be better, but if it was the second they wouldn't be missed much.

The bunch facing Siward looked like it had taken all their effort simply to walk so far away from the city. They were sitting by the side of the road, clutching sides and gasping. One of them was lying down and looked like he might not be getting up again.

'Halt.' One of the gaggle of old men raised a hand from his seated position. There was clearly nothing he was going to be able to do about it if they decided not to halt.

Siward noticed that the Vikings hadn't spotted their reception party was here at all, so intent were they on getting to Lincoln.

'Just a minute,' Siward called at departing backs.

Erik, Fregurd and Sigmund stopped and turned and saw Siward was standing by the side of the road.

'Not again,' Erik sighed and shook his head. 'You only went a few miles back.'

'No, no.' Siward gestured towards the side of the road. 'They've come to greet us.'

The Vikings joined him and saw what he was pointing at.

'This lot?' Fregurd was clearly insulted.

'Village elders, probably,' Siward explained.

'Village dead-any-minute more like.' Fregurd turned up his nose.

'I thought you respected old people?' Siward snapped, before remembering it was unwise to contradict a Viking with lots of knives.

'Yes,' Erik intervened, 'but that's our old people, not yours. Yours are disgusting. What do they want?'

Siward looked to the old men, one of whom held up a hand in that universal waving gesture which said 'give me a minute to get my breath and I'll tell you'. He quickly concluded what they wanted was to be at home, by the fire.

The Vikings and Siward waited while the old man gathered himself. Siward seriously thought this fellow had put his all into reaching the band before they reached the town. There was very little chance he would make it back without what little remained of his life petering out on the way.

'We heard,' the man gasped, 'we heard there were Vikings.' He collapsed back on to the grass by the road.

'Yes,' Siward confirmed, 'here they are.' His gesture took in the three Norsemen who looked like they were queuing up to finish off old Englishmen.

'Three?' The old man gasped with some surprise.

'Yes.' Siward nodded. It seemed cruel to try and make this ancient speak.

The wheezing, rattling lungs managed to express outrage. 'Someone said three, but we thought that wasn't very likely. When did you last hear of a marauding band of three Vikings? We dragged ourselves all the way out here for this lot?'

'More than enough for you, old man.' Erik looked down.

'I at least expected a horde. Call yourselves Vikings? Three?'

'I'm not too proud to stick my axe in the head of an old man, you know,' Erik promised.

'What do they want?' the old man asked Siward.

'They've got a meeting in Lincoln. I'm just showing them the way.' As he said this Siward realised how odd it sounded. And how odd it looked.

'Ha,' the old man managed. 'So they've burned down your village, killed your family and taken you hostage, eh?'

'Well, erm …'

'What do you want, old man?' Erik interrupted before Siward had a chance to start explaining. 'You are holding us up.'

'I'm here to tell you we will defend ourselves. Our city still has strong walls and our men are ready to fight to the death.'

Erik rested his hands on his hips and shook his head in disappointment. 'From what I hear, your men all went south with Harold which means they've already fought to the death. Even Vikings can't do that twice. We are not interested in attacking your wretched little town. It's as our guide says: we have come to meet someone.'

The old man frowned and turned to his companions, beckoning them to join him.

Those that were capable crawled across the grass and collapsed within earshot. There was some rather unhurried whispering and half-hearted and weak waving of arms.

'It really doesn't matter,' Erik put in. 'We're going anyway.'

'Storig Storigsdottir,' one of the old men croaked out, with one of the last of his lifetime allocation of breaths.

'No,' Erik responded. 'I'm Erik, this is Fregurd and Sigmund.' Fregurd waved the appropriate knife, Death-Hastener.

'I don't know how you people tell one another apart,' the old man managed between gulps. 'What I mean is, have you come to visit Storig?'

'Who's Storig?' Erik seemed to be finding this all a bit difficult to cope with.

'Storig Storigsdottir,' impatience permeated the man's terminal exhalations. 'She's a Viking.' The man seemed offended that they didn't know one another; they were all Vikings after all. 'She lives in Lincoln.'

'What's a …?' Erik, bewildered, ground to an undignified halt. 'I don't want to know,' he declared. 'I'm going to Lincoln. I am not going to attack and I have not come to visit relatives.'

The old men nodded sagely and with some comfort. One of them nodded his head down and failed to nod it back up again, collapsing instead on to the grass where he moaned quietly.

'Come on.' Erik commanded his small band to follow him into the town and they set off, the Vikings shaking their heads and muttering about useless old men.

As they left, the head old man said something, but no one could hear it clearly. Not even Siggurd could be bothered to go back and find out what it was.

◆ ◆ ◆

'Sounds like there's a Viking living in Lincoln,' Siward said encouragingly as they walked.

'That's what the man said,' Fregurd replied without any interest.

The final approach to Lincoln was quite impressive. The broad highway of Roman Ermine Street was still in relatively good condition this close to the city, and they strode quickly along it. There was no other traffic, nor any other travellers at all. The arrival of the Vikings had obviously caused a bit of a stir and it was clear, even from a distance, that the gates to the city were shut.

The old Roman walls were not in such a good state, but still constituted a better defence than most towns possessed. The entrance of Northgate Arch blocked their way, and its gates had been firmly shut. These were not the solid gates of a Roman city. These were the rather poor attempts at replacements, put in place by people who found the concept of a big gate pretty hard to accommodate. They obviously knew how small gates, and farm gates were made, so they had just made a big one of those and put it in the gap.

The resulting structure could have been climbed through by any small adult.

The walls of the city stretched off left and right, but the tops had been taken away, probably to make houses. Never mind a scaling ladder – a small stool would have been enough to mount this defensive barrier.

No uniformed heads appeared on top of the wall, and no cries of resistance rebounded from the stones. There wasn't even a man with a sword standing in the road to issue the traditional challenge, and be traditionally killed for his trouble.

◆　　◆　　◆

'What do you want?' squeaked out a voice from behind the gate somewhere.

Erik gestured that Siward should approach, while the three of them waited in the road.

Siward got the distinct impression that they wouldn't wait long before they decided to knock down the gates and enter the town anyway. He walked cautiously up to the gate, glancing all the time left and right, on the lookout for an arrow to come sweeping out of the air.

'Hello?' he called through the gaps in the woodwork.

'What do you want?' the small voice came back.

Siward couldn't see anyone inside the gate. The owner of the voice was probably hiding behind something.

'I said, what do you want?' the voice squeaked again.

Siward looked down now and saw a small child inside the gates. He was about seven, to judge from his height. It was no surprise that Siward had missed him.

'Are you all that's left?' Siward said, some horror creeping in that the entire male population of a major town might have been wiped out at the Battle of Hastings.

'Nah,' the child said. He spat. 'I volunteered. I want to kill a Viking.' He directed his glance to Siward. 'And their treacherous lackeys.' The child growled as best as a seven-year-old can growl. He waved a miniature sword in Siward's direction.

'Very commendable,' Siward nodded, 'but they're no trouble. They've just come for a meeting. They're not attacking or anything.'

'Tor, get back here.' This was a woman's voice, and it had a clear effect on the child. It nearly jumped out of its skin in its haste to do exactly what it was told.

Striding into Siward's view from one of the side streets came a woman, and his first impression was that she was magnificent. She was, in fact, the kind of woman the word magnificent had been made for. Delightful, charming, delicate, precious? No. Magnificent? Yes. She had to be at least six foot tall, but everything was in proportion – including the battle-axe she held comfortably in her right hand.

'I told you I'd see to them,' the woman called to the streets of Lincoln. 'Load of fuss about a few Norsemen wandering the countryside.' This was more of a mutter to herself as she strode up to the gates. She lifted away the lightweight and fundamentally poor cross-timber that held the doors shut, and threw the opening wide. Siward stood and gawped.

The woman was dressed in a simple brown one-piece tunic that hung from shoulders to shins. It was buckled round her neck and belted at her waist. On her legs she had boots that were laced tightly to her perfectly toned calves. Her bust was struggling against the confining cloth, but was being calmed by waves of blond curls, cascading on either side of a perfectly shaped face. The shape was mostly square, but it still suited her. Eyes as blue as sapphires shone on those around her; at least Siward assumed that was what sapphires would look like if he ever saw any.

The woman's right arm seemed to be having no trouble at all hefting her axe, which was clearly of Viking manufacture. As was she.

'Er,' Siward said. He hoped it sounded impressive.

'Who are you and what do you want?' the woman called in a clear and solid tone. A tone that went straight to Siward's knees and made them wobble. There was a hint of Viking accent, but much less pronounced than Erik and his band. And much more charming.

'Are you Storig?' Erik called from some way off.

'Who wants to know?' The woman squinted at the three Vikings who were now approaching.

'Storig?' Erik repeated as he drew close. It sounded like he couldn't put the name to the face.

'Erik?' The woman did recognise the face and the name. 'What the hell are you doing here?'

'What am I doing here?' Erik was all disbelief. 'More to the point, what are you doing here? You're supposed to be dead.' He said this in a most accusatory manner, as if the woman had done something unspeakable by being alive. 'And what's all this Storig Storigsdottir nonsense.'

'Long story,' Storig replied with a shrug.

'We're good at long stories, Vikings,' Erik said with some menace in his tone.

◆ ◆ ◆

'You two know one another, then?' Siward said brightly, hoping he could be introduced to the huge Viking woman. With any luck she was a widow.

'His wife's sister,' Fregurd explained as Erik and Storig had taken to glaring at one another. 'Vanished during a raid and we all thought she was lost. Her sister mourned for a week. And she was betrothed to Erik's cousin.'

'Did he mourn as well?' Siward tried to sound sympathetic.

'He died as well,' Fregurd said simply. 'Only he did it properly.' This criticism was clearly directed at the woman. 'And she wasn't called Storig Storigsdottir when she left.'

Sigmund was looking backwards and forwards with a very puzzled look on his face.

'Isn't that Aunty Freya?' he asked Fregurd.

'Yup,' Fregurd answered.

'So when she died she came here?' The young Viking seemed put out that this might be Valhalla.

'No, of course she didn't, you idiot. She obviously didn't die, did she?'

'Oh, right.' Sigmund fell silent, but his face said he was working hard at getting this situation straight in his head.

'I think you've got some explaining to do,' Erik instructed Storig, or Freya, or whatever she was called.

Magnificent, Siward called her.

'Come and have something to eat and I'll give you all the explanation you need.' Storig/Freya turned on her heels and walked back into the town.

Erik followed with Fregurd and Sigmund on his heels. Siward drew up the rear as no one had actually told him he couldn't tag along.

Behind them the folk of Lincoln, old men, women and boys, appeared from various hiding places. They breathed heavy sighs of relief as the Vikings left the scene – without killing anyone or breaking anything. Yet, obviously. You could never tell where, or when, or how, a visit from Vikings would end.

Chapter 13
More's the Pity

THE GATES OF GRAVESEND were closed much more effectively than those of Lincoln. These had been purpose-built and purposely closed. Perhaps word had reached the town that something bad was coming their way. It was.

The place didn't look very big at all, rather paltry really, but it did have walls of a sort and a gate set into them.

'Blast,' Le Pedvin swore as he drew his horse up, just far enough away from the walls of the town that no one could hit him with anything. 'They've already come this way.'

'At least we're here now,' Ranulf spoke up. 'I can start taking note of a town which hasn't been burned to the ground yet. Unless, of course, it's the Saxons we're after and not the details of the country at all,' he added, with a sideways look at Le Pedvin. Le Pedvin looked the other way.

'They'll never let you in,' Mabbut said with confidence.

Martel was walking his horse left and right, looking up at the walls of the town to see if there was any obvious weakness.

'We need the gate,' he said as he drew back up to Le Pedvin.

Down at the foot of the main gate was a gatehouse, with a small mullioned window looking out on to the road. The entrance to this house was clearly inside the town, so that the gatekeeper could come and go without having to step into danger.

Le Pedvin dismounted and looked the gate up and down. 'Off you go, then.' He waved Mabbut forward.

'Me?' Mabbut thought this was most unfair; he wasn't the invader. Why couldn't the Normans open their own gates?

'It's what you're here for,' Le Pedvin gave him a heavy glance, 'dealing with the locals. Or are you really no use to us at all? In which case we're probably best getting rid of you here and now. You know, cut your head off and use it to knock on the door, something like that.'

Mabbut reluctantly got off his horse. He only had one head and if Le Pedvin cut it off every time they had a disagreement he'd get nowhere. He believed the Norman. The man had history in the head-removal area.

Glancing backwards and forwards from the small band to the gates of Gravesend, Mabbut cautiously crossed the intervening space. No one threw anything at him, or shot at him, or even seemed to notice he was there. He really didn't want to be killed at all, but having your own side do it would be really annoying.

◆   ◆   ◆

'Hello,' he shouted, when he thought he was within shouting distance.

He got no reply, which was a bit odd for a place that bothered to have a gate. Someone really ought to be on lookout.

He made it to the small gatehouse without incident and looked back to his fellow travellers for some approbation. All Le Pedvin did was urge him to get on with it, using a variety of explicit gestures.

'Hello?' He spoke through the window, which was really not much more than an arrow slit.

'Yis?' a very elderly, high pitched and excitable voice replied. 'What do you want?'

'We want to come in through the town gates,' said Mabbut. It seemed best to get straight to the point.

'Oh, can't do that,' the voice said, and a little old face appeared in the small space of the window. The opening wasn't big enough for the head to pop out.

From what Mabbut could see, the voice and the face went together admirably. The old man's beard was a wispy grey thing of many years' growth, which stuck out from his chin and bobbed up and down when he spoke. His head was bald, but the beard was creeping up the side like ivy. It curled over his ears and round the back of his head, as if it had recently been driven back from covering the whole thing.

The eyes, though, were sparkling and bright. Either this man was intelligent, happy and enthusiastic for his work in the gatehouse, or he was mad. Mabbut suspected the latter, particularly when the man grinned broadly at him revealing a lone tooth, which hung in the black space of his mouth like some ancient standing stone. It looked like it could have the moss of one too.

'Why not?' Mabbut asked, as gently as he could.

'The gates are shut,' the man explained, excitedly.

While this was obviously true, Mabbut felt the rising frustration he always did when he was dealing with the stupid common man. But this was a charm offensive. He took a deep breath.

'Well, open the gate and we'll come in.'

'Oh, can't do that,' the man repeated, clearly horrified at the thought.

'Look,' Mabbut explained, 'there's only four of us and you can see that I'm a Saxon.' He held his arms out.

'Do you always dress like that?' the man asked with genuine interest at Mabbut's attire.

'Yes, of course I … that's not the point. The point is there are only four of us. Me, a chap called Ranulf who's no danger to anyone because all he does is count things and complain, and two men who are soldiers but couldn't possibly be a threat on their own. We just want to come in and have a look around. This Ranulf is doing a bit of a check on things for someone important.' He didn't like to say they were here on the orders of the Duke of Normandy who had just killed the King.

147

The old face bobbed about behind its window, looking out at the three men on horseback who were some distance away.

'Oh, yes,' the man said, positively excited by the sight of strangers. 'Are they Normans?' There was no suspicion or worry in his voice.

'Erm, yes, they are,' Mabbut admitted, hurriedly adding, 'but, as I say, they're no trouble. Only three of them.'

'They got here quick,' the man observed, clearly well aware of events further south.

'Yes, as I say they're doing a check of the country, you know, to let, erm, to let Duke William know what's going on. So you see they really can't do any harm, and don't mean to. So if we could please come in?'

'There's a fee,' the man said with a slight cackle.

'Oh, er, right.'

'Fourpence,' the man said.

'You don't know a toll-man in the woods do you?' Mabbut asked, suspicious thoughts crossing his head.

'My brother,' the man gabbled.

'Funny how everything's fourpence.' Mabbut didn't believe this. A toll on a road he could understand, but not a fee for simply opening the gates of a town. The last thing he wanted to do was let Ranulf get involved in this. They'd be arguing here for hours.

'Four men, four horses, fourpence. Stands to reason.' The man was still grinning, but the light of reason was nowhere on his face.

Mabbut sighed and headed back to the others.

'He says it's fourpence,' he reported to Le Pedvin.

'Has he got a charter?' Ranulf asked.

'Shut up.' Le Pedvin got in before de Sauveloy got going. He did some grimacing and clenching, muttering and swearing and a finger reached for the eye-patch..

'We're not going to be able to breach that gate,' Martel

observed, 'not without the rest of the army.'

Ranulf huffed. 'You'll have to just pay the toll to get on with this.'

Le Pedvin looked at him with some surprise.

'There's a considerable difference between a town with a gate and a loon in the woods with a log,' Ranulf explained.

Le Pedvin glared at them all, but pulled a purse from his waist and handed it to Mabbut. 'Take fourpence from that lot. Sooner we get the whole country on good Norman currency the better.'

Mabbut emptied the purse into his hand and saw a goodly sum of English coin. There were plain Saxon pennies and pieces of pennies where they'd been cut up to make change. Some of it still had blood on.

Mabbut gave a glare back to Le Pedvin, who took it without interest.

✦   ✦   ✦

Back at the gatehouse he peered into the window, but could see no one.

'Hello?' he called.

'Yis, what do you want?' The old man appeared again.

'We want to come in, remember?'

The old man squinted in suspicion. 'Oh yes.' He grinned widely again, as if welcoming an old friend.

'Here's the fourpence.' Mabbut held out the coin.

'What's that for?' the man asked, looking at the hand as if he'd never seen one before.

'To open the gate,' Mabbut said through gritted teeth. 'You said four men, four horses, fourpence. There you are – fourpence.'

'I can't take that,' the man cackled as if he'd been offered a bribe and was an honest man.

'I insist.' Mabbut said, thrusting his arm through the window. 'I know they're Normans, but like I say, they'll be

149

no trouble. If they were going to be trouble, why would they pay the fourpence?' He smiled encouragement. 'Here, take it.'

The man looked at the hand, considering what he should do. 'Oh, all right,' he said and snatched the coins from the outstretched hands, 'only seeing as how you say so.'

'Thank you,' said Mabbut with a sigh. He really hadn't wanted to go back to Le Pedvin and explain that despite the fourpence they still couldn't get through the gates. It would be head chopping off time again.

Mabbut waited and watched the man.

The man waited and watched Mabbut.

'Well?' Mabbut asked, after what he felt was a suitable period.

'Well, what?' The man asked equitably.

'Open the gate.'

'Oh, can't do that,' the man cackled in exactly the same tone as the last two times.

'Why the hell not?' Mabbut demanded in a barely controlled shout. 'I've paid you the fourpence.'

'I know,' the man replied, 'and thank you very much. Much appreciated.'

'So why can't you open the gate?'

'Because I'm not the gatekeeper.' The man grinned his one-toothed grin.

'What!' Mabbut actually jumped up and down on the spot. 'Then why did you take the fourpence?'

'You gave it me. You insisted.'

'What are you doing in the gatehouse?' Mabbut was beside himself with frustration. He suspected he might be beside himself physically if he went and told Le Pedvin he'd given the fourpence to the wrong man.

'I'm minding it,' the man replied proudly.

'Minding it? Where's the gatekeeper, then?'

'Don't know. Probably in the garderobe. He's always in the garderobe him. I think there's something wrong with him, myself.'

Mabbut really didn't want to know anything about the gate-keeper's garderobe habits, and wondered what they had to do with entering the town anyway. 'If you're minding the gatehouse, you should be able to open the gate.'

'You're right.' The head nodded its noddy nod.

'Good.' Mabbut nodded, just the once.

'I should.' The man nodded head and beard some more.

'But,' Mabbut said wearily and with horrible recognition, 'you can't.'

'Nope.' The man's happiness was now rather disturbing. He'd probably cackle and laugh if Le Pedvin came up and stuck a sword through him. Which was looking increasingly likely.

'You don't know how,' Mabbut concluded.

'That's right,' the man grinned. 'There's all sorts of ropes and pulleys and bits of wood in here. It's terribly complicated.'

'Well, go and get the gatekeeper.'

'I'd rather not.' The head stopped nodding for a moment and the man gave a short shiver.

There was a long pause. Mabbut didn't dare look over his shoulder. His head was feeling very insecure. He tried to calm himself, realising the only way to open the gate was from inside the gatehouse, so he couldn't afford to let things get completely out of hand. He turned and waved to Le Pedvin, trying to indicate that the entrance would open very soon.

'Look, erm,' Mabbut leant against the wall and spoke in as friendly a tone as he could manage. 'What's your name?'

'More.' The old man cackled his old cackle as if this was hilarious.

'More?' Mabbut checked.

'That's right. I've had twelve brothers and four sisters, and when mummy told daddy she was going to have me, he said, "oh

151

no, not more", and the name stuck. I think they'd used up all the names they could think of anyway. My next youngest brother's called Ohno.'

Mabbut was not in the mood. 'Well, More, let me tell you that bloke out there is a Norman, one of the nastiest, and if he doesn't get into the town he's going to be very cross.'

'I thought you said he'd be no trouble.'

'No trouble to you, that's right. Trouble to me? Very much so. Trouble with a capital sword. So, if you could go and get the gatekeeper, he can open the gate.'

'I don't like to disturb him in the garderobe.' The old man had a touch of seriousness in his voice.

'I'm sure he'll appreciate the situation.' Mabbut tried to sound encouraging.

'It's not that – it's just that it's not very nice in the garderobe when he's there. Like I said, I think there's something wrong with him. Certainly wrong with his guts anyway.'

Mabbut clenched his fists and stole a glance back to Le Pedvin. The Norman gestured impatiently to the gate, and drew his sword to emphasise his impatience.

'It is very important that we get into the town, now.' Mabbut tried to sound fierce and insistent. He didn't know how much good it would do with the not-gatekeeper safe in his house.

'Why don't you come through the side gate, then?' the man asked brightly.

'What?' Mabbut made himself speak quietly, although his inside felt as if it wanted to get out. 'What side gate?'

'The gate on the side – that's why we call it the side gate.' Old More nodded his enthusiasm for using the side gate.

'Why didn't you tell me there was side gate?'

'You said you wanted to come through the town gate. Gatekeeper told me I had to stop questioning the customers. It annoys them.' The beard nodded up and down as if it was moving the head, rather than the other way round.

'And is the side gate open?' Mabbut checked, clearly enunciating each word.

'Nope,' More nodded again.

'Then how …?'

'I know how to open that one. Just a minute.' More scuttled out of sight and the next moment Mabbut felt a tug on his jerkin.

'Hello,' More beamed up at Mabbut. Voice, face and body were the perfect expression of irrepressible madness. More's body was somehow older than his face; it was stooped and thin, and he seemed to be standing like a crab. A very happy and ebullient crab, with no obvious reason to be either happy or ebullient.

'Come on, then,' he instructed brightly. 'What are you waiting out there for?'

Mabbut controlled himself and waved to the others. Le Pedvin remounted and the three, with Mabbut's horse in tow, approached the gate.

'Is there a fee?' Mabbut asked as sarcastically as he could.

'Oh no,' More beamed. 'This gate's free. Thanks for the fourpence though.' He laughed again.

◆   ◆   ◆

'Afternoon,' More said brightly, nodding excessively at the others as they arrived.

The Normans did not reply.

'Don't they speak English, or are they deaf?' More enquired of Mabbut.

'Neither, they're just very rude,' Mabbut replied.

More seemed happy to accept this. He skipped in his crab-like manner round the side of the gatehouse to where a large door was set in the wall of the town. This was big enough for the passage of people and animals, but they would have to go in single file. This would make it easier to pick them off if need be, once they'd entered.

More hopped up to the door, grabbed the large iron ring and gave a hearty push.

'Oh dear, it's shut,' he observed looking at the door without understanding.

Mabbut dropped his face into his hands and waited for the end. He was past caring.

'Oh no, wait a minute,' More hopped happily. 'You pull, not push.' He pulled on the door and it swung open, showing the hard-won but magnificent way into the heart of Gravesend.

Chapter 14

Freya's Tale

So?' Erik demanded, when they were comfortably gathered in Freya's dwelling, gnawing on some dried fish and bread. Apart from Siward, who picked at his deer.

They weren't actually that comfortably gathered as the dwelling was very small and the Vikings were very large. Siward thought the place was a bit of a squeeze just for Freya.

Although it sat on its own, her home was like any other. A regular shallow pit had been dug and a wooden frame put up inside it. The walls were wattle and daub and the roof was thatch. The only difference from the other homes seemed to be that Freya's was a good two feet taller. Stop her banging her head on the roof, Siward assumed.

Inside was a simple rectangular space. There were two cots at one end, a small one for the child and a very large one for Freya. A fire burned in the middle of the room, its smoke winding upwards to escape through the chimney cut into the thatch.

At the other end of the space there were two simple stools and a box, presumably containing all of Freya's possessions. Into this space were squashed four large Vikings, Siward and a small boy.

Freya and the child sat on the stools while the other Vikings were cross-legged on the floor. Siward loitered by the entrance, not wanting to be noticed but not wanting to miss anything either. He scanned the place for signs of male habitation, and nodded inwardly at the stack of weapons that were propped by the entrance. He then smiled as he thought they probably belonged to Freya.

'Vad scared er?' said Erik, or that's what it sounded like to Siward.

'English, please,' Freya insisted, putting a protective arm around the boy at her side.

'What is this explanation you have?' Erik was not in a good mood. 'Your sister thinks you are dead. Your father thought you were dead; he went to his grave believing it. Gods curse it, we all thought you were dead.' He sounded annoyed to be proved wrong. There was a brief, uncomfortable silence while Fregurd laid out his knives, evenly and nicely spaced. Brain-Scratcher was given a little polish and Child-Botherer was specifically pointed at Freya's son.

'Who's this?' Freya nodded a suspicious head towards Siward, who stood up straight and brushed his hair out of his eyes.

'Just some Saxon guide,' Erik responded, without looking up.

Freya scowled at Siward. He beamed back. Building a relationship was clearly going to take some time.

'Erik,' Freya snorted, 'you know our ways better than any. Once we leave our shores we *are* dead. Only when we come back do we live.'

Sigmund nodded at the wisdom of this.

'Don't get clever with me,' Erik snarled. 'You know perfectly well what I mean. You clearly aren't dead, you never have been, and there doesn't seem to be a mark on you. Why aren't you at home?'

'I like it here.'

'You like it here?' Erik clearly thought this was most pathetic reason for being anywhere.

'Others have settled,' Freya argued. 'This whole country was settled by the Danes. King Swein Forkbeard and Cnut: the place was Danelaw, after all.'

'Yes, yes,' Erik snuffed impatiently, 'they settled after they'd killed everyone who was here in the first place. They settled when they set up a good Viking encampment, to live the Viking way and have constant war with the Saxons. They didn't settle by running away from a battle and going to live with bunch of half-heights.'

'Half-heights?' thought Siward. Is that what they call us? Bit rude.

'I didn't run away from the battle. I got separated when our glorious leader Lars lead a rather rapid retreat in the face of underwhelming odds.'

'Tactical withdrawal,' Erik mumbled.

'Pah!' It was Freya's turn to be scornful.

'You should have made your way to the coast and taken a boat.'

'That's exactly what I was doing when I met Storig.'

'Who's Storig?' Erik demanded.

'Who *was* Storig,' Freya corrected. 'He was my husband.'

Marvellous, thought Siward, he's dead. He tried to look sombre.

'You married one of these?' Erik gestured towards Siward as if Freya had become betrothed to the venison.

'Storig was a fine man and we were properly married. You'd all cleared off. How was I to know if you'd be back again? I had to make the best of it.'

'So you let this Storig divert you from your Viking ways and turn you to a Saxon?' Erik clearly thought this was a step too far.

'Do I look like a Saxon?' Freya demanded.

Siward could have answered that. No, she doesn't. Not at all.

'Of course I didn't let him divert me. I saw him in a village on the way to the coast, took a fancy to him and carried him off. I haven't gone soft.'

Siward disguised his sigh with a cough.

'And you had a child by him.' Erik still wasn't happy.

'I did, and proud of it. So it's no good you glaring and staring and coming over all Norse on me. I'm happy here and I'm staying. For one thing, it's warm.'

'Warm!' This seemed to be the limit for Erik.

'Yes, warm,' Freya snapped back. 'I no longer spend nine months of the year trying not to freeze to death and the other three stocking up food just to make sure I don't die the next winter round. The more time I spend here, the more stupid home seems.'

All the Vikings drew breath at this.

'Well, I ask you,' Freya went on, 'why do we spend so much time and effort invading other people's countries or exploring to find new lands? Because the one we've got isn't up to much. We keep sending ships west to find something a bit better than the ice-pit we live in.'

'We've discovered Greenland if you want somewhere nice,' Erik mocked, as if people who couldn't put up with a bit of cold weren't worthy of the name Viking.

'But this is closer.' Freya considered that was the end of the argument. 'Anyway, what are you doing here? Hardly likely to set up a Viking settlement with just three of you. I bet it's something to do with honour? It usually is with you, Erik. Talk about not being very Viking.'

'King Harald Hardrada is dead,' Erik intoned.

'I know.' Freya wasn't bothered.

'The battle was great and King Harold Godwinson won a worthy victory.'

'There you go.' Freya was contemptuous.

'What?'

'Losing is not worthy, Erik. I've told you this, everyone's told you this. We fight battles to win. If we don't win, it was the wrong battle. And if your enemy walks from the battlefield you run up and stab him in the back.'

'Hear, hear,' Fregurd muttered. He had organised the knives

158

into their proper hierarchy on the floor, with Gut-Slitter taking charge as usual. He would have to have another word with it later. At night when it was usually receptive.

'No one cares about your honour any more, Erik. What is it you're up to?' She narrowed her eyes in thought. 'Harold won a worthy victory and you've got the urge to do something honourable. Must be something for Harold.'

'Might be,' Erik mumbled and looked away.

'He was going south to fight the Normans last I heard. Passed through here and took most of the fighting men with him.' She frowned in thought. 'Did he win?'

Erik said nothing, but Fregurd moved his head very slightly left and right.

'He lost?' Freya twisted her mouth around in thought and gently bit her bottom lip.

Siward thought he could gently bite her bottom lip for her if she liked.

'He lost and you've come to perform some noble deed. What is it? Viking burial? Burn him on a boat? Always thought that was a waste of a good boat.'

Erik averted his eyes and studied the floor of the house with some care.

'What is it, Fregurd?' Freya asked. 'What have you really come here for?'

Fregurd looked to Erik to see if it was all right to say. Erik said nothing and didn't look up. Fregurd shrugged.

'Harold's not dead,' he explained.

'By the Gods, you've come to rescue him!' Freya clapped her knees and rocked on her stool. 'Erik, you idiot, who do you think you are? William the Norman will be looking for him and will want him dead. If he finds you've got him, he'll want you dead as well, *and* all your friends and family. You haven't got him, have you?' Freya cast a glance at Siward, perhaps thinking he might

159

be King Harold in disguise. He swallowed some venison and stood up straight again.

'Nah,' Fregurd spoke, as Erik seemed happy not to do so. 'We've got some meeting at the bishop's house in Lincoln. Don't know if we're supposed to meet Harold there or not.'

'The bishop's house?' Freya frowned. 'I shouldn't think you'll find King Harold in that den of thieves.'

Fregurd raised his eyebrows and even Erik cast a sideways glance.

'Chap called Nicodemus runs the place,' she explained, 'and no one with any sense goes anywhere near it. He'll not only have the purse out of your breeches, but you'll wind up with a contract to give him all your purses – and probably all your breeches too – for the next hundred years. Anyway, he's gone off.'

'Gone off?' Erik asked in some surprise. It must have been Nicodemus he was meeting.

'Some trouble at a monastery from what I hear. We've had nobles and monks and all sorts flapping about. Best rid of them, say I.'

'So Nicodemus isn't here?' Erik asked, serious disappointment in his tone.

'No. So if he's your contact, you'd better think again', Freya said with a grin. 'If I were you I'd think again and go home. You seem to like it there, and finding Harold will be very bad for your health.'

'What's the road south of here?' Erik asked. His head had risen and there was scheming in his eye.

'Really,' Freya urged, 'don't.'

'I don't think a woman who takes up with Saxons should be advising the likes of us.'

'Ha.' Freya grinned and obviously thought this was very funny. 'I can understand why Sigmund here is following along.'

Sigmund sat up straight and proud.

'He'd follow his own footsteps and think it was an adventure.'

Sigmund stopped being so straight and proud.

'But you, Fregurd? You don't strike me as the type for rescue missions, unless there's an awful lot of something in it for you.' She regarded Fregurd and returned to lip biting. 'Ah, Harold will be grateful if he's rescued from William.'

Fregurd held out his hands in supplication, as if he might reluctantly accept some small token of reward for an honest deed humbly done.

Freya speculated on. 'You know Harold was in the north and then he had to rush south, so he must have a good portion of his treasury with him. A good chance of him giving some of it to the people who save his skin.'

Fregurd tried to look as if such a thought had never occurred to him. He said nothing, but his straight and expressionless lips twitched in the rough direction of a smile.

'Even better if, once having rescued a lost king and his treasure, said king had a nasty accident of some sort. Say falling off a boat? With some weights round his feet?'

Fregurd widened his eyes in shock. No sincerity, just shock.

Erik looked horrified. 'Is this true?' he demanded of Fregurd. 'You're only doing this for money?'

'Erik,' Freya addressed him, 'you really are the bravest, most honourable, decent, upright and stupid Viking who ever ate a herring.' She shook her head. 'There's really nothing to be done with you. You thought a man like Fregurd was coming along for the honour? The same Fregurd who used to hide around the headland so he could jump on the funeral barges, put the flames out and sell them to the next village as fire damaged?'

Fregurd did break into a smile at this happy reminiscence.

Erik's face looked like it was a funeral boat. Another unhappy silence fell. Sigmund finished the venison and Fregurd slowly polished a handle.

✦   ✦   ✦

'So which is the road south?' Erik demanded in all seriousness.

Freya said nothing.

'If Harold is heading north, supposedly to meet here, we can go and meet him half way, or however far he gets. Agnetha's waiting for us on the coast. We'll just go south, get Harold and meet up as planned.'

'You dragged my sister into this?' Freya sounded disappointed.

'The sister who thinks you're dead?' Erik asked. 'The same sister who doted over you and saved you from the wolves on more than one occasion? The sister who's been grieving for you? That sister?'

Freya did hang her head at this. 'Where are you meeting her?'

'Due east from here, the ness of Skegg.'

'Well that's not going to work now, is it?' Freya observed.

'Eh?'

'Have you thought about any of this, Erik?' She got no reply. 'Harold is not here and neither is your Nicodemus. When was this battle lost?'

'We got the bird yesterday when we were on our way home from Stamford Bridge.'

'Good gods man, Harold will hardly be at the River Thames by now! How long were you going to wait here? A week? I doubt he'll make it this far at all if William's men are after him. Which I'm sure they will be. If you're now going to head south, you'll probably meet him somewhere round Spalding, unless his head is on a Norman spike by then. Agnetha will be in completely the wrong place. Stuck.'

Erik frowned as he worked this through. Fregurd nodded agreement. He was looking at the reflection of the fire in his knife blade, probably trying to decide which of his knives liked him the most.

'All right.' Freya had decided. 'I'll go east with young Storig here.' She rubbed the child's shoulders. 'I'll meet Agnetha, explain to her I'm not dead, apologise, do all the honourable stuff, and then send her south to meet you in the wetlands. Up the River Nene would be best, you know the place?' She said this last with some significance as if it was a renowned Viking meeting place.

'The wetlands,' Erik repeated, but he didn't sound sure.

'You really are a Viking, aren't you Erik? Put you on the featureless sea and you could find your way home in the fog. Put you on land and not a clue.'

'It all looks the same to me,' Erik mumbled.

'You,' Freya spoke to Siward, who stood up straight. 'Do you know the way to the southern wetlands, the River Nene?'

'I could guide you to the ness of Skegg,' he offered, rather hoping to spend more time in Freya's company.

'I know the way there, you addle head. Do you know the way to the river?'

Siward hadn't the first clue about wetlands or rivers. He obviously knew what wet land looked like – who didn't if they lived in England? He hadn't got a clue about any specific ones in the south, or how you could tell a river from wet land. More wet, he supposed.

He reflected. He'd done pretty well finding the way to Lincoln, though, so he'd probably sort it out. He knew it was south – or at least he did now Freya had told him. Perhaps you just kept going south until your feet got wet. As long as the sun stayed up, he could head in roughly the right direction. Maybe there'd be another monk in the woods somewhere. The last thing he wanted to do was lose touch with Freya now he'd seen her. And she had a taste for Saxon men, eh?

'Absolutely,' he said confidently.

'There you are,' Freya nodded to Erik. 'This what's his name can take you.'

'Siward,' said Siward, smiling and trying to catch Freya's eye.

Her face was turned back to the group.

'So we'll meet in the wetlands,' Erik nodded agreement.

'You will,' Freya replied. 'I'm not going there. I'll meet Agnetha and tell her and that's it. I'm not getting me and young Storig dragged into all this. I'm coming back to Lincoln. I can hear all about your pointless death in the sagas.'

Right, thought Siward, south. And then back to Lincoln to woo the lady Freya. He wasn't sure how to woo anyone, let alone a giant Viking woman. Perhaps surrender might work.

Chapter 15

Through Rain and More Rain

HERE ARE THEY?' Le Pedvin demanded once they were all through the side gate of Gravesend.

'Who?' More asked in his grinning squeak.

'The Saxons who were ahead of us.'

'Oh, we're all Saxons here.' More held his arm out to take in the magnificence of Gravesend.

From what Mabbut could see it wasn't really all that magnificent. With the main gates closed, the space inside was dark and gloomy. Timbered homes teetered above rough tracks, deep with the ruts of passing carts, horses and people. And pretty deep in the left-overs of horses and people.

There was always smell in the world. Some thinkers considered the world was made of smells; if only our minds and noses were capable, we could scent the mind of God. The mind of God had some serious problems if the streets of Gravesend were anything to go by. Mabbut supposed you'd get used to it if you lived here, but to a true Saxon, who really preferred living in the country, it was pretty thick.

The walls of the town were behind them and the gates were barred on the inside by stout oak timbers. Martel had been right. They'd never have breached those defences on their own.

The road from the gate led down a slight hill, which Mabbut assumed was towards the river. At least the slope had the effect of getting most of the filth to run down the road when it rained. Not so good if you were at the bottom, of course.

It was raining now. It was a light but solid tinkle in the face, which told the true Englishman that the sky was building up to something quite prolonged and concentrated. It was as if the more cowardly raindrops had run ahead of the bulk of the water, trying to get out of the way before the main deluge. It was not the spit of a passing shower, which emptied its mouth on those below before moving contemptuously onwards. Nor was it the strange odd drop that was quite capable of falling out of a clear blue sky, probably having travelled some distance to get here.

Whatever the humours of the sky were, they loved England. They must gather every spare drop of liquid from across the world and save it for dropping on this particular island. It made the place green and fertile, but also soggy, damp and slippery. At least it gave the locals something to talk about. In the rain they could moan about the rain, and then when it didn't rain they could moan about how it had rained and how it would again very soon. Even the brightest, warmest start to a day could be put in its place by the speculation that it would probably rain come dinnertime. And so it would.

Mabbut looked at the sky and grimaced.

'Ye gods,' Le Pedvin spat. 'Are there any days when it doesn't rain in this wretched place?'

'Not this time of year,' Mabbut replied in the face of Le Pedvin's outrageous optimism. He smiled to himself.

◆　　◆　　◆

The ground floors of the buildings on either side contained the very simple shop counters a meagre town with a ferry required. A baker and butcher, for those needing victuals, either after a long journey or just before one, and a wheelwright with livery to tend to the carts and horses likewise. Mabbut wondered about the stolen Norman horses. Had they been taken onwards, had they been sold to the liveryman? Were they even now on the butcher's slab?

'All right, where's the ferry?' Le Pedvin changed tack.

'On the river,' More replied, apparently delighted to impart this vital fact. 'That's where we keep it.'

'Bloody Saxons,' Le Pedvin muttered. 'Come!' he called to the others and urged his horse onwards. Martel and Ranulf followed and Mabbut shrugged to More in Saxon camaraderie.

'Bye, bye.' More waved them off happily.

It should be simple to follow the road down the hill, where the river must be found. The place only had about twelve houses in total, all of which had seen better days as well as better nights, not to mention better people living in them. Whether it was deliberate planning or that the householders just didn't get on with one another, the buildings had been randomly scattered over the space between the walls and the water. There was thus no simple road from the gate to the river.

The track stopped about halfway down, blocked by two houses that had been built together. The path led left and right around these before it bumped into another dwelling. So few houses seemed determined to stop anyone moving in a straight line.

They went left.

Then they came back and went right. They found a gap between two buildings which seemed to go down again, so they followed that. Until it stopped at the entrance to a pretty substantial pigsty. With a substantial smell.

'What is wrong with this place?' Le Pedvin barked.

'Very interesting design,' Ranulf nodded, looking left and right to take in his surroundings.

'A good place for an ambush,' Martel observed; they were indeed hemmed in.

'What would you know about an ambush?' Le Pedvin snorted. 'Mabbut,' he called, 'which way to the river?'

'Eh? Oh, er, I don't know really.'

'You don't know?' There was trouble in Le Pedvin's voice. 'We brought you along to show us the way, and you don't know where the river is?'

'I know where the river is, obviously. I just don't have the details of Gravesend committed to memory.' Mabbut thought it was asking a bit much of anyone.

Le Pedvin simply grunted unhappily and drove his horse back.

◆   ◆   ◆

Turning left and right almost at random, they seemed to be endlessly going round houses. It felt as if the things were deliberately moving to block their passage.

"What a wretched way to build a place,' Le Pedvin snorted as they ran up against yet another front door.

'Very clever,' Ranulf observed. 'Notice how long it's taken us to get this far, and we don't even know where we are?'

'You'll have plenty to write down then,' Le Pedvin snarled. 'Perhaps if we set the place to the torch we could see where we were going.'

'I doubt it would go up very well,' Ranulf observed, 'since the whole place is sopping wet.'

They had reached a wider path now, which seemed to go in the right direction.

'How the hell do these people get their goods up from the river at all?' Le Pedvin asked in genuine irritation.

'They probably know where they're going,' Martel put in helpfully. Le Pedvin scowled.

They managed to make a reasonable pace down the road until it too ended in another house, a rather grand one this time. In fact, the most grand in the whole town. It probably belonged to the Lord, who had an even bigger home somewhere, which meant he didn't have to live in this one.

'Oh, this is ridiculous,' Le Pedvin spat as he regarded the dwelling. It had a large double oak door that clearly opened to accept carts, and probably had a courtyard beyond. It was shut now though.

Le Pedvin walked his horse up to the door, lifted his foot out and gave the door a good kick. It swung open, to their surprise, and did indeed reveal a courtyard. Le Pedvin ducked his head and rode into the space. The others followed, although Mabbut had raised his arm to suggest that they might wait to be invited.

'I say.' A man appeared from a room off to the side of the courtyard and looked in some horror at the people trampling through the house.

'Just passing through,' Le Pedvin called, without looking.

'You can't just ride your horses through my Lord's house like this,' the man bleated, his arms raised. 'Who do you think you are?'

'The Norman conquerors,' Le Pedvin replied with another snarl. He was good at snarling.

The man dropped his arms and looked at them. As they passed he looked back up the road, through his open gates, to see where the rest of the army was. By the time he turned back to remonstrate that there were only four of them and they weren't going to conquer anything, the party had moved on.

◆   ◆   ◆

At the far end of the courtyard another gate sat open, and beyond that was the river. Le Pedvin rode on through and stopped on the far side. The others joined him and they looked up and down the shoreline.

'That was probably the toll and tax house for the beach,' Ranulf observed as he looked back up the track. 'So you can't get off the ferry or unload anything without passing through the house. Very good.'

'Perhaps you'd better go and ask them for their charter,' said Le Pedvin, who clearly didn't see anything very good about the place. 'I'm surprised there isn't a toll for standing in their rain.'

The tide was in, and the serene grandeur of the River Thames dominated the scene. At this point in its passage it seemed as wide as the sea, although the far shore was just visible through the rainy air. The fresh smell of colliding salt and fresh water filled their heads, while directly ahead of them the port of Gravesend went about its business. So to speak.

In fact, port and business were terms as out of place in Gravesend as a jeweller. The high tide lapped against a muddy shore, upon which one large boat was resting. It was clearly a river cargo vessel, capable of carrying a reasonable load over a short distance. It was open, with seating for four men at oars and a very rudimentary mast with a sail hanging limp and damp. It listed over on the shore and had two bales of something or other sitting in the prow.

A single man sat on it, dangling his legs over the side, clearly waiting for someone to come and do something or other. Or he was guarding the bales. Or he was just sitting there to keep his feet out of the mud.

Mabbut scanned the shore for anything that looked like a ferry. It could be a simple as a wooden platform, but with this expanse of water to cross, it would more likely be a solid boat of some sort.

'There,' he said, thankfully spotting a sign down to the right which said 'Ferry'.

They took their horses the last few yards to the water's edge and dismounted.

The ferry had its own jetty, which stretched from the high ground of the shore out into the water so that the boat could come and go even as the tide rose and fell. Doubtless it was constructed to allow the well-to-do on to the boat without dirtying their fine clothes in the mud of the working people. Probably as they passed through Gravesend as quickly as they could.

Nobody was dirtying anything at the moment as the jetty was bare. No ferry bobbed at its moorings, no travellers embarked or disembarked. There was, though, a small hut of half-cut logs about half way down the jetty. The thing was only about the width of one person, but it was probably where the ferryman sat when he wasn't actually ferrying. He doubtless lived on his boat and just loitered in here to take money and keep out of the rain.

The hut had an attempt at a stable door and the top half of this was open. Perhaps there was an assistant who took money and bookings when the ferry was on its way.

Le Pedvin cast a suspicious look at the local dangling on his boat, who showed not the least interest in them. Clearly not trusting anyone, he left Martel in charge of the horses and led the way down the jetty.

When they got to the shed they could see that there was a dozing figure on the inside, head slumped forwards.

'Oy,' Le Pedvin called, hammering on the side of the hut.

The figure inside the hut leaped to instant life. 'Yis? What do you want?' The grinning tooth of More beamed at them from the opening.

'How did you get here?' Le Pedvin asked in disbelief.

'I walked,' More replied, as if this was obvious.

'Then how did you arrive before us?'

'I don't know,' More replied. 'You probably came the pretty way.'

Le Pedvin didn't have an answer. He clenched his fists very hard and glared at More. Then he glared at Mabbut as if this was his fault.

'Where's the ferry?' Le Pedvin asked, getting down to business.

'Ferrying,' More nodded rapidly, obviously proud that the ferry worked properly.

'What do you mean, ferrying?'

'Out there.' More pointed out into the river.

'Damnation. Were there Saxons on it?' Le Pedvin demanded.

'Er.' More looked up into the air, as if dragging the memory

171

of who had been on the ferry from the recesses of his mind. 'Yis,' he concluded with a happy nod. 'In fact come to think of it,' he added, coming to think of it, 'they were all Saxons. There's a lot of 'em round here.' There was not a hint of sarcasm or irony about More's words; he was genuinely excited at having reached such a helpful conclusion.

Le Pedvin leaned into the hut and whispered as best a man who is used to shouting can whisper. 'Were there any well-to-do Saxons on board? Injured, perhaps?'

'Couldn't say,' More offered after a moment's thought.

'You can say,' Le Pedvin pressed. 'In fact I insist.'

'No, I couldn't say because I couldn't see.' More smiled his spacious smile. 'I was with you at the gate. When I got down here, they was already on their way.'

'Well, get another ferry, we want to cross.'

'Oh, can't do that.' More smiled and nodded some more.

'Don't tell me you're only minding the place?' Mabbut called over Le Pedvin's head.

'That's right.' More was as happy as a bald man in a hut during a rain shower. 'Ferryman will be back soon.'

Mabbut wanted to ask who was minding the gatehouse, or whether the gatekeeper had returned from the garderobe. One look at Le Pedvin told him that this was not the time.

'We want the ferry.' Le Pedvin leaned further into the hut and left very little room for More.

'That's good,' More smiled, 'you're the first in line. You're bound to get on.'

Le Pedvin leaned back a little. 'Good,' he said, although he didn't sound sure.

'Yis,' More nodded. He turned to a slate hanging on the wall next to him. He picked up a very disreputable-looking piece of cloth, and wiped the slate clean of the vertical dashes that had covered its surface. He took a chunk of rough chalk from the floor and held it in his hands.

'Four people, four horses?' he asked encouragingly.

'Yes.' Le Pedvin's teeth were clamped firmly shut, but the word managed to squeeze out.

'Fourpence?' Mabbut suggested.

'Eightpence,' More corrected.

'*Eight?*'

'Oh yes. Much more expensive to run a boat than a gate, you know.' More nodded rapidly and he drew dashes on the slate. He drew two first, looked at them and then rubbed them out. Then he drew four, and wasn't happy with that either. Finally he stared hard at each of them, while leaning behind him and scrawling a mark without looking. He was going fine while he did the men standing at his door, he then had to lean round to look at Martel and the four horses. This was clearly a challenge. More frowned hard and stuck his tongue out as he carefully made one mark for each passenger.

When he had finished he turned back to the slate, which now bore a ragged chalk mark for every passenger on the ferry. There were eleven.

'There we are, four men, four horses,' he said proudly. 'You're top of the list so just come back when the ferry's here and you can get straight on.'

'How long?' Le Pedvin asked.

'Two days,' More replied brightly.

'*Two days!*' Le Pedvin exploded and banged his fist against the shed, which shook alarmingly. 'I am not waiting two days. I want a ferry and I want it now!' His hand was on the pommel of his sword and his temper was right at the front of his head.

'I haven't got one.' More was apologetic and looked around the hut as if there might be a spare ferry in the corner.

'What do you mean, you haven't got one?'

'We've only got the one and that's gone.' A nod of More's head indicated the direction the ferry had taken.

'You don't have one coming south, while another goes north?'

Le Pedvin asked, still fierce in his annoyance.

'Oh, that's a good idea.' More nodded once more. 'I'll suggest that when the ferryman gets back.' A frown crumpled his face. 'How do you get one ferryman to work two ferries? Does he jump from one to the other, half way across?' More paused as the thought took hold. 'In which case how does he …' the thought petered out as the concept was too much for the old man's brain.

'*Arhgh*.' Le Pedvin had run out of patience. He turned to Mabbut. 'Get us across that river *now*, or I swear I will chop this stupid little man into pieces and watch him float down the river. And then I'll do you.'

Mabbut nodded silently and approached More in his hut while Le Pedvin went fuming up and down the jetty, ignoring the rain, which was now as wet as the river. If not wetter.

'Mister More,' Mabbut smiled. More smiled back, but then More always smiled, so Mabbut couldn't really take anything from this. 'The ferry will go again in two days?'

'That's right.'

'Seems a long time to cross one river?'

'Well, it's the tides, you see,' More explained.

'Is it?'

'That's right.'

Mabbut suspected More didn't know any more about tides than he did about counting above four.

'How long would it take us to ride to the nearest bridge, cross that and get back the other side?'

'London?' More was impressed.

'I suppose so.'

'Two days.' More smiled.

'I had a feeling it might be.' Mabbut looked along the river, trying to get some inspiration. 'What about the other boat?' he asked brightly, nodding his head towards the beached craft.

'Four days,' More replied.

'Four days?' Mabbut was lost.

'Yis. Get a boat to London, get off the boat, cross the bridge, back in the boat and on to Chadwell. Four days. You're better off riding.'

'We'll get the boat to take us across the river,' Mabbut announced, through irritated teeth.

'Oh, that's a good idea,' More nodded his nod. 'And I know just the man for the job.'

'You do?' Mabbut was almost encouraged. He tried to tell himself he was about to be disappointed.

'Oh yis. Shall I go and get him?'

'Yes please,' Mabbut tried to sound calm but insistent, 'and if you could hurry?'

'Be right back.' More opened the door of his hut and scuttled off down the jetty in his crab-like gait. He grinned at Le Pedvin and Ranulf as he passed, and then once more at Martel and the horses as he passed them on his way down the riverbank.

'He's gone to get us a boatman who'll take us across,' Mabbut said authoritatively. Then he muttered a silent prayer.

◆　　◆　　◆

As they waited, Le Pedvin stood defiantly in the rain while Ranulf retired to the hut and shook the water from his head. He used the moment in the dry to take parchment and quill and start making notes, presumably about what they'd seen on their way here. He looked round at the riverbank and its surroundings and made some brief scribbles.

Mabbut sidled over until he was being sheltered from some of the rain by a bit of the hut.

Martel stood patiently with the horses. All of them looked very wet indeed.

After a while they let their gazes drift towards the boat on the beach, looking for any sign of it moving and coming their way. There didn't seem to be anything happening at all. More had vanished around the other side of the boat, and the fellow with the dangling legs was still letting them dangle. They seemed to have got longer. If the thing was going to be organised to take them over the river, it would take several strong arms to push it off the mud.

Le Pedvin cast a glare towards Mabbut, who tried to look encouraging. Eventually there was the sound of oars being clattered about in a boat and the splashes of something being put into the river. It obviously wasn't the resting boat as that wasn't going anywhere.

They watched as, from behind the stern of the larger boat, the nose of something small and insignificant poked into the stream. It seemed to hang motionless in the flow for a moment before a combination of wind, tide and rowing pushed it towards them.

'At last,' Le Pedvin growled.

Ranulf looked up at the words and made another short note in his book.

Mabbut was relieved and a bit surprised that More had actually come good. He'd half-expected the man to either vanish completely, or come back and say all the ships were busy. He turned and beckoned to Martel, who started to lead the horses down the jetty.

'Oh, my good God Almighty!' Le Pedvin almost wailed.

Martel turned and saw that their transport was now in full view, swinging round on the river to come alongside the jetty. It was not impressive.

Mabbut was no sailor, but even he could see there was no way this thing was going to take four horses. It would be lucky to take the four of them, and then they'd be lucky not to drown on the way. Basically it was nothing more than a stretched coracle, able to take a couple of people at a time to a larger boat. Yes it had oars, but just the two, and they looked more like leftover planks than pieces crafted for the purpose.

It also had one person on board who was pulling the oars and who had his back to the passengers.

'Hello,' More cried out in a very nautical tone as he turned and saluted from his place at the oars. The boat lurched as he caught a crab. 'Four men and four horses for Chadwell? That'll be eightpence.'

Chapter 16
Ferry Risky

YOU SERIOUSLY THINK four horses are going to get into *that?*' Le Pedvin was directing the question at Mabbut, which he thought was a bit unfair as it was More's boat.

'I'll come back for the horses,' More explained, grinning brightly.

'How many times?' Le Pedvin was disbelieving. 'It's going to be dark soon and no horse in its right mind would put a hoof in that thing.' He cast a contemptuous glance at More's vessel. 'You may be willing to drown before we get halfway, but I'm not.'

'Safe as houses,' More grinned and tapped the side of the boat in a solid sort of way which made it rock dangerously.

'I've seen your houses,' Le Pedvin retorted.

'Oh come on, it's not far.' More looked over his back to the far shore. Mabbut was rather concerned to notice the man was squinting heavily as if he was having trouble making out that a far shore existed, let alone where it was. 'Get in, take a seat.'

'Where?' Le Pedvin asked looking at the boat.

Mabbut admitted this was a very good question. There was one seat, or rather a plank, which straddled the centre of the boat, and upon which sat More. A similar plank graced the back of the craft and that was it. Two planks in a boat.

Looking even more closely, the description 'boat' now seemed overly generous. It looked like a thing that might once have been a boat, but the outside had been taken away. This had been replaced with some sort of animal skin, and then the original insides had been thrown out as well. The result was nothing more than a floating boat repair. And a temporary one at that.

'One of you next to me, you can take an oar. Two at the back and one in the prow.' More's tones expressed disappointment at landlubbers who didn't even know enough to sit down in a boat.

'And the thing will still float, will it?' Le Pedvin asked.

'Mostly,' More grinned. 'At least enough to make it to Chadwell.'

'How many times have you made this journey?' Mabbut asked, pretty convinced the answer would be none.

'Oh, loads,' More nodded. 'I know the river like the back of my, erm, you know.'

'Hand?'

'That's it. Course if you don't want to go, you'll just have to wait two days for the next ferry.'

Le Pedvin glared hard, at the world and everyone in it. 'Get in,' he commanded the others.

'You may be mad, but I am not.' Ranulf stated this quite plainly as he joined the inspection of their transport. 'I know a little about the work of the shipwright,' he went on – no surprise there, then. 'They are skilled craftsmen, and I can confidently report that none of them has ever been near this thing. It looks like someone has hollowed out a cow and put a rudder on it.'

'Rudder?' More asked, plainly not familiar with the term.

'We can report to William that we got this far. I've made enough of a note for the trip to be worthwhile and we'll say we turned back at the river. He'll understand.'

'Yes,' Le Pedvin nodded. 'He'll understand that we turned back at the river and then we'll understand why he's killed us.'

'I think you exaggerate,' Ranulf laughed patronizingly. It was his natural laugh, but he was good at it.

Le Pedvin simply stared at him.

'All right, you don't exaggerate.' Even Ranulf retreated a little under the persistent gaze. 'But if we get in that thing we'll die.'

'You can swim.'

'Yes I can, but I don't think it's the want of swimming that'll kill us.' He pointed at the swirling brown water, which had things floating in it. Some of things might once have been animals, but a lot of them looked like they had once been inside animals. Not too recently either.

'Then you'll die in service of your Duke. Martel, just leave the horses. Mabbut, get in next to the idiot and row. I'll take the back with Ranulf. Martel can go in the prow and watch out for anything big enough to sink us.'

'Like a small, bad-tempered rat perhaps?' Ranulf asked.

'If the thing sinks within wading distance of the shore, we'll come back and wait for the ferry,' Le Pedvin promised.

More moved over to one side of his plank. He let Martel clamber past until he was kneeling in the prow, his sword laid out along the length of the vessel.

Mabbut got in and sat himself next to More. They were so tightly squeezed there was no way they were going to be able to row independently of one another. If one moved, the other would have to.

Finally Le Pedvin and Ranulf stepped over the stern and planted themselves on the plank.

An observer would have thought there were five men sitting in the river, the boat having completely disappeared from sight beneath the bulk of its cargo.

The cargo was surprised their craft hadn't immediately abandoned the idea of crossing the river and made straight for the bottom instead.

'So far, so good.' Le Pedvin tried to sound optimistic.

More and Mabbut nodded to one another and gave a pull on their oars.

'That explains that, then,' Ranulf commented, as the boat moved not an inch.

He and Le Pedvin clambered out and pushed the craft off

the mud on which it had rested. They climbed back in. This time the stern of the craft sank dangerously into the water.

'Off we go, then,' More announced with a smile, as if he was about to row them round a lake on a sunny day.

He and Mabbut synchronised movements and pulled them away from the shore.

◆   ◆   ◆

Mabbut had a strong suspicion that the first tug on the oar would simply rip the boat in half, and that would be that. To his great surprise it moved smoothly out into the body the river.

Fortunately the tide appeared to be on the turn, and so there was no great flow either to left or right just now. With two or three strong pulls they moved quite rapidly away from shore.

After the third stroke Mabbut realised his strong pulls were considerably stronger than More's. Half a dozen more like this and they'd simply turn circle and be back where they started. While that had its attractions, he knew Le Pedvin would only complain.

He eased a little and the boat returned to a straight course. Or at least the shore behind them seemed to be receding in a reasonably straight line.

Mabbut was taken aback by many things: that the boat moved across the water reasonably well, that the water always seemed on the verge of coming to join them but never did, but most of all by the fact that wiry old More rowed hard and steady.

Soon after Mabbut had dropped the weight he put into his stroke to match More, he found that he was having to up it again. His muscles were not used to this and they didn't like it. It looked like the old man could go on all day. Mabbut would be lucky to keep it up for twenty minutes.

Once Martel had to warn them to stop rowing as they were approaching a tree trunk, floating forlornly down the river. Mabbut was grateful for the rest as they watched the large brown shape float by, gently turning round and round as it headed slowly for the sea.

No one said anything as they noticed that the floating trunk had two legs and arms and looked rather bloated. As soon as it had gone, Mabbut found he had more energy for his rowing.

✦   ✦   ✦

'Half way,' More announced gleefully.

'How can you tell?' Mabbut asked, looking at the brown water in the wake of the boat and the same stuff to left and right.

"Cos I've rowed halfway,' More explained, nodding.

Mabbut dearly wanted to point out that this was the same question, but he also dearly didn't want More to explain. He kept quiet.

The rest of their journey was remarkably uneventful. There was another log to avoid, a real one this time, and some water did get into the boat when the stream got a bit choppy, but the next event was More announcing their arrival.

The boat bumped against the mud of the Chadwell shoreline and they all clambered out of the craft, muttering their own personal prayers for deliverance from evil. It was getting quite dark now and no one wanted to be anywhere on the river during the night.

The Normans and Mabbut all stood on the shore, rather dazed that they'd actually made it at all. Mabbut felt a huge sense of relief and gratitude for his life. If there had been a chapel on the spot, he'd have stopped to give thanks.

'We're across.' He had to say it out loud to make sure it was true.

'Of course.' More grinned his grin, as if he'd never doubted it for a moment.

'I never really thought we'd make it.' Mabbut breathed his apologies for doubting More.

'Me neither,' More beamed.

'What?'

'Oh yes, thought we'd drown for sure. The boat's only really made for one.'

'Then why the hell did you take us?' Mabbut put his hands on his hips and glared at More. The others joined him, staring at the boatman.

More looked at them all happily. 'Eightpence,' he said, holding out his hand.

Le Pedvin shook his head – whether in gratitude for simply being alive or in appreciation of More's single-minded approach to danger wasn't clear. He emptied the purse into his hand and held the contents out to More.

'That big shiny one's an eightpence,' More confirmed, taking it quickly.

Mabbut was about to say something, but he glanced at Le Pedvin and saw that the Norman was willing to pay anything.

'Right, Martel, you're with me. You two look around and make some notes.' Without further explanation Le Pedvin marched up the muddy shoreline, Martel at his heels.

Ranulf and Mabbut gazed left and right at the town of Chadwell as it started to vanish into the night. They saw that it wasn't a moment's work to look around and write a note of everything of value, even in the dark. Even then it would be a very short note.

◆　　◆　　◆

The ferry, the real one, was moored some way off at its own jetty and appeared to be the most valuable construction in the whole place. Mabbut felt disappointed that they hadn't crossed the river on it, as it looked far less inclined to kill its passengers.

The ferryman was sitting on a stool, planted on the rear of his solid-looking deck, resting his back on the ship's rail. An actual rail, made of real wood, was in place to stop the paying public from falling overboard. Two planks formed a ramp from the deck of the boat into the mud and up this Le Pedvin and Martel were walking.

Mabbut hoped they were making arrangements for their return journey, the thought of going back with More being too much to bear. One of those journeys in a lifetime was tempting fate: two would be inviting Fate to sit with you and introduce his friend Death.

Le Pedvin and Martel appeared to be engaged in a lively conversation with the ferryman, if gesticulation and the random waving of arms was anything to go by. At one point Le Pedvin put his hand to his sword, never a good sign, and there was much shrugging from the ferryman, which probably wasn't either.

Apparently not very satisfied, judging from the stomping way Le Pedvin came down the ramp, the two men headed back.

'What are you still doing here?' Le Pedvin asked More aggressively.

'I'm coming with you.'

'No, you're not.'

'Just into town. I'm going to see my brother.'

'Ohno?' Mabbut asked.

'No, Bother.'

'Brother?'

'No, Bother. His name's Bother. Number five, he is. I suppose mummy and daddy weren't too concerned about children at that time, so they just named him Bother.'

Le Pedvin scowled one of his very heaviest scowls, the sort that could bring down an enemy on its own. 'The Ferryman says he brought a party across some hours ago, so they'll be well on their way. We need to find horses.'

'My brother's got horses,' More announced happily.

'Why am I not surprised?' Le Pedvin didn't sound enthused by the prospect of horses supplied by More.

'Come on.' More beckoned and almost skipped up the bank

towards the sparse houses of Chadwell. He seemed as happy to have survived the river crossing as they were.

✦   ✦   ✦

The buildings of Chadwell were sparse in that there weren't many of them, and sparse in that they'd been built out of the minimum possible quantity of material. Most of the timbers which supported the teetering roofs and leaning walls had clearly been dragged from the river. They could have been shaped and crafted into decent building materials – but they hadn't been. They'd been dropped into holes exactly as they were, and buildings had been propped against them, if you can prop mud, that is.

The gaps between the timbers had been filled with whatever was to hand, and most of what was to hand appeared to be the thicker bits of the river. It had been mixed with straw in the more luxurious constructions, or just used neat when necessity commanded. This would not have been a bad method of building at all if the sun had been allowed to dry the mud to a solid. However, in the beginning God created the sun, and it had stayed away from Chadwell ever since. The damp, the gloom and the rain were permanent residents, and they weren't supporters of mud houses.

Tramping through this drooping slime of a place, Mabbut could not believe there was anywhere capable of holding horses. No stable that had been built like this would stop a horse that was intent on leaving.

There was one solid-looking place actually built of stone, but it had been put well away from the rest of the town, and certainly out of reach of the river. Doubtless it was the local lord's manor, and it sat above Chadwell like a crow on a tree above a family of fat mice.

Le Pedvin gave the place an avaricious glance, clearly tempted to storm it all on his own. He turned his face back to the north, though, and trudged on.

185

'This way.' More led them past the houses closest to the river and the place did seem to dry out a bit. There was what passed for a main street, and a few people were milling about, some of them dragging carts behind them.

'Where's your brother with the horses then?' Le Pedvin asked.

'Well, he *was* here.' More looked puzzled and his eyes wandered up and down the street, as if someone had stolen the stables.

Le Pedvin rested his hands on his hips and gazed his angry gaze at Mabbut, who shrugged.

It was clear from Le Pedvin's stance and attitude that he'd had enough. It was also clear from the way he drew his sword and laid it heavily on More's shoulder.

'*Eek*,' More quaked.

'Horses,' Le Pedvin snarled.

'Oh, Bother,' More squeaked, quite loudly.

'There will be if you don't magic some horses in the next two minutes.' Le Pedvin made the requirement very clear indeed.

'No,' More protested. 'Oh, Bother. There's Bother.' He pointed down the road to where another version of More was walking.

'Ye gods,' Le Pedvin spat, 'if he's as bad as you I'll skewer the both of you.'

'As bad as me?' More protested. 'What's wrong with me?'

'You are old, mad and very annoying,' Le Pedvin stated for the record.

'Well, no one's said that before,' More retorted in offended tones.

'That's because everyone else here is annoying as well. Horses.' Le Pedvin snapped.

More wandered off towards his brother, muttering under his breath all the way. The others watched as the two men exchanged slaps on the shoulders and then got into a huddled conversation. More emerged from the small huddle to point at Le Pedvin specifically, after which he gave a shrug. The discussion went on for a few minutes before More emerged and headed back.

'He has got horses,' More said, with an unspoken 'but' on the end of the sentence.

'But?' Le Pedvin had got the hang of this. 'Don't tell me, they cost eightpence each?'

'Oh no,' More smiled his happy smile, 'he can let you have them for a much less than that.'

Le Pedvin smiled his smile, which was more alarming than happy.

'He's gone to get them,' More nodded and grinned his grin of the lonesome tooth.

The group tried to look inconspicuous as they loitered in the Chadwell Street, with tradesmen and villagers passing by. Unfortunately the one-eyed Norman soldier was as inconspicuous as a corpse standing in the middle of the street watching people pass by. Pretty soon people started to stop and stare, and children started to point.

'Where are the horses?' Le Pedvin asked as he helped More to his own level by using his throat as a handle.

'Here they come.' More nodded in Le Pedvin's grip, which meant his head stayed still and his body swung back and forth.

Le Pedvin put the man down and looked up the road.

'Oh no,' he said, refusing the offer of the horses even at this distance, 'absolutely not. No way in heaven and earth.'

Chapter 17

Roman Down the Road

 E LEAVE IN THE MORNING,' Erik announced, nodding acceptance of Freya's plan as if it had been his own all along.

'You leave now,' Freya corrected. 'The Bishop's man may be out of town, but word of your arrival will spread. As you saw, the locals thought you were an army, and it won't be long before everyone knows there are only three of you. Then they'll gather their courage, followed by clubs, pitchforks and burning torches, and come looking. I'm not having them burn my house down, thank you very much. Quicker you're out of here the better.'

Erik scowled.

'It's no good scowling at me, Erik. If you want to go south you've got to either head through the middle of town or walk all the way round. And if you want to make it through the middle of the town, you'd better go now. Vikings who appear from across the northern sea have a bit of a reputation around here, and it isn't a good one.'

Ah, thought Siward, so we have to go straight through town then. He was getting good at picking up tips.

'Let's get on with it.' Fregurd rose from his place and shifted his shoulder to adjust the axe across his back to a more comfortable position. He gathered his knives like a swan picking up cygnets – sharp, pointy cygnets, but precious nonetheless.

Sigmund rose as well, although he then wondered whether he shouldn't sit down again as Erik still hadn't moved.

'Come on, Erik,' Freya sounded more encouraging now. 'I'll gather my pack and head east at the same time. You know the old Viking saying: "if it were done, t'were best done quickly, and violently, and with a '*yargh*' in your voice'". Her '*yargh*' was a good Viking '*yargh*', intended to send shivers of fear down the spines of opponents. It had worked for centuries.

It sent a shiver through Siward, but it was nowhere near his spine.

'Oh, all right,' Erik grumbled and got to his feet. 'What if we miss Harold, though? What if he's coming north and we're going south, and we cross?'

'You won't cross, Erik,' Freya assured him. 'This country has few enough roads and people stick to them. If he's coming from the river and you're coming from Lincoln, you'll meet, believe me. Even if you don't, there'll be word of him.'

Erik accepted this with a nod.

'Unless he's dead already, of course. But then you could probably do something honourable with his body.' Freya suggested this with a rather lewd snort.

Siward took note.

◆　　◆　　◆

The Vikings gathered themselves at the hut of Freya and clapped her shoulder in traditional Viking farewell.

Siward had been thinking about a kiss on the cheek but thought better of it. The woman would probably knock him cold.

'This way,' he called instead, heading back to the gate they had come through.

Straight through town must mean right instead of left so that was the way he headed, striding as confidently as he could. Once he got to the end of the town, however far away that was, he hoped the road would continue. Freya had said there was only one, so it should be pretty hard to lose.

Round the corner into the main track they strode: Siward the filth-man, leading his band of three large and violent Vikings. If only his mother could see him now. She'd probably shout 'run.' She'd probably be right.

The small band walked a few hundred yards until they came to the church on their right, built on the site of the old Roman Forum. This part of the town must once have been bustling with the life of the most civilised people in the history of the world. The old colonia, home to retired soldiers and the community that went with them, baths, shops, taverns – all alive and probably without a care in the world behind their high and protective walls.

Just now a small boy was weeing against the base of a Corinthian column that stuck from the mud. So much for civilisation. The child didn't even pause as a band of Vikings wandered past.

As the journey continued, on down the Bailgate towards the castle, some faces appeared at the doors of their houses. Hopefully they would remain only faces until the Vikings had passed. No one seemed to have anything in their hands ready to throw.

On to the castle square without any trouble. The Roman remains, off to their right, crumbled and teetered, left to their own devices as the feared home of the Night Legion.

To their left a building site, planned to be the next great church in Lincoln, stood silent and idle. Its builders and craftsmen also stood silent and idle among their works. With the Bishop's man, Nicodemus, out of town, there was no point in actually doing anything; they could always start again when he came back. If he came back.

One particular carpenter, lounging on the plinth for a statue of Saint Paul, did notice three Vikings and some other bloke pass by and raised a finger. 'Vikin's,' he slurred, blinking and shaking his beer-addled head to make sure the image was real. He looked round at his companions, several of whom were asleep.

'Vikin's,' he repeated, 'bloody Vikin's.' He waved his arms about to urge his fellows to action. No one moved.

Siward upped his pace and headed towards the gate out of town.

'Ah,' the drunken carpenter called as several of his work-mates eventually looked up, 'you missed 'em.

◆　　◆　　◆

Out of sight of the builders, Siward was alarmed to see the road past the castle go straight over the edge of a cliff. The way ahead was cobbled and had clearly been part of the Roman road network. In those days they must have had people who could walk down virtually vertical surfaces. Even the town went down this precipitous slope. Houses gathered on either side of the road, as if they'd tumbled over the edge of the hill in some carefully co-ordinated catastrophe. Perhaps they had.

The Vikings strode ahead, the slope making no difference to them at all. Siward had heard their land was full of mountains, most of them covered in snow and all of them with a god on top. Running down hills like this was probably second nature, he reflected bitterly.

The road was wet with a drizzling rain and Siward took his steps very carefully as he followed Erik and the others down-wards. Just when he thought he was getting the hang of it, the road tipped even steeper.

'Ye Gods, this a steep hill,' he muttered to himself. He grasped the side of a rough dwelling that had been insanely built in this location, glancing up at a sign on its side as he did so. It named the road as Steep Hill.

'Oh, very imaginative,' Siward grumbled as he almost fell.

Eventually the surface levelled off and the walking became easier. Ahead, down a now gentle slope, he could see a river at the town's boundary, its bulk of water almost indiscernible from the misty rain that was floating about in the air. He hoped there was a bridge just here, so no one would ask him, as their selected guide, where the nearest bridge was.

There was a bridge, and there was a man by the bridge, sitting on a stool planted right in the middle of the path. It was obvious to Siward that this fellow would want to gather a toll of some sort. Siward assumed, having spent some little time in their company, that Vikings didn't pay tolls. It would be interesting to see the result of this encounter.

Sadly for Siward, the encounter never had a chance. As soon as the man observed three heavily armed, if helmetless, Vikings coming his way, he appeared to decide that he really wasn't that bothered about gathering a toll and went for a stroll along the river bank instead. A stroll in the rain and completed at remarkable speed, as he was at least a hundred yards away by the time the party arrived.

The Vikings looked neither left nor right, but just marched across the bridge, intent on their destination.

Siward was also intent on their destination – most of his intent being to get some rough idea of where it might be. The road over the bridge carried straight on into the countryside, so he really couldn't go wrong.

'This way,' he nodded confidently as he caught up with and passed the Vikings.

There was very little opportunity to demonstrate his knowledge of the whereabouts of the wetlands as the journey continued. The road carried on without deviation, although the land got progressively flatter.

The rain loitered around in the air, making a good job of soaking everyone in a deviously subtle manner. The beards of the Viking dripped, Siward's leather shoes squelched and his venison joints took on an ugly sheen.

Erik was in the front once more, pressing his way to the horizon while Sigmund decisively trod the road in his leader's path. Fregurd was behind Siward, whose attention was divided. Part of him worried about the knife-carrying Viking at his back and part worried that the one in front might realise that the straight road made any sort of guide superfluous.

For the most part though, the image of Freya picking up a Saxon man and carrying him off to her fireside dominated. Despite the weather, his hunger and the dangerous company, a smile brightened his face. After several minutes of monotonous tramping it became a bit of a leer and the thoughts moved on to the actual fireside itself.

◆　　◆　　◆

After several hours more walking, some of it relieved by strips of raw roe deer, which Siward was getting quite a taste for, the light began dimming as the sun slid down the sky to their right. This at least gave Siward confidence that they were still heading south. There was no sign of the sun itself, entombed as it was in a burial mound of good English cloud.

He wondered for a moment if they'd passed the wetlands by mistake. The roadway was slightly raised above the surrounding land, and for all he knew it could be really wet out there already. He reasoned that if this Agnetha woman was going to pick them up in her boat, the land would have to really very wet indeed. Probably near the sea, and there was no sign of the sea.

He also pondered for a moment on Agnetha. If she was sister to Freya, perhaps she was magnificent too. Then he remembered that she was the wife of Erik and so, whatever she looked like, he would give her a wide berth.

'Should we camp soon?' Siward asked. He stopped and cast a glance at the darkening sky.

'Camp?' Erik asked as if he'd never heard the word before. 'Why would we camp when there's a road beneath our feet?'

'Erm, because it'll be dark soon and we won't be able to see the road?' Siward suggested.

'Pah.' Erik strode on.

'Also,' Siward said, looking up at the sky and examining his surroundings with some interest, 'I think we're not far outside

Sleaford. Wouldn't want to enter a town in the dark. Best pass through in the morning.'

Erik looked at the man in some surprise and cast a questioning eye to Fregurd. The other Viking shrugged, having no better information. He had cut his thumb on Fish-Spiker and was examining the blood with interest.

'Very well,' Erik agreed, 'another five hundred paces and we stop.'

Siward beckoned the Vikings to lead the way and they strode off. Once they were safely on their way Siward stepped away from the front of the milestone that said 'Sleaford 3 miles'.

◆   ◆   ◆

Five hundred paces must have been counted by someone because, at a commonly understood point – commonly understood by the Vikings, that is – they simply stopped walking and sat down. Packs were brought forward and more bits of fish, which looked and smelt like wood shavings, were chewed.

'Shall I light a fire?' Siward offered helpfully.

Erik just grunted, clearly not bothered one way or the other, so Siward went off the path to gather some wood.

The forest here was reasonably open and what little light there was, from a moon shrouded by rain clouds, allowed him to gather an armful of timber. He had burrowed under the top layers to locate kindling fuel that wasn't actually soaking wet, in the hope that his humble flint would be enough to ignite it.

After many moments of bashing the hell out of his humble flint he was no warmer, and the meat was no more cooked than when it was walking about on its own.

Fregurd sighed again. 'Sigmund,' he called and gestured towards Siward's hopeless efforts.

'You people,' Fregurd snapped. 'I'm surprised you manage to survive on your own at all, let alone fight off invaders.' His thumb was sore.

'The wood's wet and the flint's a bit old,' Siward explained. 'I'd normally have no trouble at all.'

Sigmund stepped over and drew his knife. Siward shied away.

The Viking took a pretty large log from Siward's little pile and hefted it in his hands.

'You'll never light that,' Siward scoffed.

Sigmund gave him the look that he was getting used to from the Vikings, implying he was comprehensively useless. With his knife, Sigmund sliced thin shavings down the side of the log, leaving them connected at one end. After just a few cuts the log looked like it had sprouted wooden hairs and had become a timber hedgehog. He then held out his hands for Siward's flint, laid the log on its side and struck the flint two or three times. The ends of the curled shavings immediately took light and spread their flames to the rest of the log. In a few more moments, with small pieces piled on top, there was a good blaze going.

Sigmund handed the flint back to Siward and returned to his dried fish.

Quite impressed with the technique, Siward brought more wood together and created a sort of cradle to hold the meat. He planted the first leg of deer on this and watched it slowly roast. As soon as the outer layer was cooked, he tore a strip off, baring the raw meat below to the heat of the flames. He stuffed the food hungrily into his mouth and closed his eyes in bliss.

'Oh,' he said, through a full mouth, 'oh, that's good, *mmm*.' He reached for another strip and looked up to see if he was expected to share with the Vikings. They were sitting gnawing on their dried stuff, apparently preferring the hard chunks to fresh meat. Siward shrugged a happy shrug and got on with his deer.

◆　　◆　　◆

The taste of cooked meat, the warmth of the fire and the fact that three large men with lots of weapons were just at hand filled

Siward with well-being. He belched, sighed and stretched out on the ground, resting on one elbow.

He dropped bits of nicely roasted venison into his mouth and imagined he was a Roman noble, being fed grapes by a strikingly handsome Viking woman. All it needed now was a skin of wine and he'd be as happy as an idiot.

He gazed into the sky as he chewed, gratified that the drizzle had stopped and the clouds were allowing a glimpse of the evening sky. It was beautiful, he thought, as a myriad twinkling lights started to arrive. Then one cloud moved obligingly aside, and Siward shivered. Revealed now was the bright star, the one with the tail, which everyone said was a harbinger of doom. Apart from the people who said it was a harbinger of great fortune, of course.

The thing had only been visible for a few nights, but, whatever it was, there was universal agreement it was harbingering its way across the sky like mad. It seemed to have faded a little in recent days and Siward followed the faint trail of its heavenly appendage as it swung into the darkness.

The tail was pointing downwards slightly now, which everyone said was a very good sign, apart from the people who said it was a very bad sign. As Siward's eyes followed the tail down, they noticed another bright object. It took a few blinks and shakes of the head to realise this one was not in the sky. This light was earthly. It was flickering, and it was getting closer. It blinked behind trees and shrubs as it moved, but it was definitely coming their way.

Probably some poacher out looking for game at eventide, he thought. Mind you, there wasn't much need to poach any more, not with all the nobles cleared off and probably not coming back. Perhaps this was just someone on his way home, lamp in hand.

Or perhaps it was two people on their way home with lamps, as a second light had appeared near the first. Or maybe three. Three people out with lights in the evening would not be up to anything good. Siward thought he would just keep quiet and they would pass him by. Then he remembered he had a good fire going with a nice haunch of venison on it. That would probably attract three people with lights in the dark. He thought about scuttling off into the darkness of the wood himself. Then he remembered he had three large Vikings on his side.

Well, they would be on his side if the lights approaching didn't belong to more Vikings, of course. If they did, it might get complicated.

Then the noise came. It was random at first, just the crunching and crackling of wood as it broke underfoot. It carried through the wood though, indicating the weight of several feet. As the lights bobbed nearer, the noise got more distinct. It was definitely the sound of feet tramping through the forest floor – but most alarming of all, they were all in step. *Tramp, tramp, tramp, tramp.* Siward's heartbeat leapt to the same rhythm and he shuffled sideways to get within kicking distance of Sigmund's leg.

Whatever the approaching group was, it had reached the edge of the wood at the side of the road. This was some four feet or so below the level Siward and the Vikings were camping on, so at least they had the advantage of high ground. Siward had a feeling they were going to need it.

He nudged Sigmund's leg with his foot and the young Viking looked up from whatever Viking reverie he was in. Nudges were passed and within the blink of an eye Erik and Fregurd were on the alert.

'Who goes there?' A deep, sonorous voice intoned from the darkness of the wood. 'Who dares camp on our road?'

'Oh my God!' Siward squeaked the squeak of someone who, if he gets any more frightened, is going to need the filth-man.

'What is it?' Erik growled.

Siward gulped and dropped to his knees.

'It's the Night Legion,' he whimpered.

Chapter 18

Fourpence Again

BSOLUTELY NO WAY AM I TRAVELLING on those things.' Le Pedvin snorted at the beasts presented by More's brother Bother.

'They're not stallions,' Mabbut acknowledged.

'Not stallions? They're not even horses.' Le Pedvin turned away in disgust.

'Of course they're horses,' Mabbut sniffed. 'They're the sort of horses the common folk use. Wouldn't do you any harm to put up with what ordinary people have to use every day.'

'As if you know anything about ordinary people.' Le Pedvin was contemptuous.

Mabbut went over and looked at what appeared to be four perfectly serviceable ponies. Yes, they were a lot smaller even than the mares they had used to get to Gravesend. Granted, if you were a Norman warlord you probably had pony in your pie rather than your stable – but if you had to get from A to B and this was all there was? And these beasts were a lot more sedate and co-operative than the monstrous creatures the Normans usually stomped about on, which behaved as objectionably as their masters.

'There doesn't seem to be a stallion merchant around,' Martel intervened as lightly as he could. 'Perhaps we could use these to get to the nearest livery?'

'I'd rather walk than be seen riding these overgrown dogs.' Le Pedvin curled his lip.

'Well, that's fine, then,' Mabbut nodded. 'Where would the nearest full livery be, More?'

'Oh, that'd be Ingrave,' said More, as if describing a place just the other side of the end of the world.

'And how far's that?'

'Be all of ten miles, I reckon,' the old man replied, with a slight whistle.

Mabbut suspected that ten miles was the largest distance More could comprehend. If he'd asked the old fool how far away Jerusalem was, he'd probably say about ten miles. On a good day.

'There you are, then,' said Mabbut. 'Ten miles. That's a good three hours walking, by which time it will be the middle of the night. Or much less on some overgrown dogs.'

Le Pedvin must be able to see that the argument was made, but that didn't stop him scowling and frowning angrily. It was not a pretty sight. Mabbut recalled his mother's warnings when he was a child and concluded that Le Pedvin's face had probably already got stuck like that. That was some excuse for it anyway.

◆　　◆　　◆

'So, More,' Mabbut turned to the old man, 'how much for the horses?'

A groan escaped Le Pedvin and he wandered off a short distance, probably so he could say these animals were nothing to do with him.

'Only fourpence the whole lot,' More nodded happily.

'Oh, right.' Mabbut was surprised at this, but thought the poor old boy probably had no idea how much horses, even ponies, cost. Odd that his brother Bother didn't know, though.

'That seems very reasonable,' he turned to Martel and Ranulf. Le Pedvin was clearly not engaging in this deal.

Ranulf looked to Martel, who shrugged the universal shrug of the man whose pockets are empty. With a sigh of disappointment, Ranulf's universal sigh of disappointment, the Norman reached for his belt and extracted the coins from a small purse tied securely to his belt. He handed them to Mabbut, who in turn held them out to More.

'Per hour,' More nodded again.

'Eh?' Mabbut was lost. What did the old man mean?

'What do you mean, old man?' he asked.

'Fourpence per hour.' More was his usual happy self.

'Fourpence per hour? What is?'

'The horses,' More confirmed, as his brother came over with the reins. 'They cost fourpence per hour.'

Mabbut still couldn't understand. 'Which hour?'

'Any hour, every hour.' More was happily patient. 'You give us fourpence and you can have the horses for an hour.'

'And then what happens?'

'Whatever you like. You can give them back, or you can give us another fourpence and keep them for another hour.'

Brother Bother nodded happily. More nodded happily. The two of them nodded happily at one another. Mabbut wouldn't have been surprised to see the ponies joining in.

'Fourpence for *every* hour?' Now Mabbut got it, and it was outrageous.

'That's right,' More confirmed.

'So if I used four ponies for half a day it would cost me …' Mabbut squinted his eyes in thought and gazed into the distance as he tried to work out this hideously complex sum.

'Sixteen pence,' Ranulf responded condescendingly.

'Sixteen pence!' Mabbut was horrified. 'One shilling and sixpence.'

'Fourpence,' Ranulf corrected. 'One shilling and fourpence.'

'All right,' Mabbut snapped in some irritation, 'twopence here or there is nothing. One shilling and fourpence for four ponies, and then we have to give them back?'

'That's right,' More was unconcerned. 'Good, isn't it?'

'It is if you own the ponies. We only want them to get to Ingrave — that's less than an hour away.'

'Ah, but an hour's the smallest time you can have.'

'Come again?'

'Well, a horse for ten minutes is no good is it?' More reasoned. 'Who'd want to have a horse for ten minutes? No, you have to take the full hour.'

'Fourpence?' Mabbut was still aghast at this robbery. 'Just to get to Ingrave?'

'Eightpence,' More corrected.

'*What?*' Mabbut had to walk in a small circle with his arms waving around a bit. He took a deep breath. 'How did it get to be eightpence?'

'An hour to Ingrave and an hour back,' More pointed out.

'But we're not coming back.' Mabbut was losing patience. He was starting to see the merits of Le Pedvin's approach to these situations.

'But the ponies have got to come back; they're no good to us in Ingrave. An hour to get to Ingrave and an hour to get back. That's two hours, so that's eightpence.'

'We'll just leave them in Ingrave. Someone can pay an hour to ride back again.' Mabbut thought this was perfectly reasonable.

'Oh, that'm nah gud,' Bother spoke up now. The man's voice was so heavily accented that Mabbut had trouble following him. He suspected the Normans wouldn't understand a word. Probably as well.

'And why not?' Mabbut demanded.

'Cos'm nah'un com frum Inguv by Chad'll. Pany'll stk.'

'What?' Even Mabbut didn't get this. He looked to More for a translation.

'Ponies would be stuck in Ingrave,' More explained. 'Bother's a bit loose in the head,' he commented, a sympathetic look on his face.

'Not too loose to charge a fortune for a bunch of small ponies. Including charging us for an hour when we don't even want them.' Mabbut's arms had started waving about again.

'Oh well.' More had a solution. 'We could always come and get them from Ingrave.'

'Right.' Mabbut saw a way out. He still wasn't at all happy about handing over fourpence and not actually having anything to show for it after an hour. Still, he reasoned, it was Ranulf's fourpence, so why should he care?

'Collection's another fourpence,' More explained.

Mabbut could only gape in disbelief now. Saying 'what' all the time was literally getting him nowhere.

'Of course,' More went on, 'if you want us to bring them back from Ingrave, we've got to go to Ingrave as well. That's fourpence for the trip. Two hours.'

'But, but,' Mabbut floundered, 'if it's fourpence for four horses, why is it fourpence for only two of you? In fact, why does it need two? Bother could do it on his own.'

'Oh, not safe on your own around here. There's robbers everywhere.'

'I know,' said Mabbut, pointing his look at Bother who didn't even have the grace to look away.

'Anyway,' More explained, 'if we have to go to Ingrave we wouldn't be here to hire the ponies. We'll be losing business. We have to charge extra.'

'But the ponies wouldn't be here to be sold – they'd be in Ingrave.' The end of Mabbut's tether was approaching fast.

'There you are, then.' More thought that was that.

Mabbut took a deep breath and tried to sort this out in his head. 'You're asking us to pay you so that we can borrow your horses?'

'That's right.' More's little beard bobbled up and down.

'And then you want us to pay you again to give them back to you?'

The beard continued its agreement.

'*And* you want us to pay you to come and be given them back?'

The bobbing beard framed the one tooth grin.

'And the fourpence for damage,' More added.

Mabbut had given up. He just gaped.

'You have to give us another fourpence in case you damage the horses. We might get up to Ingrave and discover one's sick or lame or something.'

Mabbut could feel his face reddening and he clenched his fists.

More held out placatory hands. 'Course if they's all fine, you get that fourpence back.'

'It's, it's …' Mabbut couldn't find the words for what it was.

'Very good business,' Ranulf observed drily.

Mabbut had almost forgotten the two Normans. He turned to Ranulf, as Le Pedvin was still off prowling round the locals. They seemed to be observing him with increasing interest, like some new animal that had just walked in from the forest.

Neither Ranulf nor Martel were as put out by this arrangement as Mabbut.

'It's robbery,' Mabbut complained. 'We only want the damn animals to get as far as Ingrave. We'll get rid of them when we get there and buy some proper horses. But the cost is ridiculous! First it was fourpence, now it's a shilling! Then we'll probably find full-size horses are tenpence an hour, in which case we'll be ruined before we get as far as Cambridge.'

'You can always walk,' More offered happily.

'How much to buy them?' The thought rushed into Mabbut's head.

'Do what?' Bother asked.

'To buy them. How much to buy the animals? We'll sell them in Ingrave and get our money back.' He grinned at the cunning and clever plan, which he had come up with all on his own.

More and Bother exchanged looks and began a heated discussion. Mabbut tried to follow, but they were gabbling away in the thickest local accents and he couldn't get a word of it. And it had started to rain again. He sat down to wait, feeling close to despair.

◆   ◆   ◆

Eventually the brothers stopped talking and turned back to Mabbut.

More fixed him with a beady eye. 'Twenty pounds,' he said.

'Twenty ...' Mabbut screeched. 'Twenty pounds for four ponies? Are you mad? For twenty pounds I could buy the whole bloody town – and all the people in it.' He could not understand what was going on here. These two local idiots seemed to have taken leave of their senses. Taken leave followed by a long journey, after which they realised they'd forgotten where they put their senses in the first place.

'But these are the only ponies there are,' More noted, 'and it's a business isn't it? We lend the horses to people for fourpence, and if you've bought them we've got no business.'

'But twenty pounds?' Mabbut was floundering. 'At fourpence a time, you'd have to lend the damn things out ...,' he realised he had not a hope in hell of working out this number, so deftly evaded it, 'so often they'd be dead. And I bet no one else borrows the things at fourpence a time. It's only 'cos we're here.' Mabbut folded his arms and glared.

More and Bother grinned back, clearly looking forward to getting the first fourpence any minute now.

'This is ridiculous,' Mabbut pleaded, finding himself down an alley with four ponies he didn't want.

'You can give us the other fourpence when we get to Ingrave,' More offered, as if this was some sort of generous concession.

'Tell you what.' Le Pedvin, having examined everything he wanted, returned to the negotiation. His face had lost all threatening expression and the voice was clear and calm. So clear and calm it gave Mabbut more shivers than when the man was shouting.

He leaned in and beckoned More and Bother to join a reasonable discussion. He even smiled a bit, which made Mabbut take another step back.

The Norman plonked an encouraging hand on each brother's shoulder.

'How about this,' he began.

More and Bother were all ears.

'I take your so-called horses to Ingrave and I look after them all the way there.'

The brothers nodded.

'I make sure no accidents happen on the way. The animals don't get stuck in bogs or scratched by briars or, God forbid, die of exhaustion on the way.'

Bother was still grinning, but More's expression was more thoughtful.

'And for all this care and attention I only charge you, what shall we say? Fourpence.'

Bother's face said that it was he who wasn't following this now.

'Of course, you could always choose not to pay the fourpence,' Le Pedvin went on reasonably, 'but they're horrible dangerous places roads, all manner of accidents could befall a small pony out there. We're carrying pretty large swords, for instance. Just imagine if the pony I was riding stumbled and threw me and my sword sideways suddenly, what then?'

Bother nodded happily, inviting an end to the tale of the stumbling pony.

'Headless pony,' Le Pedvin concluded with a happy slicing gesture across his throat. 'Could even happen to every one of them, and then where would you be?'

Even Bother got the situation now. The big, nasty-looking man with the eye-patch and the large sword was threatening his horses, and doing it rather well.

'And if you came with us, who's to say what might happen?'

Le Pedvin speculated in More's direction. 'Trampled to death? Another mishap with a sword? You could end up the way of the animals. In fact, if your idiot brother follows us I can almost guarantee something horrible will happen to him.'

More gulped now.

'We Normans are very fond of horses, though, so we'd take good care.'

The brothers were thinking.

'In fact,' Le Pedvin added as an afterthought, 'I'm known in court circles as someone who's very partial to horse.' He licked his lips.

More took the reins from Bother's hand and passed them over to Le Pedvin.

'Off we go, then,' he offered. 'I'll come with you and bring the horses back.'

Le Pedvin glared his glare.

'No charge,' More said brightly

Le Pedvin handed the reins to Mabbut. 'Idiot,' he muttered.

Chapter 19
Old Zeb

‘THERE YOU ARE.’ Mabbut tried to sound encouraging. ‘We're making quite good speed.’ And so they were for fairly large men on ponies that were too small.

They were definitely making northward progress faster they would on foot, but this didn't seem to assuage Le Pedvin's contempt for the mode of transport. The darkness was thick now, and it wouldn't be long before they had to stop to rest anyway. Although now Mabbut thought about it, he suspected Le Pedvin's plans did not involve stopping, let alone resting.

‘If, in the years of my life to come, anyone ever mentions that I travelled through England on the back of a pathetic pony, I will know that it came from one of you. I will then have a very good reason to put you in the stew with my next pony. Am I clear?’

The others variously nodded and mumbled, making it clear that if word of Le Pedvin's humiliation got out, it wouldn't be from them.

‘So now we go on to Ingrave and get fresh horses,’ Mabbut half-stated, half-asked a question.

‘Yes,’ said Le Pedvin, ‘and then we get after these Saxons.’

‘Which Saxons?’ Ranulf asked as they ducked some over-growing trees that loomed out of the darkness.

‘The ones that came across on the ferry in front of us. The ones who stole our horses?’ Le Pedvin said, as if so much should be blindingly obvious.

‘Why?’ Ranulf hissed. It was more than a question – it was an accusation that Le Pedvin had more in his plans than he was telling.

'Because I'm not having Saxons running off after the battle and getting away. They happen to be nearby and they've been helped across the ferry and away. I'd very much like to catch them up and kill them.'

'Perhaps then, we could at last acknowledge that we are on a Saxon hunt and not a survey of the country at all?' Ranulf proposed.

'You're on a survey of the country,' Le Pedvin replied, 'I've got some Saxons to hunt as well. When we go back to the Duke I'll be able to say I found and killed some Saxons. I just hope you can tell him all about the country.'

More had led the way out on to the northern road, such as it was, the boundaries between town and country, well-used track and open field being more suggestions than defined ideas. He stopped now and indicated the darkness beyond. Martel and Le Pedvin looked out, scanning the night for signs of activity.

'Wouldn't we be better going at it in the morning?' Mabbut suggested.

'While the Saxons get away?' Le Pedvin asked.

'They can hardly keep going all night either,' Mabbut protested. 'We hardly got any sleep in Salehurst and we'll get none tonight if we carry on. I'm sure the Saxons will have to stop as well.'

Le Pedvin gave this some thought. 'We rest when we get to Ingrave,' he reluctantly agreed, 'but not here. Not within smelling distance of Chadwell. How far?' he asked More.

'Oh, not far,' More gabbled his gabble.

Mabbut suspected this statement covered a huge ignorance of how far it was.

'How many miles?' Le Pedvin asked.

'Two,' More smiled.

Mabbut found this very hard to believe. It was ten miles when they set out, now it was two? Perhaps More did know his numbers after all: ten, four and two.

Le Pedvin took a deep breath. 'Then we will take these beasts the two miles and then get rid of them.'

'Don't worry, I'll take them away,' said More.

'We'll see,' Le Pedvin replied, which did prompt the smiling old man to stop smiling for once.

Le Pedvin's magnificent mount followed More. 'Martel, you watch the rear and see if anyone who comes our way.'

'Oh,' Martel sounded a bit worried, 'yes, right you are. No problem.'

The small caravan of small animals with big men on top tramped along in silence for some time.

'I'm supposed to make a note of this place on the basis of one stroll through the town and leaving on a pony?' Ranulf complained as they paced on.

'Oh, I can tell you all about the place,' More offered.

'I think now we're on the road you can clear off.' Le Pedvin rounded on the beard, which almost seemed to glow in the dark, hovering in the air like some illuminated web. 'You can come and get your dogs later.'

'I'm telling him about Chadwell,' More's voice grinned in the darkness. 'First of all there's old man Matthias, down by the ferry he lives. Been there all his life, does a bit of fishing now and then and he's got a little boat.'

'Boat?' Ranulf checked.

'Yes, but it's nothing like mine. Tiny little thing his is, shouldn't really go out in it, but he knows best I suppose. Used to have a wife, but she cleared off when the smell of fish got too much.'

'Tell me about the ferry.'

'Oh right, well that's very interesting because you see the feller who runs it now wasn't here at all five years ago. Oh no, he came from way off in the west, Greenwich, somewhere like that, and he had ...'

✦   ✦   ✦

And so it droned on. More had all the details of every building in Chadwell as well as their occupants, their occupants'
relatives, friends and acquaintances, the relationships that were
common knowledge and those that weren't. He knew who had
how much money and what they spent it on. He knew the
names of everyone who had left the place over the last five years,
where they had gone and how that had turned out for them.
He expounded at length about Mistress Carpenter's youngest
boy's wife's' cousin, who had travelled all the way to Bristol and
had seen the Welsh dragons flying over the great river down
that way. He also knew what the local lord's little weakness was,
and how King Harold had warned him to keep it to himself or
there would be trouble.

Le Pedvin's patience, already as substantial as a shrivelled
walnut, could not stand this drivel, and so he directed his pony
over to Mabbut.

'When we get to this next place, where's the road go on to?'
he demanded.

'After Ingrave? Depends which way we want to go. We could
head west towards London, north to Bigods or east to Wick-
ford.'

'Where would you go if you were escaping from a battle?' Le
Pedvin said quietly.

'Well,' Mabbut started, 'I think I'd …'

'I wasn't asking you, I was asking me,' Le Pedvin corrected
the Saxon. 'I wouldn't trust you to find your way out of a small
pond. I'm talking about hardened soldiers, men who know their
way around the world and the way to disappear when they have
to.' He looked around as they walked further into the darkness,
perhaps expecting there to be a clue floating in the air.

'East doesn't sound very sensible,' he speculated, 'just back
towards the sea. What's the country like down that way?

'Oy,' Le Pedvin snapped when he got no reply. 'What's the country like down that way?'

'Oh, talking to me now, are you?' Mabbut said in a high pitched and offended voice.

'Oh, for God's sake,' Le Pedvin growled.

'Got nothing of worth to say when it's about soldiers, but when you want directions it's "Mabbut, tell me what the country's like down that way".'

'No,' Le Pedvin said plainly, 'it's Mabbut, tell me what the country's like down that way or I'll come over there and stick my sword in one of your holes and push it all the way in. And twist.'

Mabbut appraised Le Pedvin as best he could in the dark for the slightest sign of camaraderie or good humour. He saw neither.

'Wet,' he said.

'What's wet?'

'The country down that way is wet. The river and the sea and the land get all sort of mixed up with one another. One moment the water seems solid and the next the land is liquid. Dangerous ground unless you know it well. Full of strange people who live in the reeds and eat eels.'

'Could be good ground if the soldier was a local.' Le Pedvin was speculating again and Mabbut thought better of interrupting. He coughed lightly instead.

'What?' Le Pedvin asked, not very nicely.

'People don't move about down there in the dark,' Mabbut explained. 'A lot of the land is floating and it does the moving about. Even the locals stay still at night.' He felt a small victory at having some information Le Pedvin didn't. He then felt bad that he was giving it to the hated invader.

'Not east then. West towards London? Might be sensible, get back to where the bulk of the population is, easier to disappear in a town. Or rouse some resistance. I still can't take on the whole of London without some help, though.'

Mabbut could almost hear Le Pedvin biting his lip as he thought. Biting his lip for pleasure, probably. Normans were like that.

'You Saxons are odd.'

'Thank you very much.' Mabbut was in the mood to take offence.

'You don't like towns, do you?'

'Not really, no,' Mabbut admitted. It was common knowledge so he couldn't see it would do any harm to discuss this with Le Pedvin. 'We prefer the country, to get out into the woods and the fields. Towns are dirty dangerous places. You never know who's sneaking up behind you.'

'So if you'd been injured in a battle and wanted to go somewhere you felt safe, it would be the country. Give yourself some space to move about.'

'Possibly,' Mabbut said carefully, worried that he was being led into some sort of trap.

'So the east is wet, the west is a dangerous town, what's wrong with north?'

'Wrong with it?'

'Yes, you people classify everything by what's wrong with it. Even your own marvellous country is too cold or too wet or too dry or too hot.' For once there was no animosity in Le Pedvin's tone. He was just stating a fact. 'Nothing's ever right, so what's wrong with the north?'

'Well, I'm not sure that's quite fair,' said Mabbut, with a small flash of recognition that he did usually think of what was wrong with something before he thought what was right. And all the Saxons he knew were the same. But then there was usually something wrong with them as well.

'North?' Le Pedvin asked. 'Tell me Mabbut, why wouldn't you go north?' There was scoffing in his tone now.

'There's the Danelaw, I suppose,' said Mabbut, as a whole list of the things that were wrong with the north sprang into his mind.

'Danelaw,' Le Pedvin repeated, but there was thought in his voice.

'Yes. I mean it'll be on the way out now that Harold's defeated the Danes, but a lot of the country north of here is still under Danelaw. Funny thing, Danelaw.'

'So it's almost like another country?' Le Pedvin half asked, half murmured.

'Well it was, obviously.' Mabbut thought Le Pedvin ought to be able to understand this, being William's right hand man and all. 'Denmark, mainly,' he added.

'So a bunch of Saxons fleeing a battle could find themselves out of the country, as it were.'

'They'd hardly be likely to go to Danelaw, I'd have thought.' Mabbut's tone implied he was stating the obvious.

'Why?'

'When you've just fought a war against the Danes? And killed their king? Not very popular just at the moment, I should say, your Saxon.'

'Hmm.' Le Pedvin clearly wasn't happy with this conclusion. 'Not very popular anywhere,' he added as an afterthought.

Mabbut ignored him. Stupid Normans, he thought resentfully. They would never make a go of things here. 1066 may go down in history as the year the Normans invaded, but 1067 would probably be the year they left again.

◆　　◆　　◆

This discussion of which direction to go had taken them the best part of a mile due north. Here the ubiquitous English trees were dominating the landscape. Copses crowded the tops of hillocks and rises, more solid growths filled the slopes and the main body of the forest filled everything else.

The track they followed occasionally sank into boggy sogginess, but became progressively drier the further they travelled.

Ranulf and More followed – and unbelievably More was still talking. Mabbut heard the lively tones as the old man went into another exciting explanation of the connections between various people and the escapades they had got up to.

Mabbut assumed Martel was still bringing up the rear, but he couldn't be seen from this distance.

'There we are,' More announced squeakily. 'Ingrave.' He sounded surprised that they'd actually come across the place.

'Where?' Le Pedvin asked, peering into the darkness.

'Over there.' More came up and pointed into the darkness.

Mabbut squinted. He could just about make out a dim lamp glowing in the darkness.

'And there,' said More, pointing in another direction.

Mabbut swivelled and saw another light. 'Ah yes,' he confirmed, 'that's Ingrave all right.'

'How can that be one town?' Le Pedvin asked. 'The lights are hundreds of feet apart.'

'We like to keep ourselves to ourselves,' Mabbut explained. It seemed perfectly reasonable. 'Just because you're in a town doesn't mean the neighbours have to be close.'

'And this place has a livery?' said Le Pedvin with rank disbelief. Shaking his head at the apparent madness of Saxons, he led the way into the town and towards the first light.

This shone from the window of a small traditional dwelling – single-storey, dug slightly into the ground and made of timber with infill of something or other. The roof was a collection of thatch and bits of wood, none of which looked particularly suited to keeping the rain out.

The single light shone from the single window, which was an opening in the wall rather than a glazed construction. In fact it looked most like a bit of the wall the builder had forgotten to infill, or had run out of stuff and decided to call it a window.

The place had a door, though – a door which had once been

the skin of a large animal of some sort. It appeared to be a considerable time ago that the thing had clothed the animal, and even then the beast hadn't taken very good care of it. It flapped, tattered and loose, but perhaps might keep out some of English drizzle which swirled relentlessly around the legs.

'Ho!' Le Pedvin called, dismounting and casting his pony adrift. He threw the skin aside and peered into the space within.

The space within contained one person who nearly leaped into his meagre fire in surprise.

'Ah,' he cried out, 'who are you? What do you want? If you've come to rob me I shall put up a fight.'

Le Pedvin looked around the inside of the building and cast raised eyebrows at Mabbut and Ranulf, who had put their heads in as well. There was nothing in this place that warranted robbery because there was nothing in the place. It was a space with a roof and walls and a fire in the corner, presumably placed there because part of the roof was missing and the hole could work as a chimney.

There was also little evidence the occupant was going to put up any sort of a fight. From the age of the skinny and ragged individual, his effort would be better spent fighting off death from old age.

The arms and legs were not in much better condition than the sticks of the house. Grey hair hung in clumps from the head, which was mottled and weather-beaten, and from the middle of which old, tired eyes struggled to gaze over the nose. A nose bulbous and red from too much of something or other. The something or other was not very healthy by the look of it.

Perhaps the man thought they were going to steal the fire. There was a look in his face that said he thought fire was magical somehow.

'We're just travellers,' Mabbut explained, putting on a bit of a local accent. 'We need to get out of the weather for a few hours, that's all. We aren't going to steal anything.'

215

'I've travelled,' the owner of the fire said, which caused Mabbut to frown at the strangeness of the comment and Le Pedvin to mutter under his breath, 'Oh God, the village idiot.'

'Really?' Mabbut nodded encouragingly. 'We'll come in and you can tell us all about it.' He stepped through the entrance followed by Ranulf, who beckoned the others to follow.

'Ooh,' said the man with the fire, 'there's a lot of you.' He frowned hard at each one of them and his lips moved as thoughts passed through them on the way to and from his brain.

'Seven,' he concluded brightly.

Mabbut opened his mouth to correct the man, but decided it would prove more trouble than it was worth.

'Oh hello,' said More in some recognition.

'Not another brother,' Mabbut said. A feeling of despair crept over him.

'No, of course not.' More dismissed a ridiculous suggestion. 'In law,' he concluded. 'This is old Zeb, this is.'

'Is it?'

'Course it is. Married my third sister.'

'Really.'

'Yis, and then the second.'

'At the same time?' Mabbut was already regretting getting into this conversation.

'No.' More looked at Mabbut as if he were some kind of idiot. 'Third sister left him and the second took him up.'

'I ...'

'I know what you're thinking,' More went on.

Mabbut was pretty sure he didn't. He was thinking that he really didn't want to know any of this. In fact he was about to say so.

'If the third sister didn't want him, why did the second pick him up?'

Mabbut said nothing, half hoping the explanation would not arrive.

'She never was too bright,' More explained.

Mabbut contained his surprise. For More to describe someone as not too bright, they must be more plant than person.

'And old Zeb's one horn short of a cow, if you know what I mean.'

They could all see what More meant as Zeb was standing against the far wall of his home, his lips still rumbling away on their own.

'No, eight,' he said eventually.

Mabbut didn't want to know, he didn't want to speak his thought, but somehow he couldn't keep it in. 'If he's so erm ...'

'Stupid?'

'Yes, stupid, why did either of your sisters marry him?'

'To get all this, of course.' More held out his arms to take in the magnificence of their surroundings.

'High ambition,' Ranulf commented unpleasantly. 'Now perhaps if we could worry less about the family affairs of idiots and just find some space, we can be out of here before a conversation breaks out.' He scoured the ground for a reasonably dry and level spot and plonked himself down. 'If there is a livery worth the name, I think we need the daylight to see what we're given. It might really be dogs next time. We can rest here.'

The others followed suit. There was just about enough room for them all to stretch out. Heads would touch one wall and feet the other, but the place was wide enough for five to lie down side by side. They assumed old Zeb would spend the night guarding the fire.

'Yes,' said old Zeb as the company sorted themselves out and removed the more lumpy rocks from the dirt floor. 'I been to Shenfield once.'

Nobody gave any acknowledgment, but settled themselves to sleep.

'All the way there and back. I went out of here and turned left and then got down to the bottom track. I didn't take the new track because that's always busy with carts and the like. No, I know this little short cut using an old drovers' road which brings you out the bottom of Kettle Hill ...'

Old Zeb's drones through the details of his pointless and unexciting journey lulled them all to sleep, even Le Pedvin. He slept with his sword clasped across his chest, looking ready to become the lid of his own tomb.

More twitched and chattered in his sleep, like a dog dreaming of rabbits who answered back.

Mabbut drifted off and dreamt of the wide-open spaces of his home. The horizon was distant and his parents were standing outside the door of his house. As he ran up to them, they turned and pushed the horizon further away. No matter how hard he ran he could never catch them up.

◆　　◆　　◆

Mabbut didn't know how long he had slept. It was one of those sleeps where he thought he had only just dropped off, whereas in fact he'd been unconscious for hours. He was woken by Le Pedvin's voice.

'What did you say?' the Norman was asking, sitting up with sword in hand.

Mabbut shook the sleep reluctantly from his head and looked around again.

Old Zeb was still in his corner chatting away, but Le Pedvin was now standing in front of the old man, staring at him.

The very first creeping light was daring to challenge the darkness, and the occasional bird tweeted its alarm that the big bright thing was coming up again.

'They come right through here,' Zeb repeated.

'No, where did they come from?' Le Pedvin asked.

'Oh, south they said, over the sideways sea.'

218

'Sideways sea?'

'The one that moves from right to left and back again. Narrow, brown, sea, sideways.'

'The river?'

'That's it. They come all the way from Senlac, they said. Been a big fight apparently.'

'There had,' Le Pedvin was encouraging. 'And they were Saxons, were they?'

'People, that's right,' Zeb confirmed.

'Any of them injured?'

'Oh, nasty it was,' Zeb dared to crouch close to his fire. 'Rested here before they moved on, they did. Expensive bloke he was, all the others fussing about him.'

'Who was?' Le Pedvin was pressing, but clearly didn't want to frighten Zeb off the trail of his tale.

'The one who was injured, like you said. It's a shame really because you only just missed them. They could have told you all about it.'

Le Pedvin now roused the others to wake with kicks and pushes. Complaints and moans came back to him.

'All about what?' Le Pedvin asked quietly.

'All about the expensive bloke who'd been shot in the eye.'

Chapter 20
The Night Legion

HE WHAT?' ERIK ASKED, looking at the lights that were now arrayed before them.

'The Night Legion,' Siward howled quietly. 'They've come for us.'

'What the hell is the Night Legion?' Fregurd asked.

Siward swallowed what he suspected would be his last swallow. 'Romans,' he whimpered.

'Pah.' Erik's snort was heavy with derision. 'There are no Romans any more.'

'We're on their road. They don't like it when you're on their road. Specially at night. They come and get you if you're on their road at night. And they take you away.'

'Where do they take you exactly?' Fregurd asked; he didn't seem concerned in the slightest.

'To join them. You tramp the Roman roads for eternity.'

'So they're spirits, then?' Fregurd confirmed.

'Of course they are!' Siward was terrified of the Legion and irritated at the Vikings' nonchalance.

'Why do they need lamps?' Fregurd asked.

Erik snorted again.

Sigmund relaxed slightly from the fighting stance he had adopted.

As far as Siward was concerned that was not a sensible question. This was a legion of dead Romans – they could have whatever they wanted.

'I mean,' Fregurd went on, 'if they're Roman spirits and all, haunting the Roman roads to take away those who dare trespass, why do they need a lamp? To see where they're going? I think if you're dead you don't need to worry about that sort of thing. And if you're Roman, and have been dead for centuries, I imagine you can pretty much do what you like.'

'Er.' Siward wasn't used to people questioning the Night Legion. Everyone knew what the Night Legion was and took it seriously. At least everyone Siward knew did so. The question of their lighting requirements had never come up.

'Do you think Thor needs a lamp to see where he's going?'

'Oh, er …'

The Vikings laughed together.

'These are not Romans,' Fregurd concluded. 'Sigmund, go and get us one.'

Sigmund bounded down from the road and headed off towards the lamps. There was much crashing of undergrowth accompanied by Viking *'yarghs'* every now and then.

The *'yarghs'* came to a definitive halt with a thump and a yelp.

Those on the road exchanged looks. Siward's was one of worry, but both Erik and Fregurd looked rather cross, which was a bit scary.

After a couple of moments, during which the lights gathered like fireflies swarming to whatever it was fireflies swarmed to, a single voice cried out through the darkness.'It's a bloody Viking!' The voice sounded offended and angry, and not at all Roman.

Erik and Fregurd hefted weapons in their hands.

'Look,' said another voice from the dark, 'there's some more on the road.'

There was a bit of mumbling from the darkness now as the lamp holders took in this information.

Some conclusion was obviously reached as a cry of 'Get them' rang out, and the crashing feet made their way straight for the road.

As one, the Vikings leapt into the black, Viking roars in their throats and courage in their arms.

Siward had heard the expression 'attack is the best form of defence', but he'd never seen it in action before. He'd thought it was pretty stupid when he heard it, however, and now he was convinced. To his mind, standing by the fire and watching for what came your way was a much more sensible tactic than leaping into the dark and hoping to bump into it first.

The roars were suddenly cut off and transformed into cries of pain and surprise. The sound of two large Vikings falling to the ground came to Siward's ears.

He knew exactly what he had to do. The short time he had spent with the Vikings had rubbed off on him: Siward was now a man of action. He promptly leapt off the road in the opposite direction and ran into the night. He had no idea where he was going; he just thought away from the lights and off the road would be best.

He had only taken three or four long strides before the ground simply fell out from under him. He pitched forward, imagining that this was the fall into the abyss. If he ever came out it would be as a cursed spirit, eternally tramping the Roman road.

In fact he landed a very short moment later in the bottom of a deep ditch. A deep and very wet ditch, and he landed head first. The softness of the watery mud, or muddy water, stopped him breaking his neck, but it was very unpleasant. The gasp of breath he took at the impact turned out to be a gasp of muddy water, or watery mud.

Siward coughed and spluttered. Then he rolled over, so that he could at least get something into his lungs that wasn't going to kill him. Getting the right way up, his feet sank deep into the ditch and he grasped at its sides to avoid sinking completely. Perhaps this was the abyss after all.

Next he tried clambering out, once he'd got over the shock of the fall, but the whole place was simply too slippery. He was just starting to think about spending the night here when strong hands grabbed him under his shoulders and hauled him upwards.

He fell forward over the edge of the ditch and saw booted feet in front of him: good, sturdy boots. Boots, he thought, what sort of Roman wears boots? Where had their sandals gone?

He clambered to his knees and now saw tightly bound leggings.

After a few more coughs and chokes he managed to stand up and face his rescuers. He didn't know whether to be relieved or disappointed. Somewhere in the back of his mind he'd rather wanted to see the Night Legion; from a distance and only as an observer, obviously, but it would be a good tale to tell. A lot of people claimed to have seen the Night Legion, but here he was faced with a bunch of Saxons – plain, normal-looking Saxons. Well-armed, strong and battle-ready by the look of them, but that wasn't so bad. Well, it wasn't until one of them hit him. Hard.

◆　　◆　　◆

A slap to his face brought Siward back to his senses, although when he opened his eyes there was no sense to be seen.

He could tell straight away that he was tied. Wrists and ankles were locked solid, but having been propped against a tree he was at least upright. He was on the edge of a small campsite, with a generous fire blazing in the middle. The lamps he must have seen were now hanging from the trees, and around this fire were about ten men, all of them very plainly Saxon.

Off to his right, around the edge of the camp, he could see the Vikings individually tied as well. None of them was happy, but they did at least look like they were used to this sort of thing. Quite a pile of weapons was collected in front of them. It looked as though every single knife of his family had been taken from Fregurd. There were an awful lot of them.

Fregurd gave Siward a very hard look. 'Romans!' He spat.

223

'They're as Roman as you are,' Erik went on. 'Just a ruse to scare travellers enough to rob them, I imagine. They're not used to people actually having a go at them.' He shouted this last to the men milling about, some of whom looked over. Rather contemptuously, Siward thought.

Of course, if he ever got out of this he could tell people he'd been captured by the Night Legion anyway. Who was to know? But then again, he might not get out of this at all.

'They haven't got a clue,' Erik cocked his head towards the Saxons in contempt. 'I don't think they've ever caught anyone before – people normally just run away. They hadn't bargained on hardy Vikings coming their way.'

'How did they catch you then?' Siward asked. His question was genuine, but he noticed Erik redden rather and realised it was a sensitive point.

'We fell in a ditch,' the Viking mumbled under his breath. 'Whole bloody country is covered in them,' he went on, firmly putting the blame on the ditches. 'Then they jumped us and tied us up. It's not the way a man fights his battles,' he called to the assembly.

Siward looked over at Sigmund who was clearly ashamed to be tied up. His head hung and he looked at no one.

'I thought this part of the country was subject to Danelaw?' Siward speculated. 'Can't be right under Danelaw to tie up Vikings surely?'

'Surely not,' Erik confirmed, 'and when we get out of this there will be hell to pay.'

One of the men of the camp, who had been moving amongst his companions, giving a word here and an instruction there, came over. He stood a few feet away and appraised them, as if trying decide which lamb to buy from the market.

This fellow was clearly a fighting man, which made Siward wonder what he was doing here instead of dead in Hastings. He was in his late twenties and very well armed, with strong-looking arms and legs. A charming scar neatly divided his right cheek; the top of this scar pulled his eye down and gave him a most alarming appearance.

Siward was perfectly willing to be alarmed by anyone just at the moment, but this man would have been fearsome anywhere. He exuded his own personal stock of alarm that dripped all over his captive.

'Vikings,' the man spat, 'just bloody Vikings.' He shook his head in disappointment. Siward wondered what the man had been hoping for. 'Still, I suppose you'll do,' he added, which worried Siward even more. He was about to say 'I'm not a Viking actually', but thought it might make things worse.

'You'll hang for this,' Erik barked.

'No, we won't,' the man replied very confidently. He beckoned to some of his fellows, who untied their ankles and then rudely dragged the captives to their feet, pushing them back to the road.

Being marched along in the dark, while tied up was not a happy experience. But then, Siward thought bitterly, apart from the roe deer and meeting Freya, his last days hadn't exactly been brimming with happy experiences. Then again, they'd had better moments than most of his days as a filth-man. It was being tied up that gave him most cause for concern. People who tied other people up almost always had something nasty in mind.

◆　◆　◆

The walking continued at a fairly modest pace through the night, but as the Saxons had all the lanterns the captives couldn't see where they were putting their feet. At least they continued south, which was handy. Siward thought they had been in the wetlands when these Saxon bandits had jumped them, but as the first hint of dawn peeped over the horizon to see whether it was safe to come out, he saw that he was wrong. He hadn't realised land could actually get this wet and still be land. It was just as well the road continued above its surroundings, otherwise they'd be getting their feet wet all the way up to their necks.

Siward's yawning tiredness greeted the sun, which revealed a horizon simply miles away. There wasn't so much as a hillock within sight, and all that was within sight was wet.

It wasn't wet enough to be the sea, or a river, but there was a flat sheen to the surface of the water which indicated something squishy just underneath. Something still wet, but just a bit thicker than the water that covered it.

If there were ditches and dykes in this part of the land, they weren't working. Siward hoped the tide was in – if any more water came from the sea, the whole country must surely sink.

They tramped on for what seemed like several more hours, with the waters on either side going neither up nor down. Siward's worries of an inundation were relieved, but he began to wonder when the water would go away, if it ever would.

As the day realised it couldn't go back on itself, the blandness of the landscape seeped into the company. There was no conversation, but even the Vikings began to lose their positive approach. They had been striding along with their wrists bound as if it was their preferred mode of travel; Saxons with spears to front and rear were simply a bonus. Now, though, they seemed slumped and disheartened.

Siward felt as though he had dropped into some sort of trance: his feet were still moving, but he was making no progress. The land was conspiring against him and lolloped along at exactly his pace. He could walk all night and day and still end up in the spot they left this morning.

After he had shaken his head three or four times to make the world move about a bit, he noticed a blur on the horizon. In the whole field of damp uniformity, which stretched in all directions, this was blessed relief. Literal relief, as it appeared to be some sort of hill, or building, or troll, or dark blob of night waiting to swallow their souls. He shook his head again.

The paces continued until the shape started to resolve itself. It was indeed a hill, and a building, and not a troll at all.

'Spalding?' Fregurd raised eyebrows, the sound of his voice breaking some of the stupor which the land had thrown about them. 'Good Danelaw town, Spalding,' he added for the benefit of their captors.

'Ha ha,' the captors laughed in a very superior manner. It didn't fill Siward with confidence.

They walked on with increased vigour. Even the Saxons seemed anxious to get out of the flat land, which Siward could now see would drive anyone who lived in it to madness. Jumping out on people in the middle of the night and tying them up was perfectly understandable.

After what felt like an interminable period, during which the walls of the town moved away as quickly as they walked towards them, they were suddenly at the gates.

These gates were not closed. They were flung wide open and looked like they hadn't moved in generations. Siward considered this very reasonable. If you lived in a place as dull as this, you'd probably want as many people as possible to visit as often as they liked. And, of course, if anyone was intent on attacking the town, they'd have to move incredibly quickly to make it to the walls without being spotted miles away. Either that or be very small, or perhaps be made of water. Siward shook his head again to stop the strange thoughts he was having from gathering together.

'Ah, there you are,' a booming, happy voice greeted them as they crossed the threshold. Looking around, Siward saw a booming, happy man approaching. He had a look of the Viking about him; height and breadth, hair and axe. He was older even than Erik, and looked like his town living days had taken the edge from his Viking terror. But he still appeared strong enough to snap Siward in half, should the need arise.

There was no recognition between the Vikings at this meeting.

'We saw you camp last night,' the greeter said as he drew up to them. 'Met my men of the marshes, eh?' He roared with laughter.

'We'd have dealt with them in a fair fight,' Erik answered gruffly.

'No point in a fair fight then, is there?' the man replied without rancour. 'But enough of this,' he held his arms wide to welcome them to the town, even though they were still tied up. 'To my halls. It's seldom we see travellers in these parts and they are always welcome.'

The man led the way off into the town and the group followed.

'I don't trust him,' Siward heard Fregurd mutter.

'Quite right,' Erik responded, 'there's something very fishy going on. Sigmund, stay alert.'

Sigmund nodded seriously while Siward looked at them all in bemusement. Didn't trust him? The man had them tied up by a bunch of bandits and was taking them into his stronghold. Of course he shouldn't be trusted. Sometimes he thought he was getting to understand the Vikings, their way of life and the way they thought. Other times he realised he didn't have a clue.

The town was simple but looked prosperous. Its location on the north–south and east–west routes would be good for trade, if you could stand the flat landscape. The buildings were solid and properly made and the streets between hardly had much muck in them at all. And the few people they saw seemed to be hurrying to do something quite important somewhere else.

Their Viking host led them up the gentle rise of the place towards the main hall. This was a large, solid, wooden-framed construction, at least sixty feet long, with smoke curling from chimneys at each end.

Light poured from the open doors as they stepped up. The Viking stood to one side, beckoning them welcome, bowing his head slightly as they entered.

Once inside the hall, as they were firmly grabbed by a larger number of their host's men, who pointed long spears at their heads. Siward hoped the Vikings could see why not trusting this man was probably for the best.

'So, my fine visitors,' the man said, apparently still as jolly as when he'd met them, 'let's have you in the dungeon then.' He watched in amused interest as a very large pile of weapons was deposited on the floor of the hall.

'What for?' Erik demanded, as only a tied-up Viking can demand.

'About thirty shillings at a guess,' the man replied. 'Don't think I'll get anything for the Saxon, but you never know till you try.'

'Hostages,' Fregurd said the word as if it was defective. 'A Viking taking hostages.' He spat.

'Don't mock it,' the man instructed, 'it's very lucrative. Specially just at the moment. Kings coming and going, you never know who's who or who's prepared to pay for them.'

'You'll get nothing for us,' Sigmund snarled.

'Wrong thing to say,' Fregurd said to the idiot boy.

'I'd better kill you now then.'

'See,' Fregurd explained.

"Course you can tell me what you're up to. Who you are, where you're going and why, but it doesn't really matter. I think long term, me,' the man went on. 'Sure, nobody wants you now; doesn't mean to say they won't want you in a year or two. If you're still alive, of course. If someone does want you now, that's best. I save money on food for my hostages by not giving them any.'

'This is the way you treat travellers, is it?' Erik was full of contempt.

'It's the way I treat three Vikings wandering along the road with a Saxon in tow. Or a Saxon with three Vikings in tow. It's the way I treat people after our good King Harald just lost a battle to their good King Harold. And it certainly is the way after their Harold went off south to fight William. So many battles, so many sides, everyone is somebody's hostage. Could be there's some rich Norse family only too glad to get you back. Could be you were on the Saxon side and Harold will want you. Maybe you're William's spies and *he'll* want you. And if not? What's to lose?'

The man looked at them on the off-chance of some sort of answer.

'No?' he said. 'Oh well, throw them in the dungeon.' He waved an arm to one of his men.

The man came over and whispered something in his master's ear.

'Well, make room,' the master commanded in some irritation. 'Get rid of the old man; no one's come for him.' He grinned broadly and held out his arms to his new captives. 'Here's hoping that you are dearly missed and well loved, so you can be dearly paid for and released fit and well. Fit and well apart from the little slice I take from all my guests.' The man roared his happy laugh once more.

With another check for weapons and even the remains of Siward's precious venison, which had travelled so far with him, removed (probably to fill the man's pot), the contingent of spear-carriers urged them out of the main hall and down a flight of stone steps into the bowels of the building. It was cold, bleak and very dark. And a long way down.

◆　　◆　　◆

Siward's first thought was that they were likely to be going under water, but the place seemed dry. Cold, damp, unwelcoming and harsh – but dry.

As it turned out, the old man who nobody wanted proved more than happy to accommodate them in his meagre cell. As the alternative was going with the guard to be 'cleared out',

Siward understood the man's choice. Even if it meant standing – as there wasn't room for them all to sit down at the same time.

When the guards had gone, they were left alone in the dark and dank. Only one small, barred window, high in the wall, let in the damp light.

'At last,' said Siward as he rested his aching legs. 'Perhaps we can get some sleep now.'

Fregurd snorted, but it was a very directed snort. Nearly a snarl.

'What?' Erik demanded.

'Well done, Erik,' said Fregurd. 'Very well done indeed. Of all the people to find in the whole of England, you lead us into his place.'

Siward looked backwards and forwards for some explanation. Sigmund looked as puzzled as normal, but no one took any notice of that.

'That's Thorold, or I'm a dolphin.' Fregurd nodded his head towards the ceiling where presumably their Viking captor was even now tucking into roe deer, probably still roaring. 'We're just lucky he didn't recognise us.'

'Thorold?' Siward asked, bewildered. 'If you know him, why don't you tell him who you are and what we're about?'

'Because of his second name.' Fregurd directed the statement at Erik.

'Second name?' Siward was finding Vikings very strange once again.

'Tell him, Erik.'

Erik mumbled into his beard.

'Can't hear you, Erik,' Fregurd prompted.

'Hostageslicer. He's called Thorold Hostageslicer,' Erik snapped.

There was total silence.

231

Chapter 21
Aefred the Absent

OW LONG AGO WAS THIS?' Le Pedvin demanded as he took hold of old Zeb by his old throat and shook him about.

'Weeks,' Zeb squeaked out.

'Weeks?' Le Pedvin dismissed the word and shook some more. Harder. 'It can't have been weeks.'

'No, no, not weeks,' Zeb struggled to recall. 'What's the shorter one?' he asked himself and the room. 'Not weeks. Hours, that's the one. Hours.' He nodded encouragingly. Presumably to encourage Le Pedvin to let go of his throat.

Le Pedvin did let go of his throat. 'And which way did they go?'

'Out,' said Zeb, pointing at the door.

Le Pedvin's teeth were clamped together. 'Did you see which way they went after they went out?'

'No,' Zeb wailed. 'I stayed in. It was raining.'

'It's always bloody raining. You must have noticed something. How many were they?'

Old Zeb screwed up his eyes, as if to picture, and enumerate the number of people who had been in his home. 'Lots,' he concluded.

Le Pedvin wasn't finding it any easier to grind his words out. 'Well, if there were lots of them you must have heard which way they went.'

'I did,' Zeb nodded, only adding to Le Pedvin's obvious frustration.

'Why didn't you tell me?'

'You asked if I saw, which I didn't. I heard, though.' Poor old Zeb seemed frightened by the fact that Le Pedvin couldn't understand him. As well as the prospect of being grabbed by the throat again, and the fact that his hovel was full of people who might mean him harm.

Le Pedvin opened and closed his hands as if practicing for strangling Zeb, which he was going to do any moment now.

'And which way was it you heard them go?'

'That way.' Zeb pointed to the back wall of his hovel.

'North,' Le Pedvin said in some triumph. 'Come.' He dropped Zeb and headed for the door, rousing the others to leave the building quickly.

'What's going on?' Ranulf asked as he rose reluctantly to his feet.

'We're off. Now.'

'Why?'

Le Pedvin didn't have an answer to this, but seemed to believe one wasn't necessary. He simply looked at Ranulf expectantly.

'Oh, of course,' Ranulf said in mock realisation, 'because you said so.'

'Exactly.' Le Pedvin nodded curtly. 'I don't suppose the livery will be open?' He directed the question to More and Zeb, both of whom looked to one another.

'No, I thought not. Still, we can always go and open it.'

'What?' cried Zeb in some horror, 'and steal the horse?'

Le Pedvin had been looking out of the door as if he expected to see escaping Saxons sneaking past. He turned back to old Zeb.

'What do you mean, *the* horse?'

'The horse in the livery. Surely you wouldn't steal the town horse?'

'You have a livery with one horse in it?' Le Pedvin's contempt was scalding.

233

'Oh yes,' old Zeb said with pride. 'She's called Morris.'

Le Pedvin's clenched fists first pointed towards Zeb, then More, then Mabbut.

'Right,' he shouted and strode from the place, muttering quite loudly about stupid Saxons and their stupid country and their stupid mares called Morris.

The others followed. Once out of Zeb's dwelling, they gathered to look to the north. There was nothing in sight, but Le Pedvin examined the ground for signs of tracks.

'Nothing,' he said, 'all trace washed away by the rain. God above, even the weather's on their side.'

With cloaks wrapped tight they pulled woollen hoods up on to their heads to keep off the worst of the rain and gathered the ponies. Le Pedvin's disgust at the mode of transport was palpable as he grimaced while mounting his beast.

Le Pedvin, Ranulf and Martel set off. After only a few dozen paces to the north they discovered that the woollen hoods were now sopping wet and freezing cold. They took them off again and basked in the slightly less cold English rain.

Mabbut hung back, feeling hungry, cold and downright fed up with Normans. He held his pony's reins and watched as Le Pedvin pressed on, trying to urge his animal to the gallop of a war horse. The poor thing didn't have a clue what was expected of it, but it did manage to get up a half-decent trot, its little legs covering hardly any ground at all, but doing it quite quickly.

Martel was once more taking up the rear while Ranulf prepared himself for a long and tiring complain.

'Oy!' Le Pedvin called back to Mabbut. He was obviously not going to get away with being left behind.

'Not coming with us?' Mabbut asked More, who had come out as well and was standing in the shelter of Zeb's doorway.

'Out there?' More asked in horror, looking up to check that the rain was in for the day. 'Not likely. Besides, your Norman seems a bit disappointed about the livery. I think I'd rather keep out of his way. I'll stay by Zeb's nice warm fire and have a chat.'

'What about your ponies?'

'Oh, they're not mine.' More nodded his grin.

'Well, your brother's then.'

'No, not his either,' More explained brightly.

'But?'

'We sort of borrowed them.'

Mabbut didn't know what to say. In his life he had seldom had the urge to punch anyone in the face, but More was a promising candidate. He looked at the old man who was grinning his happy, toothy grin and nodding his barmy beard up and down as if this was a huge joke.

'So what happens when the owner wants them back?' he asked.

'We'll say the Normans stole them.' More was happy with his excuse.

'Yes,' Mabbut said with some resignation. 'I think that'd work. I've got a feeling they're going to steal everything before long.' He mounted his horse and gave it a none-too enthusiastic prod to follow the others.

'Maybe see you on your way back.' More nodded the little beard.

For some reason these words prompted Mabbut to think beyond his current trials. Heading north with the mad Le Pedvin on a mission that made little sense was bad enough. He hadn't thought through what happened when it came to an end. What then? Would there be some fight with one side victorious and the other side dead? Would they set up some advance camp? Would they simply turn around and head back?

But if the mission failed? If Le Pedvin didn't get what he wanted and had to return to William empty-handed? He could picture the Norman, in an even more foul temper than usual, barging his way south. Unfortunately in this picture the space occupied by Mabbut was now vacant.

'No,,' the Saxon muttered to himself as he set off, 'you probably won't.'

◆　　◆　　◆

Tramping onwards at as fast a pace as ponies with soldiers on their backs could manage, Mabbut contemplated the land of his fathers, the land of his birth and the land he loved. This should have been a moment of great satisfaction. He had spent his years in Normandy telling everyone how wonderful England was, and how if he only had the chance he would be back there like a shot.

It was cold, though. And he'd forgotten how much it tended to rain. He'd often waxed lyrical about the gentle English rain, softening the landscape and misting the country into a song of growth and life. He completely missed out how wet the stuff was. And how it got everywhere. His feet were soaking and water was trickling down the back of his neck. A small patch on the left of his stomach had let the damp in and was the most irritating of all.

He'd also gone on at considerable length about the glorious English harvest time. How the bales of hay and bushels of wheat would be gathered by smiling peasants, many of whom sang as they worked. The sun would shine and there would be great rejoicing.

He now remembered that harvest was usually a battle against the elements. The seasons didn't so much meld gently into one another as get shoved aside when the next one came ripping across the land. A gentle autumn would become a snarling winter in the space of an afternoon. Even across the same field it could be summer at one end and very much not summer at the other.

Meanwhile Normandy, he knew, would be basking in the late sun. The peasants there really would be gathering their harvest in some comfort, picking the apples from the tree, squashing them into cider, drinking it and then lying down for a bit.

But this was England. That was enough.

He ploughed on through what felt like hours of rain, now being thrown about by a playful wind. It played especially with bits of him he wanted left alone.

Eventually, although those in front were making a pretty good pace, Mabbut's animal caught up with them. Perhaps it liked the company. That was more than could be said for Mabbut.

✦   ✦   ✦

They moved on in silence for some time, nobody wanting to ask Le Pedvin what their plan might be

'Where next?' Le Pedvin eventually shouted back at Mabbut. The sun was high in the sky, or at least it must be judging how bright the rain was. They must have travelled half a day.

Mabbut's pony drew up to Le Pedvin. 'We've come a good distance, probably getting near Hempstead, and beyond that Moulton or even Cambridge. A bit close to the border now.' He tried to give Le Pedvin a warning look.

'I shouldn't think there's much of a border left any more,' Le Pedvin commented.

'This part of the land has been under Danelaw for years.' Mabbut was cautious. 'Alfred never defeated them, and even Harold hadn't really taken over completely.'

'Things change,' Le Pedvin scoffed, 'especially after your King killed their King. Just like William and Harold really. William kills Harold and gets his country. Your Harold killed their Harald, so the Danes lose.'

'That's all very well,' Mabbut whined rather, 'but I've found that Danes tend to do pretty much what they want. Very little respect for Kings. Even their own.'

'That's true,' Le Pedvin agreed, which surprised Mabbut. He wasn't used to being agreed with, particularly by Le Pedvin.

They plodded on in silence for a while.

'I'm still not sure Saxons would deliberately make for Dane land.' Mabbut observed. 'I mean Danelaw,' he corrected himself.

'What?'

'It's called Danelaw, the land of the Danes, not Dane land. Don't know why.' Mabbut shrugged.

'I don't mean what is the land of the Danes called,' Le Pedvin snarled at Mabbut. 'I know that. I mean, why are you still talking?'

Mabbut swallowed. Back to normal then. A normal he was getting thoroughly fed up with. He had a perfect right to speak when he wanted to, even in the face of a mad killer like Le Pedvin, William's closest friend. As long as he was careful and kept a reasonable distance, of course.

'I mean, I'm not sure it's likely any Saxons would head back into the land of the enemy,' Mabbut offered, politely. 'Even if the enemy was defeated.'

'Then what are they doing going north?'

'Perhaps that's where they live?' Mabbut thought this was obvious. If you were escaping from a battle, wouldn't you go home? Where else was there to go?

'"Perhaps that's where they live"?' Le Pedvin seemed to find this very amusing. 'Some well-to-do Saxons who fought the Danes and then William came from Dane land?'

'Well, erm …' Mabbut could see this would be a bit odd. 'There's lots of Saxons live there,' he huffed.

'Ha!' the Norman didn't seem happy with this explanation. He dismissed Mabbut with a wave of the arm and beckoned Martel.

Mabbut rejoined Ranulf, who had a very dour look on his face. He watched as Le Pedvin and Martel engaged in quiet but earnest conversation.

'What are we doing?' Mabbut asked Ranulf, not for the first time.

De Sauveloy looked at Mabbut through the English rain. 'Chasing Saxons, obviously.'

'Won't William be cross if he doesn't get his survey done?'

'You idiot,' Ranulf observed, as if telling Mabbut he'd got two left shoes on. 'We were never doing a survey. It's always been a search for Saxons.'

Mabbut's eyes went left and right in rapid succession, apparently looking for some explanation.

'I don't understand' was all he could say.

'That doesn't surprise me, but I'm not sure I do either,' Ranulf nodded to himself. 'William could easily have sent a band out to catch runaway Saxons. Why just us? Why me and why *you* mainly?'

'I suppose I know the way.' Mabbut shrugged. 'And maybe William really does want to know what's out here.'

'Possible,' Ranulf acknowledged. 'Very unlikely, but possible. He never normally bothers finding out what's over the hill before he attacks it and kills everyone who lives there.' It was Ranulf's turn to shrug now. 'It'll come to me. It always does.' He appeared to stop thinking about the problem. 'Where's next?'

'I think Hempstead is close. It used to be on the border of Danelaw, but there's not usually any trouble. Quite a nice place actually.'

◆   ◆   ◆

Hempstead was quite a nice place and it only took them until about mid-afternoon to get there. Quite nice compared to the other places they'd been, that is. As they approached the sparsely populated area, it was clear the manor was the main reason for anything being there at all.

It was robust and defensive. It looked like it could close its eyes, fold its arms and simply refuse to play with anyone who wanted to cause trouble.

The walls were tall and solid, only punctuated by arrow slits, high near the eaves. The place was basically an elongated cube with a door at one of the shorter sides. This door was imposing, appearing to be made of something only slightly less giving than stone. Above it a small perch provided a spot from which the occupants could drop things on anyone who wanted to come in. Probably hard or hot things.

The whole place was a statement: here it stood and here it stayed. The land of the Danes could do what it wanted, but it wasn't coming past.

The time when its defences were called upon must have been a while ago, as the mighty door now stood open. Many of the arrow slits had grass growing from them, and if there were guards they certainly weren't doing any visible guarding.

'Hello?' Le Pedvin called as they drew up to the door.

There was no answer and so the band crept gratefully into the cover of the building, shivering unavoidably as the rain ceased to patter.

'Hello?' Le Pedvin repeated more insistently. 'Anyone there?'

The inside of the place was better maintained than the outside. Three or four rough tables were gathered around the fireplace at the end of the single hall, where a large and healthy blaze did its best to lift the natural gloom of a building with only weed-filled gaps for windows.

Without any discussion, everyone made their way straight for the fire. Here they gathered as close as they could while the fine English rain steamed from their clothing.

Above the fire, a pig was gently burning on its spit. The creature had clearly been put there days ago, as most of it was eaten. The occupants obviously couldn't be bothered to turn so little meat round any longer.

A number of scraps were still clinging to the bones, though.

The company hungrily tore these free before wolfing them down like men who were about to be deprived of their pig.

Around them, the rest of the space was broken up into different sections. There was clearly a sleeping area to one side, where half a dozen straw cots were laid out. A single large table was on the opposite wall, doubtless where the lord conducted his business. Finally there was a small door to the left of the fireplace, through which there would probably be a private chamber or two.

'Where the hell is everyone?' Le Pedvin asked Mabbut, finally accepting that there really wasn't anything edible left on the bones above the fire.

The Saxon was about to reply along the lines of 'How the hell should I know?' when a noise came from the small inner door.

'Hello?' a male Saxon voice called. 'Who's there? Is that you, mother?'

'No, it isn't your mother.' Le Pedvin dropped his voice to a low growl.

'Oh, I'm terribly sorry,' the voice called. 'I wasn't expecting anyone. I'll be out in a moment.'

They waited by the fire while the owner of the voice finished whatever it was he was doing in there.

'Ah, there we are then,' the voice said as its owner stepped into the room.

This was definitely a Saxon as he looked almost exactly like Mabbut. The nose was straight, but the clothes were the same and the pasty skin said this was someone who spent most of their time being bathed in rain.

To be precise, it was someone who looked exactly like Mabbut might look in about another sixty years. If he lived that long. How this individual came to be expecting his mother to call was a mystery.

This version of a Saxon was bent and thin and crooked, but he was smiling – something Mabbut hadn't done for quite some time. The fellow looked delighted to see visitors, although was something a touch vacant about his smiling, and his eyes.

'Who are you?' Le Pedvin demanded.

'Stangard Nult at your service,' the Saxon bowed. 'And who do I have the pleasure of addressing?' he enquired.

'It's no pleasure, believe me,' Le Pedvin replied. 'I am Le Pedvin.'

The Saxon beamed. 'Well, hello Le, what a charming name.'

'Eh?' Le Pedvin was puzzled.

'That's all his family name,' Mabbut explained. 'Le Pedvin. He's Norman.'

'Fascinating,' Stangard said, fascinated. 'Who's everyone else?'

'I'm Cnud Mabbut,' Mabbut bowed his head briefly. 'This is Martel,' he indicated the Norman who was still standing as close to the fire as possible, 'and this is Ranulf. I'm Saxon, but the others are all Norman.'

'Yes,' said Stangard, 'that's the most fascinating bit.' He smiled at them all. 'What's a Norman?'

There was a silence as they all looked at one another. Even Mabbut was surprised by the question.

'Er, they're, erm, people from, er, Normandy?' he explained.

'How marvellous.' The man seemed overjoyed to be having a conversation. 'And where's that then?'

'You are joking.' Le Pedvin stepped in.

'I don't get about much,' Stangard apologised. 'Charged with the manor here, I do my liege's duty and keep an eye on the feisty Danes, harrying our borders.'

'Do they harry much?' Le Pedvin asked pointedly.

'Not really.'

'And your liege never mentioned the Normans?'

'Not to my recollection.'

'Even when he was headed south from defeating the Danes to deal with someone called William?'

'William, William ...' Stangard pondered the name as if

242

trying to recall an ancient aunt. 'Can't say I'm familiar with the name. And what's this about defeating the Danes?' he wanted to know.

'King Harold defeated the Danes at Stamford Bridge,' Mabbut reported.

'Harold? King Harold? What's he King of then? I imagine King Edward will have something to say about that, calling himself a king. He always was a bad lot, that Harold.'

The group exchanged looks that were of a common intent. It was probably not worth trying to explain the recent changes in the English monarchy to this old man. An old man who had clearly been alone in his manor for far too long.

'The point is,' Le Pedvin explained, 'that the Normans have won a decisive battle. Duke William is now your King, or very soon will be.'

'The Normans invaded?' Stangard checked.

'That's right.' Le Pedvin emphasised the 'right'.

'What? Three of you?' Bewildered, the old man looked them up and down.

'No, not three of us, for goodness sake. There's a whole army at Senlac Hill.'

'Is that in Normandy?'

'Oh, forget it.' Le Pedvin gave up. 'I do not have the time to explain the world outside your manor to you. Lots of things have happened which you probably don't need to know about. You'll find out soon enough. What I'm after is a band of Saxons, one of them injured, who must have come this way.'

'Injured Saxons.' Stangard repeated the request as if he always had injured Saxons passing through and was just trying to remember the most recent.

'Yes.' Le Pedvin's tone implied that the man better remember, and quickly, but it passed the Saxon by. 'A small group probably, carrying one on a bier — had an eye injury?' He hissed this last close to the man's ear.

Nult leaned back smiling and shaking his head. 'Can't say I recall.'

'Good God.' Le Pedvin's gaze darted around the hall. 'Right, we search. Injured Saxons travelling north and didn't come by here? I don't believe it.'

'I say.' Nult seemed about to protest the invasion of his privacy.

'I'm sure you do,' Le Pedvin retorted without interest. 'Martel, you check the outside, I'll have a look round here. If they did pass through there might be some trace.'

'You can't just go barging around a man's house helping yourself to a look around.' Nult was outraged at such a breech of etiquette.

'Er,' said Le Pedvin without really giving it any thought, 'yes, I can.'

'But an Englishman's home is his castle,' Nult protested.

'No,' Le Pedvin explained. 'An Englishman's home is Duke William's castle. In fact, all Englishmen's homes are Duke William's castles, as of now. And if I want to look round them, put my feet up in them or burn them to the ground, I will.'

Le Pedvin strode purposefully to the door behind the fireplace and laid his hand on the latch.

As he did so the thing flew open and a press of Saxon warriors burst into the hall, brandishing weapons and screaming their attack.

Chapter 22
Avoiding the Slice

Ow do you know he's this Thorold Hostageslicer?' Siward asked. Then he realised what he was asking. 'What sort of a name is Hostageslicer? Who's really called Hostageslicer, for goodness sake?'

'He is,' Erik confirmed. 'Obviously he wasn't born with the name. His parents weren't called Mr and Mrs Hostageslicer.'

'I'm pleased to hear it.'

'They were the Gutrippers.'

'Gutrippers!' Siward scoffed.

'You stupid Saxons are called Smith and Butcher and Mason because of what you do.'

'I suppose so.'

'Same with Vikings, unless you're a dottir or a son.' Erik shrugged as if this was perfectly normal.

'What are your names then?'

Erik looked him in the eye, hard and steady. 'You don't want to know.'

Siward believed him. He changed the subject. 'So what do we do now?'

'Whatever you like.' Fregurd nodded at the old man who was in the cell with them and was picking his nose with great gusto. The old man grinned back, displaying a perfect set of gums, untroubled by teeth.

'His trade really is hostages?' Siward enquired.

'Oh yes, he's made his fortune at it. He'll take anyone hostage without bothering to see if they're worth anything or not. The ones who aren't, he slices.'

'Charming.' Siward was sarcastic.

'Not really, no,' Erik replied, clearly puzzled by Siward's response.

'And the ones who are worth something he slices as well, only a bit less. Hence the name, Hostageslicer.'

'Yes, I get that now, thank you,' Siward tried to stop the explanation. 'Why does he slice the ones he lets go?'

Erik shrugged. 'To keep track, I think. Otherwise he'd end up taking the same people over and over again, and those who pay get a bit fed up with that sort of thing. Thorold does well because he never takes the same person twice. He can tell who they are because they've been sliced.'

'And us?' Siward wasn't at all keen on this slicing business. It sounded best avoided.

'I don't think anyone's going to pay for you.' Erik dismissed Siward's chances.

'And no one knows you're here,' Siward retorted, attempting to make it sound just as bad for them.

'Ah well, Thorold will send word out. Probably get to Freya or Agnetha. They'll come and get us.'

'How long will that take?' Siward demanded.

'Oh, it'll be pretty quick, I should think. Six months?'

'Six months! I can't wait here six months.'

'I don't think *you'll* have to.' Erik made Siward's fate pretty clear.

'I wondered where old Thorold had got to after that incident with the King's son,' Fregurd put in, seemingly to make conversation. 'Didn't know he'd set up here though.'

Siward was dying to know what the incident with the King's son had been. Then he decided that if he was told, he'd immediately wish he'd never found out.

'But he doesn't recognise you,' he said instead.

'Never met us.'

'Really?'

'It is a big place, the north,' Fregurd explained. 'We don't all know one another.' He shook his head at Saxon stupidity.

'We can't just wait here to be sliced,' Siward was pleading. If there had been room, he would have paced up and down a bit.

The occupants of the cell shuffled around to sort them-selves out and managed to find just enough room for everyone to sit. Their knees were hunched up and feet were interlocked, but at least they could rest backs against the wall. The floor was packed, with the last remaining piece of space left to the old man, who had to sit in the straw he used as his privy. He seemed to quite enjoy sitting in his corner, and gazed at his new companions eagerly.

'What if we say we're looking for …', Siward paused and looked cautiously at the old man, 'you-know-who. If we tell Thorold that, he might let us go.'

'You-know-who?' Erik asked.

'You know.' Siward prompted.

'Who?' Erik was lost.

'The person we're looking for. The one you've come to get?'

'Harold?' Erik said it loud and clear.

'Harold,' the old man repeated, and collapsed into a caco-phony of cackles.

Siward looked about in alarm that this secret was given away. Fregurd didn't seem concerned that the name was mentioned, while Sigmund was looking round the cell as if fascinated by its construction.

'Yes, Harold,' Siward hissed quietly. 'If we tell Thorold we're on Harold's side that might influence him.'

'Influence him to lock us up for longer while he asks for a really massive ransom,' Erik responded.

'Which Harold won't pay anyway,' Fregurd put in.

'Er.' Siward got a sinking feeling in his stomach. 'Why not?'

'So many reasons,' Fregurd said plainly. 'He's just lost the battle for his country? He'll need whatever money he's got to bribe his way to safety? Oh yes, and what's the point in pay-ing to rescue the people who are supposed to be rescuing you? If Thorold ever got hold of Harold himself, he'd make another fortune from William.'

'But ...' Siward's thoughts couldn't keep up with his words, or vice versa. Both ran out and he couldn't think of what came next.

'Shall we escape?' Sigmund asked, with some enthusiasm for the task.

'Probably,' Erik confirmed.

'Escape?' Siward wished events and the words that went with them would start making some sense. 'How can we escape? You just said we were going to be sliced and sold. And I was only going to be sliced.'

"That's because you keep blabbering on,' said Erik. 'You nev-er give anyone a chance to think. Do all Saxons talk so bloody much?'

Siward did not reply.

'Hasn't shut up since we got in here,' Fregurd added.

'What do you reckon?' Erik had moved on.

Fregurd glanced around the cell as he replied, 'Single skin, stone wall with lime mortar, some of it pretty old. Door solid enough, but the hinges are on the way out. No regular patrol, very shoddy. Window barred, but seen better days. Best bet is the breeches on the middle bar.'

Siward's urge to ask what on earth breeches on the middle bar meant was almost irresistible. Almost. His urge to show these Vikings that he didn't talk all the time won the day.

'Show us your breeches,' Erik commanded.

Siward bit his lip and said not a word. He held his legs out as best he could.

'No good at all.' Erik cuffed Siward's leg aside.

He took a brief glance at the old man, but saw he had no breeches at all.

'Have to be Sigmund then,' Erik concluded.

'Again?' the young Viking complained. 'Why's it always me?'

'You've got the breeches for the job,' said Fregurd.

Sigmund grumbled, but stood and started to unlace himself.

Siward gawped and fidgeted, but still managed not to say a word. He sat stoically in a cell with three Vikings and an old loon, while a young man stood and took his leggings off.

Bare legged, with only his loose shirt to protect his modesty, and Siward's view, Sigmund approached the window.

Erik and Fregurd stood as well and indicated that Siward should do the same. He wondered what on earth he was being drawn into.

Brushing the old man out of the way, Sigmund reached up and passed one leg of his breeches through the window, wrapped it once around the middle bar, and back into the room.

'Grab hold,' Erik ordered Siward, who was rather startled at the instruction.

He observed, as Erik and Fregurd took hold of one leg of Sigmund's breeches, while Sigmund himself took the other. Siward stepped cautiously up behind the young man and grabbed a handful of breeches.

'We lean forward as one, then pull back as one,' Erik directed Siward. 'And on the pull, we pull hard.'

Now Siward got it. Two people pulling hard on each leg, while the breeches were wrapped around the window bar, might loosen the thing.

With firm grasps all round, the team leant forward at Erik's lead.

'*En, to, tre,*' Erik called, and on '*tre*' the Vikings pulled back, yanking hard on the loose trousers and the window bar. Sigmund yanked back hard, straight into Siward, who hadn't moved.

'Thor's hammer man,' Erik cursed. 'One, two, three? You pull on three?'

'Oh, right,' Siward replied, learning his first words of Viking

– apart from 'yargh'.

They re-gathered their strength.

'One, two, three,' Erik called, rather pointedly.

On 'three', the group put their combined strength into the breeches, which smacked hard against the bar of the window. Siward couldn't tell whether it moved or not, as he was still concentrating on avoiding Sigmund's backwards lunge. It was clear his strength was no match for that of the Vikings. That was probably why Erik had teamed him with Sigmund.

'Again,' said Erik, and they repeated the process.

They did this several more times. So many, in fact, that the old loon started clapping with each pull and doing a little jig.

They paused for a moment while Fregurd examined the window.

''Two more,' he said with some authority.

Siward wondered how many times they'd had to do this. How often did these people get captured?

On the next attempt there was definite movement from the bar. On the second go the thing came out completely. It flew across the room to clatter into the door, narrowly missing the old man in the middle of his dance.

'Right.' Erik nodded with satisfaction.

Sigmund gathered up his breeches, which seemed none the worse for their maltreatment. He really must have the best ones for the job.

'Out you go then,' said Fregurd.

Siward looked around the room, only to find the Vikings were all looking at him.

'Me?' he said in some shock.

'Of course,' said Erik. 'Who else is going to fit through there? We could send the old loon, but I think he'd wander off instead of sneaking back into the place and past the guards to release us.'

'Er,' Siward offered.

'I mean, we're too big to get through that.' Erik pointed at the still, small opening the window presented. 'You're built like a herring's feeble son, though; you'll be through that in no time.'

'And then sneak ...' Siward's sentence ran out of courage.

'Sneak back into the place, past the guards and let us out. And don't get caught by Thorold. He gets very annoyed when hostages escape.'

'I bet he does,' Siward said with little hope.

'Don't worry,' Fregurd encouraged him. 'He probably won't even notice you anyway. You don't make much of a hostage in the first place.'

'Very comforting, I'm sure.'

'Good,' said Erik, missing the nuance as usual. 'Off you go then.' He gestured Fregurd and Sigmund to him, to help hoist Siward out of the window.

'Er,' Siward said hurriedly, trying to think of an alternative plan. Any plan would do really, as long as it didn't involve him trying to escape the captivity of someone called Hostageslicer.

'Wouldn't it be better to go at night?' he bleated. He was quite impressed; it sounded like a rather good idea.

'Um.' Erik gave it some thought. 'No.'

'Why not?'

'Because I think it best if we get out of here quickly.'

'Really?' Siward hadn't expected the Viking to express any fear or trepidation.

'Or rather I think it best if you get out of here quickly.'

'Oh?'

'Yes. Thorold is bound to think he can get a good ransom for us – like he says, three Vikings wandering about have got to be worth something to someone. You, on the other hand ...'

'Yes?'

'Won't take him long to realise you aren't worth anything. He'll probably slice you to show us he means what he says.'

'Use you as an example,' Fregurd explained.

'And make it painful to show us what he's capable of.'

Sigmund nodded agreement.

'It's what I'd do,' Erik went on. The others concurred amicably.

Siward took a step towards the window.

'Oh,' Erik added as an afterthought as Siward was half way through the gap.

'What?' Siward hissed back in annoyance.

'If you have any thoughts about sneaking off, you know, not coming back past Thorold and the guards, but running off to save your own skin, leaving us to our fate?'

'Yes?'

'We'll all come after you and give you a good traditional Viking burial. You know – the one with your body on the burning boat?

'Yes,' Siward gulped.

'Except you won't be dead when we start the fire,' Erik said in a matter-of-fact manner.

Siward paused for just a heartbeat. 'Back in a tick,' he said reassuringly as he clambered through the window and on to the ground beyond.

The old man was now standing, gaping at the window as if Siward had just vanished in thin air. He looked backwards and forwards from window to Vikings as if one of them was going to explain how this miracle worked.

Chapter 23

Saxons in the House

E Pedvin took a rapid step back and drew his sword. Martel took a rapid step back, followed by another one.

In the gloomy firelight the Saxons pushed forward into the main hall – pushed forward with vigour and strength. They very effectively pressed Le Pedvin backwards with the advantage of surprise on their side.

They needed it. As Mabbut recovered from the shock, he appraised the attacking force. Although there were six of them, all were ragged and damaged to various degrees. They all had weapons to hand, but some of them seemed to be having some trouble holding them up. One of them, Mabbut noticed, was using his sword more as a crutch than a fighting blade.

'Get out of it,' Le Pedvin said as he backed into Mabbut and pushed him back. 'Martel, to me,' he ordered.

The lead Saxon appeared to be the least incapacitated. His left arm had clearly taken some damage as it hung at his side, but in his right he held a large sword that he swung with some ease.

Le Pedvin backed further away, partly to avoid the blade in his face, but also to get room to swing his own sword.

The four Saxons behind their leader were in progressively worse condition and looked in no state to be taking on any Normans, let alone Le Pedvin. It was the sixth man at the back who interested Le Pedvin. The man with a dark stained bandage swathing his face, a lump of material firmly tied across his right eye.

Martel stepped up quickly, well, relatively quickly. The sight of him and Le Pedvin standing with swords raised made the Saxons pause, halting their progress towards the door.

'Found the bastard,' Le Pedvin whispered in barely controlled triumph.

Ranulf now came over, apparently more comfortable behind Le Pedvin and his sword than in direct line of a bunch of armed Saxons. 'What's the meaning of this?' he demanded

Le Pedvin sighed at the stupidity of the question. 'What do you think the meaning of this is?' he asked, as he and the lead Saxon waved swords at one another, each beyond the reach of their enemy.

'Ah,' said Ranulf with some recognition. 'Saxons, of course. Perhaps now you've found some we can get on with the survey?'

'Survey all you like,' Le Pedvin said, a strange tone in his voice. It could almost be mistaken for contentment.

Ranulf now took the time to examine the small Saxon army. 'I must say they don't appear to be in good condition.' He noticed the figure in the rear. 'That back one looks in a very bad way,' he said, 'got a nasty wound to the … oh, *mon Dieu*.'

Le Pedvin said nothing.

'Now I understand,' Ranulf went on, his own contentment clear. 'I was fooled by that body in the tent. Now I see why the charade of a survey, and only four of us to examine the whole country.'

'Do you really?' Le Pedvin asked, very clearly.

'Of course, of course. I said I'd get it in the end. Now I have.'

'And you'll be telling anyone?' Le Pedvin asked, a very different tone in his voice now.

'Are you mad?' Ranulf replied. 'Of course not. What on earth do you think would happen if word of this got out? If there was even the slightest hint that, erm, this gentleman was here and not dead on the field at Senlac. I'm not stupid.'

'Good.'

'In fact, it would have been far better to tell me in the first place.'

'Then you wouldn't have played your part,' Le Pedvin explained. 'We all know what you're like when things aren't done properly.' He added a none-too-complimentary tone to the last two words.

'But Martel knew.' Ranulf was not happy.

'It was Martel who brought this gentleman's body to William at Senlac.'

'Aha.' Ranulf nodded with the glee he always demonstrated when finding the failures of others.

'Mabbut's in the dark, of course,' Ranulf stated.

'About pretty much everything,' Le Pedvin confirmed.

'What? What?' Mabbut asked, looking around to try and spot whatever it was that was raising so much interest.

'So, what now?' Ranulf asked.

The men in the room had made no moves. The drops of shoulders and drawn faces seemed resigned to their fate, as if the fact that so much running had come to nothing was too much to bear. They seemed to be using this pause to recover the strength they'd used in all that bursting out they'd done.

'Eh?' Le Pedvin asked. He hadn't thought this far.

'Do the deed here or take him back to William?' Ranulf pressed.

'I think William would prefer it we took him back.' Le Pedvin nodded at his thought.

'Back through hostile territory, with this man plainly alive and only the three of us to guard him?'

'And if we do him here at least we could take him back in a box, or a bag.' Le Pedvin liked the idea.

'Do it and bury him here?' Martel offered.

'You really want to annoy William, don't you?' Le Pedvin observed. 'Have you got some sort of death wish? First you give him the wrong body, then you want to deny him the pleasure of a body at all. Even when it's the right one.'

Martel hung his head.

'We'll have to deal with this lot.' Le Pedvin nodded at the stumbling Saxons, who seemed to have as little idea of what came next as the Normans. 'Shouldn't be too much trouble, looking at them. Of course, the old fool Nult what's-his-name will have to go too.'

At this Le Pedvin looked around to spot where the old fool was, as he wasn't with the group from the room. Le Pedvin found him behind the Normans, somehow carrying one of the benches from the eating area above his head. For a decrepit old fool he looked remarkably strong, and he seemed to know what he was doing.

He put what little weight he had behind the bench and half threw, half ran it into Martel and Le Pedvin. Both staggered forward into the assembled Saxons, who scattered before the onslaught of Normans and flying furniture. They moved round the side of the hall and made for the entrance, made with remarkable speed for an apparently half-dead group of soldiers.

Le Pedvin was naturally the first to throw the bench from his back and emerge to grab at passing Saxon legs. He threw himself full length across the floor as the man with the wounded eye hobbled past. Wounded eye and wounded leg, it seemed, which was very handy.

As his fellows escaped from the hall and out into the daylight, Le Pedvin, with a neat tap to the man's ankles, brought the Saxon to the floor. He immediately leapt up and stood victorious. 'Let's get him out into the light. I'd really like Mabbut to see this – I love disappointing him.' And Le Pedvin actually laughed. Just the once.

Martel came out from the wreckage of the dining room and grabbed the Saxon by one arm. Le Pedvin took the other and they virtually lifted the fellow from the floor and marched him out into the daylight

Mabbut rushed along, looking on in horror. 'What on earth are you doing? Is this the height of Norman nobility – not just harrying a bunch of the sick and wounded, but mistreating them as well?'

'Shut up.' Le Pedvin grinned. 'Come and see who we've got,' he beckoned Mabbut over to the door, 'before our little mission comes to a happy end.'

Mabbut looked with some distaste at the bloodstained head which was swathed in filthy bandages and now hung, comprehensively defeated. 'Poor fellow,' he said.

Le Pedvin reached out and grabbed a handful of the bandages near the chin.

'No!' Mabbut called out in alarm at this treatment of an injured man.

Le Pedvin ignored the plea and ripped the bandage from the man's face. He held out an arm to display his triumph.

'What?' Mabbut asked, demanding that the ghastly Norman explain his actions.

'What!?' Le Pedvin yelled as he looked at the face which was revealed as the bandages came away. It was definitely Saxon and it was certainly wounded, but the scratched face didn't look bad enough to warrant the swathes of bandages. What it was not was the face of King Harold.

◆　　◆　　◆

Le Pedvin took hold of the head in both his hands and tried to move it out of the way to reveal the real head underneath. He looked back into the hall and inside the bandages that were now lying on the floor. 'Where is he?' He shook the wounded man heartily, which only made him groan.

'Where's who?' Mabbut asked. 'Who did you think this was?'

'He's one of the others,' Le Pedvin announced. 'After them!' He dropped his captive as if he'd picked up a meat pie, only to find it was full of maggots. He ran round the outside of the hall to catch up with the departing Saxons. 'Where have they gone?' he screamed at the empty field, then answered his own question. 'Quick – the other side.'

They all ran back across the entrance to the other side of the hall. The injured Saxon watched with some interest as the little group ran first one way, then the other.

'By God,' Le Pedvin swore when the other side of the hall was revealed, as vacant as the first.

They returned quickly to the front door – just in time to see the man with the not very grievous eye wound scuttling around the corner like a mouse who's just escaped the cat.

'Get them, get them all,' Le Pedvin roared, and he sprinted for the corner of the hall, sword in hand.

Martel was at his heels. Ranulf made his own, more leisurely way around.

Mabbut stood where he was, looking backwards and forwards from the hall to the outside, where a dying man had just run. A dying man who turned out not to be dying at all. And what was all that about Le Pedvin saying look who we've got here? Who was the dying man supposed to be? This was all very confusing. Frowning, he made his way after the Normans.

❖   ❖   ❖

Round the corner Mabbut saw the group of Saxons on horseback, calling to one another in loud, encouraging and war-like voices. They were urging their companion to join them before Le Pedvin caught him up.

Le Pedvin was sprinting and waving his sword, with Martel not far behind. From what Mabbut could see, the Norman would make it to the man before the man made it to the horse.

Ranulf stood observing all this with interest, his arms folded.

Five horses leapt away from the manor, the men on their backs casting some very rude words and gestures in Le Pedvin's direction as they headed off into the countryside.

Le Pedvin gave a cry of anguish and ran on. The last man out of the manor was now within reach. As Le Pedvin closed in, this wounded one – the one who had been swathed in bloody bandages from head to foot, well, mainly from head – turned to face the Norman.

Mabbut gasped as he thought there would be slaughter. Almost immediately and very bloody.

Le Pedvin raised his weapon above his head as he drew up to the Saxon and brought it down in a terrible, diagonal sweep, sure to cleave the man in two.

To Mabbut's surprise the wounded man ducked sideways and held out his hand. Into this a sword was thrown by the old man of the manor. It flashed in the air to clash against Le Pedvin's and strike the point of the Norman's sword to the ground.

Le Pedvin grunted, probably from anger and frustration. He swung his head back to avoid the attack from the Saxon sword that came back his way, and then got into his fighting stance.

Martel now drew alongside Le Pedvin, his own sword at the ready, pointing towards the Saxon.

'You'll never find him,' the Saxon taunted. The Saxon who seemed to have recovered from his horrible wounds very quickly.

Mabbut noticed that this clash had given the old man the time to get around the end of the manor, presumably to another horse.

'I will when I start sticking my knife in you and you tell me,' Le Pedvin growled.

'Ha!' The Saxon laughed and launched into an attack. His sword came forward from the left, but Le Pedvin parried it easily, flicking his opponent's blade upwards. At the top of the movement he brought his own sword down. Mabbut was sure the Saxon would be lost.

Martel stood ready to one side. Mabbut expected them both to pile in to finish off the Saxon in moments: perhaps Martel had a cunning plan. So cunning it didn't require him to move at all.

The Saxon brought his sword hand up and caught Le Pedvin's attack on the cross of his own weapon. With a very neat flick of the wrist, he bought his sword over on top of Le Pedvin's and drove the point to the ground again.

As he did so, he took half a step forward to bring his right foot down on Le Pedvin's blade. His clear intention was either to break it or to snap it from the Norman's grasp. Le Pedvin was too quick for this, though, and withdrew his weapon, forcing the Saxon to stamp down on thin air. He immediately leapt forward, planning to take the Saxon off balance and finish him.

Instead of withdrawing to a safe distance the Saxon carried on forward, using the momentum of his right foot to drive himself into Le Pedvin. He was too close to raise his sword, and too close for Le Pedvin to use his. Mabbut was very impressed when he noticed that in the same forward movement, the Saxon had drawn a nasty-looking dagger from his side. Now he held a sword in his left hand and a dagger in his right.

As he stepped forward, the Saxon dagger made a beeline for the ribs under Le Pedvin's left arm.

From somewhere, Le Pedvin had drawn his own short blade. He parried the incoming dagger while bringing his right hand up to strike the Saxon's head. Yet once more, instead of ducking back, the man came forward, driving his forehead into Le Pedvin's face.

Mabbut grimaced as he thought that hitting someone like that, when you already had a nasty eye wound of your own, was probably not very sensible. It then occurred to him to notice that both the Saxon's eyes seemed to be in perfect working order. It had all been a trick. Well, what about that then?

The contact proved most effective, and Le Pedvin staggered backwards. The Saxon took the moment immediately, raising his sword to dispatch Le Pedvin. As he brought it down it clashed against that of Martel, who had finally stepped into the fray.

The Saxon had to retreat and face Martel now, although the younger Norman didn't look very keen.

Le Pedvin recovered and stepped up, his sword looking as serious as his face, which now had a livid red mark on the forehead. Martel and Le Pedvin were ready for a simultaneous attack. Mabbut couldn't see how the Saxon could survive this.

Then there was a swishing sound in the air, followed by a thud. A large arrow buried itself in the ground at Le Pedvin's feet.

'I'm not such a good shot any more,' the old man called from the saddle of his horse, where he sat holding a massive long bow, already cocked with a fresh arrow, 'but I think I'll get you with the next one.'

Le Pedvin and Martel glared at this intervention. Meanwhile the fighting Saxon raised his sword at them both and turned to cross to the old man. The reins of a second horse were deftly wrapped around his right foot.

'Not going to finish us off, then?' Le Pedvin taunted.

'Of course not,' the old man replied. 'We're going to tell the country how stupid Duke William sent four men to find King Harold. How they couldn't manage it because he was hidden from their sight by God. How these men were led a merry dance around the English countryside, in entirely the wrong direction, and how they were defeated by one warrior and an old man. It'll make a marvellous tale.'

Le Pedvin's face couldn't get any more angry. But it did anyway.

'And we all know your Duke is as mad as a squirrel with only one nut – if we polish you off, he'd probably kill everyone north of Watford.' The Saxon swordsman was on his horse now, and the two men wheeled their mounts to ride away.

'I'll find you and kill you,' said Le Pedvin in all seriousness.

'Er, no and no,' the swordsman replied, 'not till you've had some more fighting lessons.' With a laugh the men urged their horses and were gone.

Le Pedvin picked up a small rock from the ground and threw it after them. More laughter bounced back, then faded.

◆　　◆　　◆

Le Pedvin and Martel stomped to where Ranulf and Mabbut stood.

'Now I'm really angry,' Le Pedvin announced. 'We find some proper horses and we get after them.'

'I didn't get a good look at them all – perhaps he's not with them?' Ranulf asked.

'If he's not with them, they know where he's gone. And I'm not sure I believe them anyway. They didn't have time to organise anything too complicated, and they've been running since the battle. Of course we've only got Martel's word the man was shot at all, and we all know how wrong Martel gets things.' He glared at Martel, who hastily examined his sword for dam-age –admittedly unlikely, considering how little use it had had. 'If they're a decoy,' Le Pedvin concluded, 'I'm a Breton pastry. And of course I hate them and really want to kill them anyway.'

He glared at everyone, daring anyone to speak.

Mabbut coughed.

'What?' Le Pedvin demanded.

The Saxon had a very puzzled look on his face, built on a solid foundation of confusion. 'Harold?' he echoed. 'We're chas-ing King Harold? But I thought he was dead ...'

Chapter 24
The Advantages of Being a Filth-man

IWARD'S SNEAKING PAST hostage-slicers and guards was actually quite good. All those years as a filth-man, when no one wanted to know what he did, let alone see him doing it, stood him in good stead.

In his brighter moments, Siward liked to think he had some secret quality of invisibility. He could walk through the village, stand in the tavern or eavesdrop some conversation without anyone noticing he was there.

In his darker moments he thought everyone deliberately ignored him because he was widely disliked. They only tolerated him because he did all the things no one else was prepared to contemplate.

This situation would be a good test, but of course it was also madness. Sneaking around the home of someone who took – and sliced – hostages as a profession must surely rank among the most stupid things he had ever done. And Siward had done a lot of stupid things.

Running away from Vikings who were locked in a cell appeared to be a much more sensible step. He could vanish into the countryside and probably live a long life, hiding from anyone who came near and not letting anyone know who he was.

Siward reflected. He decided he'd give the sneaking a go but, if it got too dangerous and looked like it wasn't going to work, he'd revert to running away and hiding. No harm in having an escape plan.

The first sneak, from the window of the cell to the front of

Thorold's place, was easy. There was absolutely no one about to sneak past.

The building itself was not a large hall, but it was big enough to have several separate rooms on the ground floor. This was rather unusual in Siward's experience, admittedly very limited as people with large halls tended not to let him in. The place was made of timbers, but they were solid, well-made timbers, each one being the best part of a whole tree. In places the gaps between the timbers were filled with brick, rather than twigs and mud, while the floor was made of solid stone flags. It had clearly been the substantial building of a wealthy person – someone so wealthy he could afford his own dungeon.

Siward considered his surroundings. Above his head, the upper storey glowered over him, being wider than the ground floor. At least it provided some cover, he thought. He still thought night-time was best for sneaking, but knew if he didn't get back to the Vikings soon they'd assume he'd run off anyway.

At the entrance to the place, two of Thorold's men stood, loitering rather than guarding. Siward frowned at them, thinking that this place really shouldn't warrant guards who patrolled up and down and the like. They were pretty much in the middle of nowhere, after all, and could see who was coming. And anyone who'd already arrived would be locked up safe and sound in the dungeon. Unless they were being sliced.

He lay flat on the ground and peered around the corner, keeping a wary eye on the men. Even if they looked his way, they might not notice a head on the floor.

After a few moments there was a shout from inside the building. It was not a cry of alarm at Siward's escape, but just the routine complaint of someone who had found some job not done, or at least not done properly. The two men at the door exchanged resigned shrugs and scowls. Slowly they ambled back into the building to do again whatever it was they should have done right the first time.

Siward seized the moment, immediately continuing his expedition as far as the main door. He peered around this in time to see the guards disappearing through the interior somewhere.

As he looked in, he could see that the inner hall, where they'd been accosted and tied up, was deserted. Cautiously he entered and tiptoed towards the doors, which opened to left and right. They had been taken through the left-hand door, along a corridor and then down steps to the dungeon. That was clearly the door he had to use, but there were voices coming from behind it.

They were muffled in conversation rather than the exchanges of people who were walking along, about to open the door. Or so Siward hoped. Keeping perfectly still, and even holding his breath to make sure he could hear clearly, he confirmed that there were no footsteps. Then, stepping very gingerly forward, he put his ear gently to the door to see if he could make out what was going on.

He could only catch the odd word, but it all sounded very dull. A couple of men seemed to be moaning about everything. The words weather, pay, food and Thorold drifted through the wood. None of them were dressed in happy tones.

Siward was worried that this tedious exchange had the potential to go on for hours. Perhaps these men were the dungeon guards, and would stay in position until they were relieved. He was sure they were quite capable of moaning all day if they had to. Something had to be done.

He wondered about making a noise to draw them from their stations, but decided against it. He only had the outside and the other door to run to and neither of them seemed safe. So he crept carefully back and headed to the other door to see what he could discover there. Perhaps there was another way down to the dungeon, which avoided going past the guards.

If there was, he conceded, it would be a pretty poor design for a dungeon – but time was ticking by, and he couldn't think of anything else.

The other door was silent when Siward pressed his ear against it. Very slowly he pushed it open and poked his head around, prepared to draw back instantly if there was anything horrible behind it. Which there was.

The room was small, more like a cupboard than a room, and it was occupied.

'Where *have* you been?' a large man demanded as he saw Siward's face. He was not someone Siward recognised, but he must be one of Thorold's retinue. He got to see rather more than he wanted as the man was pulling his breeches back up from where they had been resting around his ankles.

'You can take it away now.' The man gestured to the leathern bucket that sat alone, steaming, on the floor. He pushed past Siward and left the room.

'Right away,' Siward replied as the man passed, recognising the situation immediately. Once a filth-man, always a filth-man. Perhaps he really was invisible. Even if he had no idea who the big man was, he knew what he'd done and what was expected.

Picking up the bucket, from which came the sort of smell that had tales told about it, Siward backed out of the room. A fresh opportunity in his hands. Too fresh for many, true, but Siward was made of sterner stuff.

He crossed the entrance. After taking a deep breath, not to avoid the smell because he was used to that sort of thing, but to gather his courage, he pushed confidently through the other door.

The room was indeed the corridor to the dungeon, and two of Thorold's men were standing guard. They looked up with little interest as Siward entered.

'Filth-man,' Siward announced, holding out his bucket for them to see. He held his head down slightly to avoid recognition, but, as expected, the last thing anyone wanted to do was look a filth-man in the eye.

'All right, all right, we don't want a sample,' one of the guards snapped at him. 'Get on with it.' He gestured that Siward should move on down the corridor. Move on as quickly as possible, taking his foul bucket with him.

'Filth-man, filth-man,' Siward continued to call as he walked on to the steps that led down to the dungeon.

'Any filth today?' he called loudly to the Vikings in their cell.

They looked out through the small, barred opening in the wooden door and gave him a very unnecessary look. Then they recognised who it was.

Siward put the bucket down and reached for the bar that was slotted across the door to the dungeon.

'Oh, that's a lovely lot of filth, gentlemen,' Siward called loudly, for the benefit of the guards. He beckoned the Vikings to exit.

As they did so, Erik turned to the old man in the cell, who was still sitting in his corner, laughing his hysterical cackle at events.

'Are you coming?' the Viking asked.

The old man looked at him as if realising only now that the door was open. He stood up very sombrely, brushed his rags with his hands and stepped forward. 'Thanks very much,' he said, with apparent sanity.

The Vikings, exchanging looks of bewildered disinterest, joined Siward outside the cell, frowning in obvious disgust at the bucket's contents. He leant in close and whispered fiercely, 'There are two of them in the corridor. After that it's clear.'

Erik nodded to Sigmund, indicating that he should go and deal with the two in the corridor.

The young Viking hurriedly and happily went to do so, casting anxious glances back at the bucket, as if it was going to follow him.

While Vikings, old man and Siward with his bucket of filth waited, a cry of 'Oy' came down the steps to their ears. This was followed by some muffled struggling and a couple of thuds as Sigmund did what he did best.

'You can leave that behind,' Erik instructed as they started to leave and Siward, out of habit, bent to pick up his bucket.

'Oh, right.' Siward felt very uncomfortable at leaving a bucket of filth un-managed. But being left behind to be sliced was worse.

◆　　◆　　◆

The group climbed the steps and along the corridor to the sleeping guards. Fregurd and Sigmund relocated the men to their own dungeon, having stripped them of their weapons, and returned to Erik and Siward.

Once more Siward listened carefully at the door. 'Can't hear anything,' he said quietly.

'So?' said Erik. Subtlety was not the Viking's strong suit. He barged through the door and out into the entrance hall.

Fortunately the space was still deserted, and Erik did exercise some discretion as he looked cautiously round the door to the outside. Just at that moment one of Thorold's men appeared. He gaped in horror at the sight of a massive Viking emerging from the building.

This fellow was clearly not a Viking as he was neither tall nor powerful – nor eager to engage in a noble fight to the death. Despite the fact the man had a sword at his side, he surrendered instantly. Erik dispatched him to the cell to join the others, taking the sword for his own.

'Where's the old man gone?' Siward asked, looking around as Fregurd and Sigmund returned from making another deposit in the dungeon.

'Run off if he's got any sense,' said Erik briskly. He stepped outside and surveyed the place.

There were only a few scattered buildings of various construction nearby. People of various condition sat chatting in doorways, or carrying out their daily tasks. They clearly weren't Thorold's men, and showed not the least interest in a bunch of Vikings making an escape.

'Back to the gate,' Erik instructed.

'Won't Thorold just get us again?' Siward asked. He had been thinking. 'I mean, he spotted us coming a mile away — surely he'll spot us leaving a mile away as well? He'll just send some more men and we'll be back in the dungeon. Well, you will. I'll probably be somewhere else all together. In bits.'

'Hmm.' The Viking seemed to be giving Siward some serious consideration for once. 'I like your thinking.'

Siward tried a knowing smile of acknowledgment. It came out as a sort of constipated smirk, but it made him feel good.

'You mean we should take on Thorold's men and harry him to his highest tower before skewering him on a mighty blade?'

'Er …' That wasn't what Siward meant at all. It was very far from what Siward meant. But he didn't like to say so.

Fregurd and Sigmund seemed taken with the idea as well, and directed approving nods towards Siward. He didn't like to admit that he'd actually been thinking about hiding until dark, then sneaking away before anyone noticed.

'And if we fail it will make a great tale,' Erik nodded, his mind clearly made up.

'Oh, but what about Harold?' Siward tried to sound regretful that something had come up to ruin his exciting plan for a fight to the death. Momentarily he thought it might be quite nice to be mentioned in a Viking saga. Then he reflected that it would be much nicer to stay alive instead.

'What about him?'

'If we were to fail, who could rescue Harold?'

'Ah.' Erik paused in thought, and nodded these thoughts

through his head. Fregurd and Sigmund looked on, their faces displaying their low opinions of running away from a fight.

The leader came to a swift conclusion. 'We won't fail,' he declared, hefting the stolen sword. He hefted it in a very disappointed manner, as if wondering why he'd been given a toy instead of a real blade.

'Aha ...' Siward tried to sound enthusiastic, but it didn't come out that way at all. His spirits quietly sank.

◆   ◆   ◆

Striding off into the town, the Vikings scanned the place, looking for someone to fight.

'Where is Thorold?' Siward asked.

'Probably indoors, writing ransom demands,' Erik snorted.

'And his men?'

'Skiving somewhere – the lazy bunch of good for nothing seagull droppings.'

Suddenly, as they rounded one building, a group of lazy, good for nothing seagull droppings stood in their way. Siward quickly counted ten of them. Even accounting for laziness and being good for nothing, Siward thought their chances of beating three Vikings were on the good side. They all drew their feeble Saxon swords.

'Going somewhere?' the leader of the group asked.

Siward would have replied, 'No, nowhere at all really, just out for a stroll. We were looking for the dungeon actually.' Buying time was always a good plan, he thought.

'Yes, we're going through your guts until we get to the head of your traitorous master, which we will slice off,' Erik replied. He didn't do buying time. Instead he yelled these last words in good Viking fashion.

'I don't think so,' retorted the Saxon. Siward believed him.

As a group, the ten men took a step forward and brandished their weapons.

The Vikings adopted defensive stances and waited for the onslaught.

Siward looked around rapidly, before Fregurd noticed he had no weapon and handed him a spare knife.

'It's only The Young Butcher, but it might give someone a nasty nick.' The Viking shrugged apologetically. 'In the right hands,' he added, clearly understanding that Siward's were not the right hands. Siward took it, trying to look grateful.

The men advanced one more step, clearly intending that the charge would come next.

'Pursold Branner, what do you think you are doing?' A well-spoken Saxon voice boomed out.

The ten men paused, and the Vikings looked round.

The old man from the cell strode into the middle of the about-to-be-battle. He looked a lot less mad and, even though he was still in his rags, he appeared to be in charge.

The Saxon leader looked very embarrassed. He half tried to hide his sword behind his back, like a child caught with an apron full of apples.

'Oh, er,' he mumbled.

'Oh, er, my lord,' the old man corrected him.

The Saxon head went down.

'And as for you lot ...' The old man had reached the line now and surveyed them all. 'Durnt Pollard, is that you?' He looked pointedly at one of the Saxons, who started carefully to examine his shoes. 'Does your mother know you're out here?'

The Saxon mumbled.

'I can't hear you?'

'No, er, no, my lord,' the man said. He was still fascinated by the ground, even moving some dirt about with the point of his boot.

'I am absolutely ashamed of the lot of you,' the old man said as he strode up and down in front of the men now. He didn't raise his voice, he didn't hit anyone or even go anywhere near them. He had presence though. The whole fighting force had collapsed into an embarrassed bunch of small boys.

'I know every one of you and I have made a note,' the man made it very clear. 'If I have any more out of any of you, there will be real trouble. Am I understood?'

The erstwhile fighting force nodded and mumbled agreeably at being let off with such a light punishment.

'Am I understood?' the man repeated.

'Yes, my lord,' the group answered in a very ramshackle manner.

'Right. Now back to your homes. Leave your weapons behind and we'll sort things out after we've dealt with this Thorold chap.'

The small Saxon army disbanded rapidly, the clattering of swords on the ground marking their departure.

Siward and the Vikings looked on in wonder and sheathed their own weapons. Siward was going to keep the dagger as a souvenir of the great battle where, with only three Vikings in support, he had fought off the combined forces of a Danish warlord. Fregurd held his hand out and took The Young Butcher back. He clearly didn't want to leave even the minor members of his family in the care of the incompetent.

'We'd have managed,' Erik said gruffly.

'Of course you would,' the old man said, approaching the group. 'I didn't doubt it for a moment. But these are my men. They served me for many years before the wretched Thorold turned up. It would have been remiss of me to let you kill them all.'

Erik shrugged that this was probably reasonable.

'So you're the true lord of this place?' Siward asked.

'I am indeed, Kenrick Baston at your service, usurped by that wretch Thorold, but only temporarily. First he took me captive for ransom, then he decided to take the whole place. Sorry about all that strange behaviour in the cell, but you do look more like

272

his friends than mine. I shall have great pleasure removing him. With your help?'

'Of course, of course,' Erik agreed, 'only too glad. But we need to get on with it. We were in the middle of a mission ourselves, before we got diverted.'

'Rescuing Harold?' Kenrick asked.

'How did you ...?' Siward began.

'The King left word when he passed through a few weeks ago. Look out for Vikings coming from the north if things go badly. Seemed a strange thing to say at the time, but it makes sense now. I assume things went badly? That might be what gave Thorold the courage to attack.'

Nobody answered him, but the assumption was accepted.

'I must confess I thought there might be rather more of you.' Kenrick looked admiringly at the Vikings, but clearly thought three was rather a small force.

'Just here to get Harold away,' Erik explained. 'What happens after that ...' He raised his shoulders in an empty shrug which said he had no idea what happened after that.

'So Duke William will be our king,' Kenrick speculated.

Again nobody said anything, and a gloomy silence fell. Eventually it was broken by Baston. 'I'd better pack,' he said.

Chapter 25
To Horse ... and Cart

ELL, I WON'T HAVE ANYTHING TO DO WITH IT,' Mabbut said in his best huff. 'I'd rather die than help you hunt down King Harold.'

'All right,' said Le Pedvin, drawing his sword.

'Now, just a minute.' Mabbut held his hands up in protest.

'I thought not,' Le Pedvin said with some disappointment as he put the sword away again. 'You two wait here,' he said to Ranulf and Mabbut. 'Martel, come with me. There must be some horses here somewhere. If we carry on with our stupid beasts, that bunch will be gone before we've got speed up.'

The two soldiers strode off around the side of the manor to see if they could find faster transport.

'Are you telling me that ever since we left Senlac Hill we've been looking for Harold?' Mabbut directed his puzzlement to Ranulf.

'Of course we have,' Ranulf replied. 'You don't seriously think four men would be sent into enemy territory just to have a look round?'

'And you all knew about this?' Mabbut seemed more offended that he'd been kept in the dark than at being expected to hunt down his own king.

'Absolutely.' Ranulf dismissed this with a wave.

'But ...' said Mabbut and stopped. There were too many 'buts'. Unsure which one to let out first, he went for the crux of the matter. 'I thought Harold died at Senlac,' he repeated. 'That's what everyone said.'

'Well, that's good isn't it? Can't have the conquered people believing their leader is still alive.'

'But,' said Mabbut again, 'if our leader isn't dead we're not really conquered, are we?'

'Details,' Ranulf shrugged. He was contemptuous, as usual. 'When all your fighting men are dead, you're usually conquered. Doesn't really matter if one man is left standing.'

'It does when he's the King,' Mabbut insisted, starting to realise the depth of the problem. Problem as far as the Normans were concerned, that is. 'If Harold is still alive, he can rally more men and drive you from our shores.' He was very enthusiastic about this option.

'Highly unlikely,' Ranulf scoffed.

'Then why did William send us out to find him as soon as the battle had finished? Probably when he realised Harold wasn't dead. He knew it was urgent.' Mabbut felt quite proud of himself as all of this sank in and he started to relish the nuances of a delicate diplomatic situation. The Norman Duke hadn't, in fact stuck a sword, or an arrow, or anything much in his opponent. That meant the Duke was still only a duke, and the King was still the King.

'And William couldn't send his whole force out to chase Harold as that would give the game away.' Mabbut folded his arms in satisfaction, both at his ability in deducing this all by himself, and at the awkward spot it left the Normans in.

'Very good,' Ranulf acknowledged. 'Would you prefer Le Pedvin to kill you now or later?'

'Eh?'

'Well, now you're aware of the situation we can't possibly let you go round talking to anyone else about it. I think Le Pedvin really wants to kill you anyway.' Ranulf sounded almost cheerful at the prospect.

'There's hardly anyone I can talk to, is there?' Mabbut protested. He really didn't know what to do. If they did find Harold, should he throw himself in front of Le Pedvin's sword? Should he cower in the face of the inevitable and betray his King? Should he just run away now? He thought he could beat Ranulf in a straight race ...

◆　　◆　　◆

The decision was taken from him as Le Pedvin and Martel returned. They were seated on a couple of old, ragged-looking horses, and were pulling two more by the reins.

It was not a promising sight. The Normans' mounts looked like they could manage a gentle stroll around the manor at best. The two for Ranulf and Mabbut wouldn't even get half way round.

'We're hardly going to catch Saxons on fresh horses with this lot,' Ranulf observed, with his usual disparaging glance. 'They're no better than the ponies.'

'These were the best,' Martel replied simply. 'You should have seen the others.' He gently urged his mount on. Very gently, in case it collapsed under him.

Each horse had a simple blanket over its back for a saddle and as soon as the beasts came to a halt they dropped their heads – not to graze the sparse grass, but seemingly because they didn't have the strength to hold them up.

Mabbut's time in Normandy had at least given him some skill with horses and he mounted with little difficulty. It helped that the back was pretty close to the ground to begin with. He wasn't sure whether this beast was a large pony, or a horse that had shrunk with age. He was alarmed when the thing sagged even further as he settled himself in.

With Ranulf mounted as well, the group set off. Mabbut considered digging his heels into his horse's flank to make it move, but thought that might prove a death-blow. He gently thrust himself forward, hoping that the animal would get the idea.

It did, but its idea was to walk forward a bit more slowly than Mabbut could have managed on his own.

Martel reached over and slapped Mabbut's beast on the rump. This did make it step up into a half-hearted trot, but Mabbut could feel the resentment coming up through his legs. The resentment combined with a clear message that this pace would not last long.

Ranulf was not doing much better. The whole contingent managed a fast walking pace as they took after the fleeing band.

'This is pointless,' Ranulf concluded as his horse tripped on a just-above-average height tuft of grass. 'We might as well put these nags on our backs. We'd go quicker.'

He had a point. Even Le Pedvin seemed to accept it as he drew to a halt. He was clearly accepting it very badly, though, as his fists were clenched and he was swearing loudly at the sky.

'We could go back and get the ponies?' Mabbut offered.

He received a Le Pedvin glare for this suggestion.

'Where will they be going?' he demanded of Mabbut.

'Looks like they're headed north again,' the Saxon responded. 'So the next place would be Wisbech.'

'And is there a short cut?'

'A what?'

'A shorter way? They'll be taking the main track with horses – can we cut across country to catch up?'

'Er, no,' said Mabbut, not understanding why there would a shorter way from A to B than the way from A to B.

'Wretched country,' Le Pedvin spat on the ground. He raised himself as high as he could on his collapsing steed and scanned the countryside. 'There!' he cried calling out and pointing to his right. 'Go that way.' He wheeled his animal around and the others followed suit. Apart from Mabbut, whose horse wasn't able to do turns.

Eventually his mount was persuaded to move forwards with a slight preference for the right, and he circled slowly round.

By the time he joined up with the Normans they had taken charge of a hay cart, being pulled by a much more likely beast. The owner of the cart had been unceremoniously dumped at the road side. Martel and Le Pedvin were in the back of the vehicle, dumping the load.

The owner was gesticulating and swearing and stamping his feet, but it seemed clear that he had been shown Le Pedvin's sword and had chosen life over property.

'What's a hay cart doing with such a good horse?' Mabbut asked as he rode up on what were plainly his own animal's last legs.

'Who cares?' Le Pedvin answered, tossing off the last of the hay. 'Ask him if you like, but he seems a bit cross at the moment. Still alive, but cross.'

Mabbut shrugged sympathy to the Saxon by the road. He received a very rude gesture in return.

'Everyone on,' Le Pedvin called as the cart was cleared of its load.

Martel hopped on to the cart. Ranulf climbed ponderously in, casting disdainful glances at the construction of the body and the circularity of the wheels, or rather the lack of it.

Mabbut stood by the side of the cart. 'What do you need me for? Now I know you're following Harold and you know the way to go? I might as well stay here.'

'You might have some conceivable use,' said Le Pedvin without enthusiasm, 'you never know. It's up to you, though.'

Mabbut's heart rose at this, even though he knew Le Pedvin's next comment would be something about killing and death.

'I can kill you here and now, or you can come with us and I'll do it later.'

Mabbut climbed aboard.

◆   ◆   ◆

The horse in the yoke of the cart was easily persuaded to move off at a pretty decent trot. Rather than being half way to the great grazing in the sky, this animal behaved as if it had been held back all its life. The group bounced and battered along what passed for a track, the uneven wheels of the vehicle finding their match in the surface of the road.

Mabbut clung to the sides, just about keeping a grip at the back. Ranulf was in a similar plight. Martel was towards the front, just behind Le Pedvin who sat on the simple seat, the reins of the horse in his hands.

'This is good,' Le Pedvin called and turned to encourage his passengers.

Mabbut noticed the man was smiling, actually smiling. First time for everything, he supposed. It wasn't a nice smile, needless to say. It wasn't comforting or gentle, warming or filled with charm. It was rather disturbing and most closely resembled one of the old horses making a desperate, wide-eyed whinny, before finally passing on.

Le Pedvin's teeth were bared and his eyes were wide. A smattering of froth around the mouth would have completed the picture. Mabbut shivered.

'What are you going to do if we catch them?' He called over the clattering of the cart.

'*When* we catch them,' Le Pedvin cried, in a very decent impression of a maniac.

'All right, *when* we catch them. What are you going to do?'

'What do you think we're going to do, Saxon? We're going to find out where Harold is, if he isn't one of them.'

'One of them?' Mabbut was lost again. 'The man with the eye wound turned out not to be wounded at all and they said Harold had gone in another direction completely.'

'And what were they likely to say?'

'Er.' Mabbut had no idea what they were likely to say. This whole situation was beyond him. First a shattering defeat at Senlac, then a pointless survey, then not a survey and not entirely a defeat, or so it seemed. He'd given up trying to understand what was going on.

'I didn't look at the other men,' Le Pedvin explained. 'One of them could have been Harold. The one with the so-called wound was just there to take my attention. They knew they were being chased, and they knew they'd been caught. What would you do?'

'Er.' Mabbut offered again.

'Of course,' Le Pedvin nodded. 'You're an idiot, you wouldn't have a clue what to do.'

Mabbut could only shrug at this.

'If you were protecting someone, you'd distract attention, give them a chance to get away. You'd hold off the enemy as long as you could while the important one was quietly removed.'

'I would,' Mabbut confirmed.

'Ha,' Le Pedvin's snort said he didn't really believe this. 'So it could be that one of their number really was Harold. Swapped places, and bandages with one of the others, and left as soon as I'd taken the man with the bandage.'

'Clever,' said Mabbut.

Le Pedvin's familiar scowl returned. It was almost reassuring after his smile.

'Maybe Harold really did go in another direction?' Mabbut suggested. 'This whole group might really be a distraction, and not have him with them at all.'

'Could be,' Le Pedvin acknowledged. 'In which case I'll just do them some damage until they tell me where he is.'

'Didn't have much luck with that approach last time,' Mabbut said pointedly, then realised he should have kept his mouth shut.

'Ah, but we'll be better prepared this time. We'll know what to expect. We know one of them is handy with a sword and one's got a bow. And Martel here will step up bit bloody smarter than he did before.' At this Le Pedvin reached back and slapped Martel heartily on the back. It was more slap than heart, but

Martel tried to grin in an enthusiastic sort of way.

'And of course we can use you as a shield.'

'Thank you very much.'

'No problem. 'Course they'll probably shoot you without a moment's hesitation, but it might give us a chance to get at them.'

'Glad to be of use.' Mabbut glared at the back of Le Pedvin's head.

He had seen that the Saxon entourage was a pretty effective fighting force. The one man with the sword had been Le Pedvin's match, while that chap with the bow looked like he could do some serious damage. And of course if Harold was with them, they would put up a good fight. Even if he wasn't, Mabbut suspected they could handle Le Pedvin and particularly Martel, who seemed happiest standing to the side and watching the fighting. And he couldn't see Ranulf making a useful contribution, unless Normans in a fight were inspired by sarcasm.

And of course in the face of superior forces Le Pedvin would just pile in anyway, being as mad as his Duke.

Mabbut's choice was clear. If they did catch up with the Saxons, if they engaged them in any way, whether Harold was with them or not, Mabbut would immediately switch sides. The more he thought about this idea, the more he liked it. He would join his king, he would be back with his beloved Saxons and he would ride off, defender of the land and opponent of the hated Normans. Le Pedvin especially.

If he followed this path there was also a much better chance of staying alive.

'And if you're contemplating joining your little friends when we get there,' Le Pedvin called happily, 'I really will kill you. Probably stabbed in the back. I'm very handy with a throwing knife.'

Mabbut said nothing, but smiled inwardly, very content with his plan. If there was one thing living in and around the Norman court had taught him, it was how – and when – to duck.

Chapter 26

The Very Short Battle of Spalding

HE BATTLE TO REMOVE THE USURPER Thorold from his stronghold proved a great disappointment.

Once they had recovered their precious weapons, and Fregurd had counted all his knives, comforting them after their horrible experience, they started the search for the Hostageslicer.

It turned out he had three or four of his own men with him, one of whom must have reported events to their leader. By the time Erik, Fregurd and Sigmund advanced on the main hall, with Siward and Kenrick supporting the rear, Thorold and his very diminished forces would have been heading for the hills, if there were any hills around here. Instead they were making swift progress away from the town and into the heart of the wetlands.

'Probably got a boat out there somewhere,' Erik commented from the roof of the Manor. The Vikings and Siward had climbed up to look for the retreating Thorold, rushing through the rushes of the wetlands.

The Viking was clearly disappointed that he had not engaged Thorold in an honest fight. He was almost apologetic that his fellow Viking had run off, instead of doing the decent thing, which was to stay here and die. Preferably horribly.

'No honour,' Erik concluded as they came down and searched the inside of the house, confirming it was empty.

'Awful that, isn't it?' Fregurd commented. 'No honour and not dead. Far better to have honour and be dead, eh, Erik?'

'Of course,' Erik answered simply.

'What do we do now?' Siward asked. He was secretly very content that Thorold had chosen to run off and leave his honour behind. Sensible chap.

'We must get back on the trail.' Erik drew himself up to his full, honourable height. 'This has been a distraction. For all we know, we could have missed Harold while we've been holed up here.'

'I can speed you on your way,' Kenrick offered. 'It is a great mission that you are on and I wish you God speed. I shall put the finest horses in my stable at your disposal.' He clapped and rubbed his hands together, clearly happy at being back in charge and able to take some action.

'Ah,' said Erik. 'Horses eh?' He didn't sound very keen.

Fregurd looked up from where he was idly comparing Kidney Finder with The Silencer to see which one he liked best 'Erik doesn't do horses,' he explained.

'Doesn't do …?' Kenrick didn't understand.

'We're Vikings, man,' Erik growled, mostly to himself.

'Seafaring folk,' Fregurd explained, 'used to lots of boats. And then when we're at home there's lots of snow and mountains. Very steep mountains. Not much call for horses.'

'But they will speed you on your way,' the reinstated lord of the manor explained.

'Certainly will,' Fregurd agreed, 'but only if we can get on to them.'

'Well …' Kenrick began.

'And it's the getting on the horse that's the problem. Then there's the staying on, and the making the beast go where you want it to go, rather than where it wants to go. Then there's making it stop, tying it up, feeding it. All terribly complicated, eh, Erik?' Fregurd said this last with a laugh. 'Oh, and apparently they look at you funny,' he added.

Erik just growled some more.

'Perhaps if we put some honour on the horse's back first you'd get on. Ha ha.'

'I was going to say,' Kenrick interrupted.

'What?'

'It's about the horses.'

'What about them, are they big and fierce?' Fregurd was enjoying himself. His knives were flickering with the fun too.

'No,' the Saxon said cautiously, 'it's just that there's only two of them.'

That stopped the conversation.

'Two?' Fregurd checked.

Kenrick nodded.

'How are we supposed to ride at God speed and good luck and all that if there's only two horses for four people?'

'They're very expensive things,' the lord complained. 'Like you said, there's feeding them and all. And then they need stables and people to look after them. You can't justify that sort of expense if you've really got no use for them. Oxen plough the fields and we just use the horses for emergencies.'

'Horses for emergencies.' Fregurd wasn't impressed.

'We'd better go on foot then.' Erik had brightened considerably. 'We can run for many miles before we need rest.'

Maybe you can, Siward thought to himself.

Fregurd studied the Saxon noble with some contempt.

The noble looked at them all one by one, rather crestfallen that his enthusiasm had come to nothing. 'Ah!' he cried out after a moment's silence.

'What?' Siward, feeling nervous, almost jumped out of his boots.

Kenrick's face had regained its energy as he announced the solution to the problem. 'I've got a cart.'

◆　　◆　　◆

'Vikings do not do carts,' Erik complained as they bounced on down the road out of Spalding. At least they bounced in a reasonably solid farm cart, pulled by two strong and healthy horses. Horses that looked like they were trying to get away from the cart as quickly as possible.

'Oh, shut up, Erik,' Fregurd instructed. 'We're getting off after Harold, aren't we? We're travelling faster than we could run, and we're not sitting on top of a horse.'

Erik sat at the bottom of the cart, holding on to avoid being thrown about against the inside, and frowned his frown.

Siward was finding the ride uncomfortable and worrying. The bumps and ruts in the road tossed them around like turnips bouncing down a hill. He thought he was going to be hurled out of the cart completely at any moment, and would be left behind on the road. He didn't mind being left behind at all; it was the landing on the road that worried him.

Sigmund was standing up at the front, next to Fregurd who was holding the reins. The younger Viking looked like he was having the time of his life. He grinned and bounced around, only holding on with one hand.

Just to make the journey even more memorable, Siward was now starting to feel sick.

Just to make it truly memorable for everyone, he *was* sick.

'Do you mind?' Fregurd asked, turning back at the sound.

As he wiped his mouth, Siward imagined Vikings saw a lot of this in their longships. He then imagined the longships bobbing up and down in the great northern sea. They might be long, but the ones he'd seen were pretty narrow and looked positively dangerous. The thought brought more of his stomach contents to the surface.

'Too much roe deer,' Siward apologised as parts of the animal re-emerged and were hurled back towards the woodland.

The Vikings did not reply. It began to rain again.

◆　　◆　　◆

The cart clattered on and its occupants bounced about, variously enjoying the experience, tolerating it or cleaning themselves up.

285

The road was relatively straight, if not very even, and they were clearly heading south. The sun actually peeked between the rain clouds now and again, although it was pretty soon put in its place.

'Where are we?' Erik asked.

Siward waited for Fregurd, who was, after all, driving the cart, to answer.

'You, Saxon, where are we?' Erik made his demand clear.

'Oh ...' Siward looked about vaguely, partly in hope that Fregurd would answer the question if given the opportunity, and partly in hope that if he left it long enough it would simply go away.

'Well?' It wasn't going away.

Siward scrabbled around in the bottom of the cart, avoiding the patches of his previous meal, and peered over at the surrounding countryside.

He saw a landscape that was universally flat and universally wet. The road they were on seemed to float on the surface of something that was on its way from being land to being water, or vice versa.

'The wetlands,' he announced confidently.

'Very informative,' Fregurd commented from his place at the front.

'Which bit of the wetlands?' Erik pressed.

'Oh, right,' Siward stalled. 'Which bit? Well, let me see.'

He peered out again, scanning their surroundings for some landmark or other. This was a pretty fruitless task as there wasn't even much land.

What he did see was another traveller on the road. This appeared to be a lone man, his back loaded high with kindling. Whoever this fellow was, he must have travelled miles from this place to find any kindling.

'We can ask this chap,' Siward suggested.

'So you don't know?' Erik did not sound happy.

'Well, I know generally,' Siward tried to make this sound as blindingly obvious as he could. 'The local will be able to give us the exact location, that's all.'

'You'll do,' said Erik coldly. 'Otherwise what use are you?'

Siward frowned, puzzled. Here was a perfectly good local almost right in front of them. The man was so laden with wood he was hardly going to run away.

'What's wrong with stopping and asking?' Siward protested.

'We don't need to,' Erik said pointedly, 'because we've got you to show us the way. You're the Saxon.'

'But I'm a long way from home now. If we just stopped and asked ...'

'We are not stopping and asking.' Erik was very clear.

'But ...'

'Vikings do not stop and ask.'

'You asked me.'

'That was bad enough. We're not doing it twice.'

Siward really didn't know what to say. They were on a mission to rescue a king from a battle, to save a man's life and possibly a whole land from the ravages of an invader. It was a do-or-die task, one in which all their lives could be forfeit if it went wrong. And there was a problem about stopping and asking the way?

As the cart approached the man with his kindling Erik glared at Siward, daring him to speak.

'You,' Fregurd called from the front of the cart.

The man under the woodpile grunted an acknowledgement, but didn't stop. It was likely that if he did, he would fall over.

'Where are we?' Fregurd asked. 'What's the name of this place?'

Erik raised his arms in despair at this breaking of his clear instruction and slumped back in the cart for a bit of a sulk.

The kindling stopped moving and a head with old and experienced eyes peered out from under the load. They appraised the cart and its occupants. 'England,' the old voice replied. 'The Danelaw bit.'

'Yes, we know that much,' Fregurd responded with a hint of menace – a hint that suggested he could set light to the kindling with the old and experienced eyes still in there. 'Which particular bit?'

'Wetlands,' responded the wood pile on top of a man.

Fregurd reached for Eye Extractor, which was always handy in situations like this.

'Is Wisbech far?' Erik reluctantly called from his hiding place.

''Bout ten miles,' the mobile kindling replied. It moved away deftly from the back of the cart, heading off to wherever it was taking itself.

◆   ◆   ◆

Siward wondered, as he watched the man go, how far the fellow would have to travel before he found a spot dry enough to put his kindling down.

'What's the significance of Wisbech?' Siward asked.

'It was one of the places Harold mentioned in his message on the bird. Half a dozen names of places he said he'd make for. Started at Senlac and ended at Lincoln. He never made it that far, clearly. Plus it's on the River Nene.'

'Must've been a big bird,' Siward speculated, wondering how heavy this message had been.

Erik gave Siward a very funny look indeed; Siward couldn't make out whether it was disappointment or disgust. He certainly wasn't amused.

'I'm not sure you're involved in this mission any more,' the Viking rumbled. 'Don't know where we are, don't know the way? That's the only reason you're here in the first place. I reckon we should throw you off here.'

Siward looked out and thought this was a very bad place to be thrown off. He could obviously follow the man with the wood, but for all he knew the kindling could still be days from its destination.

'Yes,' Erik had come to some conclusion. 'We kill you and throw you off here. Fregurd, pass me your number one gutting knife; there's no room for a sword back here.'

'Wait a minute!' Siward cried out in alarm. 'You can't kill me.'

'I can,' said Erik crossly, as if his prowess at killing small, unarmed men was being questioned.

'But, but, but,' Siward butted, 'you still need me.'

'Er.' Erik thought for a moment. 'No, I don't think we do.'

'When you find Harold, you'll need me. I'm Saxon, I can explain what's going on.'

'Harold will know what's going on,' Erik explained as if to an idiot. 'He sent the bird in the first place, remember?'

'But he won't know you're the ones who got the bird. You could just be your average pillaging Vikings, out for a bit of, er …' Siward searched for the right word. 'Pillage. If he sees three Vikings coming his way, in this part of the country, he's likely to shoot first and not ask any questions at all. If you've got a *Saxon* with you, though …'

'What if we've got a Saxon with us?'

'He'll think you're safe. He won't shoot until he's at least had a conversation.'

Erik frowned. He was thinking hard as Fregurd held out the chosen knife. It was good old Wolf Widener, not the number one gutting knife; that was far too domestic for a job like this. The others would get jealous. 'Go on,' Fregurd urged. 'I'm sure we can sort it out with Harold.' Erik did not take the knife. 'I'll do it if you like,' Fregurd offered, taking his hands completely off the reins as the cart bounced around. This caused Erik a lot more worry than the prospect of killing an unarmed Saxon.

'He could be right,' Erik said quickly, casting his eyes at the reins.

Siward sighed.

'Oh, go on, let me,' Fregurd urged. The gleam in his eye matched that on the blade.

'It could be that Wisbech is the place for our meeting with Harold. If Normans are in pursuit, it will be there we fight to the death. Another blade will aid our hopeless cause. Drive on.' The Viking nodded to himself and breathed again as Fregurd took charge of the cart once more.

Siward wondered about offering to get off the cart anyway.

'And if that doesn't come to pass, you can kill him later,' Erik promised.

The cart trotted on towards Wisbech, Fregurd smirking at the prospect of later, Sigmund still bouncing happily and Erik giving Siward very disappointed looks.

Siward tried to look happy to still be part of the team, but his thoughts ran ahead to 'later' as well. His choice was clear. If they did catch up with Harold, whether it was a friendly or a difficult meeting, whether the Vikings were greeted as a rescue party or a dangerous band of marauders, Siward's course of action was as clear as day. He would immediately switch sides.

Chapter 27

Collision Course

ROM THE NORTH OF WISBECH a cartload of Vikings. From the south a cartload of Normans. Somewhere in the middle a band of wounded Saxons, riding hell for leather. Well, riding as fast as most of their injuries would allow, which was actually pretty slow. One of them had a very particular wound, most unfortunately located. Any bouncing on the back of a horse brought tears to his eyes which made the wetlands look positively arid.

The rest of the band had grown used to his 'ows' and 'oohs' every time he moved, and did not respond. They didn't exactly leap forward offering to dress his wound either.

'How much further can it be!' the one with the wound exclaimed plaintively as another of his horse's three dozen ribs caught him right in the vitals.

The rest of the band offered no comfort, but urged their animals on.

'Please God the birds made it,' another of the band shouted over the panting clatter of the horses. 'What do we do if there's no help in Wisbech? Head east into the wetlands or keep north?'

'We head north,' the man who had fought off Le Pedvin said very clearly. 'They must not capture the King, and the further we lead them north and away from their support, the better our chances will be.'

'But the wetlands might offer escape?' the first one suggested. 'Especially if the Norsemen have sent boats?'

'And what if they haven't? If the birds didn't get through and no one is coming? We'd end up trapped in the wetlands between the Normans coming up behind us and the loons who live in the water in front of us.'

'Hereward the Wake was always a friend,' countered the man who favoured an eastward journey.

'Hereward the Wake?' The fighting man was alarmed. 'That squirrel- headed addle brain? When he's not eating mushrooms, he's talking to the water pixies. I wouldn't trust that man to stand the right way up in a puddle, let alone organise a defence against the Normans.'

The arguing man seemed to accept that this was a pretty accurate assessment of Hereward. He shrugged a grudging acceptance of the northerly plan.

'In any event, the Normans are only three,' added Le Pedvin's opponent. 'Three plus some Saxon traitor, and they caught us off guard last time. One option is to make a stand, finish them off here and then move on. Now we're in Danelaw William will think twice before slaughtering the whole country to show how cross he is. Plus if they're dead they won't be able to send word back to the Bastard of the King's escape and his continuing rule, and at least we'll have killed some more Normans.'

The rest of the band seemed very happy with this plan. They indicated their support with assorted cries of 'yargh' and 'yeah' – many of them rather strangulated and one in a much higher pitch than the others.

'Leave the one with the eye-patch to me, though. He seems the only fighter they've got. Finish him and the rest of them will fall, I reckon.'

'Aye!' the band agreed with enthusiasm.

The man drew his sword and raised it aloft and ahead. 'To Wisbech!' he cried rousingly.

❖   ❖   ❖

The cart to the north, full of rather jaded Vikings and now liberally carpeted with Saxon sick, continued to bounce its nauseous way towards Wisbech. It was late afternoon now, but they should easily make it before dark.

Erik muttered imprecations to the gods to bring him and his band good fortune. Siward prayed that they'd get there soon and that the rolling movement would stop. He had thrown up so many times that he was beginning to think a quick death by Erik's hand had its attractions.

'Pray that Harold is there,' Erik said as he stood and moved to the front of the cart to join Fregurd and the still excitable Sigmund.

Siward had never been for such a long journey at such a speed before. He thought that explained the trouble he was having with the contents of his stomach, which kept wanting to get out. As for Sigmund, he seemed never to have even seen a cart before, so great was his enjoyment.

'Time's pressing,' Fregurd acknowledged. 'If the Normans are after him, they'll be well on his tail. If he's injured he'll be slower, and if they've already caught him our efforts will be a waste.'

'We'll give him as long as we can,' Erik instructed.

'If we go much further south we'll be in contact with the Norman outliers.' Fregurd didn't seem particularly worried about this – indeed, he was stroking his knife family with relish – but it was plain he thought it wasn't the best idea in the world. 'And depending on William's plans we might bump into the main force, if they've come straight north.'

'So what do you suggest?' Erik's tone said that he expected Fregurd's idea to be useless.

'Just get to Wisbech and bed in there. If Harold reaches us, fine; if the Normans get there first, we'll have time to clear out. It's still flat land and we should see them coming.'

'And perhaps Harold is in such a rush to get here he's dropping his treasure by the side of the road as he comes,' said Erik pointedly.

'Or we could head further south.' Fregurd happily reversed his plan.

Erik shook his head in disappointment as they entered the habitation known as Wisbech.

It earned the designation because it was inhabited, just. The entire place could be taken in at one glance and the number of dwellings could be counted on the fingers of one hand. One hand of a man who had been in a battle and lost two fingers of his counting hand.

'Is this it?' Erik asked, looking around, apparently expecting some other place to be hidden nearby.

Siward had finally stopped being sick, mainly because his stomach had transferred its entire contents to the cart. He peered blearily around.

'What's wrong with it?' he muttered, through a very unpleasant taste in his mouth.

'There's a bridge over the river and a house,' Erik commented, 'then another one, and another one, and that's it.'

'Saxons don't like living too close to one another. This could be quite a big place, just spread out a bit. Towns don't have to have their houses all squashed together, you know.'

'Towns?' Erik was scathing. 'This isn't a town. It's not even anywhere near being a town. It looks more like three houses that have met by accident. It's ridiculous. How are we supposed to rescue Harold and fight off Normans in this place?'

Siward felt that this really wasn't his problem; they were the Vikings and should be able to sort this out. His stomach was still uncomfortable, though, and didn't want him engaging in conversation. He just shrugged in reply.

'Hopeless country.' Erik had had enough of England. 'Sigmund, go and see what's in these miserable hovels, get a fire going and we'll wait out the night.'

Sigmund sprang to his task, heading for the first simple building – which was really more simple than building. Finding nothing of interest, he moved on to the others. He was soon back with Erik and the cart.

'Nothing,' he shrugged, 'nobody home.'

'Where is everyone?' Erik asked Siward.

'How should I know?' The Saxon was in no mood to be criticised for things which were nothing to do with him. 'People don't hang around in their houses all day; they have to hunt and gather food and work their tithe. Saxons don't just wait until the next pillaging trip is laid on to steal everything they want.'

Erik raised a threatening finger and pointed it at Siward. 'Sigmund, light that fire,' Erik ordered, 'and if you can't find any wood, use a house.' He stomped off without giving Siward another glance.

Siward decided he would go and help Sigmund light the fire, hopefully to prevent him from using the town as fuel.

Erik and Fregurd approached the bridge that spanned the River Nene. Solid tracks approached it from north and south as it was the only crossing for miles. The tracks then tiptoed over a construction which was a bridge because it crossed a river – not because it was a safe or reliable means of crossing a river. Any drover, bringing his sheep from the south to Wisbech, would send them over one at a time rather than risk a decent-sized flock disappearing into the swirling waters. The elder sheep would probably send the lambs over first, to make sure it was safe.

Even the waters didn't swirl very convincingly. They lumbered by in a very sluggish and brown manner, as if practising for what the wetlands held in store.

The Vikings frowned at the construction, doubt on their faces that the thing would take the weight of three of them at the same time. Never mind a band of escaping Saxons and pursuing Normans.

◆   ◆   ◆

The cart to the south, the one full of pursuing Normans with a quietly scheming Saxon, was still bouncing along at a dangerous speed. There wasn't so much mess inside, but it was still unpleasant. Ranulf and Mabbut had to hang on for grim death, feeling they were going to be thrown overboard at any moment. Le Pedvin was driving the poor hay-horse forward at a speed the beast had probably only dreamed about.

In the equine dreams the pace of the gallop would have slowed quite some time ago. In the horsey fantasy there was no Le Pedvin, screaming at the animal and hitting its tender parts with the flat of a sword whenever it showed signs of slowing.

Mabbut had already pointed out that if the Norman kept this up, it would kill the horse. It was clear from the response that this caused Le Pedvin not the slightest concern. He even suggested that if the animal did die, it would somehow be Mabbut's fault.

Only when Martel touched Le Pedvin on the shoulder and pointed out that the froth from the horse's mouth was starting to coat the cart, did the pace finally slacken.

'I can smell them,' Le Pedvin growled out in a largely insane sort of voice.

'Well, that's excellent,' said Ranulf, never put off by an insane Norman soldier. 'I imagine you will lose the scent if it's overpowered by the reek of dead horse.'

The pace slowed further.

'What's this Wisbech place like?' Le Pedvin asked Mabbut, having recovered slightly from the madness of the dash.

Mabbut thought about making a smart remark of some sort. His head had several ready and waiting, but his new found plan of deceit made him want to act more soberly. He had also seen how effective the flat of Le Pedvin's sword had been on the horse, and noticed that the Norman continued to brandish the thing. He decided to answer politely.

'Reasonably large place in Roman times,' was his description of Wisbech. 'Quite a passing place on the route to the east.'

'Into the wetlands?' Le Pedvin asked.

'Well, they weren't so wet then. The Romans built great flood defences and dykes and the like, drained a lot of the area and used the fertile land to great effect.'

'Which the stupid Saxons let go, so the whole place flooded again?'

'I wouldn't put it exactly like that,' Mabbut protested. 'Let's just say Wisbech was a trading post of some significance and a stopping point on the main roads. I've never actually been there myself, but I've heard about it.'

'How can you know what it's like if you've never been there?' Le Pedvin was disbelieving.

'Perhaps because I take an interest in my country?' Mabbut suggested. 'And because I don't just go round destroying everything. I'm actually more interested in building things up and finding out about them.'

'Idiot.' Le Pedvin dismissed the concept. 'So the place could be easily defended?'

'As I say, I've never been there,' replied Mabbut tartly. 'I know Saxons tended to leave the Roman towns and move back to the country, but I imagine it would still have some semblance of defence.'

'So if those Saxons get there first and hole themselves up, there might be no getting them out.' He cracked the reins and urged the horse back to a gallop. The poor thing seemed so surprised by all this starting again that it leapt into action.

Fate now took a hand. If the horse wasn't going to able to take much more of this, the cart wasn't having any of it at all. At the next convenient pothole, which was very close to hand, the right-hand wheel departed from the company. It headed off on its own to enjoy a much quieter life.

The cart tipped immediately over, leaving the crude axle to

dig hard into the ground. The crude axle was so crude that its reaction to this treatment was not to grin and bear it in a stoical manner. It was to give up immediately and snap in half.

The horse, finding that its load had suddenly got considerably heavier and much more right-handed, headed momentarily after the wheel, before coming to a grateful stop.

The occupants of the cart, who had not been expecting the floor to be taken from under their feet, pitched violently to the right and were tossed from the cart on to the ground below.

Ranulf and Mabbut were the first to leave, but, being near the back of the cart, they had least distance to travel. They rolled rather than plummeted from their perches, ending up covered in dust on the edge of the road – just where it bordered damp bogs and pools.

Martel was thrown more backwards than sideways. After bouncing around the inside of the cart a few times, he emerged from the rear. In a remarkable piece of dexterity he landed neatly on his feet, feeling quite proud of himself.

Unfortunately momentum was right behind the young Norman. He soon realised that although his feet might have stopped, the rest of him was still moving at quite a speed. He went straight over backwards, landing heavily on Ranulf and Mabbut. They grunted a grumpy welcome as the breath was knocked out of them.

It was Le Pedvin who plummeted. He had been standing at the very front of the cart, wildly waving the reins at the horse and shouting Norman obscenities, which it was highly unlikely a Saxon horse would understand anyway. Had his weight been on his right leg he might have slid gracelessly off the cart and on to the ground.

His weight was on his left leg – the very side of the cart which pitched violently upwards as the right-hand side went down. Le Pedvin was propelled very gracefully into the air, the full force of a substantial hay cart throwing him upwards. Ranulf, Martel and Mabbut looked on with awe from their observation point on the ground. They saw him sail over their heads and make straight for the bogs and pools of the wetlands.

Not that he appreciated it, but it was only the bogs and pools which prevented Le Pedvin breaking several of his bones.

In other circumstances, a detached observer would have derived great entertainment from the sound of a Norman soldier falling from a significant height into a good Saxon bog. But these were not detached observers. Le Pedvin's travelling companions well knew well that he would not respond positively to this experience. On the contrary: the results woud be dire. So they watched in some horror as the man landed, face first, into a particularly soggy and distasteful stretch of bog.

✦   ✦   ✦

Water is light and lively stuff. It is joyous and flamboyant. When something falls into it, it leaps and bounces in sheer exhilaration.

The Saxon bog of significant vintage, into which Le Pedvin fell, did none of this. Instead it gave an imperceptible gloopy shrug and absorbed the latest creature to fall into its grip with disinterest.

After the shortest of moments there was no sign that anything had happened at all. The bog closed over Le Pedvin's skinny frame and got on with life.

'We must get him out,' Martel exclaimed, trying to leap to his feet.

'Do we have to?' mumbled Mabbut resentfully.

'He'll drown,' Martel protested as he untangled himself from the other two, neither of whom was showing much enthusiasm for a rescue.

'Well, yes,' Mabbut said more clearly. 'If he hasn't already, that is.'

'Accidents happen,' Ranulf added, which surprised Mabbut.

'You …' Martel didn't seem to quite believe what was being suggested. 'You mean we leave him there?'

'Could get him out, I suppose,' Ranulf went on. 'Then he can make us resume the chase for half a dozen angry and well armed Saxons, let alone what else lies in wait for us in the north.'

Martel did pause now. 'You mean if he doesn't come out, we could give up and go home? Tell William that we couldn't find Harold and that Le Pedvin fell by the wayside.'

'Actually he fell *in* the wayside,' Mabbut pointed out. He could not resist a smirk that his homeland had taken Le Pedvin quite so literally.

'I wouldn't fancy telling Duke William that we've failed in the mission he gave us,' Ranulf reasoned. 'The fact the whole thing was supposed to be a secret won't blunt his beheading sword. It won't help Martel when he has to explain why Harold isn't dead. Again.' He arched an eyebrow at Martel.

'So we do have to get him out,' said Martel, clearly confused about what he was supposed to be doing. He was torn between the twin perils of William, who was miles away, and Le Pedvin, who had vanished into a bog.

'Unless you'd rather never go back to Normandy and spend the rest of your life in hiding here,' Ranulf replied.

'Live in England?' said Martel, as if he'd been asked to spend the rest of his life sitting in a bucket of worms.

'Do you mind?' Mabbut objected. 'It's actually very nice here.'

'It might be for you,' Martel responded coolly. 'You're used to it.'

They all stood and gazed into the bog, perhaps hoping that if they waited long enough the decision would be taken from them. Without Le Pedvin to lead them, or more importantly, to protect them, there was no way they could advance on the Saxons.

'In point of fact,' said Ranulf, pondering, 'we don't know that Harold was one of those Saxons at all. They could be right and he's gone off in a completely different direction. We could say we did catch them, we interrogated them and that's the information we got.'

To Mabbut's suddenly shrewd ear it sounded as if Ranulf was rehearsing his conversation with William, rather than arguing for a course of action.

As they continued to gaze at Le Pedvin's resting place, the bog unexpectedly belched. When the skinny Norman went in he must have trapped some air, which now found its way to the surface. Two or three very distasteful bubbles rose and burst, with revolting slowness. The skin of the bubbles dropped back into the bog to rest on the top like fetid scabs. The contents sighed into the air, the unwanted exhalations of corruption.

Except that one of the bubbles contained a cough.

The three observers watched in nervous anticipation as the bog moved and the grave of Le Pedvin gave up its dead.

Ranulf sighed with irritation that the man couldn't even fall into a bog and drown properly. Martel rushed forward to help their leader extricate himself from the cloying mess.

'Typical,' Mabbut said out loud. 'The man's so revolting even a bog won't have him.'

◆   ◆   ◆

After much slipping and sliding about in the slime and filth of the bog, watched by Mabbut and Ranulf from the dry of the road, Martel and Le Pedvin stood once more by the wreckage of the cart.

Le Pedvin cleared as much of the muck from his face as he could and glared his hatred at everyone and everything.

'Right,' he said, spitting wet bits of England from between his teeth. 'They're not far ahead.'

'How could you possibly know?' Mabbut asked. The man had been stuck head-first in a bog, for goodness sake.

'Because when this stupid cart threw me into the air I could see them.' Although just what Le Pedvin must have wanted, he clearly wasn't happy about how his information had been obtained. 'And there were about three houses just ahead of them and a bridge over a river. If that's Wisbech, it's not just been deserted since the Romans left – it's been dismantled. If they stop there we should have them well before nightfall.'

Mabbut, Ranulf and Martel exchanged glances of resignation, tinged with disappointment.

'Come on,' Le Pedvin called. He set off at a run.

'You bastard,' Mabbut mumbled. It wasn't clear whether he was addressing Le Pedvin or the bog.

Chapter 28
North or South?

IGMUND HAD BEEN PERSUADED to light the fire from some kindling taken from one of the houses, rather than use the house itself, and the thing was just starting to take, throwing its first substantial smoke into the air, when Siward noticed they had company.

'Erik,' he called. The Viking emerged from one of the other houses, where he had plainly found nothing worth stealing.

He joined Siward on the edge of Wisbech and looked down the road to the south. Fregurd and Sigmund came to stand at his side.

They squinted into the afternoon light to make out the figures that were approaching on horseback. With the land so flat, it was hard to tell how far away they really were.

'Saxons,' Siward announced.

'How can you tell?' Fregurd was dismissive.

Siward shrugged. 'When you live near the coast, subject to pretty constant attack from the sea, you learn to recognise people when they're coming at you from a distance.' He didn't say the word Viking, but they all knew what he was talking about.

'Harold?' Fregurd asked.

'Oh, come on,' Siward pleaded. 'Be reasonable. What more do you want? The names of the horses?'

'You know the longer you've been with us,' Fregurd observed quietly, 'the more irritating you have become, and the more I want to kill you.'

'You're not exactly my chosen company either,' Siward

retorted. The sight of mounted Saxons was giving him some confidence.

'No,' Fregurd agreed, 'but I'm the company with all the knives and a lot of experience in killing people.'

'Shut up,' Erik instructed. 'If this is Harold, we need to be ready to head for the boat. If it isn't, we may need to defend ourselves. Sigmund, get up on the roof. See what you can see.'

Sigmund sprang away and nimbly climbed up one of the small houses. He perched on the roof and peered towards the arrivals.

'Definitely Saxon,' he called down, 'and they're being followed.'

Erik pulled the axe from his back with one sweep and Fregurd drew his sword. He also made sure all his knives were where they should be, and were awake.

'How many followers?' Erik called up to the roof.

'Impossible to say,' Sigmund replied. 'They're a way off, but there's one man in front running and more behind. They aren't running though.'

'Come,' called Erik, and he leapt forward on to the road, axe in hand. Fregurd followed and Sigmund jumped down from the house. 'We'll get to the Saxons before they're caught.'

The Vikings set off at a significant pace – not a sprint, but pretty fast all the same. Siward got the impression they could keep this up all day. As the man without any weapons, never mind fighting skills, he loitered at the back for a while. Then he followed at a pace which he was sure would guarantee his arrival at the fight once any actual fighting was over.

The Vikings all dashed over the bridge before they realised they were on it. They actually stopped on the other side and looked back to confirm that the thing hadn't fallen into the river. It was still there so, with shrugs of grateful surprise, they ran on. No point risking a return journey to get the cart – not that the bridge would be able to cope with such a load anyway.

The route to the rescue seemed to go on forever. The land really was flat and distance was deceptive. Siward had to stop three or four times to gather his breath, which had the advantage of letting the Vikings get even further ahead.

When he finally arrived at the meeting place, introductions had been made and Erik was speaking. Siward scanned the Saxon band to see which one was the King, quickly realising he had no idea what the man looked like. Nor were any of them wearing a crown, which was rather disappointing.

'We head for the river. A boat is coming and we can take you away.'

'We deal with our followers,' one Saxon said, an experienced fighting man by the look of him. 'Then we stay to rally an army and drive the Normans from the coast.'

'There could be a good force on your tail,' said Erik, with some enthusiasm for taking on a good force.

'There's four of them,' the Saxon confirmed brusquely. 'We dealt with them once already. And only one of them's a real fighter.'

'Only four that you saw. Perhaps they were an advance party. They could have sent for reinforcements once they knew they were on to you,' said Erik hopefully. He relished the prospect of grappling with reinforcements.

'We need to gather our strength,' a voice came from the rear of the group. This was the man with the leg injury, the injury very high on the leg, so high that he couldn't walk with anything like comfort. Still using a sword as a crutch, he stepped forward – well, sort of winced and hobbled forward.

He was a short fellow, dressed no differently from the rest of the party, but the other Saxons at first tried to prevent him coming forward. When it was plain they were being ignored, they stepped back.

'This boat will take us where? To Norway or Denmark, where we can gather forces?' the injured man asked.

'Ah,' said Erik in the voice of a man who knows a problem that no one else does.

'"Ah"?' The man gave him a quizzical look.

'It's just that with Harald dead, the new King, Magnus, has said we're not to get involved.'

'Wasn't your last king called Magnus?'

'Popular name,' Erik shrugged.

'So we can expect no support.'

Erik tried to look apologetic for his country.

'And after Senlac there aren't exactly many good English fighting men left.' The Saxon was clearly sad and angry.

There was a silence involving a bit of glaring, some sighing and a general air of disappointment.

'We must re-group,' the Saxon said, half to the men, half to himself. 'I shall talk to the Welsh and the northerners.'

'If I may say so, your Majesty,' Erik spoke up. He sounded a bit tentative.

So that's King Harold, Siward noted: doesn't look much like a king. What kings were supposed to look like was a bit of a mystery to Siward, who had never given it much consideration before. He just thought they ought to be different somehow. Not more legs or arms or anything, but perhaps a bit taller.

'You may,' Harold answered.

'You do not seem in the best condition to be traipsing across the country to gather new allies. Better perhaps to take time to recover, then re-group. Once you have your fitness back?'

Harold didn't answer immediately, plainly giving the suggestion some serious thought. He winced as he moved his weight from one leg to the other. The group waited respectfully for his decision. 'You could be right,' the King acknowledged at length. He was obviously feeling sorry for himself. Siward knew the signs.

'Some bastard shot me in the thigh,' the King complained. 'I mean, is that fair, I ask you? Still, better than Borton here.' He gestured to one of the wounded Saxons who had a large bandage over his eye. 'I told him not to look up when the arrows were coming down. Idiot.'

The man called Borton shrugged his shoulders stoically and directed his one remaining eye to the ground.

'How far away is this boat?' Harold asked Erik.

'I don't know, your Majesty,' Erik replied confidently.

'That's not much good, is it? How are we to know where to go?'

'The boat will come as far as it may, Majesty, depending on the state of the tides and the water levels. We shall follow the river to the east and meet up with them as they come up to the west.'

'Perhaps leaving about now would be a good idea?' Fregurd suggested, nodding his head towards the approaching Normans. They were still some way off, but figures could be made out now.

'To horse!' Harold cried. He looked at the Vikings questioningly.

'We've, erm, we've got a, er, cart,' Erik mumbled, clearly ashamed of the fact.

'To horse and to cart then,' Harold announced without a blink.

'Oh, great,' Siward mumbled. His stomach churned unhappily at the prospect.

Sigmund ran back towards the bridge and the sparse houses to bring the cart, while the Saxons remounted their horses.

Harold did so last of all, and very slowly.

'If I do anything,' he said through gritted teeth, 'I will have my revenge on William for despoiling the English land, for attempting to usurp the English throne from its rightful King and for slaughtering so many of its good men.' Then his tone, rousing and declamatory, fell to a much more personal and intense level. 'And I shall save the best bit for shooting me in the leg.'

'Bit higher than the leg, Majesty,' one of the Saxons pointed out. The man almost immediately realised his mistake as his fellows all made gestures of silent anger at him. He tried to look somewhere else.

'Yes, thank you,' Harold retorted with some bitterness. 'And if I don't do it, my sons and daughters will,' he vowed.

'I rather think sons and daughters are out of the question now,' muttered the impudent Saxon, but this time only those nearby heard him. Some of them snorted and Siward detected an undercurrent as eyes were rolled skywards. It was as if, by leading them to defeat at Hastings, Harold had lost some of his majesterial authority. But he was King. Put there by God. Surely everyone respected the King – until he died, of course.

◆　　◆　　◆

The route towards the boat followed the south bank of the River Nene. The Romans had the right idea, navigating the river until it met Ermine Street going north and south. It was a sensible and profitable arrangement.

The flood defences ensured the river was navigable to this point, so boats carrying goods from all parts of the known world could sail right up to the road. Here carts would be waiting to take them to the very furthest reaches of Britannia.

It was a magnificent system: a feat of engineering, of planning and of organisation. It meant that Roman Britain could prosper and develop. Of course the Saxons completely ignored it when they arrived, soon after the Romans sailed away, and the whole thing fell swiftly into ruin.

The floods came back and flooded. Then the roads fell apart. After this the Saxons gave up and spent their time running round in the woods chasing boar.

This decline meant that the route to the east was no longer as easy as it had been. The river was certainly not navigable even this far inland any more, and the road at its side had never been made to carry heavy goods. Siward hardly had the time to be sick at all before it became clear the cart would get no further.

'Get the horses out of the harness,' Erik ordered. 'We'll leave the cart here. Push it across the path, it might hold them up a bit.'

Fregurd, Sigmund and Siward did as they were told. Although Siward put his weight behind the cart, he didn't feel he was contributing much.

'Fregurd, you and Sigmund can have the horses,' said Erik. 'I will keep the pace of these slovenly Saxons without any bother.'

'What about me?' Siward asked. He looked down the riverside path after the departing King.

'Yes,' said Erik, 'what about you? What are you still doing here anyway? We've found the King – you can clear off.'

'Oh, Erik, you promised,' Fregurd said with heartfelt disappointment. He lightly touched Navel Gazer, who had been selected for this task some time ago – after a long debate with all the others of course. 'What, into the hands of the Normans?' Siward objected, quickly ignoring the Fregurd option.

'You don't have to go that way,' Erik explained, his patience at an end. 'Cross the river and head north again.'

'Where?' Siward scanned the river for any sign of a crossing place. There was none.

'Swim,' said Erik simply.

'Swim?!' Siward was aghast. 'I can't swim.'

'You live by the sea, man, how can you not swim?' Now it was Erik's turn for the aghastness.

'Yes – I live by the sea, not in it.'

Fregurd had a constructive suggestion. 'If I throw him in, he might learn. Then again, he might not.'

'Why can't I just walk along the path with you?' protested Siward. 'I mean, it's not your path. I'm not getting in the way.'

Erik clearly had no time for this discussion. He bade Fregurd and Sigmund mount their horses. 'Let's be off,' he snapped, 'the Saxon can do what he likes.'

Fregurd unhappily put Navel Gazer away and climbed on to his horse. He spared some threatening glares for Siward as he did so. Calming the disappointed knife was going to take some time.

The horses, with Viking escort, pressed on along the river path. Years of overgrowth had been stamped flat by the Saxons, who had gone ahead.

Siward drew up the rear, just that distance from the group occupied by a younger brother who has been told that no, he can't play with the older boys. Later they will turn on him, but he will explain that he's not with them, he just happens to want to walk along the same path as them and they can't stop him.

They will then show that they can stop him, and he will run home to one parent or another, complaining about how mean everyone is to him.

Siward had already concluded that everyone was mean to him. After all he'd done for these Vikings, for goodness sake. He had taken them across his own land, helped them with a mission that almost went the length of the known world, and what gratitude did he get? None at all. Once they'd found the King it was 'Clear off, Siward, you're no use to us anymore'. And Harold wasn't even their King. He was Siward's King and he'd really met him.

His mother had always told him to stop feeling so sorry for himself, even when he got the job of filth-man. He felt at the time, and he was sure now that he was right, he was bloody well entitled to feel sorry for himself sometimes. No one else was going to do it for him. Siward rumbled and grumbled along, kicking fallen nettles and stomping angrily. Every now and then he noticed that the group had got ahead of him a bit, and would discreetly speed up.

◆   ◆   ◆

The river path wound on and on. The Vikings soon caught up with the Saxons and the group pressed on. Siward hung back and followed at a distance that he felt said pretty clearly that he was part of the band, but not a troublesome part.

As they rounded yet another bend in the river, the vista opened up as the reeds and rushes fell back. It was still some considerable way to the sea, but the breadth of the stream meant they could see some way ahead.

Siward had never in his life, never even in his imagination or his darkest nightmares, conceived that he be would glad to see a Viking longboat coming towards him. He was now.

As he took in the sight of this one, still some way off but gently rowing its cautious way upstream, he had a very pleasurable anticipation that perhaps Freya might be aboard.

'There, Majesty,' Erik proclaimed. He stretched out his arm to indicate the boat that every one could see perfectly well.

'Yes,' said Harold, turning back to acknowledge Erik's prowess at spotting the only boat on the river, and a big one at that.

'And there.' The King held his own arm up and pointed back down the river path.

Erik turned. 'Normans!' he called. 'Go.'

They went, leaving the crashing lead Norman still some distance behind but closing. He appeared to be on his own, but who knew how many of his men were behind him in the cover of the undergrowth?

The Saxons set off at the best pace their respective injuries could manage, all of them trying hard not to out-run their King. Erik and Sigmund easily kept pace, but Siward was pretty rapidly left behind.

'Wait for me,' he cried.

'No,' Erik replied.

'What if I'm caught by the Normans?'

'I'd like to say it's been nice knowing you,' Fregurd called from his horse, 'but it hasn't really.' He waved Navel Gazer, at least giving it the chance to see whose insides it had been going to gaze at.

'They're not after you,' Erik called from the distance. 'Just keep out of their way. And if we do escape with Harold ...'

'Yes?'

'...keep *right* out of their way.'

Chapter 29
Heels, Hard on the

IF ANYTHING COULD BE GUARANTEED to give Siward an extra spurt of energy, it was being chased by a Norman with a sword who clearly wanted to do something horrible with it.

When the Norman started hollering the most explicit threats of physical harm, Siward found he could up his pace quite considerably. Obviously he wasn't fighting fit, not like the Vikings who would be in their element: regular pillaging requiring a lot of effort. None the less, keeping up with some gently cantering horses when death is snapping at your heels turned out not to be a problem.

Siward had to admit that his life had been a pretty lazy one up to now. Clearing filth didn't need much in the way of strength, and people tended to leave him alone, understandably, to get on with his job. When he wasn't clearing filth he was laying about, foraging half-heartedly for food or hanging about in the tavern.

He told himself that if he ever got out of this he would make a bit more effort. He also considered this would put him in better stead with Freya. If he was fit and a hard worker, he'd make a better impression.

He also promised God that he would pray every day, would clear filth for the priest for nothing and would lead a good and pious life – if only God would arrange for the nasty Norman not to kill him.

◆　　◆　　◆

'Martel, will you keep up,' Le Pedvin called back from his advanced position. 'I can see the buggers and there's only so much I can do on my own.' He stopped on the river path, a path only created by the passage of those he was chasing, and put his hand on his hips, waiting. 'It's no good you hanging around on the left flank now. Get up here and fight.'

Martel appeared out of the undergrowth, sword in hand.

'And put that thing away,' Le Pedvin ordered. 'There's no one to fight here and it's only getting in the way.'

Martel sheathed his sword and stole a glance backwards, up stream.

'And it's no good looking for help from that pair. Ranulf wouldn't dirty his hands if he stuck them up a cow, and we all know Mabbut is useless.'

Martel now drew up to Le Pedvin and tried not to look out of breath, or terrified.

'At least the useless lump hasn't got the brains or bravery to come at us from behind – that's something, I suppose.'

Martel peered around Le Pedvin and looked out into the swell of the river. 'Is that …?' He started.

Le Pedvin turned to see what Martel was looking at. 'It's a bloody longboat,' he wailed, as if about to claim that it wasn't fair. 'These cheating bastards have got the Vikings on their side, and it looks like some of their friends have turned up to take them away.'

'Oh dear,' said Martel, in the tone people use when news of the death of a much-hated relative has been received, six months after the happy event.

'So this is my plan,' Le Pedvin began, generating a look of bewildered horror on Martel's face. 'Well, you needn't think we're letting them get away,' Le Pedvin stated for the record. 'That's Harold up there, I'm sure of it. Do you think we should let the prospect of death stop Duke William's sworn enemy escaping our grasp?'

'Well …' Martel sounded like that was exactly what he thought. Which it was.

Le Pedvin glared his one-eyed glare and Martel looked away.

'How many are they?' Martel asked.

'Not too bad,' Le Pedvin sounded confident. 'Six Saxons, but all wounded to one degree or another. Harold might have an arrow in the eye, so he'll be easy to take. Three Vikings, I reckon, plus some Saxon.'

'Sounds quite a lot then,' Martel commented.

'And then on the longboat probably about a dozen.' Le Pedvin grinned at the prospect.

'What's going on?' Ranulf now appeared through the rushes, with Mabbut in tow.

'We're just planning our attack on the fleeing coward Harold.'

Ranulf looked down the river. 'And his Saxon friends, some Vikings and … is that a longboat?'

'It is.'

'And a longboat. I see. Well, good luck with all that.' Ranulf was clear that he had found a comfortable spot from which to watch the battle. Which would not be a long one.

'We're going inland and will circle round on them. When I give the signal, you two cause a distraction.' Le Pedvin's plan was clear in his head. The unwavering cooperation of the others was simply assumed.

'"Cause a distraction"?' Mabbut was incredulous. 'Just how are we supposed to distract a band of soldiers escaping on to a Viking longboat? They don't strike me as the sort of people who are easily distracted.'

'I don't care how,' Le Pedvin said, leaning really close to Mabbut's face. 'Throw yourself in the river and drown. If that distracts them, it's a job well done.'

'What's the signal, anyway?' Mabbut asked, ignoring this.

'An owl hoot,' Le Pedvin replied.

'An owl hoot?' Ranulf was contemptuous. 'It's broad daylight in the wetlands! What sort of an owl is this?'

'The sort that has a bloody big sword and gets what it wants.' Le Pedvin's glare must be wearing out.

'Can you only do owls?' Ranulf enquired.

'What does it matter?' Le Pedvin was adding frustration to his perpetual glare.

'Any Viking worth his salt is going to wonder at an owl hooting in the day. Especially coming from a landscape with a marked absence of trees for owls to live in.' Ranulf's tone implied that idiocy could go no further.

'For God's sake!' Le Pedvin seemed on the verge of doing something very physical.

'Martel,' Ranulf asked, 'what can you do?'

'Eh?' Martel was baffled. He was also puzzled by Ranulf and scared of Le Pedvin.

'What bird sounds can you do? Can you do a marsh warbler?'

'I don't think so.'

'Oh come on.' Ranulf couldn't believe this. 'A marsh warbler's easy. You must be able to do a marsh warbler. Everyone can do a marsh warbler.'

'I can't do birds,' Martel confessed, shamefaced. 'I can do a cow though,' he offered.

'That's something, I suppose.'

'Oh, is it?' Le Pedvin demanded. 'So much more likely to find a cow out here on its own plodding around the marshes than an owl, eh?'

'Maybe the owl's resting on the cow?' Mabbut volunteered.

Le Pedvin could stand no more. He simply punched Mabbut hard in the face.

'*Ow!*' howled Mabbut as he went down. 'What was that for?'

'Everything,' Le Pedvin snarled, 'absolutely every bloody thing.' He pointed a pointy finger at them all one by one. 'There will be an owl hoot. When you hear the owl hoot, you will make your distraction. We will then attack the boat and get Harold.'

Martel blinked unhappily. He looked like the sort of soldier who would have trouble taking on an owl with its legs tied together.

'Come.' Le Pedvin beckoned Martel and stepped off into the undergrowth of the riverbank.

Ranulf helped Mabbut back to his feet.

'Did you see that?' Mabbut asked, clutching his face and examining his hands for traces of blood. There was only one trace, but it covered both his hands as his nose disgorged a good head-full of the Saxon bloodline.

'Of course I did.' Ranulf was puzzled by the question. 'Le Pedvin hit you. So what? It's the sort of thing he does.'

'Well, I'll be damned if I make his distraction for him,' spluttered Mabbut. 'He can hoot all he likes.'

'You forget one thing,' Ranulf observed coldly.

'Oh yes,' Mabbut was scornful through his bleeding nose. 'And what's that?'

'That I'm Norman? That I'm on Le Pedvin's side, idiot though he is, and that if you don't cooperate I shall have to let some more of your blood out.' Ranulf drew a short dagger, concealed somewhere in his clothing. It was a small blade, more use for cutting up a meal than a man, but it would do a good enough job.

'What do you suggest, then?' Mabbut asked. He was even more determined that if the chance came, he would be on that boat with the Saxons.

'I think we ask for a lift,' Ranulf said, quite seriously.

'Ask for a lift?' Mabbut wasn't serious at all. 'Oh, great idea. We call out to a Viking longboat and say, "Excuse me, could you give us a ride to the nearest shop?"'

'Something like that, yes.'

Mabbut snorted his derision.

'We're out in the reed beds,' Ranulf explained, 'probably doing something Saxon and unspeakable. I wouldn't know.

317

Anyway, we've got a long journey ahead of us to the coast and we spot a boat.'

'A longboat.'

'Yes.'

'A Viking longboat. Have you any idea how many Saxons call out to Viking longboats and ask for a lift?'

Ranulf shrugged.

'None at all. Never. Ever. It wouldn't happen. Never mind an owl hooting at the wrong time of day. If a Saxon sees a longboat, he heads in the other direction. Fast. He does not shout out, "Excuse me, mister Viking, can I come aboard while you chop my head off?" The whole thing's ridiculous.'

An owl hooted.

'Ahoy!' Ranulf called out to the boat, waving his arms and running along the path.

Mabbut dropped his head in despair. A lot of blood came out, so he held it up again. He tramped after Ranulf, muttering darkly about the stupidity of Normans. As he followed, he did wonder if this might be his chance. It was unbelievable that the Vikings would let them on board, of course – but, if they did, he could declare his allegiance to King Harold and have Ranulf, Martel and Le Pedvin thrown overboard. After he'd punched Le Pedvin in the face. Or better still, asked a very large Viking to do it for him. Mabbut was warming to the idea.

◆   ◆   ◆

The Viking longboat had drawn up as close to the riverbank as it could without grounding itself. This was not close enough to climb straight on, so a long plank was sent out from the bulwarks to rest on a solid piece of ground.

Erik went first. He escorted Harold to the safety of the boat and then supervised as the rest of them were brought over. The horses, stripped of their saddles and harness, were left to their own devices. Then Fregurd and Sigmund came aboard.

Siward was the last, but as he stepped on the plank they started to pull it in.

'What are you doing?' he called.

'Leaving you behind,' Erik replied, puzzled at the question.

'I'm a Saxon,' Siward wailed, mostly for Harold's benefit. 'You can't leave me here.'

Erik grimaced at the words, but did catch a very kingly glance from Harold. Reluctantly he put the plank back, just long enough for Siward to climb on. He dragged their tame Saxon aboard and threw him on to the deck.

The boat lurched as the oarsmen put their backs to pushing the craft away from the riverbank and out into the stream.

'What do they want?' Siward looked over the side of the boat as soon as he got his feet steady.

Erik looked to where Siward was pointing as two figures appeared down the path, waving their arms and calling. One of them seemed to be dressed as a Saxon.

The Viking glanced back over his shoulder and grinned. 'They're probably the distraction for this pair,' he said, nodding in the opposite direction. Here two men with swords had emerged from the bushes and appeared to be trying to creep towards the boat.

When it was clear they had been spotted – clear from the fact that anyone who wasn't rowing had gathered at the rail to observe the approach – the two with swords stood up and walked to the riverbank closest to the boat.

'I am Duke William's liegeman and I have come for the traitor Harold,' Le Pedvin called to the boat, now gently moving out into the stream. He called with as much pride as he could muster, given that he was still more bog than man.

This prompted much laughter from the party in the boat.

While the hilarity went on, Martel came up to Le Pedvin and stood at his side.

Mabbut's heart sank as he saw the boat move away. He could

319

swim, but he didn't fancy it in this river, weighed down with his fine Saxon clothes.

Ranulf drew up to Martel and the two of them took a couple of steps back – having made a simultaneous decision that they weren't going to get too close to a boat full of armed Saxons and some large-looking Vikings.

'Where is Harold?' Le Pedvin demanded.

'Who wants to know?' came a voice from inside the boat. Harold strode up to the rail, if shuffling with your knees firmly clamped together can be called striding. He caught Le Pedvin's eye.

'So you are here,' Le Pedvin said, with some satisfaction. 'You know me, Harold. Marcel Le Pedvin.'

'Marcel?' Mabbut sniggered to himself.

Le Pedvin peered across the distance to the boat. 'I thought you'd been shot in the eye?' he called.

'The eye?' Harold frowned. 'No, not the eye.' He reflected for a moment. 'The thigh, perhaps?'

Le Pedvin turned his frightful glance at Martel.

'Well, my man swore ...' Martel started.

'I bet he did.'

'The eye sounds better, though,' Harold taunted. 'More kingly, isn't it, to get shot in the eye and still survive?'

Le Pedvin decided to move on. 'You know me as the representative of Duke William of Normandy, conqueror and rightful King of England.'

'Really?' said Harold with interest. 'You don't look much like Le Pedvin. Though last time I saw him he wasn't covered in mud, it's true. Anyway, I'm the actual King of England, so I think it's *you* who bows to *me*.'

Mabbut dropped to his knees and looked up. 'Your Majesty,' he cried out in pleading relief, 'they've tricked me and made me come along with them. The evil William holds my parents hostage.'

'I have told you ...' Le Pedvin began. He gave up with an exasperated shrug.

As Mabbut did his pleading, he noticed another Saxon on the boat. This one was not in fighting gear. He was secretively beckoning to Mabbut and pointing to a rope he was dangling over the back of the boat.

'Well, master Le Pedvin,' Harold went on, 'it seems the Norman force consists of you, not in a very good state if I may say so, and another one with a weapon who looks like he really doesn't want to use it,' he nodded at Martel. 'Then finally, if I'm not mistaken, you have Ranulf de Sauveloy.'

Ranulf nodded a brief acknowledgement, the one he used to condescend to kings.

'So unless you're proposing to use him to bore us to death, us being three good Vikings and six Saxons, oh and a boat full of other Vikings, I suggest we leave you with the thought that we will be back. We will recover what William the Bastard has taken and deal with you all. You personally, I think.'

Sigmund brandished his axe and sword. He gave a happy smile.

'Well, *you* could, I expect,' Le Pedvin replied equitably, 'but you know how William is when things don't go his way. He's likely to lay waste to the whole country, kill every Saxon he can lay his hands on and then lay siege to the Norsemen for helping out.'

'True, true,' said Harold, in just the same light, conversational tone. 'He is, as you say, completely mad. The first thing he'll tear into, though, is the person who brings him the news that I've escaped. And that would be, oh, let me think. Yes, that would be you. That's right.'

There was a splash in the water and a flash of pink leapt from the bank and into the river. Mabbut had chosen his moment and quietly slipped all his clothes off while no one was looking.

He ran the short distance to the river and dived in, hoping

that he would land in some water and not a good grounding of mud. He expected a knife in the back at any moment, but none came. Throwing himself into what he assumed was an effective swimming stroke, he headed for the boat.

The whole company, Saxons, Vikings and Normans, watched in fascination as the naked man grasped the rope that Siward was dangling over the side. With the man at the bottom trying to climb and the man at the top pulling, it didn't take too long before the new Saxon was aboard.

He stood, naked and shivering, hunched slightly and clasping his hands strategically so as not to offend the King's eye.

He clasped even harder when he noticed two Viking women appraising him with what could only be described as amused disappointment.

Siward quickly gathered up a skin that was draped over one of the side shields and handed it to the new arrival.

'Afternoon,' Siward said as he handed the skin over. 'Longstone, Siward Longstone.'

'Pleased to meet you, Siward,' said Mabbut, holding out a hand. 'Mabbut, Cnud Mabbut.'

They shook hands and looked at all the other people on the boat who were looking at them. They paused.

'This is a fine pickle, eh?' Mabbut commented.

'*Cah*.' Both men made similar noises and raised their eyes to the clouds in shared sympathy for the things Saxons had to put up with these days.

'If we could get back to business?' Harold enquired.

'Sorry, your Majesty.' Siward bowed, and turned to Mabbut. 'The King,' he mouthed an explanation.

'Well, cheerio,' Harold called to Le Pedvin from the boat, now well out into the centre of the river.

Le Pedvin was standing up to his knees in the water – as if about to wade out, or command the river to empty itself so he could reach his enemy.

All he could do, however, was slap his sword ineffectually against the stream and swear, loudly and often, as King Harold sailed off into the distance.

'What do we do now?' Martel asked as he slumped on to the riverbank.

Le Pedvin turned and looked him straight in the eye. 'We go back and tell Duke William that Harold has escaped. Again. Well, *you* do. And I think he mentioned what he was going to do to you if that happened.'

Martel looked as frightened as a very frightened man.

'Of course, I could always tell him you took your own life out here, out of shame.'

Martel wasn't believing this. 'You would do that?'

'Of course,' Le Pedvin nodded.

'You'd let me go, and tell William I was dead?'

'No.' Now Le Pedvin was puzzled.

Martel looked puzzled back.

'You kill yourself out here, out of shame, and I'll tell William.'

'Oh,' Martel stole a wistful glance towards the boat, now sailing out of sight.

'Or you could just run off,' Ranulf offered.

'I wouldn't,' said Martel in a tone that said yes, he would.

'And then we could tell William that you ran off and were in fact Harold's spy. The Duke could then confiscate your family lands and kill your father and most of your relatives. He likes confiscating land and killing people's relatives. It's what he does best.'

Martel's shoulders fell. His feet fell into step with Le Pedvin and Ranulf as they turned from the river and started the journey south.

Epilogue 1

THE RETURN JOURNEY of Marcel Le Pedvin, Ranulf de Sauveloy and Giles Martel is a tale for another time. A tale to be told around a warm winter fire with the doors firmly bolted and the children sent to bed.

Tales of a violent Norman with a very bad temper, who has just suffered a major disappointment and is looking for someone to take it out on, do not make comfortable listening.

Suffice to say the trio arrived back at William's camp safe and sound. Safety and soundness not being noticeable in the trail they left behind them.

The return journey was a particular disappointment to old More. He had to ferry them back across the river – the last ferry he ever operated.

In the few short days since the battle at Senlac, William had retired to Hastings and was planning the steps that would take him to the throne. Knocking off Kent came first.

When the three travellers entered the Duke's tent, Martel had gone beyond fear. He had passed through terror, taken a left at gibbering and howling, and had finally arrived at completely numb. He hadn't eaten for days or slept more than about ten minutes at a time. Even then, all his dreams had a duke in them.

'Ha ha!' William rose from his writing desk and greeted Le Pedvin, who had at least cleaned himself up. He nodded at Ranulf and looked at Martel, as if trying to remember who he was.

'News of Harold, sire.' Le Pedvin dived straight in.

Martel tried to swallow, but couldn't even do that.

'I know,' the Duke replied. 'Good, isn't it?'

324

Le Pedvin frowned.

Martel dared to look up. Sideways, at an angle.

'Harold escaped,' Le Pedvin said bluntly. He sounded disappointed at his master's reaction.

'Yes – but only into the hands of the Norsemen. Meanwhile everyone here thinks he's dead. Even his mother. Shot in the eye, they say. I've refused to hand over the body. Just told them he was never really King and he'd got a bit damaged in the battle anyway. Putting his body back together again would be too much trouble, that sort of thing.'

'How did you know he was with the Norsemen?' Le Pedvin was clearly not happy that his disappointing traipsing around the country appeared to have been for nothing.

'Their new King Magnus sent word. Apparently one of their more ... what was the word he used? Honourable, at least I think that's what he said. Their honourable men set off on the rescue mission.'

'But if he's escaped to the Norsemen, he'll gather forces and come back,' Le Pedvin protested.

'I don't think so.' William was smirking now. 'I've exchanged birds with Magnus. Harold's going to vanish, permanently this time.'

'Why? What?'

'Magnus owes me a favour. Well, he does now. I've promised not to take advantage of the fact that most of his army was killed at Stamford Bridge and invade.'

'Have you?' Le Pedvin asked. 'Were you going to?'

'No, but Magnus doesn't know that. Everyone thinks Harold's dead, and soon he will be. Happy ending all round.'

'So what are we going to do to Martel?' Le Pedvin sounded bitter in his disappointment.

'Who?' William asked.

'Martel.' Le Pedvin gestured to the quivering Norman who shivered in the corner. 'The one who brought you Harold's body,

325

except it was the wrong one. The one who told us he'd been shot in the eye, when in fact it was the thigh.'

'Really?' William was interested in this.

'Yes,' Le Pedvin confirmed impatiently.

'Nice and high, I hope.' The Duke winked. Then he shrugged. 'It's too late to change the tapestry now. The eye it will have to be.'

'And Martel?' Le Pedvin persisted.

William thought for a few moments. 'Hm. It would look a bit odd chopping some of his bits off for letting Harold go when the world thinks Harold is dead anyway,' he mused.

Martel risked a smile. It was a slightly deranged smile, but it contained a scintilla of hope.

'I've an idea,' said William.

Martel's smile shot back where it had come from.

'He can be our emissary, almost an ambassador, if you like.'

'Really?' Le Pedvin asked, dubious at such a reward.

'Yes,' said William, looking at the now smiling-again Martel. 'He's had experience of the country now. He can go and take word of the Norman Conquest to the farthest reaches.'

Farthest reaches sounded quite promising to Martel's ears. Anywhere away from Le Pedvin and William would be good.

'Yes,' William went on, nodding to himself in agreement. 'He can boldly go where no man has gone before – or gone and come back, anyway. We'll send him to Wales.'

Martel fell to his knees and started begging his Duke to take his eye instead.

◆　　　◆　　　◆

Leaving Martel to his sobs at the thought of death in the mouth of a dragon, or on the altar of a Druid, William beckoned to Ranulf.

'So, master Ranulf,' William sat back at the desk. 'This plan I concocted for finding out what's in the country. The more I think about it, the more I think it's actually quite a good idea. Perhaps you could put a plan together to do the job properly.'

Ranulf smiled a smile of pleasure.

'And I like the name Doomsday Book. Has a nice gloomy ring to it, don't you think?'

'Excellent, sire,' Ranulf replied, smirking smugly. 'If, for once, I am allowed to organise a job properly, I will make you a book to last for a thousand years.'

'Ha!' William laughed. 'A thousand years.' He slapped Ranulf playfully on the shoulder. 'You really are an annoying idiot, aren't you?'

Epilogue 2

THE JOURNEY ACROSS THE GREAT NORTHERN SEA was a trial for all concerned.

Most disappointing for Siward, any chance of a blossoming relationship with Freya came to a swift and sticky end. She had actually cast her eyes over him when he first joined the Saxons and found Mabbut some clothes. As they moved down river he had joined her at the side of the boat. She had even not moved away. He had dared to nod an acknowledgment of her, and she had nodded back. Then he had risked a brisk smile, and she had not walked off. He had prepared some simple, general conversation about events that was neutral but engaging, and had opened his mouth to speak.

Then he was sick on her.

He quickly detected that his chances of becoming the next mister Freya were gone. She became quite distant after that, and awfully keen to be dropped off up the English coast and return to Lincoln. She didn't even say goodbye.

Mabbut and he had been asked if they wanted to stay behind as well. Mabbut replied that he would rather die a thousand deaths than live under the Norman yoke, which seemed to impress the Saxons on board.

He didn't mind really. He knew that going back to being a filth-man in England would be very dull after his adventures. Erik had told him filth men were respected where he came from, for doing vital and dangerous work. And perhaps the place was full of Freyas.

Siward hadn't managed to say anything, as his mouth was full of his stomach's empty contents, so everyone assumed he wanted to tag along too.

He went on to discover cart sickness was the feeble younger brother of boat sickness. Things came up out of his stomach that he was convinced had never gone down there in the first place. He was sure he'd never seen them before.

He was pushed from one part of the ship to another as his vomiting threatened to turn him inside out. Even the slave oarsmen would have nothing to do with him. Eventually he found a spot by the rail where he could hang his head over the side and watch the water roll by. The water rolling by did nothing to help his retching, but at least he could do it without being cuffed about the head.

His fellow Saxon, Mabbut, had offered some sympathy to begin with but it ran out in very short order.

As land came into sight, after what felt like weeks of pounding torture, Siward sought some relief at the prospect of being able to stand on something that didn't keep moving.

The rest of the ship's company was very happy to let him be first off the boat and on to dry land.

He immediately found his legs didn't work any more. The world went spinning round his head and he threw up again.

'That's a shame,' someone said as they passed him by and clapped him on the back. 'You've just found your sea legs by the look of it.'

❖   ❖   ❖

Siward was still lying on the dock, very unsure as to why the earth, which he knew to be solid and still, continued to roll like the deck of the boat, when Mabbut came up. He was clearly full of news.

'We're moving on,' Mabbut said excitedly.

'*Urr*,' said Siward, half-interest, half-groan.

'Apparently the King won't let Harold stay. There's been some deal with William and Harold's got to go.'

'*Nooooh!*' Siward howled at the thought of getting on the awful vessel once more. 'Why does this King have to do what William says, anyway?' He was outraged at these wretched kings making life wretched for him.

'They're all related, aren't they?' Mabbut said simply.

'Are they?' This was news to Siward.

'Yes, of course. Norsemen? Sounds a bit like Norman?'

'Well, I never noticed that before,' said Siward in wonder. He sat up with the shock of it all. Then the ground spun again and he lay down.

'So this King can either let Harold go or he has to kill him. But he's said he won't do that. Honour or something.'

'And what about us?' Siward tried to say. He found that his throat wasn't capable of getting more than a few words out clearly. The constant flow of messages from his stomach seemed to have rubbed it raw.

'We have to go as well, otherwise we might tell.'

Siward beckoned Mabbut to come closer. 'Kill me now,' he croaked into his countryman's ear.

◆　　◆　　◆

Back on the boat, once it started to roll on the swell once more, Siward found things had actually got a little bit better. He wasn't sick at all any more. Well, not at all compared to how often he'd been sick before, which was constantly. He only had to rush to the side of the boat every few minutes, and in between felt almost normal.

It seemed the boat was now sailing north up the coast. Siward had no idea what was north of the Norsemen. God, perhaps?

'Where are we going?' he asked Mabbut, when some of his vocal function had returned.

'Some island out in the northern sea, apparently,' Mabbut replied. 'We have to sail north up the coast and then out due west.

Magnus said Harold couldn't stay with them as William had his spies. This island would be safe. Quite a few Vikings live there, it seems.'

'Doesn't sound very nice,' Siward commented. 'An island stuck out in this cold sea.'

'It's not all that bad, so some of the crew say. It's got geysers, I think they are sort of hot springs, and there are volcanoes.'

'What's a volcano?'

'No idea. From what I could make out, it's some sort of out-door fire.'

'Sounds like you'd need them.'

'I don't think Harold's very keen either,' Mabbut went on.

'Really?'

'Well, he's not happy about the whole business, but he definitely wasn't keen on somewhere called Iceland. He said it sounded a bit, you know, icy.'

◆　　◆　　◆

The sea rolled on and the boat rolled with it. Siward stopped being sick at all, and even managed to eat something, keeping it down for nearly an hour. He did at least start drinking again and offered to help out with the filth from the boat. It was good to be back in harness somehow.

The bulk of Iceland appeared to them through the dank mist and rolling sea. Siward was surprised to see that it wasn't even made of ice. It appeared to be made of rock.

When they got close, some of the rock even seemed to be steaming, as if it had just been made.

The boat sailed on around the coast until it approached the main town and harbour, at which point it stopped.

The Saxons and the Vikings got into a serious and prolonged discussion. There was waving of arms and raising of voices. The general consensus, as far as Siward could tell, was that the

331

Saxons didn't like Iceland at all while the Vikings thought it was lovely.

Soon the paltry sail on the boat was raised again and it turned its back on the harbour.

'What's happening?' Siward asked Mabbut, who had been eavesdropping on the conversations.

'Iceland's no good, it seems. Harold didn't like it at all. Very grim, he said, and he'd be blowed if he stayed there.'

'Oh dear.'

'Some of the Vikings said they could put him off anyway, or let him swim to shore, but he went on about the King's honour and Erik backed him up.'

'So what now?'

'Seems there's another place a bit further west.'

'Further west?' Siward was amazed. 'How much further west can we go? We'll be in Ireland before we know it.'

'I know – it is amazing how far these Vikings go. Anyway this next place is nicer. The Vikings have only been there a while themselves.'

'And what's it called?'

'Greenland.'

'Well, that sounds a lot better.' Siward smiled in relief.

◆　　◆　　◆

Greenland was not better. It was worse. A *lot* worse, and there was another even more heated discussion between the parties.

Mabbut, who was spending more and more time in the company of the King and his men, kept up constant reports to Siward, who was spending more and more time with the crew. He had even been given odd maintenance jobs on the sail and the oars.

'There's been a lot of debate about how Vikings name places,' Mabbut explained. 'The one not covered in ice is called Iceland

and the one not at all green is called Greenland.'

'I've never seen so much ice,' Siward agreed, looking out at the coast that was slipping by on their right. You could hardly miss it as a wall of ice rose out of the sea and touched the clouds. Sometimes the clouds dipped down out of the sky and touched the ice. 'There's even big chunks of it floating about in the water, all on their own,' Siward commented with wonder. 'I hope the helmsman's paying attention. If we hit one of those things, we could sink.'

Mabbut nodded and wrapped his coat around him. It was a nice sealskin coat, which only a couple of days ago had been in active use by the seal. 'The Vikings are worrying about the winter now. They say it will close in soon and they won't get back till the spring.'

'And what does Harold think of Greenland?'

'Not a lot.'

'So where *do* we go?'

'Further still. There's one more land to the west.'

'Another one?' Siward really couldn't believe this. 'If we go any more west we'll end up back in Lincoln.'

Mabbut tutted his agreement. 'The Vikings have agreed to take him there, winter with him and then head back in the spring. If he doesn't like it, they've offered to shoot him in the eye themselves.'

'I thought my Vikings would have the run on the Saxons,' Siward commented, neatly splicing two hemp cords together.

''Course they would, there's so many of them.'

'So what's the new place called?'

'Vinland.'

'What's a vin?' Siward was wary.

'I think it means pasture.'

'And I suppose the Vikings say that this Vinland is all green and fertile and full of food and drink?'

'They do,' Mabbut confirmed, 'although they were a bit

difficult. Almost like they didn't want anyone to know about it. But Harold's a persuasive man.'

◆　◆　◆

The days to Vinland were grim indeed. Winter was howling its anger from the north, blowing snow and ice into their faces and into anywhere else that got exposed.

The sea tossed them about like salmon in a stream, but the longboat held firm. Some of the Saxons now started to suffer 'Siward's sickness', as it had become known. Yet the progenitor of the ailment seemed to have become proof against anything the elements could throw at him. He would even climb the mast when the boat was almost on its side, to untangle the sail.

It was on one of his excursions up the rigging that he looked out and saw something on the horizon.

'Land ho!' he called.

'What?' One of the Vikings called back.

'Land ho!' Siward repeated the call.

'What does that mean?'

'It means there's land over there, where I'm pointing.'

'Why don't you just say so?'

'It's quicker to say "land ho",' Siward insisted.

The Viking stomped off muttering about stupid Saxons.

'Well, you climb up the mast and look then, Henrik Henrik-son,' Siward called down. 'Oh, sorry, I forgot, you can't.'

Siward hung by one hand, gazing out over the grey rolling mass of the sea, and wondered at how far he had come. From humble filth-man, sneaking in the back of the tavern in the hope that no one would see him, to hanging from the top of a long-boat as it pitched in a winter sea, shouting insults at Vikings. Real Vikings. He grinned in the face of the screaming wind.

The boat drew closer to the land and turned south.

'Aren't we landing here?' Siward asked Mabbut. 'It looks nice enough.'

'Apparently it gets frozen in the depths of winter. We'll stop off and get water and some game, but then we head south for a bit longer. Just to where the snow is manageable.'

And so they did. The boat was driven up the shore by the powerful arms of the oarsmen, and a hunting party disappeared into the all-encompassing woodland.

Siward hardly had time to re-calk the hull, mend the sail, splice together some fresh rigging and cut a new spar from a tree before the party was back.

'That was quick,' Siward observed as six big and strong Vikings strode from the wood, laden with meat and skins of water.

'How much game is out there?' he asked one of them in some wonder.

'A lot,' the man replied, 'and most of it stands still while you kill it.' He shrugged and walked off carrying a simply huge leg of something or other. Siward didn't like to speculate what sort of deer it had come from. He knew he wouldn't want to meet one in the dark.

Back on the ocean the vessel continued its southward trek. It seemed Harold was much happier with this offering and was congratulating the Vikings.

In their turn, the Norsemen were still cautious. They seemed slightly to regret revealing this place to the Saxons at all.

◆　　◆　　◆

As well as his seamanship, Siward's command of the Norse language had grown. He had first learned words for parts of the boat, then insults for parts of his own body and finally the in-between words which drew them all together. He couldn't keep up a long conversation, but if they talked slow enough he could follow.

'What's the problem with bringing the Saxons here?' Siward asked, as if he wasn't one of them.

'They'll ruin the place,' a Viking replied. 'They always do. Normans, Saxons, they're all the same. They just ravage their way across the land, destroying everything in their way.'

'You're a fine lot to talk,' Siward objected, having experienced several rounds of Viking ravaging.

'Ah, but that's only other places, where someone else lives. We always manage our homeland well. You lot, you end up killing all the game in one spot and then wonder why you starve to death. Give you a lake full of fish and in six weeks it'd be just a lake.'

'But surely a handful of Saxons couldn't destroy a place this big.' Siward looked out at the passing land which stretched beyond eyesight.

The Vikings continued to mutter and complain as they eventually offloaded Harold and the entire ship's company on a convenient beach.

With the boat dragged well up the land, covered and staked down for the winter, the party moved on.

They didn't have to go far. Over the dunes of the coast was a wide plain. A plain so wide it knocked the Saxons into stunned silence.

'I've never seen anywhere so ... so big.' Mabbut eventually spoke.

The grassland they saw did indeed seem to go on forever. Even in the wetlands of England the horizon was never too far away. Some river or the sea would break the vista.

This land was simply so vast that it defied the eyes. The horizon was out there somewhere, but it gave the distinct impression there was simply more of the same after that. The grass was high and waving in the breeze, inviting the observer to walk out into it, and to keep walking until death. Even then you probably wouldn't have crossed the space.

As the party brought possessions from the boat, some other people appeared. Mabbut and Siward had no idea where they had come from, but they seemed to be friends with the Vikings. These new arrivals were very strangely dressed and spoke in a language that made absolutely no sense at all. A lot of arm waving and pointing was required before messages could be exchanged.

The boat's contents were sorted out into piles, ready to be made into some sort of dwelling, or so Siward hoped. Probably tents would do to begin with.

Harold and his group of Saxons were still awestruck by the scene, and Mabbut and Siward went over to join them. As they looked, Siward swore the ground began to rumble.

'What was that?' he asked.

The others gave him sympathetic glances until they felt it too.

'The land is moving,' Siward said in some panic. He could now tell the difference between moving boats and stationery land.

'Where have these Viking traitors bought us?' Harold cried, apparently convinced that death was just around the corner after all.

The Saxons looked around in a panic, but neither the Vikings nor the locals seemed bothered about this strange phenomenon.

This didn't stop the noise and the shaking getting worse. Eventually Siward had to go over to one of the strange men to find out what was going on.

'What is it?' he shouted, waving his arms about.

The local man looked at him from under his unique hat and frowned.

Siward held his hands to his ears and mimed his legs shaking with the vibration of the land.

'Ah.' The local man got it and pointed out into the distant grassland.

Siward peered after him, but couldn't see anything.

The local man indicated that Siward's eyesight must be defective, or that he was some sort of idiot. Or both.

He peered harder and could just make out some dust rising on the horizon. How could dust make such a noise? Perhaps it was being disturbed by something.

'What is it?' Siward said again, nice and loud so the local would understand. He pointed out to the horizon and shrugged a shrug to demonstrate he wanted to know the name of the phenomenon.

The local under the hat frowned again.

'Me Siward,' Siward clapped his hand to his chest. 'That?' He pointed out to the distant dust cloud.

'Aha!' The local smiled and nodded that he understood what Siward wanted. He held an arm out and pointed to the horizon. Then he moved the arm left and right, indicating that whatever the dust cloud might be, it was covering a mighty distance.

'Yes?' Siward nodded.

The man nodded back. 'Buffalo,' he said, from under the feathers in his hair.

Epilogue 3

As More sat on the old Roman road south of the river, warming his hands by the fire of his burning boat, he cursed Normans in general and those with only one eye in particular. The man had returned from the north in a very bad mood. When More asked where the ponies were, the wretched monster set fire to his boat – only after he'd taken them across the river again, of course. Without paying.

As he grumbled and moaned in the evening, wondering whether he could borrow Matthias's boat, faint words drifted out of the darkness and circled his head on a zephyr of silent wind. Sparkles of light floated in the air, like fireflies, but somehow with more intention to their movement.

Breeze and light seemed underpinned by a faint, rhythmic tramping sound, as if thousands of weightless feet were walking ceaselessly. '*Qui ambulat in nobis via?*' the voices asked in a hopeless sigh.

'Look at my boat,' More wailed at the night. He picked up the end of a nicely flaming bit of boat and hurled it towards the lights. 'Sod off!' he cried. 'You're never around when we want you.'

The lights wavered uncertainly and whispering voices could be heard, voices in a strange tongue not heard on these shores for hundreds of years. The wind bubbled across the night, brushing More's face but strangely not disturbing any of the flames, which suddenly danced high and blue in his fire. A sorrowful moan circled the road and seemed to launch itself away high over the river, heading due north, in a very straight line.

FINIS

Howard of Warwick

will continue to interfere with History in 2015 with

The Magna Carta (Or Is It?)

Also available,
in
The Chronicles of Brother Hermitage:

The Heretics of De'Ath

England 1066...

During an utterly pointless debate at the austere monastery of De'Ath's Dingle, a monk dies in mysterious circumstances. Standing accused is Brother Hermitage, who needs to work out who did it before he's executed. More medieval than detective, he finds a companion in Wat the Weaver, producer of tapestry to make Beowulf blush. Naive and blindly deferential, Hermitage is helped through events by Wat, coming to a conclusion as startling to him as anyone. With monks, nobles and even a King, The Heretics of De'Ath does for the medieval crime genre.

Read the first chapter →

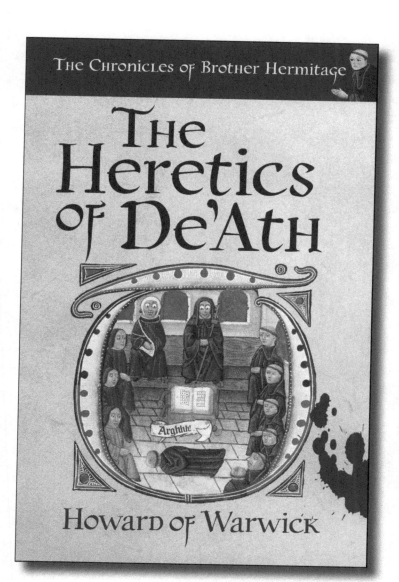

THE
HERETICS
OF DE'ATH

Arghhh!

HOWARD OF WARWICK

ISBN 978-0-9929393-0-4

£7.99

After Vespers

ND THUS I REFUTE THE PROPOSITION in all its blasphemous impudence. I say yes, the Lord did get sand in his shoes during the forty days and forty nights in the wilderness. Any other belief is HERESY.' Brother Ambrosius hurled the final word into the rafters of the refectory.

Young Brother Hermitage who was in the front row – or who, more accurately, *was* the front row – nodded with admiration and respect as the elderly bulk of the orator sat down in exhaustion. The argument had been long and complex, and despite a warming fire which made this the most comfortable place in the whole monastery, only three monks remained alert at the end of the four-day exposition. And that's allowing a very broad definition of 'alert'.

Hermitage was surprised the official opponent in the debate had given up after only the first five hours. He said he was retiring to his chamber for private prayer and took the novice Thabon with him. Their prayer was pretty vigorous, judging from all the grunting noises. Thus there were three contemplations on the case of Brother Ambrosius.

He glanced at the others to encourage their reactions. First was Brother James, and his was clear and instant.

'Oh, bugger,' he muttered, 'back to the garden.'

Hermitage frowned, but recalled that interest in the debate was an exeunt from daily labours. He smiled, trust Brother James.

Casting the old monk's carefully constructed arguments to another mind in the room, that of Brother Francis, meant they fell not so much on stony ground as on extremely large boulders. All of them stupid. His response was the same as always.

'What?' he said, as if accused of something distasteful.

Hermitage shook his head lightly in disappointment, not at the reactions of his Brothers, which was frankly no surprise, but at the loss they suffered through not engaging with this marvellous topic.

Leaving them to their own devices, Hermitage returned to the pose of those in profound thought, or profound boredom. He hunched almost double, propped his elbow on his knee and buried his face in his left hand. Thus he demonstrated deep concentration, or that he was dozing off.

Hermitage was so excited he could not have slept, even if he had been up all night writing a short summary of yesterday's proceedings – which he had. After a while he raised his head and lifted his bright and wakeful eyes to the massive and complex timbers of the roof. He stroked his chin and began to order the many significant ideas accumulated over the last four days. He considered the argument had weight and a certain beauty, although the premise that sand was a work of the Devil was perhaps a weak spot. Most impressive was the passion of Ambrosius for this rather obscure area of theological research.

Deep in his own thoughts, carefully constructing his observations and responses, Hermitage failed to notice that Brother Ambrosius was looking around in some agitation and anger. With a strangled gasp, the old man suddenly clutched at his chest.

The Lord above, perhaps having heard all that he needed, spared the world from further debate by recovering Brother Ambrosius to his bosom. Far from having the opportunity to respond to any questions Hermitage might have come up with, the poor man stopped responding to anything.

Hermitage also failed to notice that Brother James, alert to the ways of the world, looked around to confirm that no one else had noticed this event and slipped quietly out of his seat and away into the darkness.

Hermitage thought on in quiet satisfaction, relishing a rare opportunity for intellectual activity in this austere institution. The monastery in De'Ath's Dingle had a sparse population and provoked little interest from senior figures in the Church – in fact, it hardly attracted any attention at all. That this debate of Conclave was assigned here, while literally a Godsend to Hermitage, was a sure sign the result was of absolutely no interest to anyone.

The all-pervading ambience of isolated misery explained why it was some time before the dark of the autumn evening brought another monk to the great hall to light the sconces. Only then was the blindingly obvious fact of Brother Ambrosius's death revealed.

Sconce lighting at De'Ath's Dingle was a serious and sombre duty, to be completed with quiet devotion. It was a privileged task, given to those who would not use the opportunity for frivolous discussion with other monks, or as an escape from the natural labour of life. It was not meant to be a pleasure and so the Prior, Brother Athan, was the perfect choice. He had told Hermitage on many occasions that the unending toils of this life were a precursor to the hereafter, where things would be really tough. It was accepted wisdom that the man wouldn't take pleasure if it was carried by a flea and injected into him.

Even Brother Francis, who knew very little, had learned to move away from Athan when he saw him coming. He followed his instincts now, looking round in apparent puzzlement at where James had got to and why Ambrosius had stopped talking.

As Athan entered, Hermitage turned towards the distant door and saw surprise on the monk's face. Athan didn't like surprises. Apparently it was only a short step from a surprise to a joke, and then where would we be?

'Brother Hermitage,' Athan boomed.

'Yes, Brother.' Hermitage stood and responded loudly.

'What have you done?'

'Erm.' This was not what Hermitage had expected at all. Some cutting remark about the debate being a waste of breath perhaps, or the oft repeated accusation that Hermitage was a self-indulgent enthusiast. What had he done? He hadn't done anything. Yes, he'd been thinking deeply, but that counted as doing nothing as far as Athan was concerned. He gaped a little, hoping that there would be some further explanation.

'Brother Ambrosius,' the new arrival barked. As if this was sufficient explanation.

'Erm,' Hermitage repeated, uncertainly.

'Brother Ambrosius is dead,' Athan said, never one to beat around the bush. Beat the bush maybe, set fire to it as a sinful luxury, but on all occasions get straight to the point.

Hermitage wondered who Athan meant for a moment. There was a Brother Ambrosius at Peterborough, but why would Athan be concerned with that? He glanced back at the large shape of the old monk who had so recently completed his argument, and considered. He did look a bit dead now it was pointed out, but that couldn't be. Surely nobody died just like that. He had seen dead people, and was sure they hadn't sat down in a chair to do it.

Dead bodies were the result of run-of-the-mill domestic mishaps. Usually they'd been chopped up, or mangled by some piece of machinery or a horse's trampling hooves. Ambrosius looked quite normal: very still and rather staring, but apart from that normal. His pose in the chair was a touch more slumped and the look cast solidly on his features was of outrage, which was a bit odd considering he had just finished his debate.

The longer Hermitage looked the less normal it became. Ambrosius didn't move. At all. His huge chest and stomach no longer made their wheezing way in and out, and he hadn't farted or belched for at least a minute.

Hermitage looked around the room to see if there was anything that might account for a death. Across the length and breadth of the chamber he didn't really know what he was looking for. There was certainly no horse or suspect machinery.

'Are you sure, Brother?'

'Yes. I'm sure,' Athan snapped. 'Don't go anywhere,' he added, pointing a finger at Hermitage

Hermitage hadn't been going to.

Brother Athan strode across the room as if it were insulting him by being in his way, and peered closely at the defunct monk.

'Yes, definitely,' he spat into the room, as if accusing Hermitage of something.

'Oh,' Hermitage replied, 'that's strange.'

There was a pause while Athan did some glaring. Only Hermitage felt pauses needed filling.

'We must pray for the departed, although it's a bit too late for unction *in extremis*.'

Then Hermitage was puzzled. He liked being puzzled.

'I wonder when he died.' He puzzled away.

'Oh you do? You've been here for his entire pointless ramble, the best part of a week. You've given the old fool your undivided attention, and you wonder when he died?' The older man had suspicion in his voice. He also had it in his look, and probably had some spare in his habit should it be required.

'Well, I didn't notice anything, and as you say, I've been here all the time.' Hermitage blinked in the face of the inevitable consequences of this statement. He had never learned the technique for hiding his light under a bushel when situations got awkward. He was incapable of keeping his mouth shut.

Athan paced back to where Hermitage was standing and took up his usual position, just too close to be comfortable. As he did so Hermitage squirmed under the gaze, every stain and ragged thread on his well-worn habit calling out for punishment.

Hermitage faced his Prior. His bright blue eyes were wide and honest. He smoothed the unruly lock of chestnut hair that tufted from his tonsure, despite the best efforts of the barber. The open and fresh expression that sat perpetually on his handsome and even features bolstered the intelligent enthusiasm, bubbling like a fresh spring from every pore.

'You make me sick,' Athan said. 'You were here all the time, and so?' He gave Hermitage a moment to answer, a moment which went over the head of the enthusiast like a heron in a hurricane.

'And so how do you explain a dead monk and you in the same room?' Athan screamed helpfully.

'I was contemplating the argument and preparing to raise a few questions,' the younger monk answered honestly, wondering why Athan was so excited.

'Raising the Brother himself would be a miracle, never mind getting any answers,' Athan waved his arms at Ambrosius. 'I walk into the room of a most important debate of Conclave and find a dead body with you leering over it.'

Hermitage was offended. 'I wasn't leering over it. I wasn't anywhere near it. I didn't even know it was there.' He paused as he thought of something else. 'Anyway, what do you mean important? You've always said the debate...'

'You were the nearest one.' Athan cut Hermitage short. 'I want to know what you're up to.'

'I'm not up to anything.'

'You were engaged in the debate.'

'Well, I was listening,' Hermitage said, wanting to be strictly accurate. As usual.

'He was talking, you were listening?'

'Yes.'

'Now he's dead, you're not.'

'Well, yes.' Hermitage really couldn't see where this was going.

'Very suspicious. You have ruined the Conclave.'

'Ruined the Conclave?' The accusation knocked Hermitage back a bit.

'Yes, you idiot. The reason Ambrosius was here in the first place?'

'I know what the Conclave is, Brother. I just never knew you had an interest.'

'Of course I have an interest in what is important to the Church.'

'But you said this debate was a complete waste of time and the lives of those who would fritter away their minutes listening to the interminable drivel of a demented old man.'

'Don't quote me back at myself, Hermitage. I might get annoyed.' Athan thumped his fist into his palm for emphasis.

'I'm still not sure I follow, Brother,' Hermitage said, so meekly that lambs would have lain at his feet.

'Ambrosius's ramblings were just that. It doesn't mean that the decisions of Conclave are not of vital importance to the future of the Church.'

'But I thought you said the Conclave itself was a steaming pile of...'

'And now Ambrosius is dead, this particular decision cannot be made and you seem to be in the middle of it. That is extremely serious.'

Hermitage blundered on. 'I think you may be exaggerating a little, Brother. The wilderness footwear issue is not of mainstream significance. Obviously in Matthew caput four reference is made to stones in sandals, and while Ambrosius's point about the existence of demons is granted, there is doubt that they should be manifest upon the body of...'

'No, no, you fool. It's no good you carrying on the debate with a dead monk, is it?' Athan gestured once more at the slowly stiffening Ambrosius. 'The major problem is how this vital Conclave can resolve itself.'

'Vital?' Hermitage had thoroughly enjoyed the debate, but even he wouldn't have called it vital.

'Vital.' Athan emphasised the word. 'The vital debate is halted because there is a dead Brother in a room with only you in it.'

'But I hadn't noticed,' Hermitage pleaded. 'He must have simply died. He was old. Perhaps the exertion of the debate was too much for him.' As he spoke, he reflected that it hadn't really been much of a debate. Arguing with three monks, none of whom answered back, could hardly be described as testing.

The message was not sinking in, so Athan trod on it a bit harder.

'That will be of little comfort to the Abbot, will it?'

Now the blinkers of enthusiasm were torn from Hermitage's eyes by the overhanging branch of mortality. The wheels on his cart of fervour cracked on the stones of self-preservation, and he wanted to go to the privy. Understanding flooded through him from brain to bowels, and his mouth opened and closed a few times of its own volition.

Hermitage had chosen the Benedictines as they were a very flexible order. Yet this Abbot considered flexibility something to be frozen solid, preferably into some sort of weapon. He was a man of severe countenance, severe habit and a severed leg from some accident long ago. He nurtured great bitterness – and his only spark of generosity was to nurture it so well that it could be shared with everyone around him

'The Abbot?' Hermitage swallowed hard. 'The death of a Brother is a regular occurrence and we simply give the Abbot the old habits. I don't see why he would want to be involved now,' was the rather pathetic argument he came up with.

He waited for Athan's response and watched. The pockmarks and lines on the man's face seemed to squirm under the intolerable pressure of reasoning, while already small and pinched eyes tightened further. Athan drew in his breath and delivered his riposte.

'He wants to be involved, because he does.'

'But the other Brothers will bear testimony to the situation,' Hermitage whined slightly.

'Other Brothers?' Athan's voice lightened to a point in which Hermitage detected a hint of pleasure.

He looked around the room and noticed there were no other Brothers.

'I think you'd better come with me, young Hermitage. The Abbot will want to determine how the death came about and what to do to you. I mean with you.' Athan thought for a second. 'No, I mean to you.'

He helped the young man up by the elbow, if using the grip of a blacksmith to drag someone along can be called helping.

As the pair walked out of the room, exchanging the glow of the large fire for the cold of advancing evening, Hermitage offered a short prayer for the departed. It seemed the prayers of those under suspicion are incapable of ascending to the ears of the Lord. This one must have rebounded from the refectory roof and landed on Brother Ambrosius, as the corpse chose this moment to slide gracelessly to the floor, cracking its head on the flagstone.

Hermitage jumped and spun hopefully, expecting to see Ambrosius fully recovered and dribbling his familiar smile. He winced when he saw what had happened. Even Athan drew in his breath as if sharing the pain. Hermitage muttered a short blessing. Athan added his own contribution.

'Well, if he wasn't dead before, he is now.'

Hermitage grimaced.

'To the Abbot,' Athan said, with what passed for glee.

Hermitage cast a final glance at Ambrosius, being quite clear that he would prefer a night in the company of a corpse than half an hour with his Abbot.

Also available
in
The Chronicles of Brother Hermitage:

The Garderobe of Death

England 1067...

... and the King's favourite hunting companion has been murdered. How anyone actually did it is a mystery, given the intimately personal nature of the fatal wound. Robert Grosmal, a Norman of disordered mind, sends for a monk to investigate. Medieval monks are supposed to be good at this sort of thing. Brother Hermitage is a medieval monk, but he's not very good at this sort of thing. Motivated by the point of a sword, he and his companion, Wat, weaver of adult tapestry, set off to solve the crime. Oh, and King William is arriving that night so they'd better get a move on ...

And the Chronicles will wander on with:
The Tapestry of Death
Hermitage, Wat and Some Murder or Other

The Garderobe of Death

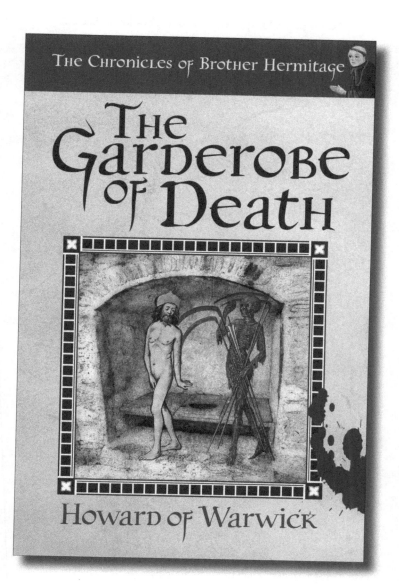

Howard of Warwick

ISBN 978-0-9929393-1-1

£7.99

Notes pages for questions you might like to discuss
at your book group:
Why? Why not? Who and where? How come? Never again?

Notes pages for questions you might like to discuss
at your book group:
Why? Why not? Who and where? How come? Never again?

Notes pages for questions you might like to discuss
at your book group:
Why? Why not? Who and where? How come? Never again?

Notes pages for questions you might like to discuss
at your book group:
Why? Why not? Who and where? How come? Never again?

Notes pages for questions you might like to discuss
at your book group:
Why? Why not? Who and where? How come? Never again?